KING ALFRED'S DAUGHTER:

The Lady of the Mercians

By

Marjory A. Grieser

First published by Dog Ear Publishing
4010 W. 86th Street, Ste H
Indianapolis, IN 46268
www.dogearpublishing.net

ISBN: 978-160844-306-2

Printed in the United States of America

In Memory of Daniel R. Grieser

TABLE OF CONTENTS

Introduction 1

Part One:
The Early Years; London and Winchester........................5

Part Two:
The Middle Years; The Later Wars Against the Danes 93

Part Three:
The Later Years; The Fortress Builders.........................155

Epilogue...235

Source Materials...239

Brief Genealogy Of The House Of Wessex 242

INTRODUCTION

*R*esearching the historical background of this story of the life of Lady Aethelflaed presented many challenges: first, there was the difficulty presented by the lack of extensive historical records of this period; secondly, there was an even greater scarcity of records concerning Aethelflaed's life and exploits. I did as much as I could here in the States. At the time I researched and wrote this book, the internet had not yet been invented. I decided that I needed to go to England to find more information. I took several trips, with my husband, in the 1970s, and the basic draft of this book was written between 1972 and 1976.

In England, I had access to archaeological reports at the sites of her fortress-building. Many museums had small scale models of her fortresses, based on the results of archaeological digs. There were also interviews with Museum staff members, which obviously could not be conducted long distance.

I have followed the available historical records as faithfully as possible. I believe that the dire situation in which Aethelflaed, daughter of King Alfred the Great, and her family found themselves called forth a remarkable response of bravery, cunning, and wit that overcame the Danish occupation of England and eventually united the seven kingdoms of England under one crown.

My historical sequence is based on the *Anglo-Saxon Chronicle,* which record was ordered to be written by King Alfred. I relied primarily upon the Parker Manuscript A (Canterbury) and the Laud Manuscript E (Peterborough). Especially I have made use of Manuscripts B and C, the *Abingdon Chronicle,* which includes a short account known as the *Mercian Register.* The *Mercian Register* runs from 902 to 924 C.E. and is an account of Aethelflaed's resistance against the Danish and Scandinavian invaders. To ensure some degree of accuracy, the other versions of the *Chronicle* were consulted, and both the modern translation and Plummer's edition of the Anglo-Saxon text were employed.

The account of the battle of Chester is based on the work of the late Professor F. T. Wainwright, who made a major contribution to the existing information on the life of Lady Aethelflaed. His book, *Scandinavian England,* edited by Professor H. P. R. Finberg, takes up the matter of "Ingimund's (Hingamund) Invasion" and also reproduces in translation (from Old Gaelic) an ancient Irish source called *The Three Fragments.* In this account of the battle of Chester, Aethelflaed is extolled as the "Queen of the Saxons" and her treaties with the Irish, Welsh, and Lowland Scots are brought to light, illustrating her role as a military tactician. Nowhere in the *Chronicle* is Hingamund mentioned and there is only a note that in 907 Chester was fortified. Aethelflaed's role is not mentioned.

The role of feudal women in society deserves especial attention: my sources authenticated the importance of their many roles in feudal times, not the least of which was the production of goods upon which the society depended. Monastic women played prominent roles. Abbesses held the power of Absolution and often presided over double monastic houses. They also functioned as ruling magistrates over the towns in which these monastic orders were situated. St. Hilda of Whitby was such a one: confessor to two kings of Northumbria, she presided over the first synod of the western Church in the seventh century.

At Aethelflaed's death her daughter, Elfwyn, briefly assumed the Overlordship of Mercian London and its territories before being deposed by Aethelflaed's brother, King Edward the Elder. Professor Wainwright's dating of Elfwyn's deposition (918) was used instead of that given in *The Anglo-Saxon Chronicle* (919). He places this action at six months after Aethelflaed's death. Wainwright maintains that Aethelflaed knew of Edward's intention to rule Mercia and appeared never to have opposed his plans. The records show that Athelstan was raised in Aethelflaed's household. This fact was the basis for my supposition that the rule of Mercia by the throne of Wessex may have been a long-term plan with the House of Wessex, having probably started with Alfred.

Wainwright also mentions Elfwyn's single state, wondering if it had political significance. For the sake of the plot, I assumed that it did. A reading of *The Mercian Register* of the *Chronicle,* for those who might care to pursue it, indicates the deep loyalty the Mercians felt toward Ethelred, Aethelflaed, and their daughter. The deposition of Elfwyn was obviously deeply resented by the author of *The Mercian Register.* The entry for 918 makes it very clear that the writer thought of Aethelflaed as the rightful Overlord of Mercia, and much of her following must certainly have transferred their loyalty to Elfwyn at her death. The tone of the other manuscripts of *The Anglo-Saxon Chronicle* is vastly different. Aethelflaed's death is mentioned quickly and records of her exploits are virtually nonexistent.

At her death, Edward was strongly aware of her influence and he appeared to have made certain that Aethelflaed's following was secured to himself before he deposed her daughter. A show of force by Edward was probably necessary to ensure submission immediately following Aethelflaed's death.

Aethelflaed, Wainwright goes on to say, was strong enough to have formed her own Mercian nationalist party before her death, but the evidence of mutual cooperation and fortress building indicated that she backed Edward and his plans. Furthermore, separation of the provinces of Wessex and Mercia would have left the English open to renewed threat from the Scandinavians, whom they had recently subdued. Such a division was intolerable and to prevent an uprising from forming around Aethelflaed's daughter two things needed to be done: first; Elfwyn had to be deposed, and second; the record of Aethelflaed's contribution had to be expunged. This was unfortunate but necessary to prevent an internal uprising that might undo years of Aethelflaed's work with Edward and Ethelred in bringing the Danelaw under English control.

Military records of the time give the impression that Aethelflaed was a thoughtful planner, a formidable foe, and above all, a person who commanded intense loyalty from her followers. The Mercians and Irish regarded her in the light of a savior: she successfully held her territory against the Scandinavian Vikings ruling in Dublin and the Danes. All that survives of her exploits are the *Mercian Register* of *The Anglo-Saxon Chronicle,* and the *Irish Annals (The Three Fragments).* My story is based on the sources previously mentioned, as well as Sir Frank Stenton's *Anglo-Saxon England.* The maps at the head of the three major sections are based on information found in these sources.

One last note: Aethelflaed requested that she be buried in the Church at Gloucester, the lands of this community having been given to her by Ethelred as a morning-gift. It is also possible that Lord Ethelred had been buried there. The *Chronicle* says that she was buried in the east wing of the Church in Gloucester. When I visited Gloucester Cathedral, hoping to glean what information I could, I asked the guide about Aethelflaed's grave. She led me to the apse behind the high altar and told me that the Saxon church lay directly beneath my feet, underneath the foundations of the present-day Cathedral. She then left me alone in the apse to think about the Lady whose life so fascinated me.

My source materials, including those referred to, are listed at the end of the book. I have followed the events as recorded in the *Anglo-Saxon Chronicle*, but have conjectured the lives of the historical figures from the record of their exploits, so this story should be read as historical fiction. Where contemporary accounts, such as Asser's *Life of King Alfred the Great,* related personal facts, I used the information, knowing that some historians questioned its accuracy.

I am indebted to many for their help: the staff of the combined London Museum and London Guildhall Museum in Kensington Palace for their assistance with material on early London and tenth-century hand weapons; the staff of the Stafford City Museum, not only for the excellent display on which the descriptions of the fortifications in this book are based, but also for showing me a palisade point which they recovered from Aethelflaed's original fortification of Stafford; the staff at Tamworth Museum for their guidance in pointing out Saxon artifacts and reconstructions of Aethelflaed's fortifications of that city; and to the Worcester City Museum for allowing me to study some of their excellent material, especially the plans of the Saxon Burgh. Despite four centuries of Saxon occupation of Worcester, little evidence of it remains. My reconstructions and descriptions of Worcester, as is the case with the other descriptions, while based on museum materials, are entirely of my own devising.

I am also indebted to my Anglo-Saxon tutors, Dr. Dean Baldwin and Dr. Margaret Hartshorn, who guided me through the Anglo-Saxon versions of *Alfred's Will, The Grant to Worcester Monastery,* and *The Dream of the Rood,* among many other works. Excerpts from my translations are used in this book. My thanks also to my good friends Dale Weisman and Esther Kash, both of whom are practicing editors and writers, for their encouragement and invaluable suggestions during the preparation of the final draft of the manuscript.

I am indebted above all to my late husband, Dan, who encouraged me to write this book, and chauffeured me around England, helping me search for the mostly lost sites of Aethelflaed's fortresses. He also gathered material for me on the Roman foundations of Saxon forts and collected and detailed the numismatic material used in this book.

PART ONE

THE EARLY YEARS:
WINCHESTER AND LONDON

Historical Notes

In 886 King Alfred laid siege to London and drove out the Danes. The English people there swore allegiance to him and to Ealdorman Ethelred, who was the exiled leader of Mercia, and who had been fighting for some years alongside Alfred. Alfred then gave the rule of Mercia and London back to Ethelred.

The Early Years: Winchester and London.
The Division of England, 886

CHAPTER ONE

(886)

*T*he air near the top of the hill was crisp, sharpening the harvest scents fading in the autumn air. The dense undergrowth on either side of the steep trail impeded the determined climber as she made her solitary way to the summit. The girl, climbing sturdily, pulled her cloak impatiently from the grip of the brambles, and despite the steepness of the upper slope of the hill, sprinted the remaining distance to a small clearing just below the summit. She blew on her cold fingers and rubbed her hands briskly to warm them.

She was bareheaded and the chill air nipped her cheeks to a pleasantly ruddy hue. Her knees below the short tunic were also bare and the strapped sandals provided only token protection against the rough edges of the jutting rock on which she stood. Her hair, in contrast to her military garb, tumbled loosely over her shoulders as she straightened up and drank in the crisp morning air. Against her wind-buffed face, her eyes were a startling gray-blue that gave her gaze a quality of penetration, unnerving in one so young.

She yawned and looked westward over the city, moored to its riverside in the valley beneath her perch and etched in misty detail in the growing dawn. Here and there, a finger of light stirred the veil of fog guarding the walled town. Plumes of dying mist rolled lazily upward from the river, disappearing as the sun met and warmed their upward progress. In the shadow of the hill, the river lapped softly at its banks, barely breaking the silence that shrouded it.

As the sun, with a sudden burst of effort, heaved itself over the treetops, the river took fire, breaking into ripples of gold and silver streaked with deepest sapphire. The trout stirred their flickering, red-gilled bodies within the molten depths of the river and cavorted in their beds, loosing upon the crisp air jeweled sprays of water as they rose to greet the sun. Just as quickly, the trout disappeared with a flick of the tail, leaving only swirling eddies written on the polished surface of the water in memory of their presence.

She sighed, for the peacefulness and beauty of the scene drained her mind, even for so short a time, of the troubles that pressed hard upon her family and the scattered villages under their protection.

The great walls of Winchester now shook off their draperies of mist and set the city they delimited sharply apart from the surrounding countryside. Cheap Street, the main thoroughfare that cut a path westward from wall to wall, was already stirring with life as the city awoke. The rubble-stoned grey walls of the palace, to the south of Cheap Street, loomed starkly in the slanting light. Hard by the palace, the three churches of the Cathedral city strung themselves away from the rising sun like dark gems on an invisible chain. Closest was St. Mary's Abbey Church, small and cruciform. Next was the great rectangular Cathedral of Saints Peter and Paul, raised in the seventh century.

Furthest along the chain lay the monastery of St. Martin's, its squat stone tower raised like a stubby sentry to heaven, its solitary bell now calling the monks to the daybreak Office of Matins. The brown-robed monks would be shuffling two by two in answer to the summons, disappearing silently into the arched doorway to give thanks for this chilly autumn morning in the year of our Lord 886 and to beg deliverance from the pestilent enemy, as ordered by the King. They needed no royal decree to do so, having heard of the Northmen's penchant for rich monasteries. Such was their own, richly endowed by Alfred, so great was his gratitude to the Sovereign God of the new belief.

These Northmen were as pagan as the wild spirits that still inhabited, so it was believed, the forested sides of the great terraced earthwork looming darkly to the south, casting its long shadow on the morning as it brooded silently on its mysterious past. No one went up there: the new faith had not yet cast out altogether the old ways and the old spirits, and it could be seen that no hand of God had shaped that hill. Did the pagan spirits of the hill, offended by the churches in the vale below them, send some silent invitation to their northern kindred to come and ravage the land that had abandoned them? The Church viewed the spirits as evil; the common folk thought otherwise. But the times were bad, and it behooved Church and noble alike to fight the old beliefs. The common folk said the spirits were angered with the new beliefs and had called upon their fellow goblins among the Northmen to avenge them; indeed, the folk considered the Norsemen themselves to be inhabited by demons.

Certainly the bear-sarks were, those dreadful Vikings whose badge and costume was the bear pelt. They charged into battle, wearing their bear-sarks, with cries and screams more hideous than all the others taken together. They fought more viciously, killed more brutally, if such were possible, and invariably died themselves in the accomplishment of their mission. They were feared above all the Norsemen for they feared nothing, and death least of all. The fearsome legends they left behind them multiplied and terrified the common folk into secret offerings to placate the angry spirits who had sent them.

Her eyes swept northward to the village of Winnall, with its mud-and-wattle huts. No smoke trickled from the chimneys here, as it did from the buildings in the city. These were peasant dwellings, free, but lowly farmers, herders, grindingly poor, too much so to burn their precious gatherings of twigs before the deep cold of midwinter. Woodcutting privileges belonged only to thane and king alike, but the twigs and falls were left to the poor.

From Winnall, the countryside undulated down to the Itchen River. Her eyes followed it and she saw the small band of men leave the East Gate, cross the wooden bridge spanning the river, then turn northward toward a clearing. Two of the men were on horseback. The tall one at the head of the group would be Ethelred, Ealdorman of Mercia, ten years her senior. A strong, practical man, disciplined by many battles, he was her father's most trusted friend. Ethelred controlled the levies of Mercia. Even so disorganized as that harassed kingdom might be from raids and starvation, the strong will of the Ealdorman held the levies together. King Burhred of Mercia had long since fled to Rome, the invasions of the host having broken his fainting spirit.

Ethelred was of noble origin and had ranked highly in Burhred's court. Only fourteen when Burhred went to Rome, he was seasoned by more than a year's campaigns, and bid fair even then to take his dead father's command. The senior Ealdorman's lands were overrun, but the father had packed the son off to Burhred's service before he, himself, was killed defending his manorial lands from the attacking horde. Ethelred fumed inwardly at the indolent, indecisive king's court and spent his time in the field at training whenever he could escape the duties of attending the royal family.

They were inattentive to his frequent absences, fortunately for themselves. His skill as a tactician and a leader had grown rapidly with each campaign. By 883, this ealdorman, though not possessing royal blood, had earned the loyalty and devotion of every Mercian of Saxon heritage and the respect of his enemies. The King of Wessex, hearing of his reputation, sent for him and proposed that they should join forces and unite Wessex and Mercia militarily. Ethelred, fatherless son and lordless noble, was drawn to the King instantly and adopted the sad-faced man as the father he had lost and the only overlord he had ever respected. The King, seeing in this stalwart young soldier a sense and purpose second only to his own, embraced him gladly as an adopted son.

Aethelflaed smiled thoughtfully as the Ealdorman turned to the youngster at his side: Edward, her brother, who was as impatient as the young stallion under him, waiting to be turned loose. Fourteen years old, he was high-spirited, headstrong, and possessed of a robust intelligence not yet firmly under his own control. Ethelred, into whose capable charge Edward had been delivered, held a firm rein and exercised an unrelenting authority over the King's heir. She sighed, preferring greatly to have joined the preparations below, but this time, the King forbade it. Her only recourse was to seek out her hillside aerie before dawn so that she could at least watch from a distance.

Edward paused and looked surreptitiously over his shoulder and raised his arm in salute. She smiled to herself, but did not return the salute, knowing that he could see only the thicket that concealed her. But he would know she was there.

If Ethelred and the King were as close as father and son, Aethelflaed and Edward were closer still, for no lord and noble servant relationship pertained here. They were, if anything, as two ends of the same thought. Where Edward was headstrong and willful, she was calm and deliberate. Where Edward's personality rushed like a spring freshet, tumbling headlong and noisy with careless disregard for obstacles, she flowed quietly in her own course, like the Itchen below her, carving a deeper track each year. However calm a surface she presented, the depths glinted with currents unknown even to her. The gray-blue eyes through which she studied the world hid from those around her a maturity grown beyond sixteen seasons; a maturity induced by a childhood filled with battles, retreat before the Norse scourge, and times of hiding in the wilderness as the House of Wessex fought for its survival and the survival of its tiny band of followers.

The King, when he studied her thoughtfully from the shadows, glimpsed occasionally the strength and depth of the undercurrents as they surfaced in unguarded moments. God had given her a woman's shape, shrouding from careless view the mind and heart of the warrior that Alfred saw in those rare moments. He knew that Edward would have need of such a mind: it was as well that his first-born was a female. Two brothers with such spirits as theirs might one day come to bloodshed. It had happened before in the House of Wessex, when his ageing father Ethelwulf had been deprived of part of his kingdom by his sons, and the remaining kingdom had been split into separate factions.

Two spirited and able leaders they would be, for Edward already attracted loyalty the way nectar attracted bees; two such leaders contending for the same throne could wreck a kingdom. And Edward was contentious, of that there could be no doubt. No man would wrest a kingdom from him.

Of the King, his father, he stood in absolute awe, even as he chafed at the restrictions laid upon him by Alfred. He was fortunate, though, in his father's choice of a mentor and companion. Ethelred understood the high-spirited heir as did no one else. His elder sister, if she did not always understand him, tolerated his sometimes peevish energy with good humor. From these two only did Edward cheerfully allow criticism: from Ethelred because he was, next to his father, the best soldier in the kingdom and minced no words with the heir, and from his sister because she handled her sword and shield as well as he handled his own. This was also Ethelred's tutelage.

The riders and their retinue disappeared around the hillside, and she remembered that it was well past breakfast and she had brought no food with her. She made her way quickly down the rocky path to the bridge, bade good morning to the grizzled old warrior at the gate. Life had been hard on him. He was part Mercian, like herself, and had served under both Ealdorman Ethelred and her father. Both of his sons lay buried in Mercia, and his wife and daughters he had seen, as he lay on the ground left for dead, carried off by the Danes into East Anglia as hostages, which meant thralldom. More likely, his wife was dead, fervently to be hoped under the circumstances, and his daughters transported over the northern seas to the slave markets on the Dnieper, there to be sold into Muslim hands after their desirability as harem property was proved to the satisfaction of both Viking trader and Mohammedan buyer.

"Have you eaten today?" she asked him. He shook his head. "We will send you something then," she promised. Not many had more than one meal a day, if that. Old retainers deserved whatever their Lord could give them, and it was the King's obligation to feed them.

Ealhswith glanced up from her tabby weaving at the light tap against the open door. "We missed you at breakfast." Her fingers plied the shuttle swiftly with a sureness born of long experience. Aethelflaed watched the design taking shape in fine silk and gold thread. Weavers of peace, the Saxons called their women, and her Lady Mother was certainly such a one. The Queen carefully hung the weaving tablets by their knotted threads on a small pegged board. The task took all her concentration for a few moments as she held the knotted ends firmly with one hand and ran the fingers of her other hand through the hanging threads to remove twists and tangles.

"Your father has given you too much to think about, perhaps?" She nodded knowingly as Aethelflaed bestowed a quick, dark look on her. "You will give your answer soon, I expect?" She snipped a loose thread with a pair of iron shears suspended from her girdle, then drew the girl to the settle bench beside her.

"Child, even had you been the first son, you would not have found it easy, not with your mind and heart. You and Edward are very different and that is fortunate for you both. He is well suited to his place in life. He will be a good king. He is strong-willed and he shall command the loyalty of his thanes. No." She shook her head at the look on Aethelflaed's face. "He is not like the King, but he will command devotion. You are the thoughtful one, and you are the one who is like your father. If we had peace…." She paused and looked through the arched window. "If we had peace, it might be different. Still, you would not rule Wessex but your life might be easier and the decisions you would be asked to make would be less bitter."

"I do not envy Edward, Lady Mother." It was through the Queen's good offices that she was still with her family. Other daughters were married early, as early as eleven or twelve years, before nature had given them their womanhood. As soon as that event occurred, they were wed and bedded quickly, for the fortunes and alliances of countries depended heavily on the outcome of royal unions.

She might have been married overseas to a foreign king, to one whom she did not know or could not possibly care for, to cement a treaty between two families. Betrothal could mean leaving all that was dear and familiar to go abroad forever, to serve the political needs of others. Yet her mother had done just that when her father arranged her marriage to Alfred, the brother of King Aethelred. The King had thus far forborne to press duty on his daughter, but time was no longer on her side. She studied the Queen's profile, the face of this quiet Lady who had borne nine children and buried four of them.

"Mother," she asked, "Do you know what the King wills for me? Has he spoken to you?"

"He asked me if you might have shown a preference for someone."

Aethelflaed smiled ruefully. "No, I have none. It is as well, else I might be troubled to put my feelings aside." She looked up as a slight movement in the doorway caught her eye. "Look, your slave brings you dinner."

A boy, one of the Queen's thralls, stood silently in the doorway, holding a steaming pot wrapped in cloths. The Queen nodded to him and he slipped into the room and fixed a table for them. He turned to go but Aethelflaed stopped him.

"Know you the old guard at the gate?" He nodded. "He has not eaten today. Ask the kitchen to prepare a meal for him; then you shall take it to him."

She noticed the iron slave ring on his arm, wondering how the palace came by so young a thrall. Sometimes children were sold into slavery by their parents when famine struck. It was one way to ensure that the children survived. The palace rarely bought slaves, for they had more than they needed of hostages, prisoners, and men who had lost their freedom by criminal acts.

"He was born here," said Ealhswith, reading her thoughts. "His mother was a Welsh girl taken in the wars beyond the *wealasdic*, the Welshdyke."

"His father…?"

"Was English," finished Ealhswith, lowering her eyes.

Aethelflaed looked at the boy with sudden pity, but the steady, waiting gaze that he returned showed no trace of pity for himself. He simply waited, as he had done all his short life, on the actions of those above him. "Tell him the Athelinga, the princess, sent you. Be quick about it and you will have a piece of mutton and a barley cake with honey for your supper. And you shall also have half a silver penny."

Ealhswith and Aethelflaed ate silently, each wrapped in her own thoughts. Aethelflaed dabbed at the chunks of steaming mutton in her earthenware dish though she was not very hungry. The Queen refused to eat meat from the joint as was done in the Great Hall below. Her own servants prepared the dish for her, cutting the meat from the bone, drenching it in drippings mixed with wild herbs, finally serving it on a thick trencher of bread to soak up the succulent drippings. The trencher would be left in the dish along with any scraps of meat not to the Queen's taste for her servants to enjoy later. She was always careful to leave a morsel or two; otherwise, her servants would rarely taste meat.

Aethelflaed smiled as she watched her mother eating so daintily. It was as well that women were not present at the meals in the Great Hall. The manners of the retainers were rough and boisterous, and, as the evening wore on and drinking horns were filled and refilled, the men became quarrelsome, bawdy, and loud. The King tolerated much. These men, he reminded his wife, had little enough pleasure in such troublous times and he was inclined to envy the man who could lose himself in drink, as he could not, being much bothered by his digestion. The King's Peace, however, was rarely violated, for the penalty was severe. At worst, a man could lose his freedom if he started a fight or perhaps injured another at the king's board or in the king's household. So Alfred allowed the thanes to work off their pent-up spirits in raucous laughter, drink, and shouting. But when the King stood up, the din dropped to a whisper, for no one wished to anger the King or disturb the King's Peace.

With such power at his ordering, it was remarkable that her father had asked her consent to be given freely. Of course, she reflected, free consent was by law a woman's right, though not many parents observed it. Daughters who refused their parents' choice might be openly abused, or at best, hounded into submission. But Alfred was not one to disrespect a law, whether it be of his own making or not.

"Daughter," Ealhswith broke the long silence. "You need not fear that your father will not choose wisely for you."

Aethelflaed shook her head. "No, I have no fears there."

Ealhswith chuckled. "My love, all that is asked of us is consent. But," she added placatingly, "if you are not pleased, your father would not insist on the match."

"Did you love the King when you married him?"

"You mean, did I fall in love with him as soon as I saw him? No, I did not. It was not required." She saw the unspoken question in Aethelflaed's eyes. "Of course, I was nervous. Later on, I did come to love him." Her tone softened with remembrance. "The King is a most unusual man, and I bless my father, fared forth that he is, I bless him daily for having bestowed me beyond my hopes. If you consent to marriage, your father will surely treat you as well as mine treated me."

A rustle at the door informed them that the boy was back to remove the dishes. "You have finished your errand?" He nodded, staring at her with wide, dark eyes. "Good." She took a silver half-penny from the bag at her waist. "This one must be for you. Young thralls must be rewarded as well as old ones."

The boy continued to stare at her, this time in amazement instead of curiosity. He was too young to be paid for his labors, and he had never owned hard coin in his short life. He stared up at her, and then dropped to his knees by way of thanks.

"Stand up," she ordered, not unkindly, for she was strangely discomfited by the sight of the slave boy on his knees. "You have earned it." Ealhswith nodded quietly to herself, again absorbed in her tabby weaving. The boy quickly cleared the table and left, with a backward glance at his benefactor, which almost caused him to bump into the slender figure standing unnoticed at the door.

"Dearest sister!" A clear, musical voice floated to her from the shadows of the doorway. "You will turn the child's head with such a gift and make him the envy of the kitchen. It will cause him no end of trouble." The owner of the voice stepped into the light of the room. "But I have no doubt," she continued, "that he'll not care. He will be your slave for life!"

CHAPTER TWO

*A*ethelflaed turned and held out her arms to her sister. She hugged her warmly, then stepped back and scrutinized her. She wore a coarse woolen cloak and hood over her sashed robe, which accentuated her delicate frame. A heavy wooden cross around her neck proclaimed her ascetic disposition, for it was not ordinary for women of royal blood, pledged to the Church from birth as was Elgiva, to take the vows of poverty so strictly. Indeed, had not both the Abbess and the Queen ordered other-wise, Elgiva would have indulged her ascetic nature to extreme.

To the Queen, Elgiva, at thirteen, was still a child, and memories of the girl's delicate babyhood brought quick concern to the Queen's face as she noted the pallid cheek and slender frame.

"Nonsense," said Aethelflaed, noting her mother's expression, "she is as sturdy as an ox. Besides, she is a woman now according to the law, and she may choose to follow a discipline. None but the Abbess can stay her."

"Nevertheless," the Queen said, "both of you will dress as becomes your station. You, Elgiva, will put off the hair shirt under your robe. I know you wear it, the Abbess tells me so."

A barely audible sigh escaped Elgiva. Aethelflaed took her sister's hand and begged the Queen's leave before Elgiva could protest. To dress in the manner deemed fit by the King for a member of his family was truly a penance for Elgiva, who abhorred personal display of wealth or rank, and to whom the austerity of convent life was a pleasure. She shepherded her younger sister to their adjoining apartments.

"You like Shaftesbury?" The question was unnecessary, for Elgiva's small face shone at the mere mention of her adopted home.

"Ah, dearest sister." She took Aethelflaed's hand. "It is beyond expec-tation. We have finished the Chapter House, and the Church lacks only a year or two of finishing. I would so much rather have stayed there." She paused, blushing at her sister's smile. "I didn't mean that I do not wish to see my family," she faltered, "but the Abbess insisted that I must return to Winchester for a while before I take my vows."

"She is very wise. And do not blush. I know you love it there." There was no reason to suppose that Elgiva would change her mind. The King had professed her himself at her birth, and was graceful enough to seek her consent on her twelfth birthday, but no flicker of doubt had marred his con-viction that monastic life was Elgiva's calling. Even had it not been so,

15

Aethelflaed doubted that the girl would have gone back on her father's word, for the Church was to be wooed and won with royal gifts, such as her sister, just as patronage was won in the courts of Paris, and Flanders, and in Rome, with worldly brides. Nevertheless, Alfred was secure in his judgment: he had seen an unworldly happiness shining in her, even from the cradle. The family saw it as she grew up and knew her to be one the Lord had marked for himself.

Alfred had ridden out to Shaftesbury when Elgiva was seven and surveyed the tiny village perched high on its escarpment. It was most suitable. Shaftesbury, the Fortified-Place-On-A-Cliff, commanded a stunning view of the vale of Blackmoor and no more lonely or beautiful a place might be found for a soul promised to God. Thick forests protected the northern approach to the hamlet. To the south, the escarpment dropped sharply away from the low wooden wall surrounding the village to provide an unencumbered view as far as the eye could see or the mist, swirling at the base of the hill, would permit. Such a landscape would yield lessons in joy to a contemplative spirit, as Alfred knew. But contemplating it also from a more worldly point of view, Alfred did not fail to see its excellent potential as a fortress.

Elgiva would be elevated to Abbess on her twentieth birthday: until that time the sisters of the Abbey of St. Mary, Nunnaminster, in Winchester, supervised the building of Shaftesbury and much of the fortification of the village as well. That Alfred's purpose was twofold disturbed them not a whit, for they were practical folk. If anything, they were well pleased, for it was better to be protected from surprise attack whilst they carried out their duty to God and to his representative, the King.

"She is wise," Aethelflaed repeated. "It is better to be sure of your mind and heart." She smiled a little enviously. "You are fortunate to know your destiny from the cradle." And fortunate, too, she reflected silently, to be so certain. It was as well that she would have the protection of an abbey to surround her, for the calm, unbroken rhythm of the Daily Offices would suit the girl.

Both girls had changed to long robes of finely woven white wool, decorated with Ealhswith's elaborately delicate embroidery and sashed at the waist with red and gold tabby-woven belts, also the Queen's handiwork, worked in designs of twined vines and animals. Aethelflaed's cloak, worn loosely over her shoulders, was fastened at the front with a circular, jeweled brooch. Heavy gold ringlets adorned both arms, which were bare to the shoulder under the cloak.

Elgiva balked at so much finery, though she had consented to wear a gold cross inlaid with garnet and colored enamels. Her cloak was fastened with a gold brooch chased with figures and scenes from the Bible, both gifts of the King. She disapproved of the Abbess' habit of wearing elaborate ecclesiastical jewelry, suspecting that the woman had never conquered her personal vanity.

Elgiva studied Aethelflaed narrowly. "Your thoughts may be hidden from me, but the feelings of your heart are not. I am come home to witness your betrothal, am I not? No," she added quickly, seeing Aethelflaed's look of surprise, "I have not been told. It is long expected."

Aethelflaed's lips curved in a wry smile. "Indeed, as you say, long expected. Since I am twelve, I think."

"The King asks for your consent?" She nodded. "You will give it, of course." Aethelflaed was quiet. "Ah," Elgiva's eyes widened knowingly. "You do not like our father's choice of a husband?"

"I do not know who the King may choose for me." She twisted the silk tassel of her belt irritably. "I mean, perhaps, I would rather not marry, for I think sometimes it is good to be alone."

"Nonsense." Elgiva's tone was decisive. "It is never good to be alone." Aethelflaed raised her eyebrows, knowing Elgiva's penchant for solitary meditation in her cell. "Even I am not as alone as you would think. We are not allowed to withdraw. Anyhow," she radiated calm certainty, "you will find your answer."

"My Lady Mother and yourself are of one mind about me," Aethelflaed replied dryly. "I wish I could share your conviction. I pray often but I have no answers yet."

"Well, you cannot wait forever," Elgiva said, unhelpfully. "You must decide soon. Besides," she added, "you are getting quite old, you know."

"Enough!" Aethelflaed laughed and held up her hand. "I will decide forthwith, lest I become so aged no man would have me."

"I suppose you have considered the convent." Elgiva was suddenly serious.

"If I choose not to marry, it could be an acceptable life for me."

"Never!" Elgiva smiled with some amusement. "It is quite otherwise. The daughter of a king can be more useful elsewhere. Besides, you would never consent to be ruled by the Abbess. You do not understand the discipline of the Church."

"I understand the soldier's life. Surely you would own that to be discipline." Aethelflaed's cheeks reddened with momentary anger.

"No offense, pray, sister." Elgiva's voice was soothing. "I only meant that you are used to giving orders, not to taking them." She paused a moment to let that sink in. "Why think you that you be not subject to Providence even as I am? You may not yet know your fate, but certainly it knows you." She touched the gold circlets on Aethelflaed's arm. "You are a ring-giver; that is your Providence."

Aethelflaed disagreed firmly. "That is for kings, not for such as myself."

Elgiva nodded but she was prevented from pursuing the subject further by the look of withdrawal in her sister's eyes.

"What have you heard of the host?" Aethelflaed asked abruptly.

"Nothing. We are very much alone on the cliff."

"It has not escaped your attention that there is more being built than a monastery?"

Elgiva shrugged. "A sensible precaution."

"It is more than that. The Danes still camp at London."

"They have been there a long time." It was obvious that she did not understand the danger.

"The King is preparing to march on London," Aethelflaed said slowly and deliberately, and saw Elgiva's eyes widen in comprehension.

"That is why I am sent home, it is not a betrothal after all. Will you go with them?"

Aethelflaed sighed and shook her head ruefully. "No, nor Edward either. We will stay here with the Queen. Ethelred, of course, will go with the King."

"Edward will not go? Then it is more dangerous that you are saying."

"If it goes well, Edward and I will join them at London. If not, we will escort you and the Queen to safety at Athelney." The advantage was always, in a siege, with those inside the walls.

"I would rather die at Shaftesbury." Elgiva raised her head defiantly.

"You will not die at Shaftesbury or anywhere else," Aethelflaed replied curtly. "You will come with us. We can no more afford your death than we can Edward's. If the King does not come back from this, if he is either killed or taken hostage, we must have the family safe. We cannot continue fighting without Edward, and his success will depend on the rest of us."

Elgiva suppressed a fleeting smile at the commanding tone, but Aethelflaed took no notice of it. She was thinking, without relish, of dismal Athelney in the marshes of Somerset and hoping desperately it would not come to that. Elgiva would have few, perhaps dim, recollections of Athelney, though Aethelflaed remembered it all too vividly herself. She had been only eight years old and Elgiva not yet five when the bitter defeat of the English at Chippenham drove Alfred, his family, and his retinue of thanes into Selwood forest beyond the Parret River in full retreat.

Never had the Danes attacked midwinter. They stole secretly, after Twelfth Night, into Wessex, taking the army completely by surprise. They pushed on, south and west, into Devon and beyond, driving many of the people over the water to Europe. The King escaped, because the hidden marshes of Selwood had been known to him for many years, lying as they did in the country near Glastonbury and Cheddar.

The King's despair and brooding silence had pained her as they crossed the deep woods and then into the marsh by boat. In later years and other difficulties she never saw her father so beset by doubts and fears as he had been in those days. Grim and desolate though it be, the isle of Athelney was the one place in England secure against the invader if only because they could not find it. Even had the Danes known it was there, the forests surrounding it were trackless and the marshes inside the forest remained under a thick curtain of mist. It was said to be haunted by water spirits and elves, and even if the men of Somerset believed that, and there was no doubt that many did, they nevertheless knew their way around the forest. The King had no fear of betrayal. The folk would shrug and roll their eyes if asked about the spirits and cite endless cases of goblined horses and possessions by demons. No one dared enter. So they were safe.

Certainly Elgiva would barely recall the chill misery of that winter, living in mud-and-wattle huts like the peasants instead of the stone and wood palace at Cheddar. It was almost Easter of the following year before a wooden building had been raised for the King and his family. Nor would Elgiva remember the spitting hatred with which the thanes of Wessex pronounced the names of Ivarr the Boneless and Halfdan, whose brother was slain by the men of Devon. The raven banner of Sigurthr, despised jarl of the Orkneys had been captured and hope glimmered, though Ivarr ravaged Northumbria, and Halfdan still harried Wessex.

The fortification at Athelney proceeded. Countless times Aethelflaed watched as the thanes of Somerset and Devon, Wiltshire, and the near side of Hampshire stole silently into the marshes to meet with Alfred. Then, guided through the secret tracks in the marshes and forests by the same folk who professed to fear the spirits and elves, they rode out as stealthily as they had come, back to the rolling hills of Wessex that were now held by their enemies.

For seven weeks, Alfred and the thanes of Wessex harassed the Danes with raids, striking quickly, disappearing like phantoms back into the mists and fog of the forest, only to return as swiftly to strike again. Between raids, Alfred gathered his men around him and planned. And prayed. Seven weeks after Easter, the King rode out with the thanes of Wessex and met the entire host at Edington: he put them to flight, pursued them, and laid siege to them in their own fortification. After two long weeks, they surrendered, and the much-hated Guthrum, their king, submitted to Alfred.

Alfred's terms opened wide many eyes: baptism for Guthrum and his men. Furthermore, they must leave Wessex forever. Traitors, all of them. Men who mouthed honor whilst their hearts reeked of treachery. The King's honor, as he bestowed gifts of gold and food on the newly baptized Christians, came from deep within his spirit. Nevertheless, she knew he regarded his newly baptized brothers with considerable caution.

Alfred gathered strength on his knees for whatever trial confronted him. She often stood in the shadow of the tiny stockaded church on Athelney and watched her father wonderingly, for he appeared deep in conversation. She saw no others there, and for many years after, puzzled that he should spend so many hours talking to himself. She overheard him speak to the Queen about St. Cuthbert, but that holy man had been dead for many years, and she knew herself that there had been no one there. Later she understood, and marveled that a man of such a religious disposition, who was granted speech with the faithful dead, could rise from his knees, don his helmet and byrnie, and swiftly rally his thanes to the attack. As the Queen well knew, it cost him dearly.

Aethelflaed came back to herself with a start. Athelney was far behind them, and with God's help and their own determination, it would stay behind them. St. Mary's bell, insistently tolling Vespers, recalled her. Elgiva was regarding her solemnly. "Perhaps you are not so sure now that what you will do is right. Yet the day will come that you will be certain in your heart that what you chose was ordained for you," she said, misreading Aethelflaed's musing. She rose, dropping a caressing hand on Aethelflaed's head before she left for Vespers, leaving Aethelflaed to her own thoughts.

The nuns had finished Vespers and the chapel was deserted when Aethelflaed entered and knelt on the cold stone floor. Stout timbers overhead pressed upward against the heavy roof. A candle burned dimly in the sanctuary and light from the setting sun filtered wanly through small, arched windows high in the nave, throwing into deep relief the carved stone angels on the wall that guarded the entrance to the sanctuary. Little light would be needed, for the nun's priest knew his Offices by heart.

It was well for the priest that he was musical by nature and had an inborn knack for the rhythm of the Psalter and the Responsory. He was willing also, at the King's urgent suggestion, to learn to read and understand the words he mouthed so roundly. The highly born nuns were taught to read, paint, and embroider, and to chant their Offices gracefully and in tune. The Book of Offices, reposing in unread splendor on the altar, had been translated by them for their own use.

She shifted uncomfortably. The rough stone floor dug into her knees. Unlike the King, no visions would attend her at prayers. Such things might be for him and perhaps Elgiva too. They knew their hearts and thoughts better, and, unlike herself, knew how to withdraw from worldly concerns when they were on their knees.

She bowed her head and began. *Our Father, thou that art in heaven, be thine name hallowed...*

She felt the urgency behind the simple wording of the prayer. A desperate request was woven into the acknowledgement of heaven's greatness, for to the heathen, nothing was holy. The gods of the Danes were like the Northmen themselves, adventurers, seeking what they might destroy. No church in all of England was safe from them, no person secure from the heavy double-edged battle-axe, murderously wielded with both hands. These glory-seekers, when conquered, took holy oaths and baptism to prevent English reprisals against them. As quickly as they swore on the sacred armlets, they broke the oath and returned to pillage and murder. They would never hold sacred any oath or obligation.

Thy kingdom come, thy will become on earth as in heaven...

It was hard to see God's will in the ravaging of England. Even harder to imagine how it might be fulfilled in the fate of London, shortly to be seen. Either way it went, London and its people would suffer. The Danish camps were sprinkled around the countryside outside London, and Aethelflaed knew that her own countrymen would set these tiny burhs to the torch. Was the will of God written in the scorched land and the stench of wasted countryside that would sear the nostrils of the King's men as they marched on London?

Give us our daily loaf today...

The burned-out wheat fields would force the Danes to flee or starve. The English who set fire to their own fields, helped by Alfred's thanes, would starve too. For years it had been thus: invasions, fires, destruction, starvation, then a pathetically short period of respite to coax the fields to bear again before there were more invasions, more deaths. Many would go without their daily loaf. Not her father's armies. The men who pledged their lives to the King received his pledge of arms and provisions in return. But the peasants would scratch a living from the soil as best they could, and when they could not, they would go begging at monastery gates, where starving monks would share their own pitiful crusts with the folk. Aethelflaed more than once saw her father weep for the fate of his poor and knew, as he did, that the depredations of the Danes, in the eyes of the poor, were hard to tell apart from the reprisals of the English.

And forgive us our guilt as we forgive our offenders...

The brutal slaughter of Dane and countryman alike weighed heavily on her mind, though it was accepted stoically by others; indeed, it was seen as part of the natural order of things that so few should die peacefully in their sleep. The monasteries, with their treasures of books and gold, were eagerly sought and raided by Vikings. The books were tossed aside and later used for kindling, as they lit fires to warm themselves among the ruins they created. Treasures of jeweled golden chalices and rich furnishings beckoned. Helpless monks were felled by the dreaded long-handled, double-edged axe, their skulls split open at the foot of the altar where they had mistakenly fled for refuge.

Her stomach wrenched with nausea as her memory reminded her of Danish bloodguilt. No *wergild*, no man-gold, was paid by the heathen for the lives they took: they were not subject to Saxon law. Instead, they exacted peace payment from the people whose kinsmen they murdered and whose country they ravaged. Without the peace payment, they would not leave, and even when they got it, if indeed there was any precious coin left when they finished their pillaging, they would soon be back to terrorize the helpless villages again and again. The Lord commanded that she forgive this dreadful enemy and love him.

Her countrymen were not so squeamish as she. Hate festered and burned in their hearts as they knelt at Mass and prayed fervently for a great kill on the battlefield. Was not Christ God's great young warrior, as the poet sung? Did he not of his own will embrace a bloody and terrible death, as did the thanes of Wessex, for a greater glory? Did he not fight the heathen even as they? And without the burning hatred that they carried into battle, so unlike God's Warrior, could they have fought the host so bitterly and even successfully? She thought not.

The agonized English repaid the Danes in kind for their bloodlust. She had seen ghastly reminders of their hatred. Such hapless Danes as were unlucky enough to stray into English villages without the protection of their fellow Vikings were killed and flayed. Killed first if they were fortunate. Their skins, still running with blood, were nailed to minster doors as a grisly threat to any heathen who might again violate holy places.

"Forgive us," she murmured, tears staining her cheeks. "We are pressed past prayer, past reason, past even despair." She raised her head and finished:

And do not thou lead us into temptation, but lead thou us away from evil. Truthfully.

She rose and turned to leave. Her father was standing quietly in the shadows behind her. He came closer and studied her face.

"These are not ordinary prayers. You are much troubled."

She rubbed the wetness from her cheeks. "Yes, my Lord."

Alfred took her hand and drew her to a bench. "I cannot put off plans for your future much longer, daughter, but if it distresses you so, I can perhaps delay a little. Is that the matter that weighs on you?"

"Ah, no father. At least, that is not all of it. It is," she shrugged her shoulders helplessly, "it is this enemy, this wretched necessity. I can neither love nor forgive these people."

He nodded heavily. "We must destroy them before they destroy us. They are still God's creatures, and we must learn to love them some day, even if we can't now."

"How shall I love, seeing the things they do? And if I could love, how then kill them?"

"You have not yet done so! I have tried to spare you that burden."

"I am grateful, My Lord, but the time will come that you will not be there to spare me. Then I will have to kill or die."

Alfred regarded her thoughtfully. "You are not a child any longer, neither are you a coward. When such a time comes, you will do as you have been trained to do. One cannot escape one's burdens." He lapsed into silence, then addressed her softly. "Aethelflaed, would you rather I sent you to monastic life? Even that would not guarantee protection of yourself or others against the host. I will gladly consider that life for you, if you wish it."

"I have thought of it."

Alfred's eyes were dark with compassion and understanding. "Once I might have preferred to stay in the monastery, to read Latin as easily as the abbots and to spend my hours chanting the Offices."

"You could not! Did not my grandfather take you to Rome when you were only four? Were you not then anointed king by His Holiness in Rome? A king must be a warrior. Your father raised you thus!"

He shook his head sadly. "Ah, but everyone was. It was necessary."

"You said 'once.' Even though you were anointed a king?"

He smiled. "I may have been anointed, but there were others ahead of me. No one expected to see me here, least of all myself. Indeed, once I thought of monastic life, but it was mostly learning that I loved." He paused, thinking momentarily of that first trip to Rome to which she had referred. "It was before the marriage to your mother was arranged by my brother and before the Witan chose me. What I am is God's will, not mine."

"Ah." A thought lay half-formed in her mind. "The bishops and thanes in the Witan, did you see their will as God's will for you?" The King nodded. "Then they chose for you. You did not choose for yourself. Yet you ask me to choose for myself?"

He laid his hand over hers. "Only to say whether you will marry or no."

"That is it, My Lord. Must I say yes without knowing who it shall be?"

"My dear, have you a preference? Is there someone you love?" His eyes narrowed imperceptibly. It was not lost on her.

"No, Father." Her forehead wrinkled with perplexity. "And I don't really think of monastic life. But I see Elgiva's happiness."

"Elgiva is not Aethelflaed."

"Elgiva will not be sent over the sea," she blurted out. "She will stay near her family and her home. But if I marry, I will go to some nobleman in a strange land among strange people, whose ways I do not know!"

"If I had planned that, I would have sent you there long ago to be raised among them so you would not be ignorant of their ways or their tongue. You are much too old for that now."

She stared at him, hoping against hope. "If I marry I would not have to leave Wessex?"

"I cannot promise you that you will not leave Wessex, but you shall not leave England. I promise you, I shall not send you to Frankia or to Flanders, though you could do worse than to live at Baldwin's court. Judith is my kinswoman and friend and would not fail to be kind. No." He patted her hand, comforting her. "You shall not go to Flanders. I have already arranged that Aelfthryth will be married to Judith's son. Now, do you still wish for a convent?"

She smiled her relief and exhaled softly. She had not realized she was holding her breath as her father spoke of the youngest sister's marriage. Part of the burden dropped away from her and she squeezed the King's hand gratefully. "No, My Lord. You will choose a husband for me, and I will accept, even as the Witan chose a kingdom for you, and you accepted."

He smiled at her reassuringly. "You will not be displeased. The convent does not suit you. There is something else in your thoughts. What else remains?"

"I am tired of war, I am tired of hating the Danes. But how can one keep on fighting unless one hates? I understand nothing of what is meant by loving an enemy that we must nevertheless kill." She paused, puzzled. "The new belief says we must destroy the heathen."

"You will work it out in your own way. There is no other path."

She studied the King's face in the deepening shadows, seeing for the first time some of the burdens he bore. Perhaps the hours he spent every day chanting the Offices with the monks helped to ease the guilt she saw etched on his brooding face. Of the depth and sincerity of his faith in the new God who led him forth victorious from Athelney there could be no doubt. He believed himself called to kingship by this God with a childlike faith and simplicity. But behind the deceptive simplicity burned the mind of a king; shrewd, intelligent, zealous for the good of those entrusted to his care, even to the killing of another of God's *mancynn* who threatened all he called his own. It was not only charity that drove him to insist on Guthrum's baptism. God might order the Christian to spread the gospel among the heathen, but the king in him whispered that this enemy might eventually be brought to heel more easily if he were a believer. Christian might be less likely to raise arms against Christian. A vain hope, perhaps, but worth the effort.

The moment of insight passed, not fully comprehended, but something in her heart pondered the fleeting insight, and she sensed dimly that the future unseen in her thoughts was by the king beside her clearly seen in all its detail and color. It remained to him somehow, and perhaps even to her, to fill that vision with form and substance, with all the dimensions of reality.

The King smiled suddenly, breaking the somber mood. He put his arm around his daughter's shoulders. "Do you think, my child, that you could find Lord Ethelred acceptable?" She caught her breath and stared back at him.

Then the King told her of his vision for Wessex and Mercia.

CHAPTER THREE

*E*alhswith allowed herself to smile happily. She knew her future son-in-law well and was pleased. He was a good man; truly he and her daughter would be equals in the old Saxon tradition. Privately, she deplored the practices of the Frankish and Flemish courts, where women were in bondage to their husbands. The Saxons had brought their own customs of freedom and responsibility and their old gods to this island before the new religion swept the lands they had left behind.

Nevertheless, changes came. The new faith came to the island of the Angles and the Saxons. It was a slow process. The old gods were not officially honored any longer, not at court. Still, the ancient customs and laws prevailed among the folk, to the chagrin of the clergy, and even the baptized nobility trod as carefully as any peasant if they thought that *Tir* or *Woden* might be watching. The new faith had not changed everything, if only because it had not been around long enough.

Perhaps a woman and her betrothed no longer exchanged shields and spears as wedding presents, as they had once done in the old country. Women were no longer expected to fight at their husband's sides, though some did still. But women could still own and bequeath property as they saw fit, and they could not be deprived of what they inherited from their male kinfolk. It was often tried but Saxon law forbid it.

This was not so overseas. The new religion, with its strange Eastern customs, discouraged and even forbade the giving of power and riches to women, and the Frankish clergy preached that women were too foolish to be entrusted with such important things. The Franks and Gauls listened and did as they were told. The Saxons and the Celts held back: they had a long history of powerful women. Still they accepted the new faith. It offered a hope that the old Gods did not.

When Aethelflaed's betrothal writs had been signed, and property settlements and powers were entered, the couple found a few moments alone, their first in several days.

"Do you mind?" asked Ethelred. "Might you find you have a preference for me?"

"My dear friend," she responded, "I have always had a preference for you." Indeed, she realized she had. How much better to be betrothed to a man one knew well as a friend, instead of a stranger. She breathed a sigh of relief and squeezed his hand.

His face relaxed into a genial smile. She held up a warning finger. "I do not know if I love you. Even my mother did not know that before she married my father, because she had never met him. Do you mind that very much?" He smiled and slipped his arm around her shoulders. "I had not expected that you love me now. I am happy to find myself acceptable. But," he promised, "you will love me someday. And we shall get on very well together."

There was, of course, no doubt about the intention of the match. Wessex and Mercia were to be welded into one kingdom with one loyalty: The House of Wessex. Ethelred was popular among his own people, and though Alfred was much loved by the Mercians, they would follow their own son, soon to be married to a princess descended from both Mercian and West Saxon royalty. A good arrangement for both sides.

There was no time for Ethelred and Aethelflaed to enjoy any time together at all, for the preparation for the coming campaign proceeded, if anything, more swiftly and urgently than before. Edward's distress at being excluded knew no bounds. He displayed it plainly enough in the private company of Aethelflaed and Ethelred, and with great effort, forbore to show his impatience elsewhere; showing it to the King would bring stern reproof. Edward clearly had inherited none of his father's patience.

"I could take a division south of London while my father attacks from the north." His eyes glowed with excitement as he paced the floor of Aethelflaed's chambers nervously.

Ethelred shook his head. "The Ealdorman of Wiltshire will do that." "Besides," Aethelflaed put in gently, "Ethelhelm has many seasons of fighting behind him."

Edward sighed his dejection and ran his hand though his hair. He was still growing and because of that, still slender, but without a trace of awkwardness. Two years of battle since attaining his manhood at the age of twelve had given him some toughness, but he was too young to be entrusted with a command, which he knew as well as they. He chafed silently at the inactivity of palace life, and silently endured the long Offices required by the King for all members of his household, restraining with great effort the restless energy of youth. His relief was heartfelt and visible when the levies were called to prepare for battle.

The King's sense of mission made him a firm disciplinarian and he found it to both his and Edward's advantage to put his rough-edged heir in Ethelred's hands. The King would not tolerate a breach of manners, public or private, from any subject, not even his son. Royal blood did not come ahead of military discipline, and in the field, Ethelred's word was law: the Ealdorman was subject to the King and to no other. Of this Edward was aware and consequently accepted Ethelred's command as he would have the King's. In spite of this, Ethelred wore his authority easily, as one who had earned his right to it. Unlike the King, who was approachable only when he chose to be, Ethelred was a man whose manner invited openness and confidence.

"I could wait at Eastdene," Edward suggested hopefully.

Ethelred threw back his head and laughed. "You will not give up, will you? No, again. Eastdene is to be left empty and the royal manor will be barricaded." Aethelflaed nodded agreement. Eastdene was too close to the channel and too open to invasion if the Danes brought support from Frankia again.

"You will have enough to do here," Ethelred assured him. The Welshman, Asser, will be coming from Eastdene to join us soon. He will find much to keep you busy."

Aethelflaed repressed a smile. The priest's arrival would not be hailed by Edward, for bondage to the schoolroom would be viewed by him as a poor substitute for the battlefield.

"Nevertheless," Ethelred bent a stern eye on Edward, who opened his mouth to protest, "you will be wise to attend to him. A king needs more than skill with a sword and spear and scramasax to rule." Edward pressed his lips firmly together, recognizing both the look and the tone of voice. "I envy you," said Ethelred. Edward looked up in surprise. "Yes," he looked speculatively at Edward, "it is a good thing to know more than weapons and war. I would have such knowledge myself, for I know I will stand in great need of it. But matters press too hard upon us, so I must rely upon your sister to make up for my failings." Neither Aethelflaed nor Edward understood fully this last remark, but Edward, shrugging it off impatiently, begged to be allowed to join the King and his thanes at war council, promising absolute silence.

It was a promise he was hard-pressed to keep, for some of Alfred's plans surprised him and Aethelflaed as well, though as she mulled them over later, they shed some light on Ethelred's remarks.

Alfred and Ethelred would lead part of the levies eastward to the northern approach to the city. "We will clean out the villages and destroy the crops here," Alfred pointed at dots on the roughly drawn parchment map, "and here. Ethelhelm," he nodded at the thane across the table from him, "will do the same to the south."

"We will leave a small party at Eastdene to keep watch on the coast-line," Ethelhelm added. The chalk cliffs, not far from Eastdene, provided a clear view of the channel. Viking ships could be spotted easily on a clear day, and riders would relay the news to Ethelhelm long before the host could drag their dragon-prowed ships onto the beach and spread out across Surrey. The dense forests between the coast and London were the English defense. It would only take a few men hidden in the Weald to stop the advance of support sailing in from Frankia.

Ethelhelm, with the Weald secure behind him, could reduce the Dane-infested hamlets to the south of London without fear of attack.

"I will go only this far," Alfred indicated a line several miles outside of London, "and Ethelhelm will take up his position on the south bank of the Thames across from the south wall. We will block the westward approach to the city with some of our own ships. The only exit from London will be the estuary. Rochester is in English hands, and our men there will see to it that the host do not attempt to leave by the river."

Edward looked stunned. "You will not lay siege to the city yourself?" Aethelflaed sent him a warning glance, then looked at Ethelred, who was lost in thought, apparently oblivious of Alfred's statement.

"No." Alfred turned to the Ealdorman of Mercia. "This town belongs in Mercian hands. Ethelred will lay siege and enter the town, and I will support him. As soon as we reach London, Ethelred will take command."

The King turned his head and looked at his daughter. "This is my wedding present, Aethelflaed. The city of London belongs to Ethelred and to you as long as either of you live." He turned again and studied Edward, transfixing him with the intensity of his gaze. "Do not forget that." Edward swallowed hard and nodded silently, although his face showed his bewilderment. He did not understand the King's refusal to set foot in London. It was Mercian land, not West Saxon: the King came as a liberator, not as a conqueror. The House of Wessex would someday rule London and all of Mercia, but this was not to be accomplished entirely by sword and spear.

Aethelflaed met Ethelred's eyes for a moment before she turned back to Edward's puzzled face. The fleeting glance told her what she had already sensed as she listened to the King's instructions. All the thanes present were meant to clearly understand his intentions. Edward would one day receive Mercia as his rightful inheritance, without the shedding of blood and by the acclaim of its inhabitants. Together she and Ethelred would pave the way that would unite these two great kingdoms.

She laid a restraining hand on Edward's arm, and nodded her thanks to the King. With such an incentive, Ethelred could not fail. When the host was driven out, a strong rule would keep them out: that meant Ethelred. The throne of Mercia was empty and the land abounded with men claiming royal blood. Such a situation promised civil war, unless, of course, Ethelred's wife happened to be of unquestioned royal blood herself. It never failed to strike Aethelflaed that the King's plans were a blend of political necessity and inspired wisdom. Edward must certainly rule Mercia one day and it was to be hoped that it could be accomplished by peaceful means. Ethelred's remark to Edward earlier that day began to make sense to Aethelflaed. London would require a ruler well versed in matters other than warfare. London would need both a military commander and a governor, and Ethelred knew he could not be both. His wife must carry part of his burden.

CHAPTER FOUR

*I*t was with great eagerness that Aethelflaed awaited the arrival of Asser. Edward was reconciled to studying with the Welsh bishop and had displayed some enthusiasm. Though Edward, Aethelflaed observed to Ethelred, was undoubtedly more avid for intelligence of the Danes that Asser might have gathered from the Kentishmen where he had served than for his instruction in Latin grammar. Asser had gone to East-dene, leaving his Pembrokeshire community only after repeated entreaties on the part of the King. Wales had not many great scholars, for it had suffered as much as England from the constant invasions. Even so, the state of learning encountered in England by Asser shocked him as much as it did the King.

Aethelflaed expected to find Asser somewhat remote, a quality she found common amongst monkish scholars. Her own teacher from St. Martin's had been a myopic priest who spoke in a whisper. He was uncomfortable in her presence and it was a relief to them both when the lessons were over. The somber-garbed bishop from St. Daffyd's who replaced him, however, brightened the sober West Saxon court with his winsome disposition and set about his teaching duties with an enthusiasm that won the interest of even the restless Edward.

"Your father has taught you well," Asser remarked to Aethelflaed, looking up from the parchments stacked on his table. He inspected the neat characters, carefully copied. "It surprises me that so busy a king takes pains to instruct his own children."

Aethelflaed smiled. "He thinks himself ignorant. He did not learn to read until he was eleven, and he vowed we would learn earlier than he. I was set to copying when I was five."

Asser agreed. Setting children to copying, even what they could not read, was a practice he firmly believed in. When the mind was ready to understand what the hand was doing, it would. Meanwhile, the fingers learned their chores properly. "I see you are fond of your English poetry." He smiled, his dark eyes twinkling. "It is not like Welsh poetry, of course, but it is very good," he said affably, "very strong." She looked up at him quickly, but he only smiled cheerfully back at her.

During the morning hours, she found her mind wandering from the text to the activity at the camp at Winnall, and the pen would slip from her fingers, unheeded.

"Perhaps you have been copying too long?"

Aethelflaed stared at Asser blankly, then looked back at her parchment in confusion.

"Your thoughts are far from St. John's Gospel?" The brown eyes were serene and a smile curved the corners of his mouth. He nodded as if encouraging her to speak, but a slight movement in the corner startled them. Aethelflaed turned and saw a small shape huddled in the shadows. Asser moved swiftly and pulled the terrified boy from his hiding place. He glared down at the child, still holding him by the arm, and would have boxed his ears, but Aethelflaed stopped him.

"It is only my mother's thrall. He comes here often when his work is finished."

"What is his name?" Asser gave a boy a little shake.

"He hasn't any name," Aethelflaed explained. "He was born a thrall and no one ever gave him a name."

The priest was shocked. "He has not been baptized?" The boy looked at him blankly, not comprehending. Aethelflaed shook her head. Asser's lips set in a prim, determined line.

She looked back at the child. "Do not be frightened," she said. "Why are you here?" The boy looked up at Asser. "Ah." She followed his glance with understanding. "Because he is Welsh?" The boy's expression relaxed.

"I do not understand." Asser's puzzlement demanded explanation.

His mother was a Welsh thrall." She felt a small twinge of regret that any of Asser's fellow countrymen should be enslaved. If only they did not harass the western borders so, it would not be necessary to capture them. "I am sorry. He has never seen a Welshman before, but I imagine his mother told him much of your country."

The bishop studied his small countryman for a moment. "Life is harsh with all of us, Lady. No one escapes." There was no accusation in his voice, only sadness. "At least allow me to baptize him." He released the boy, who rubbed his arm and continued to stare up at him. "What name would you like? St. David is the patron saint of Wales, and the name of my community at Pembrokeshire. Would you like to be called David?" The boy nodded mutely.

"Good." Asser smiled suddenly. "With your leave, My Lady, I will take David and baptize him." He took the boy by the hand. "I would like your leave also to teach him to speak his own tongue."

She nodded. "If you will teach him to read English also. You may bring him here to do it, but," she shrugged, "see that he is quiet about it. Cook will beat him on the sly if she finds out."

Asser turned to Aethelflaed. "You may take the rest of the day as you choose. Perhaps you wish to think about your betrothed?" He took the boy by the hand and left.

Asser's cheerful disposition, as he busied himself with teaching duties, eased the tension now pervading the palace. The King had set up a palace school for the children of his retainers, and as an inducement to the thanes to send their children to lessons, he promised preferment to those who came and learned their lessons well. Ethelhelm's only child, his daughter Elfled, came, as well as Ecgwin, the orphaned daughter of the thane of Devon, and Ethelwold, the eldest son of Alfred's late brother, King Aethelred.

The lessons were presided over by Asser, and Aethelflaed often helped the younger ones with their copying. Asser attended to the older children, though to call them children was an injustice. Elfled was not yet fourteen, cousin Ethelwold, who was gone now since he was training with the Ealdorman of Wiltshire for the coming march, was one and twenty. For Aethelflaed, the hours spent in lessons surrounded by the children of Wessex nobility went quickly and pleasantly. Under Asser's tutelage, an atmosphere of benign calm prevailed, and so much had the Welshman's charm and sincerity disarmed her that she was quite unprepared for the personality of John, the Old Saxon, who arrived shortly after Asser.

John came to Winchester from the west of Germany, from the land of their ancestors and because of this, did not suffer the problems of the strange English tongue suffered by his fellow priest, Grimbald, sent from northern Frankia by Archbishop Fulk. One thing John and Grimbald had in common: they both saw the Church in this strange, and to them uncivilized, country as sadly wanting in order and discipline. The laxity of the rule horrified them, and the negligence of the clergy appalled them, especially in the matter of wives.

The English clergy, particularly the lower clergy in the villages, saw nothing amiss with the taking of a wife. It was not expressly forbidden; it was a comfort to them, besides being very practical. They were not living in an abbey so they had no one to cook or wash clothes, or make ale for them, or otherwise tend to their wants. The King disapproved, of course, because the celibate Roman clergy sternly pointed out the error of these ways, but he had little control over the villagers, much less the clergy who lived among them. Furthermore, the Roman attitude toward women was alien to the older ideas of shared responsibility that the Angles and Saxons brought with them from the old country.

But John, Old Saxon though he was, came from a monastery firmly regulated by the See of Rome. Here in England it was apparent that there was corruption. If the English saw nothing wrong with a clergyman with one wife, they assuredly saw something amiss with more than one. Such depravity as John beheld among the clergy and laity alike in this half-heathen land hardened his inflexible resolve to reform it. There could be no doubt, to him at least, of God's intent that he should be the instrument by which the ragged Church of this war-torn land would be set to right.

To Aethelflaed, blooming under the warmth of Asser's Celtic faith, John seemed as cold and harsh as the homeland from which he had come. True, he spoke almost the same language as the English, but there the resemblance ended. She could feel no kinship with this bitter stranger. Tall and gaunt, his eyes burned darkly in his sallow face. He could encompass everything in a single sweeping glance, leaving the impression that all he saw was corruption, meriting the deepest wrath of God.

She and Asser, deep in their studies and unaware of the nature of John's preoccupations, looked up one day to find the Abbot contemplating them darkly from the door to the hall that served as a schoolroom, discontent burning in his eyes.

"Why," inquired the Abbot coldly, "does the Lady Aethelflaed not pursue her studies in the company of the nuns, as her sister does?"

Asser looked up, smiling. "Good day, my Lord Abbot. Your presence here honors us." His tone was mild and unsuspecting. "My Lady's sister is promised to the convent. It is to be expected that she take her studies with the Abbess. Lady Aethelflaed prepares for a worldly life and has other needs," he offered by way of reply.

"Her need for Latin cannot be great. Certainly she can learn all she needs to know by translating the Altar Book. It is dangerous folly to put more in her head than she has need of or can comprehend."

Aethelflaed felt the anger rising to her cheeks and burning there. The Welshman's calm remained unshaken. "Come now, my Lord Abbot. Surely you know the King's passion for educating his children?"

"Certainly." John's voice was chill and hard as marble, his eyes glittering with reforming zeal. She gritted her teeth and clenched her fists under the table, determined to say nothing. The man's insolence was boundless.

"Certainly," John repeated, "though in my country, we do not see fit to waste lessons on women. The Holy Church has reformed our ancient and mistaken customs, for which we are thankful. It is obvious, even to you, that it is men who must be taught, for they must rule. Women have no head for this."

Asser's dark eyes were beginning to sparkle dangerously. "The Lady Aethelflaed," he replied, with growing annoyance, "must be able to help her husband administer justice in a land which you know yourself to be ignorant of the law. This cannot be done by one who is herself ignorant."

The Abbot's face remained set. "One must then abide by the King's will. His judgment in educating a daughter to rule must not be questioned." He clearly thought otherwise. "It would be wiser to invest such authority in a man." Aethelflaed gasped involuntarily at the man's effrontery. Asser's face drained of color and he looked up at John in disbelief. Alfred had made it clear that in England, whatever might be the case overseas, the clergy received their power from the King as God's agent. When they accepted gifts of lands and monies from the King's hand this was understood. An abbot did not question the King's word here.

"I must advise the King, nevertheless," John went on, "that it is unseemly for young women to be educated in the company of the young men. Many of these boys are destined for the priesthood and for the monastery. It is of great importance that that they not be corrupted by the world before they come to their profession. They are most unreconciled to the duties and requirements of monastic life once they have been turned."

Aethelflaed jumped to her feet before Asser could restrain her. "My Lord Abbot," she said, containing her anger with difficulty, "your attitude at Athelney will be most fitting, but the King's household is not a monastery. We are quite aware of our Christian duties and responsibilities here. We are also not in the habit of questioning the King's judgment, nor should you, because he is your Lord as well as ours!" There was no mistaking the sudden hatred that flared in the Abbot's eyes, but she was too angry to be intimidated.

John bowed stiffly by way of apology. "I merely felt it my duty to offer such instruction as appeared necessary to me. The King has given me his confidence that great discipline is necessary to repair the ravages inflicted on the Church by the enemy."

"Quite so," she replied coldly, her anger unabated. "Your concern is well-taken, but Bishop Asser and I are not in need of further instruction." Her clipped tones were a blunt, discourteous dismissal. She did not care. The man was a vicious fool. John bowed again, lifting his eyebrows in a gesture so arrogant as to belie his token humility.

"Aethelflaed," said Asser, when John's footsteps had receded out of earshot, "you should not have spoken so to the Abbot."

She glared at him. "How can you say that? He all but accused the King's household of venery!"

"That is his duty. He believes himself a reformer, and so he must look for such things wherever they may be found."

"But not here!"

"It is not unusual to find such things in royal households. Even in the House of Wessex, as you already know!" He cocked his head to one side, as she bristled.

"I hope this will not bring you trouble," she said ruefully.

Asser shook his head. "But it will undoubtedly bring you your portion. When this reaches the King's ears, as it will, though not by me, you will be asked to do penance for your temper." She agreed, grimacing. The King had rules. "You have made yourself an enemy, Aethelflaed. It is unfortunate. He is an Abbot and so he must be respected. He is consecrated to the Church and that must always set him apart, even if he is not always right." She noticed that he did not outright declare him wrong.

Asser suddenly burst out laughing. She looked up in surprise. "Lady," he explained, in answer to her puzzled look, "the man addressed you as an inferior and found himself rebuked by a woman of the first rank. He will think twice before he crosses you openly again. Ah, but we must be patient. He gets his contempt of our ways from his own abbot. I daresay he is worse than John."

"I forgot myself. I should not have spoken so sternly."

Asser smiled. "You are made of stronger stuff than to be intimidated by such as he. I expected you to chasten him for insulting the King." He raised his eyebrows. "It is not likely your father will believe that the Abbot of Athelney would insult the King who gives him lands, wealth, and authority. I suggest you do not try to explain yourself but take your penance silently." He opened the Vulgate in front of her. "Now we must work harder. You must finish this soon. You are ready for other studies."

She did not doubt that he was right, nor did she doubt that she would be reprimanded by the King for ordering the Abbot from the hall. As Asser pointed out, it would not do to explain why. She apologized to John, as sternly commanded by Alfred, but to her surprise, she was turned over to Asser for her penance. It was a comforting penance. Asser took the finished Vulgate away from and gave her the Laws of Ine to study, and that was all there was to that.

Though she was to know many men of the Church in her life, she came to love Asser the way one loves those who are a happy part of one's quickly vanishing childhood. He was a mentor of unparalleled understanding and sympathy. Asser's capacity to love and his astonishing ability to accept without condemnation the like of John the Old Saxon, and above all his affectionate understanding of her, endeared him to her forever.

She followed his advice about silence before the King. Alfred was, for once, blind in his anxiety to restore learning and discipline to the broken monasteries. He saw in John a man with a firm hand to deal with monks who kept the Rule badly or not at all, a man devoted to the love of God. He did not see the cruelty lurking behind the deceptive firmness, nor the hatred of life lurking in the Abbot's deep-set eyes.

CHAPTER FIVE

*N*ews came regularly by rider and the days lengthened toward winter. Edward fidgeted, and muttering to himself that he was of age for battles, complaining bitterly that one would think he was an unseasoned child. Aethelflaed finally rounded on him abruptly, begging, if not ordering his silence. Her own nerves suffered as grievously as did Edward's though she was determined not to show it, and Edward's constant fretting irritated her into exasperation.

"If it should fail, do you think it good we should lose yourself as well as my Lord Ethelred and the King?"

He clamped his lips together, seeing the concern behind her impatience. He was now aware that it was more than the safety of the King that troubled her. Of course she would be concerned about the safety of her future husband and the King; the safety of not merely the two most able leaders of Wessex, but that of the kingdom of the West Saxons as well.

If Ethelred had driven his men hard in anticipation of the grueling march on London, he had driven himself harder. He and the King counseled together until late, after the Great Hall below was darkened and deep in slumber. The thanes slept on the floor, wrapped in their fur rugs and snoring, around the King and his most trusted ealdorman.

When not in council, Ethelred spent what few free moments he could find with Aethelflaed. He had not rested from the exertions of the previous week, and when he came to her chambers to bid her farewell, she saw the weariness crinkling at the corners of his eyes.

In the short space of time since their betrothal, warmth had bloomed between the two of them, and Aethelflaed longed to know her betrothed better. The thought that she might never see him again cut through the moment, sending a shiver through her. She raised her head to speak tentatively to him of her feelings, but he forestalled her words, bending his head to kiss her. There was no polite distance in this kiss, as if they were plighted strangers. She relaxed against him, enjoying the unaccustomed feelings.

"I will keep your father's word," he whispered against her hair. "You will have London as a wedding gift, and all of Mercia for your morning-gift." He held her close again, then turned and was swiftly gone. She sat down, pondering these things.

She sought out Edward's company and together they waited for news of the advance on London by the King and Ethelred. The rider who brought them the news was exhausted from the hard ride. "The King has crossed the Kennet into Reading." He spoke wearily to Edward, who was waiting for him in the yard. He had not bothered to dismount and kneel before the Atheling, for Edward had run quickly to his side, grasped the bridle and forestalled ceremony in his eagerness to hear the news.

"Is the village there secure?" Edward held the bridle firmly and steadied the horse. The man nodded. "But the fields are reduced." He passed his hand over his eyes in a gesture of exhaustion, as if it could wipe from his memory the vision of the havoc wreaked by his own companions as they made the land useless to the enemy. "Now the King and Lord Ethelred march eastwards to London. Lord Ethelhelm goes from Arundel to Lewes and will fortify Eastdene at once." Aethelflaed hurried to join them and overheard with satisfaction his last statement. The trap was being readied.

"Has the King any message for us?" Edward fingered his sword hilt impatiently. The man shook his head. "Only that food and other supplies are needed."

"We will see to it at once." Edward, his hand still on the bridle, led the messenger into the Great Hall and called loudly for a thrall to bring food and drink. Aethelflaed mounted the stone steps quickly and made her way to the upper hall schoolroom to find Ethelhelm's daughter. The girl worried and must be told that her father fared well. She smiled to herself. Elfled would surely prefer to hear it from Edward, but if he noticed her at all, he only saw the childhood playmate, not the young woman she was becoming.

Elfled showed a marked partiality for Edward, which was understandable. He was growing taller and stronger and his liveliness and good looks had captivated the spirited girl. She followed him like a pet hound. Edward was only peripherally aware of her presence, for to his indifferent eye her attention was claimed as much by a score of other handsome young nobles as by himself. He had not remarked her preference his own company.

Among the young and hopeful nobility whom he saw as contenders for her attention was his cousin, Ethelwold, some five years his senior. Ethelwold was among the oldest of these and second only to Edward in rank, being the son of the late King Aethelred, Alfred's brother. He would not have been in the classroom at all except upon order of his uncle. The state of Wessex during his own father's beleaguered reign was such that there had been no opportunity to learn to read and write. After his father's death, such woeful events befell the kingdom that no one was taught anything except warfare. Thus came Ethelwold in his young manhood, skilled with sword and spear but unhandy with learning to Alfred's schoolroom.

Alfred did not intend to allow the late King's son to remain ignorant for he wished to place him highly. Ethelwold, in the service of the Ealdorman of Wiltshire, was left behind with Edward on the King's order. He was disgusted. In vain did Alfred point out that his excellent training under Ethelhelm and his skill as a swordsman made him a valuable asset in the King's absence to the less-experienced Atheling, Edward. However ungraciously, Ethelwold stayed behind.

Ethelwold was covertly jealous of Edward. It was to be expected, for Edward was clearly regarded as heir to the throne of Wessex, despite Ethelwold's demonstrated ability, while he, Ethelwold, was looked upon as an Atheling without a kingdom. He grudgingly understood the need for his uncle to be placed at the head of the kingdom he believed rightly to be his own, and that the Witan was the ultimate authority to determine kingship; nevertheless, it should have been made plain that he, not Edward, was the rightful heir. In intelligence, they were a close match: both shrewd, quick-witted, and cunning. Good soldiers both, Ethelwold's only advantage being a few years' more experience. The family resemblance was striking in facial features as well: they were similarly handsome men. But the quirk of fate, the Providence that left Ethelwold barely out of infancy when his father died, leaving a throne too large and unsteady for a child to occupy, rankled in the deepest recesses of his heart. Nevertheless, Ethelwold had no doubt that when the time came, the Witan could not fail to pass over Edward and choose himself instead.

Lately he had come to find another grievance against his cousin. It was not Elfled that captured his fancy, but another. Her name was Ecgwin, the orphaned daughter of the thane of Devon. She had caught his eye, and quickly thereafter, his starved affections as well, for they had both lost noble fathers. It seemed to him they ought to have much in common. He filled his daydreams with thoughts of Ecgwin, not seeing that the strength of his fantasy did not penetrate her awareness.   Delicate and shy, Ecgwin rarely raised her eyes from her copybook. He watched her hungrily, almost as a hawk studies its prey, with frustrated affection. Then he noticed the direction of Edward's attention.

Edward, while he talked often with Elfled, since he could hardly avoid her slavish attentions, found his eyes coming always to rest on Ecgwin. He was as unconscious of the stir he was causing in his envious cousin's breast as he was of Elfled's devotion. He saw only Ecgwin and she soon began to notice him. This was not lost on Ethelwold, nor was it lost on the daughter of the Ealdorman of Wiltshire.

Aethelflaed had barely time to relay her own news when Edward joined them. He nodded to Elfled briefly, but settled himself opposite Ecgwin and demanded her attention merely by sitting there and staring until she was forced to raise her eyes to his. She blushed furiously. Ethelwold turned quickly away, his face dark with anger. Aethelflaed, seeing his face before he turned and walked away from them, realized for the first time that more went on under her cousin's normally smooth façade than she had imagined. Edward's increasing maturity was bound to cause some hard feelings but Ethelwold, being older than both of them, had received their admiration, even adulation, as children. Surely he could not forget their affection.

Elfled, at her elbow, was close to tears. Edward's indifference she could tolerate, but his absorption elsewhere filled her heart with despair, which flickered briefly in her eyes before she, like Ethelwold, turned her head away.

"Come," said Aethelflaed kindly, putting her arm around Elfled's shoulders and propelling her gently toward the door. If Ethelwold was beyond her help, perhaps Elfled was not. "I need your help." Elfled followed her dutifully to her chambers and Aethelflaed set her the task of straightening the sheaves of parchment littering her worktable, then left the girl to recover her composure in privacy.

It was evident before long that Edward's infatuation was not merely a passing fancy. He sought out Ecgwin frequently enough to cause at first a mild stir, then discreet silences and blank looks in his presence. Aethelflaed watched his progress with amused indulgence, and Elfled was spending more and more time in her chambers, busying herself with nonexistent chores.

"Elfled," she said finally, "your devotion to my needs is appreciated, but I would be pleased to see you spend more time with your companions."

Elfled's eyes reddened ominously. "I am certain they do not notice my absence."

Aethelflaed repressed a smile, for Elfled's face was tragic. "You mean Edward, don't you?" she asked gently, determined to put a stop to Elfled's self-imposed isolation.

The girl turned her back and sniffled audibly. "Can you not help me with Edward?" The kerchief she held to her face muffled her voice. Aethelflaed knit her brows thoughtfully.

"You know I cannot do that. He would not tolerate my meddling." The girl was more serious than she had imagined, but she had forgotten that Elfled, though a little younger than Edward, was recently of marriageable age. Had Ethelhelm been at home instead of marching to battle, he would have been busy arranging a marriage for her, and it was clearly this that was on her mind. Edward was not a passing whim with Elfled.

Elfled rounded on her suddenly, resentment flaring in her eyes. "My father's position in this household is second only to Lord Ethelred's, yet Edward does not see me for Ecgwin," she said hotly. "She has no family left and no position. Certainly you can see she is no fit match for Edward. Can you not persuade the King to marry her to Ethelwold? His rank is almost as high as Edward's and besides," she faltered under Aethelflaed's astonished stare, "Ethelwold would gladly have her, even though she is landless." She lifted her chin stubbornly.

Aethelflaed held back the reproof that rose to her lips. Maneuvering for position among the King's retainers was as inevitable as death. It had not occurred to her before that a girl of Elfled's young years was planning so far ahead. Certainly the faithful and unassuming Ethelhelm would not have filled his daughter's head with fancies of power and privilege: privilege was already hers in abundance. Somewhere in all this, there was a corner of the girl's affection for Edward that was real, carried away though she was with the idea of marriage to the Atheling. Aethelflaed had known her too long not to believe that.

"It is not my place to suggest marriage arrangements to the King, nor to interfere on anyone's behalf." Her tone was final and she saw anger hardening on Elfled's face. It saddened her to see her old playmate, once so open and cheerful, now masking her feelings. Aethelflaed sighed. Even if the childhood ties did not dissolve, people changed. Friends changed. One could not expect all bonds to survive unchanged the rigors of adult demands. The expression of stung pride on Elfled's face told her that the girl was aware of her own lack of reason. She regarded Elfled a bit sadly as the girl stiffly begged leave to withdraw.

She refused to distress herself about Elfled's self-imposed silence, although the guarded relations between them made Elfled's service difficult to bear. In deference to Ethelhelm she would keep Elfled in her service. Edward grew daily more enamored of Ecgwin, Elfled grew daily more sullen, and Ethelwold grew daily more remote, which made the already tense waiting period close to unendurable.

It was with relief and thanksgiving compounded that Aethelflaed received the news that London was under siege at last, and that she and Edward were to set out at once so that they might witness for themselves the deliverance of the town from the Vikings. The duration of the siege was expected to be short, since the food supply had been destroyed in the fields where it stood awaiting harvest. They must leave quickly.

The Queen joined her in making lists of herbs to be prepared by the kitchen thralls; there would be many in need of remedies. They studied the

Leech Book, memorizing instructions. Extra linens were laid by to bind up wounds. There were other sicknesses, too. Soldiers suffered more than physical wounds. Weeks of marching and fighting, if one escaped other disasters, could work unseen harm. Possession by demons after battles was not uncommon, nor were the flying venoms that drifted on the winds, lit upon the body and made it deathly ill. Three pennies' weight of mandrake root in warm water for witlessness and possession by demons; wormwood and lupin, to be made into a salve with fresh butter and honey, such would be proof against elves and goblins, especially when accompanied by the prescribed prayers and Masses.

Aethelflaed picked up the great Leech Book, a gift to Alfred from the Patriarch of Jerusalem, and read from it the list of herbs to cure the flying venom, and Ealhswith copied it carefully on a piece of parchment, to be included with the pack of medicinal supplies.

"Mugwort, plaintain, watercress, chamomile, nettle, crabapple, chervil, fennel, and roots of water dock." The Queen's pen scratched quickly across the parchment. Aethelflaed peered over her shoulder. "Take an eggshell of clean honey, let someone mix these into new butter for a salve." Ealhswith scribbled industriously, repeating each word as she wrote it, then laid aside her quill and took the book from Aethelflaed.

"We have enough now." She embraced her daughter briefly, then stood back. "It will be a terrible journey, child. The King will understand if you choose to stay here."

"I am no longer a child, Lady Mother." She held up the hand with the gold betrothal ring on it. "In less than a year I will be in Mercia with Ethelred. I must suffer with these people myself as the King has done with his people. I will know them as they know themselves."

The Queen studied her daughter's face, musing silently, her reluctance to release her first-born to the winds of fortune tugged at her heart. She looked up at Aethelflaed, who was now some inches taller than herself. She would be wearing her soldier's tunic when she left in the morning, and a sword and scramasax. Her tumbling blonde hair would be tied back and well-hidden by her hood and cloak, and from a distance she would be taken for a soldier of obvious rank. She must not worry. Her oldest two *bearns* would be well guarded, for they would take with them some of the finest of West Saxon nobility. She took Aethelflaed's hand. "Let us say our Vespers together with Bishop Denewulf tonight. We shall wish you proper God-speed." She turned to the doorway and called for David, and when he appeared quietly, sent him for Edward. "Tell Lord Edward that his mother and his sister would have his company at Vespers."

CHAPTER SIX

*T*he peaceful green of Winchester lay behind them, sparkling with dew under the cold morning sun. At Winnall the villagers lined the narrow street to stare at them as they rode through the hamlet. A few villagers entreated them to stay, but the party pressed on, since it was some sixty miles to London. Everywhere the name of Guthrum filled their ears. Alfred's baptized godson he was, who, after his defeat at Edington, had been content for a while to rule East Anglia and leave Wessex to the English.

But in 884, Guthrum was joined by a new army from Frankia and together they sailed up the Thames to besiege Rochester, building a wall outside their siege line to protect themselves. It had not availed. Alfred came, relieved the siege, and the Danes fled back to Frankia. It seemed that Guthrum could no longer tolerate the English peace he had sworn to honor at his baptism. In reprisal for Guthrum's part in the siege, Alfred sent his fleet to East Anglia and captured sixteen of Guthrum's ships at the mouth of the River Stour. Guthrum's vengeance was quick. As Alfred's ships toiled homeward, Guthrum attacked with still more ships, and in a single battle, destroyed the English victory. Now the vow-breaker controlled the port city, and again the host threatened Wessex. Alfred's siege of London would end that once and for all, and Guthrum would be made an example to the Danes.

Aethelflaed and Edward left their horses on the south bank of the Kennet and crossed by boat. Their horses would be rafted across. They had deliberately chosen the northern route, following the King's *fyrd*, since the approach from the southwest through Guilford and Chertsey might still harbor a band or two of Danes. The villages and hamlets there would be full of Danish sympathizers. They camped inside Reading for the night, at the confluence of the Kennet and the Thames. London was now forty miles east of them and in the morning they would set forth along the bank of the Thames for the village of West Minster.

For the moment, Aethelflaed thought only of the clean straw that had been spread for her in a mud-and-wattle hut. She was tired from the slow, jolting ride and it mattered little to her where she slept. The straw was fresh and smelled sweet, and she sank quickly into a refreshing sleep. Morning brought a disturbance which left both Edward and herself angry and shaken, though they were to see more, and worse, before long.

They emerged from their huts and washed in the river, hastily, for the water was stinging cold. They soon became aware of an angry mumble coming from the tiny common on which the huts fronted. They walked back, surprised to find a knot of people collected there murmuring ominously. Edward turned to the soldier at his side, his eyebrows raised in question, but before the man could respond, a slight figure bolted out of the crowd. Angry hands quickly dragged the ragged creature back.

"Bring him to me," Edward commanded. The reeve dragged the figure forward, a filthy boy of perhaps nine or ten years, a child with mud-caked hair, and threw him on the ground. The boy's dark eyes and hair marked him as a Dane.

The reeve's expression was vengeful, and he kicked the boy viciously. "Viking *nothing!*" He spat on him and pulled a knife from his girdle. The boy began to tremble violently and his eyes widened with terror. Aethelflaed followed the boy's horrified look and saw that the man was brandishing a flaying knife, used on the hides of animals, and that, with any provocation at all, he would use it on the child.

"Mercy," the boy whispered thickly, choking with fear. The reeve kicked him again, bringing the knife closer to his head with a fearful gesture. Aethelflaed stepped forward quickly and gripped Edward's arm.

"You must not let them do it," she whispered urgently, for the reeve's rage was boiling, dangerously excited by his own bloodlust and that of the villagers.

Edward's eyes were unaccountably hard. "Why not? He is a Dane!"

"No!" screamed the boy, "My mother was English!" An angry rumble arose from the villagers. Aethelflaed turned to the reeve.

"Is this true?"

The reeve stepped back reluctantly, nodding. "He is a rape-child, a Danish bastard and belongs to no one." He threatened the child with the knife again and sneered as the boy cringed before the blade.

"Is he baptized?"

The reeve exploded. "We do not waste Holy Rites on enemy bastards!" he screamed.

The acid taste of nausea rose in her throat and Edward's face blanched under its tan. In spite of his hasty remark he was as revolted as she was at the prospect of a human flaying. However much they were familiar with public torture, neither relished it; certainly not that of a boy still in his miserable childhood. They looked up and studied the faces of the villagers, strangely inhuman as they shuffled and circled their helpless quarry. It made no difference that the terrified child was innocent of any crime. Were not also their own children innocent of any crime? Yet had not the host inflicted as much or worse on them? They could do as they chose with this filthy animal. No one would avenge his torture and death.

"Call the priest," Aethelflaed ordered. "Bid him bring parchment and ink." Edward's face relaxed with relief. When the monk elbowed his way fearfully through the crowd, Edward signaled to the thane at his side, who went to the boy and yanked him to his feet. The reeve brandished the knife angrily again. The thane drew his sword with careful deliberation and coolly eyed those closest. The crowd pulled back, still buzzing, but submitted at the thought that the blood shed might be theirs.

Aethelflaed exhaled softly as the villagers lapsed into a hostile silence under the cold stare of the thane. She dictated quickly to the monk, who hastily scribbled her words on the parchment, pausing only to cast furtive glances upward at Edward and herself. She took the quill from monk's nerveless fingers when he finished, signed the parchment, and silently handed the document to Edward. He read it with a quick glance, took the quill from her and set his name carefully at the bottom of it.

"Henceforth this boy belongs to the monastery. We have set our hands to it in the King's name." The crowd buzzed like a nest of hornets. "There is a *wergild* on his head now. Whoever kills him must pay the *wergild* or forfeit his own life." He handed the parchment back to the monk and bid the thane escort the boy and his new master back to the monastery safely. Terror had erased all other expressions from the boy's face, and while he comprehended dimly the fact of his escape from a ghastly death, the eyes he turned on his benefactors registered only dumb shock.

Surely this wretch was nothing more than an animal; their own thanes made sport of these creatures. Even the lowest villager, the least of the freemen and his lowest slave, looked down on such as this boy. His kind slept among the cattle and sheep and shared their filth, for he was a *nithing*, not human, scarcely more than a beast. Yet the eyes he had turned on her were human and the terrible hopelessness she saw in them belittled her impulsive generosity. What she had done had cost her nothing and had given him his life, little though it was worth to him. He offered no gesture of gratitude as the monk dragged him off, and she owned secretly that she deserved no gratitude.

By the time the caravan reached the outskirts of the hamlet of West Minster, both Aethelflaed and Edward were worn from the hard ride. The stench of the burned-out fields filled their nostrils and seared their lungs. The carcasses of stray cattle and animals, scorched black, littered the fields. By noon the stink was nauseating even in the cool October air. Most of the peasants had fled as far north as they dared and taken haven in the Chiltern hills; only a few remained to poke disconsolately about the ashes of their baked huts, looking to salvage a pot or two, or trying to guard a tiny grain horde from friend and foe alike.

They followed the Thames closely, staying near the water, since the seared land still smouldered intermittently and frightened the horses. Puffs of smoke scudded darkly across the sky toward the east. Such tattered peasants as remained scuttled away in fright at their approach, and those too bewildered to move eyed them gauntly with hollow stares.

No shouts of victory greeted them as they approached the west edge of the village of St. Peter's Church, the West Minster, which had been an enemy stronghold, hard by London. Now it was no more. Aethelflaed dismounted and felt her knees buckle under her. Edward caught her before she slid to the ground.

"My God," she moaned against her brother's shoulder. Her eyes were scratching from the acrid air and too dry for tears. The late afternoon sun glared like baleful eye at the blackened ruin of what had once been houses and the Church of St. Peter's, from which the village of West Minster took its name. The tiny monastery had crumbled to the ground and all that remained were its stone and earthen fireplaces jutting starkly upwards. The air was as still as death and stinging with ash. Nothing remained alive and only now were the rats returning, seeking and scurrying among the cinders, their progress marked by occasional puffs of ashen smoke that swirled upward.

Nothing could be heard from the eastern edge, the riverside of St. Peter's, though they knew Ethelhelm's men were by now lined silently along the stretch of the Thames from the West Minster to Southwark and beyond.

"We cannot stop here." Edward's voice was insistent. "We must go on. It is less than an hour's ride to the camp."

She looked wearily up at Edward's resolute face. Whatever he felt this time, he kept it to himself, though she could see that the fourteen-year-old youth who had left Winchester a week ago was no longer. His face had changed in the past three days, as hers must also have, reflecting the mind-thoughts aged by the sights they had seen. She leaned gratefully on his shoulder as he helped her to remount. The sternness of his face, the urgency in his voice as he ordered the party forward left no doubt that he had shed his boyhood somewhere along the Thames between Reading and West Minster. She mourned her own loss of innocence as well. No one can witness such things and remain untouched.

The watchful glow of campfires scattered east to west along the Chiltern Hills appeared ahead of them, shortly after sundown. Clayhangra was their destination, the sight of which revived their desolate spirits and spurred them forward. Although it was too dark to see the walls of London two miles to the south, its position was clearly outlined by another ring of campfires. There was no need for the English to hide their position from the Danish sentries posted on the walls. The fires had been there in exactly the same places every night for several weeks. They would be there as long as necessary.

They approached the center of the camp and a tall figure detached itself from the group huddled around the fire. Exhausted as she was, Aethelflaed felt a warm flush of recognition when she saw Ethelred hurrying toward them, and with great relief allowed him to lift her from her horse. She clung to him, needing comfort, before he set her on her feet. The King received them silently, with open arms, sadness and suffering written on his face. The attacks of colick, she guessed, tormented him and though he would admit nothing, the look of relief that swept across his face as the precious cargo of medicinals and herbs was unloaded was obvious to all.

"How much longer will they hold out?" Edward asked his father.

"No more than a few days. They have been cut off for only two weeks, but they had no time to bring in the harvest."

Edward frowned. "Even so, could they not hold out many weeks longer? Surely the city is well-stocked." He drained the horn handed to him by the King.

"It is." Alfred agreed and sat down wearily. "But they have too much to lose. The townsmen would surrender tomorrow if Guthrum's men would let them."

"If you went in now, would you find many willing to help you?"

"Without doubt," Ethelred responded to Edward. "We know there are many English in the town. A few come out each day." He filled his own drinking horn and held it out to Aethelflaed, thirsty from the long ride. "We must wait until those who wish to join us have time to get out safely."

"Besides," the King put in wearily, "the men are tired and need the rest. Waiting can only help us now."

She noticed how the King's mouth drooped with fatigue and she rose. "We are tired, father. We beg your leave to rest." She said no more than that for she did not wish to distress him further with her reflections on the devastation of the land they had seen. She had seen his eyes and could not bear the look in them. She nudged Edward to his feet. The King nodded absently, the guttering candlelight casting long shadows on his face.

"How often has he had the colick?" she asked Ethelred when they were out of earshot.

"Almost daily. He suffers greatly."

Edward shook his head, puzzled. "He seemed well enough at Winchester. This is not like him to be ill now."

"He was well, but not in good spirits when we left Winchester." Ethelred paused to speak to the guard outside his tent. "But," he continued as they stepped into the tent, "it torments him to destroy his own land for the sake of driving off the host. He is the most compassionate man I know."

"He is a born soldier." Edward's tone was emphatic.

Ethelred shook his head. "No, Edward, I am the born soldier. I sorrow, too, for the misery we inflict on our own people, but is a thing I must and can live with, however much I hate it. The King is a great soldier, but only of necessity. In his heart he is God's thane, not a king. Killing goes against him more than most. Surely," he said, fixing Edward with an intense look, "surely, you have seen the bloodlust that rules these men!" The sweep of his arm described the arc of campfires. "They come to life in battle. Without this, they might be fighting each other."

Aethelflaed watched Ethelred's face as he spoke, seeing on it the concern and devotion he accorded her father. He was not so simple a man as he believed himself to be, for he had seen and understood, as she had herself, the guilt that preyed upon the King's mind. Yet he was a man of firm decision and swift action once the course was decided. He did not equivocate about it, nor boggle at the necessity that impelled him to do what must be done. He accepted the grim facts of war, not coldly or heartlessly, but with the resignation of a soldier. Edward by training and natural disposition reflected Ethelred's outlook, not his father's. It was perhaps as well. When Edward ruled, he would do as well as Alfred; with his natural capacity for single-mindedness honed and polished by Ethelred, he would be a formidable enemy. He was not experienced enough to share Ethelred's sensitive appreciation of the King's unusual personality.

It struck her, as Ethelred rose from his bench to bid her goodnight, that some of the qualities that inspired his devotion to the King were also her own. It had not occurred to her before that Ethelred might come to love in her the same qualities that he loved in the King. She hoped in time that he might find other reasons as well, but for now, she was content. When he took her hand and clasped it firmly in his own, she smiled up at him with new regard. He had earlier returned her fierce embrace of greeting, sensing her need and communicating his own strength to her. He flushed with pleasure at her smile, then turned and gruffly addressed Edward. "We will sleep on the ground by the fire and leave the tent to your sister."

Morning came quickly. Aethelflaed splashed water on her face, rinsing the sleep from her eyes. Three days had they been here and while the exhaustion had quickly lifted from her young body, her mind was responding more slowly. The water of the River Lea sparkled in the half-light of dawn as it fell through her fingers. She watched the river flow quietly and swiftly toward its confluence with the Thames, eager to be out to sea, lapping softly past the hulls of the English longboats riding at anchor across the entrance to the estuary.

The full extent of the siege showed itself in the clear light of day. Ethelred quickly sketched a map on a patch of bare ground as he told the story of the march from Winchester. Alfred's forces had marched swiftly downriver toward London. Longboats from Reading followed his progress along the river, carrying supplies and picking up loads of grain not consigned to flames or hidden by hungry peasants along the way. The King met Ethelhelm's forces at St. Peter's Church and the two levies razed the town.

The English fleet then divided: half the ships were sent down the Thames past the unwalled city riverfront, where they burned and sank all the Danish dragon-prows they found along the quays, then took up positions along the city front to a point east of the mouth of the Lea. The rest of the ships blocked the estuary and rode at anchor off St. Peter's Church, cutting off escape both seaward and upriver. Alfred marched his levies north to the camp on the west bank of the Lea at the edge of the Chiltern near the hamlet of Clayhangra. Ethelhelm's forces spread themselves eastward from St. Peter's Church along the south bank of the Thames to the blockade at the Lea. The single bridge from London to Southwark was heavily guarded. Ethelred's siege circle to the north, a few hundred yards outside London's ancient wall, commanded the five entrances to the city.

As he sketched in the dirt, Aethelflaed saw that the encirclement by the *fyrd* was complete. At night she had seen only the campfires dotting their circle, as the guards atop the wall would also see. During the day, part of the *fyrd* remained in the woods behind them, guarding Ethelred's siege circle from the rear. This was Dane-infested land. Now in the growing light she saw some of the men emerging from the woods behind them. She watched with surprise and curiosity for she had not realized how great was this levy that the King had brought with him. They were moving steadily out into the open. The English would wait no longer. The walls of London would be breached today.

Ethelred, following her gaze, nodded. "No English have come out to join us the past three nights, so we will storm the gates today. We will breach the north gate and one of the west gates."

"What about the gate to the fortress?" She pointed to the dimly visible jog in the northwest wall.

Ethelred shook his head. "Too dangerous. It will be heavily timbered and guarded. If we come in from the north and west, the two arms of the *fyrd,*" with a quick movement, he sketched two pincers from north and west into the heart of the city "will meet at the inside entrance to the fort. We can storm it from the inside. When they open the gate to escape, they will fall among the English waiting for them."

She squinted up at the brightening sky. "Then you will attack within the hour?" It surprised her that he still lingered at the camp. He saw her confusion and smiled briefly, shedding for an instant his grim concentration.

"The *fyrd* is more than doubled this morning. You slept so soundly that you did not hear the men moving forward during the night. The King ordered that you not be wakened, but he has been up for several hours himself." He embraced her briefly and called for his horse. "I must leave now. You will stay here," he ordered, brushing her cheek with his lips before he mounted. He looked down at her only a moment before he rode off. She watched him until he reached the forward circle. He turned and raised his arm in a quick salute before he melted into the mass of men gathered there. "Godspeed," she whispered.

"Give me your blessing also, sister." Edward stood at her elbow, a shirt of loose ring mail over his leather byrnie. A wooden shield, its polished bronze boss gleaming in the sun, was slung over his left arm. "The King gives me leave to ride behind Ethelred." His voice throbbed with excitement. She knit her brows with concern. He saw the look and laughed, reaching out to give her arm a little shake. "You must not worry. I have looked forward to the day that I might share more fully the glory of battle."

"You may share the bloodletting, too," she said evenly, though her heart pounded in her ears. Edward put his arms around her. "You shall not fear on my account." Before she could reply, he was gone. She slipped into her cloak and hood and ran the short distance to the King's tent. "Father," she cried, "they are gone already."

"Then I must prepare to join them shortly. You," he signaled curtly to the thane beside him, "are charged with her life. Stay well behind the circle and move back to the edge of the forest to the camp after the wall is breached. It will be dangerous if too many come out, for we are not leaving many men behind in the camp." Only the King's eyes showed when he pulled the iron and leather helmet down over his face, the barely curved nosepiece giving him a look of grim ferocity. Pain showed in those eyes, physical and spiritual both. He sat his horse as easily as if he were riding out to hunt with a falcon on his glove, but his leather-clad hand rested instead on the hilt of his finely hammered sword.

Once inside the gates, the fighting would be on foot and though they were reasonably certain of the outcome, none doubted the savagery with which the trapped men of the *here* would resist. They could be killed or they could be fought to a standstill and be brought to terms. One must never underestimate the strength of an army that counted itself lost at the outset: some would never put themselves at Alfred's mercy.

A moment's fear gripped her as she saw them spur their horses forward: her father, her brother, her betrothed, never separated in battle, always together. Together also they might die.

From her vantage point she could see the planking that had been laid across the ditches at the north gate. The heavy log ram, lifted on the shoulders of a score of men, swing into position before the gates. Wood slammed heavily against wood and the sharp report of its contact rolled across the field seconds after she saw the ram pulled back for its next assault.

The gates held firm under the battering as time and time again the ram was thrown against them. The reports ceased while the second crew came in. They began again, pouring fresh energy into the assault. Slowly, hesitantly, the sound of tearing wood and the screeching protest of hinges, straining in their mounts, rolled across the field. The battering continued. The third crew took its place and rushed the gates with renewed force. There was a shuddering wrench as the wood screamed and parted. A roar rose from the massed army as the gates gave way, crashing inward to the ground in a cloud of dust and splinters. Seconds later, another cry told her that the western gates had given way and the pincers were set to close on the city. She strained to see Ethelred's banner as the levies streamed into the gap behind him, but the clouds of dust stirred up by the pounding of running feet obscured her view.

Hours passed and the fighting sill went on. She wrapped her cloak tightly around her against the chill. Cries reached her faintly from the walled city but little occurred on outside. Part of the *fyrd* remained outside, restlessly milling to and fro along the walls. She looked up at the sun and grew uneasy, for it was now well past midday. Surely a messenger would be coming soon.

"Look!" Her guard pointed to the top of the wall. Stricken, she watched thin trickles of smoke winding upward, darkening the air, and grim memories of their ride from Winchester overtook her. Alfred had planned to use fire only if he met with strong resistance: the Danes were not giving up the city easily. Figures now appeared at the top of the wall, arms spread wide in terror, before they either fell or threw themselves into the ditch below. Screams reached her ears, mingled with the piercing, triumphant blasts from the antler horns of the English.

The thane touched her arm to draw her attention. "Come Lady, we must go back. Some are getting through and it will be dangerous to stay so close."

Her horse pawed the ground nervously, and she stroked his neck speaking soothing nonsense to him. "No," she said, with determination. "I will stay." The blasting of horns sounded more frequently now as fresh troops poured into the city. Her heart quickened at each note, for surely the sound of horns meant that things fared well. The weakened city could not hold out much longer, and she prayed it would not for the sake of the town as well as for the safety of her family.

"Now," said her guard firmly as Edward rode toward them, his helmet under his arm, his young face streaked with dirt and smoke. His eyes were more grim than she had ever seen them as he reached over and took her horse's bridle.

"We will have no argument, sister. Both the King and Lord Ethelred command me to remove you back to camp." Edward wiped the sweat from his face, leaving a white streak across his forehead. "The worst is yet to come!" She followed him reluctantly, looking backward as she rode. The last levies to ride in carried torches, like huge candles, high over their heads.

All night the city burned, in huge patches here and there. Not all went to the torch, for they did not wish to occupy a ruin. The crackling of fire on dry timber muffled all other sounds and the flames threw up great billows of smoke, etching ghostly patterns in the sky. She could think only of the scorched animals they had seen in the field on their march to London. Then she had felt most revulsion for the ugliness of the dead forms. Now she imagined the pain of the living souls, and it bore heavily on her heart and filled her with ghastly pity.

They went to the King's tent, where a single candle flickered before the crucifix that was Alfred's altar. The King's Mass priest, holding the open Book, mumbled his ceaseless vigil softly, as he did throughout every battle. Edward knelt, and threw his helmet on the ground. His face was expressionless, almost mask-like, as he fought for control, but tears coursed silently down his soot-grimed face. She knelt beside him, and he put his arm around her, gripping her shoulder painfully. Even Edward, the strong, insensitive stripling soldier, who had never seen a siege before, was shocked and sickened.

Together they gave thanks for the victory and begged forgiveness for its fearful price.

CHAPTER SEVEN

(887)

*A*way from its shallow marshes inside the north wall, Walbrook stream flowed lazily and uncluttered under the midsummer sun. Further south in the heart of the city, where the damage had been the greatest, the stream was clogged with garbage and debris. Barely a year had gone by since Ethelred had stormed into the city and still the townsfolk dug themselves out from under the ashes and rubble.

Aethelflaed rose early, as soon as the sunlight flickered through the windows of the rebuilt timbered fortress. Ethelred slept deeply and did not stir as she slipped out of bed and dressed quickly, pausing only to kiss him lightly, so as not to wake him. Her habit of early morning walking was ingrained, and the cool banks of the Walbrook that now replaced Winchester's Itchen afforded her a moment alone with her thoughts before the day bustled into restless activity.

It was not yet a month since she and Ethelred joined hands in Winchester's ancient minster over the golden casket containing Pope Marinus' gift of a fragment of the true cross and received Bishop Denewulf's blessing on their union. Their vows had been given earlier in the Great Hall of the palace as was customary, for marriages were a family matter and subject to civil law only. This important part was done before the assembled thanes of Wessex, for it was their witness and their approval that was sought.

There, in the Great Hall, with ceremony and with feasting, did Alfred give his eldest daughter into the keeping of the Overlord of Mercia, and well did he wish his nobles to mark this, for Ethelred now ruled a large and unsteady kingdom. Ethelred's authority and closeness to the throne of Wessex were not to be left in any doubt. Nor was there to be any doubt, at least among the family, of the position of the eldest daughter. Agreements and dowers were drawn up by both Ethelred and the King, and Aethelflaed was given certain family lands in Wessex which would revert to the throne on her death. Ethelred, for his part, presented to Aethelflaed a parchment, witnessed by both Edward and the King, which placed her in charge of the courts of Mercia in Ethelred's absence and gave her rights to the overlordship of Mercia in the event of his death. English Mercia was again in the hands of the Mercians, though the connections with the House of Wessex were strong. Mercia could not, for now, stand alone. Nevertheless, Alfred wished it plainly to be seen that the overlordship of Mercia was a gift from the King of Wessex.

In this spirit of political unity and amity were the vows exchanged, the Bishop's lengthy blessing given, and the marriage ring of heavily worked gold surrounding a large, glowing ruby slipped on her finger. The feasting went on for several days, and somewhat decorous as long as the newly wedded couple was present, becoming more raucous when she excused herself and went up to her women, happy to escape the toasts of wine and mead. The longer this went on, the noisier and bawdier it would grow. Ethelred would stay to receive, good-naturedly, the brunt of their humor. He held her hand under the table to encourage her lest, like the Queen and her ladies, she grow faint with the noise, the mingled smells of roasting venison and mutton and the sweat of too many people crowded into the Great Hall.

She appreciated the warm, strong clasp of his hand, but she was neither faint with the heat and smells, nor repelled by the growing slyness of the jokes. She was instead exhilarated, for these rough men loved Ethelred and the King, and for their sakes, they loved her also. A dreadful battle had been fought quickly and with great dispatch for the capital of Mercia, and backbreaking hours of labor rebuilding it had been given unstintingly for the sake of this wedding. Not for her sake, personally, or Ethelred's, but for the cooperation of two great English kingdoms in the hope of forestalling a common foe.

So she smiled at their jokes and applauded their antics. They truly deserved a celebration. When Edward rose to toast the couple, she rose also, pulling her husband to his feet. She knelt and then kissed his hand, then laid her hands in both of his in the traditional sign of fealty. A political gesture only, but it brought, as she knew it would, a great roar of laughter from the assemblage, and catcalls when he kissed her warmly on the lips in return. She clapped her hands for silence, and when she got it, turned wordlessly to the King and knelt before him. She took his hands, outstretched in blessing, laid her hands in his and gave to her father, the King of Wessex, the same sign of fealty she had given her husband. The thanes were silent for a moment as the meaning of her action penetrated their awareness; the shouts it brought from their throats this time were not of laughter, but of loyalty, pledging also their lives and fortunes to the King and his son-in-law. Her honors done, she left the hall, smiling to herself at the cheers that followed her up the stairway.

When she received her husband in her chambers not much later, she was still smiling, and this time it was he who knelt. It was a good beginning. She had honored and enhanced his already great reputation in the eyes of his own nobles and he would not forget it. She accepted the consummation of the marriage at first with curious docility, then with growing delight, for Ethelred was not remiss in expressing his gratitude for her public display of esteem.

If she had only been vastly fond of him the night before, by morning the bond of mutual pleasure had established in them a growing bond of love. When Ethelred arose from his knees on his wedding night, he dismissed her giggling ladies, who had arrayed her in a fine robe of embroidered linen, and closed the door firmly behind them. He blew out the candles and kissed her gently, undemandingly. This time her response flowed quickly.

When they awoke the next morning and rose to enjoy their traditional wedding breakfast, they looked into each other's eyes, and smiled warmly at each other, remembering, and silently acknowledged the bond that now tied their two lives together and would hold them forever.

Ethelred's *morgengifu*, his morning-gift, to her followed an ancient tradition, one not often still seen: a ceremonial sword, with a hilt of braided and interwoven fine gold wire, sparkling with a few great gems. Hundred of years ago, he told her, Saxon men and their brides exchanged swords and shields as wedding gifts, as a token of their willingness to share their responsibilities. And surely, he went on, raising to his lips the warm hand he held fast in his own hand, she could not doubt his need for her, as a wife, a comrade-at-arms, trained by himself, and as a ruler equal with himself. In the newer traditions of Mercia and Wessex, his morning-gift also bestowed on her lands in Worcester and Gloucester. He had kept his promise: a wedding gift of London and a morning-gift of Mercia.

There was little time for privacy. For Ethelred, his wedding was a brief respite from his duties in London, and they very shortly returned to London and the rebuilt, refurbished garrison that was to be their home for the rest of their lives. Ethelhelm stayed in London during Ethelred's absence, but the ealdorman was carrying the King's alms to Rome and could stay no longer. The passage through the Alps must be made before winter closed the route. He was gone before they arrived, taking Elfled with him, to Aethelflaed's unspoken relief.

Ethelred joined her at breakfast, kissing her heartily before he sat down at the long trestle table that David had set with wooden plates, bone-handled knives, and drinking horns. He reached for the earthen jug of Frankish wine and filled the drinking horn, taking a long draught from it. He set the empty horn down, a look of wry distaste on his face.

"It is almost vinegar!" He wiped his mouth as if to remove the offensive flavor. David, anticipating his wants, brought a flagon of ale and removed the jug. "I hoped we might have better wine by now," grumbled Ethelred. He saw the extra plates and raised his eyebrows in question, but before she could explain, Edward appeared, respectfully guiding an elderly man.

"My Lord Heahstan!" She jumped quickly to her feet and grasped his hand warmly before he could bow. The monk's robe fell loosely from his bent shoulders, ill-concealing the gaunt, once-tall frame of the Bishop of London. His hand in hers was bony and roughened with hard work, but his grip was as firm as his voice.

"We give thanks for your safe arrival and for the deliverance of the City of London."

"Surely," she said, her voice tinged with regret, "the English deliverance is no less harsh than the Danish rule?"

He studied her face. "Yes, deliverance," he repeated quietly. "Perhaps it may be harsh, but it is not so terrible as it appears to you. We are of good spirit." His eyes were calm and sparkled with innate good humor.

"I might have thought otherwise," Aethelflaed replied a bit drily.

"My dear," he said mildly, still retaining her hand, "some things can be worse than death, as I'm certain you know. One must accept difficulties at the hands of one's friends as well as one's foes. We are well accustomed to these things here, and there is little our friends would refuse to suffer for the sake of being amongst their own again."

The old bishop had weathered many storms from both sides. His fellow churchmen, several of whom fought at Alfred's side, criticized him openly for his friendship with the Danish overlords of London during its occupation. "My duty is here," he wrote the King briefly and without apology, "for without the comfort of the Church, our people will not survive." The King agreed and bid him continue, urging him with all speed to baptize as many as would receive it. It was a wise decision, she reflected, for the loyalty of the Londoners to the faithful bishop prevailed against the will of the Danish masters.

"You are young," Heahstan broke in upon her thoughts, "and cannot yet accept suffering as inescapable. But we are Mercian and will gladly suffer what may come for a Mercian king," he nodded at Ethelred, "rather than suffer without hope under Danish rule."

"My Lord Bishop," interposed Ethelred a little wearily, for he had heard these lines of talk before, "the throne of Mercia has never been empty. I rule in the King's name."

"Perhaps." Heahstan smiled. "But Burhred left Mercia to the invaders, and now he will never leave Rome." He scowled to himself. "He has no taste for kingly duties," he finished with infinite tact.

"I do not speak of Burhred," Ethelred replied softly, "I rule in King Alfred's name. At his hand I received this city, and as his son and ally will I govern and defend it."

Heahstan smiled again. "Have it as you will. The people look on you already as their king. You are Mercian and were of high position in Burhred's court. The King of Wessex shows great wisdom in placing the safety of Mercia in your hands. He knows a West Saxon ruler of Offa's kingdom would not be acceptable."

"Then they do not know when they are well off. Mercia cannot defend itself without his help. It were better if Wessex and Mercia were united even now under one crown for their own safety!" Ethelred pushed his bench away from the table and paced the room. Aethelflaed eyed Heahstan thoughtfully, considering his relentless needling.

Heahstan was not to be put off. "Who sits as head of the Mercian council?"

"I do, as you well know," Ethelred replied.

"And who receives the King's taxes?"

"They are remitted to me by the King of Wessex. That does not make me King of Mercia, only the Overlord."

"Your authority is without question!"

"And well it should be," retorted Ethelred, though without heat.

Aethelflaed regarded the Bishop with undisguised concern. "Are you suggesting that my Lord Ethelred set himself up as King, opposed to my father?"

"Not at all, My Lady. The Ealdorman is a good leader, a good soldier, so good that he does not realize the extent of his influence."

Ethelred turned to Aethelflaed, smiling at her distress. "Come now, dearling, surely you see my Lord Bishop's game? He touches on my ambition." He turned to the Bishop, a wry smile curling at the corners of his mouth. "You have been outspoken in the past. I trust in the future, you shall not be less so!"

"You may indeed trust me." Heahstan's eyes twinkled with amusement at the friendly barb. "However," he rose from the table, "I am here to fulfill my promise to your Lady to show her the city. She should know the people she has taken for her own."

Ethelred smiled again at Heahstan, some inward jest lighting his eyes. "Rest easy, my friend. I do not intend to overstep my limits, if I understand your mind rightly?"

"You do, My Lord." Heahstan bowed to Ethelred, who acknowledged the bow as he turned to the door with Edward. They left together, their minds quickly intent on business elsewhere.

Heahstan extended his hand to Aethelflaed. "Come dear Lady. We have much to see." They rode out through the gates of the heavily timbered stockade.

CHAPTER EIGHT

*E*thelred's efficiency in rebuilding the fortifications in so short a time astonished even the King, who had the highest opinion of Ethelred's ability. Two considerations perhaps had stirred the Ealdorman to surpass himself. He would shortly be bringing a bride to London and although he himself might have been content to live in a mud-and-wattle hut while he and his men struggled out from under the rubble, it would not do for a royal wife. So the fortress and its sturdy wooden palisade were rebuilt with all speed from huge logs dragged and rolled from the Chiltern. It was not a palace. It was what it had been for centuries and would continue to be throughout their lifetime—a military garrison. There were no bowers around the main building for the women of Ethelred's retainers. Instead the garrison was large enough to house the women and families in the rooms that surrounded the Great Hall.

The main consideration was the protection of the city against the Danish province of East Anglia, close by the broken city. A bitter pall of defeat hung over London when Guthrum, his face worn and haggard, signed the treaty. He would never again break a treaty with the King of Wessex, if only because he would not live long enough, but others after him would. Alfred and Guthrum exchanged hostages to ensure the peace. Guthrum, his eyes occasionally holding the vacant, hopeless stare that presaged impending senility, agreed to the boundaries that would keep him east of the River Lea and east of a line northward from Bedford and along the River Ouse to Watling Street.

Furthermore, Englishmen living under the Danelaw were to have equal rights with Guthrum's own subjects. Alfred's strength would no longer be underestimated by the host now that London was again in English hands. With Ethelred in London and Alfred and Edward in Wessex, it was plain that Wessex could now limit the power of the *Vik* in England.

But as Ethelred set about restoring the devastated city, it was also plain to him that the *Vik* would not accept limitations easily: their submission to the treaty was not to be relied upon. So he pressed urgently the rebuilding of the city and the restoring of trade. The rebuilding of the fortress made the ancient walled town a stronghold and a place of refuge, and, with the goods-laden ships plying the harbor, restored trade now made its principal citizens wealthy. It was not in the least surprising that the Londoners looked to Ethelred as their rightful Lord and regarded Alfred as merely the instrumentality by which Ethelred, and thereby peace and prosperity, had been restored to them. The Bishop's warning, if such it was, was not without foundation.

If Ethelred's sympathies were with his fellow Mercians, he gave no sign of it. Indeed they were in the minority in London, whose inhabitants now comprised many Danish-English as well as Mercians, and perhaps more than either of these were the Frankish, Flemish, and Moorish traders. The ambitions of a handful of Mercians were not likely to cause a ripple in London's ocean of mixed loyalties and ambitions. So Ethelred set about his business of refortifying London, rebuilding its bridges, and mustering men for *fyrd* service, the three main duties of an overlord, with vastly more concern about the Danes of East Anglia and Kent than about the throne of Mercia. Alfred, for his part, quietly waived all claims as conqueror, a fact gratefully accepted and quickly forgotten by the wealthy traders, and remitted the King's food rent to his son-in-law. Thus Ethelred was, in fact, if not in title, king.

Ruling this great province, which extended northward out of London and westward along Watling Street into the heart of the midlands, would not be easy. To the west and south lay the protection of Wessex, but to the east, English Mercia was bordered by Danish Mercia and the Danelaw. For the time, the treaty would hold the land and would hold gold-hungry Danes in check, but even Guthrum could not be held accountable for the ambitions of his Northumbrian brethren.

"Guthrum is old," Edward had reminded her during the intense rebuilding activities, "and the treaty will be binding only so long as he lives. London must be brought well under the law, for when Guthrum dies the Danes still living here may no longer wish for English control."

"Ethelred is a strong man! They will have English rule regardless of their wishes."

"He is a soldier first. He said so himself. But he is unschooled in the law." Edward rubbed his forehead wearily, for Ethelred had set him a strong pace that day. "There are no shire courts here as there are in Wessex for the hearing of civil complaints. We are still under military rule. We must have civil rule as well."

"Surely the Lord Bishop knows his duties in the courts?"

"Aye," Edward responded, "and he does the best he can, but he and his monks are busy tending the sick. They have little time for governance. You have been appointed praefect. This job is now yours."

Constant thievery plagued the city as much as disease and starvation. Food was pitifully scarce during the first winter after the siege, despite the loads of grain brought in from the west. Money, normally scarce in peace, had all but disappeared except into the pockets of the wealthy merchants. London was a study in extremes: abject poverty and misery against lavish wealth. Lawlessness of every variety abounded, and without stern measures to curb it the uneasy peace was threatened. Their East Anglian neighbors could well bide their time, for Mercia might yet fall to them by weight of its own seething internal disruption.

Now Heahstan affirmed Edward's words as they rode along the riverside, where ships from Rouen and Flanders busily plied the Thames or waited to dock at the water-gate. "Mercia was never divided into shires." He reined in his horse briefly as a wharf rat scuttled across his path. "Besides, we have paid heavily in silver and slaves to the Danes, and they have controlled everything. We have had no rule of our own for many years." He shrugged. "One cannot expect much. Thievery is a way of life for many here, and not just for the poor."

Aethelflaed nodded. "Military rule, though, cannot address the complaints of the citizens."

"It has been just so for many years now," he reminded her. "And until the host was driven out there was no hope of aught else, at least not for the English. For their own kin, they have one law, and for the merchants, being foreign, another law. They drove hard bargains, those heathen." This last was given musingly, for if the Danes excelled at fighting, they also excelled as merchants, though not all the goods they dealt with met with the Bishop's approval. "We do not intend any longer to ignore the complaints of our English. Nor of any man who lives here, be he English or no. We have heard of the folk moot established in Wessex by your father. We hope you will follow his example here."

She nodded. "The host have it also. They call it the *hustings*. But the folk moot is not a shire court," she pointed out, "and it requires a royal minister as praefect."

Heahstan slanted an approving look at her. "That is where you can help. You have studied the laws of Wessex then?"

"A little, though I do not know them all. We follow the code of Ine, but it is three hundred years old, and the King is drawing up a new code."

He nodded in agreement. "We need such a model here, but these heathen folk have no respect for Christian oaths." He paused and grinned wryly, "Not that our own brethren are always as observant as we might wish them to be."

"Aye," she agreed quickly, "we have seen enough of that. It is needful that we set up civil courts soon that will suit Mercian needs."

"London must come first. It is the gateway to all of Mercia. Your presence at the courts in the boroughs would lend authority to them and your voice would be greatly respected."

Aethelflaed reined in her horse and studied the Bishop. "I am praefect only in Ethelred's absence."

"Exactly." Heahstan smiled blandly at her. "But," he persisted, "it is important that the courts be ruled by one who knows the ancient codes. We have enough of ignorant thanes and merchants sitting in, each delivering his own justice."

"My dear Lord Bishop, need I remind you that women are not allowed such authority? Not since Queen Eadburh, Offa's daughter, poisoned her husband, King Beorhtric of Wessex, have my people allowed a woman to share her husband's throne." She paused thoughtfully. "Of course, my grandfather Ethelwulf put his Judith beside him. It caused much trouble, so my mother tells. But my Lord Asser tells me too, that it is a wrong custom of the West Saxons not to share the throne with a wife. Hateful, he says of it."

Heahstan brightened. She had made the point for him. He pursued the subject further. "And he is right, you may trust that. A most learned man. You must also bear in mind that West Saxon customs do not carry so much weight here." He glanced sidewise at her, sly humor glinting in his eyes. "Eadburh, you say. She was Mercian and perhaps they do not trust the Mercian strain in the House of Wessex." She looked quickly at him stiffening slightly, but he was laughing at her. "If you wish," he continued, "you might sit over the borough in Ethelred's name, since he is occupied elsewhere. I am certain he would be pleased to give you that honor."

Aethelflaed pushed her hair back from her forehead, where it had been clinging in curling tendrils, and let the cool breezes from the river play across her face. Edward had hinted at what the Bishop voiced openly. Aethelflaed had imagined a different role for herself. She foresaw helping Ethelred in private to the decisions and actions he took openly. She had not contemplated directly taking the authority herself. Yet this was what Heahstan was asking of her, saying in the same breath that this is what Ethelred would wish of her, since his military duties kept him occupied elsewhere. It was not altogether an unpleasant idea. The King himself had educated her in Saxon law. For that reason she hesitated. "I am a West Saxon."

"You must think of yourself as a Mercian, which you are now," Heahstan reminded her. "London will accept you easily, not only for Ethelred's sake but also for your mother's bloodline. But we will pursue the matter some other time," he continued. "Right now," he waved his hand at the docks ahead of him, "I must show you London's most important gate, for this one, more than any other, rules the city." What occurred that day reinforced Heahstan's words. The incident that took place, into which she stepped without hesitation, settled her direction. Further pursuit of the matter by the wily Bishop was unnecessary.

They spurred their horses out of the slow and lazy walk and trotted briskly the short distance to Billings Gate, where the merchant ships discharged their cargoes for inspection. To the left of them, rows of stone buildings housed kegs of Rhenish wine, delicate glassware, and intricately wrought iron swords from the Gaulish provinces. Slaves and ox-drawn carts labored past under bales of precious silks from the East. At the dockside, port reeves, attended by armed guards, read the writs of landing permission presented to them by merchant captains from Frisia and Rouen, and supervised unloading of the ships granted entry. All cargoes, no matter how small, were required to go through the toll gate and pay the appointed taxes before they could be carried off to the warehouses.

It astonished Aethelflaed that the town, so recently wracked by fire and destruction, showed little damage on the waterfront. The canny traders had much to lose by resistance, and she now understood the quickness of the town to surrender. The precious cargoes brought at great cost and danger to the trader-captains had to be protected from fire and plunder. It mattered little to them, be it Dane or Englishman, who held this gateway to Britain. As long as they had goods to sell and were permitted to do so, they were content. But to allow territorial bickering to endanger their warehouses, bulging with exotic goods, was unthinkable.

"War," Heahstan observed drily, "encourages money to change hands swiftly. Those who have goods to sell care naught where it is sold."

They dismounted, giving their horses to the charge of the retainer who followed them and approached the wooden tables where the reeve's assistants studied long bills of lading and calculated cargo taxes. The coins she saw heaped at the counting tables were Frankish gold, destined for the royal coffers. The English paid in silver. There had been no gold coin from English mints for centuries, though the English silver penny was highly valued. A gold mancusa was worth thirty silver pennies, enough to buy an ox. There were few who saw that much in a lifetime.

Heahstan guided her to a nearby table and pointed to bales of cloth waiting to be loaded. "Our English cloth is in great demand in Frankia and Spain. Flanders merchants buy the wool for their own looms."

She pointed at the papers being perused intently by the clerks. "Be these bills of sale? It seems they take uncommonly long in reading."

"Aye," he agreed. "Perhaps more so than those for the goods coming into London. These goods will be loaded for the return trip to Flanders and must be checked carefully before they are allowed out of the port to be certain that the market tax is paid and that the wool is charged at the decreed price." That she understood, for it was the overlord who set the price of goods sold in the markets. It was a way of controlling the flow of taxes into the royal coffers. "If the merchant has paid less than two hundred shillings for a *wey* of wool," Heahstan continued, "both he and the one who sold it to him will be fined."

"We cannot afford to do it otherwise, if we are to discourage thievery of royal taxes. Besides, these merchants are given good measure. There are no longer any short weights here. Ethelred brought the official measure for wool from Winchester so that London wools shall not be wanting."

Her attention was drawn to the third table by a sudden commotion. The stacks of gold at the counter's seat far exceeded those on the other tables. The guards dragged forward a ragged, sturdy man, and she understood at once the large stacks of gold.

"It is the thrall table!" she exclaimed, full of curiosity and was surprised to find herself slightly repelled at this method of acquiring slaves. She was accustomed to war hostages and their offspring or to those to had forfeited their freedom by committing serious crimes.

They stepped closer. Slave trading with the Continent was brisk and drew much gold from Frankia. The merchants were eager for slaves and were often not concerned with the legality of their choices. She had never seen a slave market before and moved closer, curious to know more about the brief altercation.

The reeve jumped to his feet and bowed as they approached. "My Lord Bishop," he appealed to Heahstan without preamble, "this merchant claims the slave was sold to him as a Danish captive!" He was greatly agitated and Aethelflaed understood why as he waved his hand toward the merchant, a dark-complected, black-bearded man, richly robed in white woolen and colored silk.

"Then what is the trouble?" Heahstan's voice was cool.

"The thrall says he is English." The reeve knit his brows in consternation; he was vaguely aware of the law, but uncertain as to its application. Had he not caught the Bishop's approach out of the corner of his eye, he would have ignored both the thrall's protest and the law. The Bishop's presence demanded that he consider the problem in a different light.

"He is lying!" The merchant spat contemptuously in the thrall's direction. "I paid a good price for him because he is strong."

"What proof have you that he is a Dane?" Heahstan's face was stern.

"My Lord," replied the merchant smoothly, "the word of your countryman who sold him to me is proof enough."

Heahstan ignored him and turned to the slave. "What is your proof?"

"I have none, My Lord." The thrall's eyes were fixed on the ground.

"Have you been a slave all your life?"

The man nodded, not lifting his eyes. "All but a few years. There was a great famine when I was a boy. My father sold me for bread when I was four."

Heahstan eyed the ragged creature grimly. "You are still a thrall then." It was a statement. "If your parents were English, then were you baptized?"

"Aye, My Lord, I am that." He pulled a crude wooden cross on a dirty cord from the neck of his tunic.

"Surely you do not believe this tale," the merchant sneered. "Even the English do not take the word of slaves."

Heahstan ignored the statement. "Where are you bound?" he asked the merchant, who did not answer. "To Cordoba, I'll wager." Heahstan's eyes narrowed.

The merchant bowed, his drooping lids hiding his eyes. "My word, Sire. I am Moorish, but I trade only among the Franks."

Heahstan studied him with distaste. "Oh? Because you are aware of English law concerning Christian thralls?"

"I do not understand you, Sire."

"But I am certain you do," replied Heahstan softly, clipping each word. "If you trade only in Frankia, then I am certain you have paid with Frankish gold. May I see it?" The man demurred. "Shall I call the guard?" There was an edge of impatience in Heahstan's voice. The merchant sullenly produced a leather pouch, reluctantly extracting a few coins, which he handed to the Bishop. Heahstan studied them, then passed the lot to Aethelflaed. It took her but a quick glance to understand what the Bishop's aim was.

"These are dinars," she exclaimed. "There is not a Frankish mint among them." The merchant averted his face.

"We do not sell Christian slaves to infidels." Heahstan's voice grated with anger as he returned the coins to the merchant. "Give back the purchase price," he commanded the flustered reeve.

The Moor intervened angrily. "You have no right to interfere with this purchase. I have paid much gold for this slave."

"Most certainly he has the right." Aethelflaed stepped forward. "As bishop, he is acting as the Overlord's praefect. The code is also clear. Your gold will be returned."

To her astonishment, the Moor waved her off. The reeve's face turned ashen as he plucked nervously at the merchant's sleeve, all the while watching Aethelflaed. "You must listen," he whispered urgently to the Moor.

The merchant turned away from him and said to Heahstan, "Many pardons, My Lord, but in my country, women are kept at home. Our women do not question the word of a man."

She regarded the merchant distastefully, her eyes glinting with anger, and motioned to the nearby guards, who quietly stepped to either side of the Moor. "The laws of my ancestor, King Ine of Wessex, are well known to English and foreign traders alike." She stared coldly at the man. "As you fully understand. No Englishman, bond or free, may be sold overseas by his countryman. The Church adds weight to the law when it is a baptized Christian, for no baptized man or woman may be sold to an unbeliever."

The Moor turned to speak to Heahstan, but he had stepped back, and the guards prevented the man from moving away from her.

"Your manner," she continued, "suggests contempt of the law, not ignorance of it."

"I will take it to the Overlord of London," the man replied angrily. "A woman's word will not be taken against mine."

"It will indeed," interrupted Heahstan. "Lady Aethelflaed, to whom you speak so unwisely, is praefect to the Overlord of London and is his wife."

Aethelflaed caught the quick glint of triumph in Heahstan's eyes as he turned to her, waiting for her pronouncement. She looked back at the Moor, who plainly disbelieved Heahstan. She was becoming exasperated with his arrogance. "This sale is not legal, and in the name of Ethelred, Ealdorman of London and Mercia, whose praefect I am, I will attest to that." She had the satisfaction of seeing the look of shock erase all other expressions from the swarthy countenance. The reeve quickly counted out the gold coins and shoved them at the Moor. "Your permission to trade at this port is also revoked and will not be renewed until you pay the fine for your contempt of the code." She signaled to the guards, who escorted the angry merchant back to the dock. She turned to the reeve. "See to it that this bondsman is returned to his owner, and also that his owner pays his own *wergild* for trying to sell him."

Heahstan smiled at her as they moved away. "I could not have done so well myself, Lady. In fact," he said thoughtfully, "I dared not say more on the matter since you were here to settle it. You yourself saw how he argued with me! Of course," he said blandly, "as Ethelred's appointed praefect, he must not argue with you."

She eyed him a bit primly, then laughed aloud. He had counted on her to intervene. Nevertheless, she understood Heahstan's sense of urgency, for the flustered reeve, whom she lectured severely before they left Billings Gate, was not capable of administering justice, much less of knowing the law. The foreign traders were better educated than the London reeves and were quick to take advantage of them. Even the clerks who could read, as many of the reeves could not, were ignorant of the laws of their own country and knew only of taxes on wool, or glass, or wine. Worse still was the cupidity of many of the English, who were all too eager to satisfy the foreign traders' appetite for slaves, to say nothing of their own for gold.

In the next few months she found, as Heahstan predicted, that her presence in the city was easily accepted and especially so at the markets, which she took to visiting frequently. The extent of the violations of the king's taxes became evident when she undertook occasionally to check for herself the bills of lading and tax calculations against the goods piling up on the dock. The discrepancies appalled her and she called Ethelred's attention to the lost revenue.

"See to it," he advised her briefly, for he was busy. So she did, finding that her continued visits to the dock greatly discouraged violations of the law. She noticed that she was recognized more and more as one who spoke for the will of the Ealdorman. Now no trader on the dock dared deprecate the presence or the word of the young woman who watched intently the hustle and noise of the markets. She had, after that incident, begun to single out the thrall market for her attention, since thralls were the greatest and most lucrative export, and it was the code restricting the selling of slaves that was the most frequently ignored.

The imports of wine and fish, and ironwork and silks also, were carefully scrutinized. There were taxes on the goods themselves and tolls to be paid by the vessels that brought them in, for the privilege of tying up at Billings Gate or of passing under the bridge. No one was allowed to sell goods except at a market place, for this was where the taxes were levied. The traders, foreign and local, found ways around the market place. There was also a toll for entering the city for the purpose of setting up at market, and this was collected infrequently, if at all. It did not take her long to see how much revenue was being lost.

She set guards and scribes at the gates, especially at Cripplegate and Aldersgate, who collected entrance tolls for the cartloads of local goods that poured into the city and registered all merchants entering the gates. There were butter and cheeses, salt, honey, oil and vinegar, fish, eggs and live pigs and cows and chickens, brought to market by the women who produced them. They paid their toll in fresh eggs and butter and a live hen, for they had little coin, and came to barter for cloth and spices. It was exciting, and her daily excursions into the market place were no chore. She scrutinized bills of lading and watched the toll collection at the gates and found herself fascinated by every detail of the city. And when she had finished all this, she drew up lists and brought them to Ethelred.

"It would seem," he acknowledged "that your head for these matters is keener than mine." He studied her sheets of parchment, shaking his head.

"I had not known so much was slipping past or being stolen. You are putting a stop to it."

Her duties were to be interrupted for a while. By October she was expecting her first child, and Ethelred's delight was boundless. "I am twenty-eight," he said. "A long time for a man to be childless!" It was his wish that she return to Winchester until the child was born. The city vapors, to say nothing of her long excursions into the market place, he insisted, were bad for her. In vain did she argue with him, at last prevailing on him to let her stay a few weeks longer, long enough to appoint the best of their retainers and Heahstan's men to oversee her duties in the market and borough courts. She left Ethelred regretfully, and just as regretfully did she leave the bustling city she had come to accept as her own. Heahstan pointed out the compensations.

"I will offer daily Masses that you be delivered of a healthy heir. London will be at your feet when your child is born!"

Aethelflaed knew he was tired from his own work, and affectionately acknowledged her debt to him. "My Lord Bishop, without your devoted counsel, I should still be a stranger here." She brushed the old Bishop's cheek lightly with her lips.

She left the walls of London behind her, reflecting with some astonishment that it had been little more than a year since the siege, and half as long since her marriage to the ruler of one of the largest kingdoms of the English. In that short time she had become absorbed in the life of city, its administration, and the busy fortress that was her home. She recalled with surprise that not once had she found the time to feel homesick for Winchester and knew that this was greatly owing to Heahstan's aid and companionship. Wise old man! Well, she liked it. She would be happy to see her family and to immerse herself for a while in the life of the court of Wessex. But London, the city and its life had taken hold of her. Ethelred had handed it to her and she was too honest not to admit that she enjoyed the exercise of power. Ethelred had made it plain to her that she would share his rule of Mercia, not after his death, but now, and as she turned her face toward Winchester it occurred to her that this had also been her father's intention from the beginning.

CHAPTER NINE

*T*he fields, heavily blanketed with ripening wheat, rippled in golden waves under the autumn breezes. Asser was exultant. "God has been merciful to us," he exclaimed, greeting her joyfully. "He has held back the rains until we bring in the harvest."

"Your influence with God is no doubt as great as your influence with my father," Aethelflaed laughed, "for I saw no offerings to the old spirits as I passed through the shires."

Asser smiled benignly. "The King has forbidden the old harvest offering, and we have celebrated All Hallows according to the rule of the Church. We cannot wipe out old customs, so we must use them as best we can." He shook his head regretfully. "Perhaps you did not see the offerings to the pagan spirits, but they are out there nonetheless."

She scanned his face as they entered the Great Hall. "Dear friend, your eyes are not as happy as your face. Do things not go well with you?"

"Ah? It shows, then." He mused silently, staring absently at the wool hanging that covered the damp grey stone of the walls.

"You are too long away from Wales?" she prompted and noticed the quick response in his eyes. "Surely my father will let you go? Has not Grimbald arrived to continue the work of the Palace school?"

"I have asked him, but he begs me stay until Twelfth Night is gone. I must stay until he can work without my help."

She smiled reassuringly. "You may trust the King. He will reward your devotion well!"

His face relaxed into a rueful smile. "The King rewards all his servants well, including myself." He was solemn again. "It is not that I am unhappy here...." He broke off. "Have you seen the hills and forests of my country?" She shook her head. "If you had," he went on, "you might understand. One must always go where God calls, but," his face was wistful for a moment, "I think of my hills often."

She thought of her own brief touch of longing for the rolling countryside of Hampshire before the life of the city absorbed her. "I used to dream of Winchester, though perhaps it is not the same. I am happy to be back here, but now that I am here, I see that I have become a Mercian, for I have grown to love London."

"Then you will have the company of a Mercian countryman. Werferth of Worcester came shortly ahead of you and there is not a nobler man of

God to be found anywhere, excepting it be Pleymund, from Cheshire." She would have pressed him further, because she had heard much of Werferth from the great See of Worcester, but Asser begged her leave to retire and she gave it to him reluctantly.

The See of Worcester lay west of Watling Street near the western boundary of Mercia and extended westward to the restless border of Wales. The position of the city of Worcester on the banks of the Severn River was strategic, for now that entry into Wessex by way the Thames was blocked, the Vikings would be plotting another route into the midlands. The Bristol Channel and the rivers that poured into it, the Severn and the Avon, were guarded jealously by those who had the most to lose: Wessex to the south, Wales to the northwest, and Mercia to the north and east. With the ruling families of Wessex and Mercia closely united, the back door might be effectively closed to the Vikings across the Irish Sea, regardless of what the fractious Welsh might choose to do.

Then there was the eastern border. The headwaters of the Avon, which joined the Severn below Worcester, lay to the east of Watling Street in the Danelaw. Ships launched east of Watling Street could be sailed down the Avon through English Mercia to the Severn. She shuddered involuntarily. There could be no doubt that the Danes of Northumbria eyed Worcester enviously, for the ancient city, brooding majestically over its river, was a stronghold guarding the entry to the rich lands of Wessex. Worcester in the hands of the host would cut the southern midlands off from the strong leadership of Wessex, leaving the northern midlands and Cheshire open to both the Northumbrian Danes and the Irish Vikings. Then if Haesten should return.... The thought of Haesten always lurked unpleasantly in the back of her mind.

"My Lady, you seem greatly thoughtful!" The familiar voice with its southwestern accent startled Aethelflaed out of thought. She turned and extended both hands in greeting to find the younger woman, closely attended by Edward. Ecgwin's beauty gave her a look of other-worldly innocence. Aethelflaed repressed a swift pang of premonition. Such a child appeared too delicate to bear a queen's burden, and queen she would probably be some day.

For Ecgwin's sake she was glad that Elfled was still in Rome, though when she returned, her position at the court of Winchester would be stronger than ever. Her father, Ethelhelm, had been chosen to take Peter's Pence to Rome: Elfled's journey to the Holy See, was a signal honor and could only enhance her influence.

Edward cut into her thoughts. "Sister, whatever solemn thoughts you have must be put aside. Advent is upon us and we have much to celebrate."

He hesitated. "I have a favor to ask." He glanced self-consciously at Ecgwin, then fell nervously silent.

"Ah!" Aethelflaed repressed the smile hovering at the corners of her mouth. "I must have a companion for my waiting and lying in?"

"It, it is customary," Edward stammered.

"Then I shall be content with your choice." She put her arm around Ecgwin's shoulders, to Edward's open relief.

"She has much to learn," Edward whispered.

And so do you, little brother, she observed silently. Nevertheless she applied herself to Ecgwin's training.

However seriously she doubted that Ecgwin could be of help at her lying in, there was no doubt that the girl was as cheerful an attendant as anyone could wish for. Ecgwin's surprising skill in organizing palace tasks proved to be of great value. Aethelflaed provided her with half a dozen women of the court, who, under Ecgwin's patient supervision, wove and stitched diligently the embroidered hangings for the Christmas feast in the Great Hall. It had to be done quickly for Alfred decreed that no unnecessary labor be done from the first Christmas Mass until Twelfth Night was past. Every morning, nevertheless, Aethelflaed firmly dispatched Ecgwin to the school quarters, presided over now by Pleymund and Grimbald, despite the girl's protests that her head was not meant for Latin.

"Besides," Ecgwin pleaded, "I must see the hangings finished by Christmas."

"I will attend to the women until you return from your lessons," Aethelflaed promised, giving her a gentle push in the direction of the schoolroom. "It is Edward's wish that you continue your education." That was always the talisman. If Edward wished it, it was unquestionably to be done, and Aethelflaed used it shamelessly to keep the girl at her studies. Ecgwin turned obediently to leave, but not before Aethelflaed caught a glimpse of the glow at the mention of Edward's name.

"You keep the child so busy, she has no time for the Atheling," Asser remarked bluntly, though the sparkle in his eyes belied his tone of voice.

"A little separation is good for lovers," she replied, a little wistfully. "Or so I'm told."

"You bear your separation well." Asser knew. His mistress, his Wales, was still a far-off dream. "It is my turn then to beg you to be of good cheer. Lord Ethelred will be joining us soon?"

"Aye," she laughed, "and none too soon for me. I grow tired of the company of the women and you can be sure they tire of me. I am not used to such a quiet life. To make it worse, the Queen pampers me as if I were her favorite pet."

"You do well enough. But are you not a little hard on the girl?" He looked thoughtfully after Ecgwin.

Aethelflaed was emphatic. "She must learn the ways of the Court quickly and well. There is always competition and she must be prepared for it."

"I see." Asser refrained from commenting on the bluntness and finality of her tone. "Competition?"

"There are others," she replied shortly.

"Lady, the matter is not yet decided." Asser's eyes sparkled. "If you are displeased with Edward's choice, surely a well-chosen word from yourself would direct matters more to your liking?"

Again the corners of her mouth twitched with a longing to smile. She repressed it, knowing he was baiting her into admitting what they both already knew. "I would do no such thing," she reprimanded him sternly, struggling against laughter, "and it is not a question of 'others', which you know yourself." Asser raised a doubtful eyebrow. "If Edward is decided," she went on, "I will do as he wishes. I must trust that my brother's heart will not change or be swayed. He may be headstrong, but he is also faithful and single-minded."

"Let us pray for her sake that he is. And pray there are no other rivals."

She regarded him with astonishment. "Other than Elfled?"

He smiled enigmatically. "I do not speak of rivals for Edward's affections, but for Ecgwin's." The expression on her face stopped him. "No," he said, misreading her face, "I shall speak no more of it, for it is probably an old man's imagination."

It was not an old man's imagination. Her mistake had been in assuming that once Ecgwin's choice was known, the matter was henceforth closed. Asser patted her shoulder as he rose to take his leave. "See to it that you do your job well. It is better for all of us if the heir to the throne marries someone he loves. In the old days...." He shuddered. "If there is no love, or at least acceptance, God's will is set aside. Then the bitterness that happens between a king and his queen may tear a land apart." The Welsh, she reflected, were incurably romantic; about love, about God, and above all, about their mountainous homeland. Nevertheless, he knew the House of Wessex was not without its failings in this respect.

Asser's hopes were not to go unfulfilled. At Christmas, the King granted to his tutor the properties of the monasteries of Congresbuy and Banwell in Somerset. Best of all, he granted his permission to return to Wales. Asser's longing for his mountains would be fulfilled come spring, and no one, save her father, was more unwilling to part with so dear a friend than herself.

Before Christmas overtook them, an incident occurred which recalled to mind Asser's warning about a rival, and it took her completely by surprise, as had Asser's remark. Why had she been blind to what the Welshman had so plainly perceived? But then he had the advantage of her. He visited the schoolroom daily, and she was in London with Edward and Ethelred. Of course, with Edward in London, Ethelwold could pursue his advantage unhindered.

From the day Edward left for London until the day he returned, Ecgwin languished. Ethelwold assumed the sighs and downcast countenance were all owing to love of himself. Then Edward returned, and with his return Ecgwin's lagging spirits fled. Ethelwold could not help but notice and he was anxious to be near her, to tell her of his plans for their future. He also noticed that Edward was with her constantly so that he had no chance to do so. He fumed, first inwardly, then outwardly, and finally, one day brought the matter to a head.

It happened as Aethelflaed and Ecgwin were returning to Aethelflaed's apartment. They had barely entered when Ethelwold appeared at the door begging leave to speak to Ecgwin.

Aethelflaed knitted her brows thoughtfully. "I shall see if she wishes to speak to you. You wait here." She turned to go back into the room, but instead of waiting, Ethelwold followed her inside.

Before she could reproach him for entering without her permission, he said, "You would not have me wait outside to speak to my betrothed?" By this time, he had caught sight of Ecgwin, whose expression, when she saw him, changed from polite indifference to dismay.

Aethelflaed whirled around so suddenly that he took a step backward in surprise. "Your what?"

"My betrothed," he said mildly in the face of her surprise. "Surely she has spoken to you of it?" Aethelflaed looked back at Ecgwin, whose face registered the same amazement as her own.

"Surely, she has not," replied Aethelflaed caustically, "since she seems not to be aware of it herself."

"Not aware?" He checked himself midsentence and strode across the room to Ecgwin, taking her hands in his. He did not seem to notice that she pulled back, trying to avoid his advance.

"My dear cousin," snapped Aethelflaed, thinking briefly of Asser, "surely you can see that she is ignorant of your feelings. I think it best that you go, and quickly."

Ethelwold looked at her first with mild annoyance, then with growing anger as he discovered that she was serious. "You would deny me leave to speak with my betrothed?"

"She is not your betrothed, and since she obviously does not wish to speak to you, yes, I certainly deny you leave." She turned to Ecgwin. "Forgive me for being so hasty. Do you wish to speak with Ethelwold?" Ecgwin's eyes were large with growing comprehension of Ethelwold's behavior. She shook her head. "No," she whispered.

"But my dear," said Ethelwold, urgently, retaining his grip on her hands. He was interrupted by a curt voice from the doorway.

"She said 'No'."

Aethelflaed closed her eyes and drew a deep breath, for Edward's tone was icy. She opened her eyes again and saw Ethelwold turning to the doorway, anger flaming on his cheeks. He had turned too quickly to see the relief springing to Ecgwin's eyes.

"It is no affair of yours!"

"But it is. If she does not wish your company, then I cannot allow you to stay." Edward eyed Ethelwold with some distaste, which only served to whet his cousin's anger.

"She is my betrothed." Ethelwold lifted his chin insolently and stared at Edward. To Aethelflaed's great relief Edward did not strike him. He merely stared at Ethelwold for a moment, then threw back his head and roared with laughter. Ethelwold watched him helplessly, his face growing darker by the second.

Edward finally wiped his eyes. "She cannot be betrothed to you, cousin. I have already spoken to the King, who is her legal guardian, with her consent. Have you done likewise?"

"That cannot be." Ethelwold clenched his teeth. "I have not spoken to her but she knows my feelings." Ecgwin shook her head vehemently at Aethelflaed.

Ethelwold was goaded beyond endurance by the sight of his two cousins and his imagined betrothed ranged firmly against him. He could stand it no longer. "You have stolen her affections from me," he exclaimed angrily. "It was me she loved until you returned!"

"No!" Ecgwin's voice cut in on him. He stopped and stared at her, not comprehending. "No," she repeated, moving to Edward's side. "I have never given you a single word of encouragement. I have cared for no one but Edward."

Her words had the effect of arousing him to fever pitch. He saw Edward move closer to Ecgwin's side and fury took him. It was without his own awareness that the hand resting on his sword hilt drew the weapon and pointed it at Edward.

"No," he said hotly, "You shall not touch her. Stand away, for you will fight me."

Edward wordlessly thrust Ecgwin away from him in a quick movement and laid his hand on his own sword hilt, but did not draw it, seeing the forbidding look on his sister's face.

She turned to Ethelwold. "How dare you unsheathe your sword in my chambers? Put up your sword immediately, for you are in violation of the King's Peace in his own household." He stood there, breathing hard, his eyes glazed. "I said, put up your sword," she commanded him. "I will not be ignored!" Ethelwold in a daze complied, but slowly.

Edward relaxed his grip on the hilt of his undrawn sword. "Ethelwold and I will settle this elsewhere." Ethelwold nodded grimly, assenting.

"You will not!" she snapped at both of them. She turned a cold look on Ethelwold. "You have tried my patience beyond endurance. You heard Ecgwin herself say she did not know of your feelings and yet you persisted. You shall not be given a chance to settle your supposed differences, for you have tried to provoke a fight and threatened bloodshed in the King's household." Ethelwold blanched, knowing the penalty, death or slavery, at the King's pleasure. "You have threatened the life of the Atheling," she continued.

He interrupted her. "I am the Atheling!" he said coldly.

She stared at him, beginning to comprehend, and said, "You will remove your sword at once."

"And if I will not?" Edward, hearing this started forward angrily. She waved him back.

"You will or you will present yourself to the King under guard." Ethelwold slowly unbuckled his sword belt and it slid to the floor with a clatter. His face remained flushed and angry, but he said nothing. She escorted him to the King's quarters with only the lad, David, in attendance, after beseeching Edward to remove himself and Ecgwin and not to interfere.

"He is not a common criminal, after all," she said. "He is our cousin." Ethelwold did not respond even then, but she saw him wince at the pity in her voice.

She wondered after it was over, if Ethelwold realized his good fortune in having an uncle of such compassion. Alfred contemplated his nephew's face sadly as Aethelflaed recounted the incident. He turned to Ethelwold. "Is this true?" he demanded. Ethelwold nodded, grimly silent.

"But why did you draw your sword on my son?" the King persisted. "Surely you know I cannot countenance that."

Ethelwold's eyes suddenly blazed. "I am the Atheling," he repeated as before. "My wishes should be given attention over Edward's."

Alfred studied him silently for some moments. "My dearest nephew," he said softly. "I know your feelings better than you think I do. Your father was a great king and a loving brother to me, and for his sake I can even consider your claims, though you know as well as I do that only the Witan can make the decision that binds us all upon my death. It is for them to say, and you and Edward both will abide by their word when the time comes."

"They will uphold my father's succession and they will uphold mine!"

"They have upheld your father's succession in his time, but even they cannot say now if they will uphold yours. That will depend upon the time and necessity. I did not wish to be king, but I had no choice but to abide by the decision of the Witan." Ethelwold scowled, but said nothing.

Alfred's eyes rested meaningfully on his nephew's face. "For now, Edward is accepted as the Atheling, though in the end, it will be decided for him. You must accept it, too. I do not wish you to say again that you are the Atheling, for you may stir up problems that we cannot afford to indulge. The kingdom must be united if it is to survive these invasions. We cannot afford the divisions of power that happened in Ethelwulf's time."

Ethelwold looked intently at the King. "What punishment must I undergo?"

"You are my brother's child," replied Alfred sadly. "I shall not impose the law on you." Ethelwold's sigh was barely audible. "But I will send you away for a while. If the Witan should decide in your favor, then there are many things you must know. If they do not, then the lessons you will learn will uphold you well. You must learn patience and humility. You must learn to curb your temper. Above all, you must learn to listen God's voice directing your life and to accept what He has laid out for you. I can think of no better place for you to learn these lessons than at Athelney, and no man more capable of teaching you than my friend, Abbot John."

Aethelflaed drew in her breath sharply, but otherwise remained silent. Ethelwold was fortunate to be left with his life. Any other king would have seen the danger to his own line and removed it without a qualm, for the provocation was certainly there. Alfred instead chose to honor his dead brother.

She hoped her father was right; that John, harsh as she deemed him, would indeed be the man to break Ethelwold's pride and presumption. Nevertheless, she felt uneasy. She glanced at Ethelwold, whose face was rigid as a mask. He went stiffly to his knees and kissed the King's outstretched hand, mumbling his thanks. There was nothing of compliance in the bent knee, the hanging head, or the downcast eyes. There was nothing of gratitude in the stiff, tight voice with which he thanked the King for sparing his life.

CHAPTER TEN

(888)

Spring of 888 came early. Trees unfurled their tender buds to the warm rains and gentle sun and mantled the hillsides with feathery plumes of palest green, and Aethelflaed felt the strong stirring of life inside her. Ecgwin's fingers trembled slightly as she pressed her hand against Aethelflaed's swollen belly. Aethelflaed smiled happily to herself, for each prod of a tiny elbow, each kick, assured her that her child would be born alive. Ealhswith, still praying for her own stillborn, relaxed and shared her daughter's confinement with a pleasure born of experience, at which Aethelflaed rejoiced silently. The Queen had been silent and withdrawn since Christmas when the family, together with the whole court, bid the youngest daughter of the House of Wessex a fond farewell.

The Queen was sad, though her beautiful child was leaving Wessex with every promise of a good marriage and a happy life. Aelfthryth, at ten years of age, was going to Flanders. When she came of age, she would become the wife of Baldwin the Second, Count of Flanders. Alfred was now a king of some renown, though it was Countess Judith's fondness for her old friend that prompted her to seek his daughter's hand for her son. Alfred, in the past two years since the siege of London and the consequent taming of Guthrum, had gained respect in Frankia and Flanders. They, too, had contended with the host, and admired the King of Wessex. The child was a great prize, and Alfred's daughter would be given great honor over-seas. So Aelfthryth must leave, to learn the ways of her husband's people before she took her place in his bed.

Judith was delighted. It was her link to her first husband, Ethelwulf, whom she adored as a child, and a gesture of respect to his son, whom she admired. Her grandchildren would be great, with the blood of her beloved Baldwin Iron-Arm and the strength of Alfred of Wessex mingled in their veins, they would surely be invincible.

She wrote Aelfthryth warm letters, full of affection, describing the splendors of the court of Flanders, the beautiful clothes she would have. She sent Aelfthryth a cloth-of-gold dress embroidered with jewels for her wedding, accompanied by rolls of fine woven stuffs from the fabled looms of Flanders. For the Queen there was a box of the finest silk threads of all colors for her embroidery. Aelfthryth forgot her early distress at the prospect of leaving and dried her eyes as Judith's letters and gifts poured into Wessex. The child's eyes sparkled with anticipation, eager for a court filled with gaiety and luxury. The Queen was mournful as Aelfthryth read her letters to them.

Aethelflaed for once was annoyed with the Queen. "Look! She is happy and eager to go. Would you send Baldwin a sorrowful, languishing child? Or one filled with happy spirits and laughter, the better to capture his heart? A long face will encourage him to seek comfort elsewhere."

So the Queen put a good face on the matter and Aelfthryth wept only a little at parting with her family. Wise Judith had sent her a gift to distract her mind from the leave-taking, presented with great deference by the escort sent to fetch the diminutive bride. The Countess wished no one to underestimate the high estate which her daughter-in-law was to be accorded. A generous and forgiving heart had Judith, forgiving, considering the way the English had treated her when she was the aged Ethelwulf's child bride. Aelfthryth, if Baldwin had inherited any of his mother's disposition, might one day count herself most unusually blessed.

Ealhswith, however, had retreated, brooding silently until Aethelflaed's child one day awoke in her womb and announced its presence with a lively kick. Aethelflaed jumped up, startled, her hand against her belly. Ealhswith looked up from her embroidery, recognition dawning on her careworn face, and for the first time since Aelfthryth left, smiled.

As the new life waited eagerly to be born, two more hung in the balance. Athelred, the doughty, aging Archbishop of Canterbury, took to his bed and despite the vigil of prayers by his monks, weakened daily. Convinced that his work was finished, the Primate wrote his king and dearest friend a last letter, begging him to consider carefully the appointment of his successor. The English church, he affirmed, was fallen upon desperate circumstances. The monastic system was a shambles in the face of constant invasion. Some progress in converting the Danes in Kent had been made, but heathen practices still abounded in Kent as elsewhere. He had heard of Grimbald, the holy monk from Saint-Omer, sent by archbishop Fulk to Alfred, and with all respect for the King's own choice, begged that Grimbald be consecrated in anticipation of his, Athelred's, death. The King, with a heavy heart, advised Grimbald of the Archbishop's request, and though he knew Grimbald had a great distaste for high office, begged his prayerful consideration.

Another life, too, was fading. The once-dreaded Guthrum was sick, ill with his final defeat, long years of battle, and the indignity of senility. While the Archbishop's death would be a great loss, keenly felt, Guthrum's death posed a certain threat to the peace of Mercia and the security of London. In spite of this, Alfred was openly saddened by the impending death of his Danish godson, but the danger of renewed hostilities prompted him to summon his family and Werferth to council.

"Worcester," he said grimly, "must be fortified quickly. Haesten prowls the Frankish kingdom, waiting only for news of Guthrum's death. Guthrum is toothless these past two years but Haesten...." His voice trailed off as he looked around his council table and saw his own concern reflected in the intent faces. Haesten was anything but toothless. There was no need to remind anyone of Haesten's vigor and ambition or his quickness to take advantage of every situation. Alfred's family knew the Frankish woes as well as he did. Charles the Fat, King of the Franks, had died earlier in the year, and Arnulf, his nephew, wrested the throne from him as he lay dying of his excesses. Foolishly, Arnulf consented to divide the kingdom into five parts and consecrated himself and four others as kings, with himself as overlord, since he alone, so he claimed, had paternal rights. The five kings fought each other incessantly, ravaging each others' territory.

Alfred shook his head in disbelief; Rudof, Odo, Berengar, Guido, and Overlord Arnulf, all fools, overestimating their strength, and all consumed with unquenchable greed. Haesten, clever as a marauding wolf, saw his chance clearly and rode upcountry and over the bridge at Paris virtually unopposed. Haesten would never waste his energies on a united, well-prepared foe. There were lessons of great significance to be learned from his example, the King said, studying his council and family with his intense, blue-eyed stare, as if he could transmit to them the working of his mind by a moment's impaling with his gaze.

Ethelred stared back thoughtfully. "His kinsmen in Northumbria and East Anglia are restless. There is much talk of recapturing London." The open border between East Anglia and Mercian London worked well for both sides and Ethelred was reluctant to close it any sooner than necessary. Even Northumbrian Danes entered the city, as Guthrum's subjects, ostensibly for the purpose of trading, but once there, eyed the wealth piled up quayside enviously. They could also see the strength of London's fortifications, which Ethelred knew would present a deterrent to their lusty ambitions. Like Haesten, they were unwilling to attack what they knew to be well defended, since they could not afford great losses.

Furthermore, their loquacious habits in the mead halls supplied Ethelred with a constant flow of information from the north and east. Once well-drunk with the potent brew of fermented honey, their tales of Danish daring and cunning flowed as freely as the mead that was poured into them by Ethelred's hand-picked men. Encouraged by applause, of which they never wearied, they would turn to future exploits when the past was exhausted. Thus it came to Ethelred and the King that Haesten was itching to be back.

"Werferth's duties here," the King went on, "must be put aside for now."

"I shall leave at once for Worcester."

The deep voice belonged to the man with the craggy, bearded face, who was sitting next to Ethelred. He stood up as he spoke, as if he meant to leave upon the moment, and looked down at them with his deep-set eyes. The strong face and his great height and bearing gave him the aspect of a soldier. Aethelflaed had become accustomed to Asser's gentleness and Heahstan's open friendliness and thought it typical of men of God. But there was nothing gentle in this man's restless intensity. It surprised no one who knew him to find that he was an accomplished scholar; it did not take one long to discover that Werferth possessed a many-faceted depth of personality.

His appearance of strength was also the reality for there was nothing deceptive about the man, and Aethelflaed would discover and rediscover both his strength and depth many times in their long and close friendship. In more than physical stature did Werferth tower over others, and perhaps his only equal in breadth and depth of learning was the King himself. He showed his respect for his Lord King with great humility, and it was also evident that Alfred returned Werferth's homage with equal deference.

The King rose also. He was tired and there was little else to detain them from bed. "Ethelred will accompany you to direct the fortifications."

Aethelflaed looked up quickly. "I am strong enough to go with you."

Ethelred dissented. "Your time is near. You must stay here at least until you are safely delivered. Edward will go with me until then. Ethelhelm has returned from Rome and will stay in London until you are able to return there."

In spite of her disappointment, she silently acknowledged the wisdom of his decision. She would eventually get to Worcester, for the stay in London would be brief. Her body was heavy now and the trip into hilly midlands of Gloucester and Worcester would be hard, though she was not afraid of birthing. It should come easily to one of her strength. So it was with mixed feelings that she bid her husband and brother goodbye. She must learn patience.

Ecgwin, deprived of Edward's company, hovered solicitously close to her, charged by her beloved with the care of his sister. In spite of Aethelflaed's private doubts about her usefulness in the lying-in chamber, she found Ecgwin to have a calm, reassuring strength, for Ecgwin was a born nurse.

When Aethelflaed unwillingly took to her couch for what turned out to be a long period of hard labor, Ecgwin remained with her, offering her dainty hand to Aethelflaed's hot grip as the pangs of childbirth bore in upon her. Between the waves of labor, Ecgwin brought steaming bowls of chamomile, to comfort her Lady, and wreaths of pennyroyal and borage, the one to ease her pain and the other to give her courage to bear those that remained. When at last Elfwyn squirmed her way in the world and into the Queen's waiting arms, it was Ecgwin who sent the midwives away and herself fed Aethelflaed a hot broth of mutton and barley laced with aromatic herbs and strong, Rhenish red wine.

When Ethelred returned a few weeks later to gaze on Elfwyn's pink face, he was rapt in admiration of the tiny being who clung tightly to his finger and stared curiously into his face. He delighted in his first-born. Aethelflaed watched both of them with great satisfaction. No more spoiled child existed. The King's pleasure in his first grandchild brightened his voice and made his footstep lighter and more lively. Ecgwin attended the child as if it had been her own, and when Aethelflaed departed in midsummer with Bishop Denewulf for Shaftesbury for the consecration of the Abbey, Elfwyn was already thriving, well past the dangers that afflicted the newborn. Aethelflaed prayed that her daughter would survive the ills of babyhood without her, for though she stopped at Winchester on her return from Shaftesbury, she would quickly depart for London, and the child would be left in Ecgwin's and the Queen's care.

Edward returned from Worcester and Aethelflaed privately prevailed upon the King to make a formal declaration of his betrothal. She did not divulge the reason for her feeling of urgency, and her father accepted her vague explanation that it was best for Edward. Who knew Edward so well as his sister? He would not, of course, connect it with the fact that Ethelhelm and Elfled would shortly be on their way to Winchester from London. The betrothal would put fatherless Ecgwin firmly under the King's protection and Aethelflaed could go to London with an easy heart. She had grown to love Ecgwin as a sister during her confinement, and maternity had made her fiercely protective, not only for her baby daughter but for Edward's guileless betrothed as well.

She was eager to take up her duties again in London, however briefly, before rejoining Ethelred in Worcester and was thankful for the strong constitution that permitted her to recover quickly from the strenuous birth. Inactivity made her restless, and though she had whiled away the months of her confinement with study, Elfwyn's birth came as a blessed relief from the constraints of pregnancy. She longed to see London's busy streets again, to hear the Mass chanted by Heahstan at St. Paul's. Above all, she longed for Ethelred. Despite the intermittent separations of their short marriage, they had become close, united in their affection for each other and now in their delight in their child.

She held her daughter closely, delighting in the warmth and strength of the baby's sturdy little body, before relinquishing her to Ecgwin.

"See to them both," she whispered quietly to the Queen. "Elfled returns with an ambitious heart." No word had passed between them about Ethelhelm's daughter, but Ealhswith was too wise to remain in ignorance of anything that occurred in the family or the palace.

"Indeed," she promised, "Ecgwin shall be as my own daughter in your absence." She kissed Aethelflaed fondly, then drew back a little sadly. "Godspeed and strength, dearest *bearn*." She turned away abruptly, though Aethelflaed saw the veiled premonition in her eyes. Her own heart was light at thoughts of London and her husband and to the upcoming journey to Worcester.

One matter intruded upon her rising spirits. Ethelwold had returned from his sojourn at Athelney. If he was any the better for it, none could tell. Not that he was still sullen and moody. Outwardly he was polite and greeted Edward and herself with aloof respect. To the King he was a loyal and devoted subject, and Alfred responded joyously, relieved that the period of solitude at Athelney had apparently healed his nephew's wounded pride.

It had delighted the King that John had highly praised Ethelwold's behavior, and as his appointed confessor and mentor, had steered his prayers and meditations into the proper paths. They had become great friends, these two unlikely persons, the Abbot of Athelney and the King's nephew. That was, to Aethelflaed's way of thinking, no recommendation for the nephew. She still distrusted him.

Edward, openly betrothed, had forgiven all. He happily clapped his cousin on the shoulder, welcoming him as a brother. Aethelflaed saw a warning flash in Ethelwold's eyes as the acknowledged Atheling embraced him. It was quickly extinguished and the expression that greeted Edward's outpourings of good will, was one of bland remoteness and discreet withdrawal.

It was no matter though, for no further traces of outward bitterness marred Ethelwold's punctilious deference to the King and his Atheling. But the momentary flash surprised by Aethelflaed in her cousin's eyes signaled that the fires of envy, far from being out, were merely banked, awaiting some future opportunity. He had acquired at Athelney a finely polished veneer of false humility, arrogant modesty, and an icy reserve.

Aethelflaed was ready for her return to London. She could hear the horses, waiting outside the Great Hall, stamping impatiently on the dirt underfoot, snorting and anxious to be off. Edward locked his hands together for her foot when she was ready to mount, and when she was settled, she kissed her fingertips lightly to him in salute. Only Ealhswith, now brooding again in the shadow, had any inkling of the terrible year that awaited her before she would again return to Winchester.

CHAPTER ELEVEN

(889)

*A*ethelflaed picked up the parchment and studied the words wearily: *To Almighty God of the True Covenant and the Holy Trinity in Heaven be praise and glory and deeds of thanksgiving for all the good things that He has given us. For the love of whom in the first place, Ethelred Ealdorman and Aethelflaed, and for St. Peter and the Church at Worcester, and also at the prayer of Werferth, their friend, commanded the fortification at Worcester to be built to protect all the people, and also God's praises therein to exalt.*

Nothing in those words, so carefully devised by Ethelred and herself, would ever convey how much of themselves they had invested in this bitter year in Worcester. Grindingly hard, even for one of her constitution, it had been. It rained in the spring of 889; it rained until she thought she would scream. The mighty Severn, under the steady downpour, washed over its banks again and again, flooding the east bank where the city lay rooted in its ancient origins. No hint at all of the price she paid for the fortification showed in the formal wording of the Charter.

The city was barely three-quarters of a mile from north to south, and scarcely half a mile wide, if one included the flood bank of the river. Her first sight of Worcester had filled her with gloom and dismay. The Church of St. Peter's in the center of the town and the Bishop's small stone palace, hard by to the south, stood on high ground, a little above the flood waters that surged and receded every spring. North of St. Peter's was St. Helen's, of sturdy timber and stone. Both churches had been here for at least two centuries. The Romans walls were long since gone, for the city's folk quarried them for the stone with which to build their houses. It was far simpler to use the neat, well-shaped blocks than to carve the stone from the hillsides and drag it back. Traces of the wall remained underground though, the top was covered with a thin layer of sod. This would form a support for the palisade, which they would raise against it from the inside.

Most of the city in the area inside the remaining walls was open. Whatever streets had been laid out by the Romans were gone. Wide dirt tracks wandered aimlessly about the town, though it soon became apparent that there were several well-traveled tracks. Most of the them led eventually to the Cathedral and its small attached abbey, as did the road leading in from the East Gate. That road was intersected by another running some-what north and south, connecting the gates that lay at either extremity. Without fortification the town was open to easy invasion on all sides. Aethelflaed saw that their work was cut out for them.

And there was, strangely, considering all the merchant-thanes in the burh, no market place. Trading was carried on in the streets or from door to door. Worcester was vastly different from other burhs of its size in one significant respect: most of it was owned by the Bishop and when revenues could be collected they were remitted to the Bishop or Overlord for the town's defenses.

The burh's key position on the Severn made its fortification impera-tive; moreover, something else made it doubly attractive, and that was the salt furnaces at Droitwich, not far to the northeast. Wagonloads of precious salt came into the city daily to be traded or sold. It was a necessity without which no one could survive, for the salt preserved their meat and fish for winter food and was necessary for the survival of the animals. Droitwich, with its briny springs, was the largest inland salt pan in the country.

The salt furnaces of Droitwich put her in mind of another matter; the salt trade was always taxed, and if a way to avoid paying the salt tax could be found, the townsmen would certainly find it. There was little taxable land in the burh, and no market place where taxes could be collected.

Even so, the fortification had to be paid for. She, Ethelred, and Wer-ferth set about correcting the situation. Plans were laid out for a market-place at the northwest corner of the burh, inside the wall and fronting on the river. This would make the market accessible by water as well as by land. The market-plot would eventually be given to Ethelred and herself, for these parcels of land, called *haga*, were a common feature of town life. The *haga*, until they took part of it for a residence, would be rented out to merchants. A wagon toll on salt from Droitwich, would as always, be required, and the market place meant that there would also be a tax on live-stock, wool, and dairy products sold there. There would be much grum-bling, but fortification was a costly matter and the burh's inhabitants, as well as the farmers and small landholders and their households who crowded into the burh for protection against the host, knew they must pay for it.

The merchants and thanes would pay in silver, the farmers in live-stock and produce, which would feed the Mercian army there to protect the burh. Silver was scarce. Even Werferth's treasury had little hard coin. In 873, when he had succeeded to the See, he had been forced to sell some of his lands, as he wrote, *to raise money for immense tribute each year to the barbarians seated in London.* Despite all the great lands he yet had left, the

See was drained of coin by the Danes. But they still had Droitwich, far more valuable than hard coin.

Aethelflaed and Ethelred lived in private quarters in the Bishop's palace with their own retainers, and though it was small, it was passably comfortable. In the early, chill spring, the Severn constantly swelled, the air perpetually swirled with mist, and the stone walls of the palace ceaselessly sweated and dripped. The brightly colored wool tapestries hung over the mildew-streaked walls did their unsuccessful best to lighten the gloomy atmosphere.

The fortifying of the burh began with a ditch, dug around the entire length of the old Roman wall. As soon as the ditch had been dug, the rain washed the silt back into the trench, and the next day, they would start again to dig it out. A few mud-and-wattle huts scattered along the banks, much too close to the river, were weakened with each new downpour and soon washed into the swirling muddy waters of the implacable Severn.

Werferth, his cheer and energy undiminished, set the homeless to rebuilding their huts to the east of the church. "Come summer," he explained, "they will again build their huts too close to the river. They never learn."

Aethelflaed shivered involuntarily, longing for the sunshine of Wessex. Werferth laid his heavy woolen cloak around her shoulders. "The rains will give way before long," he prophesied. "I have lived here many years, and every year it is the same."

He was right. One day, the clouds at last parted, the sun appeared, and the Severn docilely returned to its channel. The ground drained, and Ethelred's men began again to dig the protective trench around the city. The palisade rose slowly as woodsmen and soldiers, guiding their oxen carefully through the gates, dragged heavy timbers cut from the surrounding hillsides. The logs were hewn to shape and sharpened, then set on end, pointing upward, in the trench. A double stockade now enclosed the burh, with inner platforms covering the gateways to guard the approaches into the town.

Worcester, though still damp and misty, warmed to the sun, and spring finally proceeded. The bare, rugged shoulders of the Malvern Hills rose steeply to the west like gloomy sentinels, watching the Welsh mountains from afar. At their feet nestled lush forests and meadowlands burgeoning greenly from the wet spring.

Aethelflaed was with child again. This time there was no lazy stretch of confinement for her. Instead she was busy helping Ethelred plan the fortifications. She inspected the progress of the walls daily as they rose behind the sloping, muddy trenches. When the palisade was completed and the inner trench into which it was set filled in, a platform ringing the inside of the wall was built, where sentries could patrol and watch the hills to east and west alike. Another trench would be dug outside the stockade, stretching only from gate to gate, as an added deterrent to entry. The openings were boxed over to limit the number entering at any time, giving the soldiers on the platform the advantage of either survey or attack.

She poured her energy into securing the position of the burh, not sparing herself or others in the process. If Ethelred noticed how hard she drove herself, he had little time to say so, for the maintenance and training of the *fyrd* kept him well occupied. She privately worried that she had overspent her vitality, for this babe did not seem at all lively, like Elfwyn.

She pushed her concern aside, because too many lives depended on the safety of the brooding river fortress. Besides, this country grew on the spirit and she found herself contemplating its possible loss with pain. She arose early in the mornings while the town was still quiet and walked the inner platform, planning the day's work as she surveyed from her vantage point the terrain in which the burh was set. The land sloped away from the town to the horizon on all sides, where it again turned upward at the edges. Unlike Hampshire, with its gently rolling hills, Worcester presented to her gaze a view of wild and rugged beauty, a countryside of unpredictable moods.

Summer increased, and when the lush hillsides ripened into fall, the work was nearly complete. She and Ethelred drew up the Charter granting to God, St Peter's, and the Lord of the Church half of the rights belonging to their Lordship, those rights in the market and the street to help the community, except that the wagon shilling and the load-penny, the salt tax at Droitwich went to the King. But *otherwise both rent and fines for fighting and fines for theft and fines for every crookedness which allows of compensation, will belong half to the Church of the Lord for the sake of God and St Peter, as it was settled for the market place and the streets, and without the marketplace, the bishop be entitled to the value of his lands and his rights.*

For these gifts, the bishop, his village, and his community of monks would appoint daily Offices to be said in perpetuity, and at every Matins and Evensong, at Tierce, the third hour, during Ethelred's and Aethelflaed's life, the Psalm, *De Profundis*, would be sung:

Out of the deep have I called unto thee, O Lord: Lord hear my voice.
O let thine ears consider well: the voice of my complaint.

For the heavy burden of duty she took upon herself at Worcester, she paid dearly. When she left late in the fall, carrying the Charter to her father, winter breathing its chill warning at her back, she left behind her a tiny casket that held the fragile remains of her son. Labor came upon her untimely, and when she looked upon the tiny body, she grieved. The bluish pallor of his skin bespoke his fragility, his untimeliness. His little being could not yet withstand the harsh vicissitudes of life.

Werferth chanted Mass over the little casket, and himself consigned it to the high burial ground of St Peter's yard among the remains of the noble Mercian ancestors. *Trust in the Lord,* the monks choir chanted, *For with the Lord there is mercy: and with Him is plenteous redemption.* This wild, terrible place claimed her infant son before he had even a chance to live.

Sorrow darkened her spirit as illness descended on her exhausted body. Ealhswith's pain-filled eyes haunted her fevered dreams. She saw again and again in her delirium the sad look bestowed on her at their parting the year before and understood finally that the Queen's foreboding had been for her, some knowledge that her eldest would share her own grief most intimately. Ethelred comforted her as she struggled with grief and sickness, and when the fever at last broke and her delirium quietened, she remembered only that each time she regained consciousness, the firm pressure of his hand was on hers, and his voice called her urgently back to the world. He coaxed her out of the dark recesses of her spirit, where she might have been content to yield to the firm grip of nature upon her body. "The will of God," he whispered close to her ear, "lies ahead of you. There is yet much to be done." His words found her where she lay hidden deep inside her aching spirit and sickened body, and followed her insistently, entreating her return. Finally, listening, she acceded to his demands and fought the silent spectre that beckoned in her fevered dreams.

By late fall she was well enough to travel to Winchester, at Ethelred's insistence. She knew he watched her anxiously as she made her daily pilgrimage to the churchyard, where she stood, lost in grief, over the grave of her son. He might have prevented her visits had not Werferth intervened.

"My Lord," said Werferth, "you must give her time." His voice was quiet and reassuring, as one who dealt constantly with death. "Each soul works out acceptance in its own way. You cannot hurry the matter."

"She broods." Ethelred's tone was edged with compassionate desperation.

"It is to be expected," was all the Bishop would say.

She continued her visits, sometimes alone, sometimes with Ethelred beside her. He too, mourned, of that there could be no doubt, but his discipline and responsibility to his thanes held him firmly. She knew that he allowed her to indulge her grief where he did not indulge his own. She longed to explain to him her feelings, but checked the impulse. How could she explain her confusion? The dead child was now safe from the certain hardships of life, and most probably a violent death, too, but he would never experience the warmth, the joys, and the laughter that could make the harshness of life worth the price of one's birth. She had longed to give Ethelred a son to fight by his side. That was beyond hoping for. She had, miraculously enough, survived the deadly childbirth fevers, but those, who like her, came back from death that way, never bore again.

"She will make her peace," Werferth assured Ethelred. "But it is between her and God. I do not understand women, My Lord, and I expect you do not either. I have buried many a child, and it is always the same with their mothers."

She was quietly grateful to Werferth, who never approached her with either kind words or advice. His silent compassion lightened her despair. As her mood slowly lifted, she saw the burden that absorption in her own grief had placed on Ethelred. It was not until after Edward's wedding, that she could bring herself to speak of it to him. Then when she had at last unburdened herself and spoke painfully and haltingly of her grief, he expressed only his relief.

"You are alive," he said simply, holding her close. "I prayed only that I would not lose you." His eyes spoke a need that she knew he could not put into words. Pangs of guilt assailed her again at her own thoughtlessness. Indeed, Werferth had reminded her gently, when she showed herself ready to listen, that her loss was Heaven's gain and her sorrow must be put aside.

She smiled at her husband for the first time since the child's death, touched by the strength of his love, silently promising to attend to his needs more closely. The grief receded, and though it would never be forgotten, they found the experience had deepened their dependence on each other and their joy in each other. She loved the wild country of Worcester now with an anguish too sharp for words. Part of them had died at Worcester; but something greater had been born. They returned to Winchester and lavished on their sturdy Elfwyn all their frustrated care and solicitude.

They returned in time for Edward's wedding, and when she saw her brother's glowing face as he embraced his bride, her sadness evaporated. She rejoiced to see him, to whom she and Ethelred had grown so close, so happy. He was as tall as Ethelred now, a large, rawboned young man, sinewy and straightforward in looks and in manner, and possessed of a driving, uncomplicated intelligence.

When Denewulf ended his lengthy blessing, the couple was escorted to the Great Hall for the feast. They paused at the doorway, and there was a moment of silence. Edward was tall and splendid in his brightly embroidered robes, his hand on the jeweled hilt of his sword, his face wreathed in smiles; but the awed silence was for his dainty bride in her deep-blue, gold-embroidered gown, the train of her mantle billowing out behind her. The King's gift of a necklace of gold cloisonné inlaid with sparkling garnets glittered around her throat, but nothing outshone the radiance of her face.

A roar of approval broke from the throats of the assembled company, and they jumped to their feet waving their drinking horns over their heads, crying *Hael*! to the Atheling and his bride. The feasting would last for days. After several hours of eating and toasting, Ecgwin looked tired. Aethelflaed caught her husband's eye and raised her eyebrows faintly. He nodded and moved to Edward's side, raising his drinking horn in still another toast. In the ensuing shouts and clamor, Aethelflaed drew the bride unobtrusively from the Great Hall. No one saw them leave, except Elfled at the far end of the Hall, her face a study in bitterness and despair. Aethelflaed's eyes rested on her face momentarily. What anger she saw there was directed against herself, not Ecgwin.

Nor did the situation change in the weeks following the wedding, despite her efforts to ease Elfled's wounded pride by requesting her presence as often as she could. It was taken as a mark of favor by everyone except Elfled. During the time that Elfled somewhat grudgingly attended her and spoke with her, she discovered that what she had earlier suspected was indeed true. Ambitious and proud she might be, but her feelings for Edward were genuine. However much she might covet the honor and position given the Atheling's wife, as she most certainly did, she loved the Atheling himself more.

"You could have prevented the marriage," Elfled burst out bitterly one evening as she waited upon Aethelflaed. She did not seem to understand that far from preventing the marriage, Aethelflaed was more inclined to encourage it. She could not tell Elfled that she had grown to love the girl who had nursed her through her first birth and had been a loving stepmother to her daughter in her absence. Ecgwin was as a sister to her and now by marriage, had become her sister.

Instead, she told Elfled, "Never fear, my dear, you will marry well when your time comes." She was prophetically right about that, though she had no way of knowing it as she spoke, not even by the smallest flutter of premonition. As it was, she followed Werferth's advice to herself and left Elfled to work it out alone. She could not be hostile forever and certainly a good match could be found for the daughter of so esteemed a retainer. She gave it no more thought, for urgent matters shortly presented themselves.

Chief among these was a letter from Asser at Sherborne: the letter was stern and uncompromising. She read with disbelief the Welshman's words that the deed he wrote of merited the utmost of contempt and punishment. In the dead of night, the ill-fated community of Athelney had risen against its despotic Abbot. It had been difficult to find monks willing to join so isolated a monastery. The tiny building was damp and miserable, surrounded by forests and cut off by floods. Novices naturally preferred the monasteries of Cathedral towns, for in spite of their vows of poverty, the larger abbeys were enriched by many gifts of wealthy, productive lands and tax exemptions by the King. To get the community on its feet, young Franks, mere children, and even captive heathen Danes were brought to Athelney to be trained in the rigorous conditions of life in the swampland.

She looked again at her father's grief-stricken face. Why could not the King understand that his devotion was not shared by others? The venture was doomed from the start.

She picked up the letter and read on: "He was ever a quick man, easily stung to action; indeed it has come to my ears that he was knowledgeable in fighting. He would have made a good soldier had he not been set on a higher profession." The community, enraged at John's harsh rule, bargained with two Franks of the monastery, a priest and a deacon, to kill the Abbot. The Abbot heard them creep into the chapel where he was engaged in his private devotions. He rose from his prayers, shouting that they were sent from Satan and rushed them boldly. But his attackers were armed with stolen swords and John was defenseless. His soldier's skills served him well, otherwise his attackers would certainly have accomplished their purpose. The commotion roused the entire community and the Abbot was found bleeding, half-dead on the floor. The Franks escaped into the forest.

"It is unpardonable!" Alfred burst out, "To turn against a man of God." Part of his vehemence came from his distress at the failure of Athelney, his own gift of thanksgiving, to become a self-sustaining house. He could not understand why Athelney, so great a refuge for himself, could not become so for others. Now it was desecrated by the attempted murder of its Abbot. A more terrible blasphemy neither he nor Asser could imagine. She thought that it was inevitable and even as she longed to tell the King just that, she knew it was not possible for him to listen. She had once, long ago, been chastised for criticizing John. She had seen the man's innate cruelty when he first came to Wessex, a cruelty only thinly masked by his monastic vows. She was certain that he had harshly enforced a discipline of a more rigorous nature than was called for by the Rule. He would have, she observed silently, been better off as a soldier. He would have been a bitter, implacable enemy to any who opposed him on the battlefield. Such as he went into religious professions only for power and, once in possession of it, wielded it with a vengeance.

"It is a heinous crime," she agreed, keeping her thoughts to herself, "and the guilty must be punished."

"I must leave that to Asser," Alfred responded grimly. "I have set him over the See of Sherborne, and the Church must discipline its own."

John recovered, as Asser later reported, but did not stay to take revenge on the community. As soon as his wounds were healed, he disappeared, apparently unwilling to risk his life further in what he condemned as a barbarous land. It was rumored that he returned to his homeland, a fact Aethelflaed secretly doubted. John was too proud and unyielding to return home in failure to Archbishop Fulk. No, she decided, that was not it. John was a born plotter and of such a nature that vengeance would come as naturally as breathing to him. He would turn up again; of that she was certain.

The murderous Franks were never found, and if the monks of Athelney knew of their whereabouts, they maintained an unbroken conspiracy of silence. Nor did anyone hear of John. All that came to Aethelflaed's ears was that her cousin, Ethelwold, had possibly helped John to escape, though he denied it, saying he had no knowledge of John's whereabouts. Something in his eyes, too blank, too innocent, belied him and though nothing came of it, Aethelflaed could not rid herself of suspicion.

Alfred, who craved solitude, even that of a dismal swamp, was in a state of despair and bafflement. It was a noble effort that had failed dismally and the King took it as a personal judgment upon himself. Her father, she reflected later, when Werferth had skillfully drawn him out of his despondency, was a realist in battle, but incurably hopeful about human nature. His respect for the Church, and for the sorely needed order which it could, when judiciously administered, impart to a land steeped in violence, blinded him to the inordinate cravings for power that motivated too many of God's elect. So desperately did he wish for peace and so intensely did he long to cultivate in his people the love of learning he himself possessed that it did not occur to him that the aims of the clerics were not always one with his own.

It was a relief to everyone when the King put aside his gloom and buried himself in his books and writing. She renewed her study of Ine's Code and begged the King's help, urging him to complete his own Code. Ine's Code was useful, but it was too old, and English life, beleaguered from enemies within its own territories, needed the new laws to strengthen its defense.

When she set out for London, for home, late in 890, she carried the precious papers, the new Code, with her. The King himself lifted Elfwyn, still his only grandchild, to the front of her mother's saddle. The child's eyes were sparkling with excitement, and for a moment, Aethelflaed regretted that her daughter would not grow up in Wessex as she had. But Elfwyn was a born Mercian and must grow up in Mercia.

Aethelflaed now thought of herself as a Mercian and less as a West Saxon. With time, she reflected, one's childhood memories recede from view and are recollected later as events that happened long ago, almost as if to someone else. It must be, for it would not have occurred to her before this to think so critically of the King. When first the thought of her father's lack of judgment in placing John over Athelney overtook her, she was shocked with herself. But the thought persisted, and she finally accepted that a great king could also be a human being and subject to error in private. Childish thoughts of unquestioned wisdom of others must be put aside sooner or later. After the first twinge of regret at seeing the King as merely a man, she welcomed the freedom that greater awareness brought. Happiness and tragedy mellowed a person, the way the ebb and flow of seasons weathered a timber, testing its strength and integrity, making it sound and capable of bearing its burdens faithfully.

If she was reluctant to leave the past behind her, she was, nevertheless, eager to explore the future. She embraced the King fondly, grateful for her childhood. One day her own daughter, now gazing worshipfully up at her, would realize that her mother and father were, after all, human, and far from perfect. Hopefully, Elfwyn would judge them gently when the time came.

PART TWO

THE MIDDLE YEARS:
THE LATER WARS AGAINST THE DANES

Historical Notes

*I*n the year 892 after Easter a comet was sighted. The English often called it a "long-haired star" because of the way the light trailed out behind it. Even more commonly, it was called a "firedrake" and omens and portents were attached to its appearance.

In 899, shortly before All Hallows Day, Alfred, son of Ethelwulf, now King over most of England, died. He had ruled his kingdom for nearly 29 years. Edward his son was elected King by the Witan. Ethelwold seized lands at Wimborne and Christchurch illegally.

PART TWO
THE LATER WAR AGAINST
THE DANES
892 - 896

0   40
MILES

• YORK

NORTHUMBRIA

CHESTER
(893 - FALL)

(893)
BUTTINGTON
R. SEVERN

BRIDGNORTH
(895-896)

LEAVE FOR
EAST ANGLIA & GAUL
(896)

R. OUSE

WORCESTER

BRYCHEINIOG
(894-WINTER)
GWYNLLWG

ESSEX

(894)

OXFORD

THORNEY
ISLE
(893)

LONDON

BENFLEET

MERSEY ISLE
(893-894)
SHOEBURY
(893)
SHEPPEY

THAMES

(893)

BRISTOL
CHANNEL

FARNHAM
(893)

ROCHESTER
ALFRED'S ⊗ POSITION

MILTON
POSITION

WINCHESTER

R. LYMPNE
APPLEDORE
(892)

EXETER

POOLE
BAY

WIGHT

The Middle Years; The Later Wars Against the Danes

CHAPTER TWELVE

(891)

$\mathcal{W}$erferth had been granted an ancient stone palace in London near the waterfront where the Walbrook emptied lazily into the Thames. If the stalwart Mercian minded the stench of garbage and offal that was thrown into the meandering stream as it coursed through London, he made no complaint. It was, in spite of this, a good location. For one thing it was not far from the Billings Gate, where Frisian merchants docked daily looking for English wool to feed the looms of Flanders.

Worcester produced a quality wool, sturdy enough to weave and wear well, fine enough to be spun into delicate thread for embroidery. At Billings Gate market, the Bishop of Worcester tended to the economic health of his See with the shrewdness of a born trader, and for this purpose he needed the London residence. Through the London market, bales of Worcester wool flowed into Flanders and Frankia to return in the form of hard gold coin. In gratitude for his enterprise and guidance; worldly, scholarly, and spiritually, Alfred remitted to him the taxes itemized in the Charter. Werferth, in his turn, poured the taxes and monies from the wool trade into the fortification of his burh, repairing bridges of his See, and maintaining the *fyrd* required by the King.

"Lady!" Werferth rose from his writing table as she entered and extended both hands to her warmly. David, who had accompanied her, silently removed her cloak and himself knelt for the Bishop's blessing. Werferth laid his hands on David's head, murmuring the Latin benediction. Aethelflaed smiled at David when he rose.

"My Lord Bishop's kitchen is warm and well provisioned. You must avail yourself of the comforts and companionship you will find there."

"I am ashamed that a mere Bishop's kitchen should surpass that of the Ealdorman's household. I will gladly share it with you, with your leave." Werferth's tone was rueful.

"You do not appear to have taken advantage of the benefits of your kitchen," she replied, noting the more than usual leanness of his spare frame. "Besides," she relaxed and accepted the silver cup Werferth held out to her, "it would be useless to urge Ethelred to adopt the ways of my father's court. He would not be happy growing lazy on the riches of London."

"He is wise. London is full of retainers eager to flatter and fatten off his service."

"That, dear friend, is why the palace remains a fortress." Aethelflaed stared absently at the silver goblet of obvious Flemish origin. Werferth had carried touches of the court life at Winchester with him, mostly for his guests and those in his personal service. Werferth believed, as did Alfred, that those in power must display their wealth. It was undoubtedly necessary as a means of demonstrating authority and commanding respect. A king would command loyalty only if his thanes believed that he was more wealthy and powerful then they, or if they believed him more skillful and cunning than themselves. It was fortunate that there were always those whose loyalty was not to be bought for any treasure. Nevertheless from the king's hand flowed rewards for service. A king who was poor and weak could attract no followers.

While neither Alfred nor Werferth were cynical men, as experience might have made them, neither did they delude themselves about the short-sightedness of the retainers at court. Their lack of imagination, even their worldliness mattered not a whit, for Alfred had visions of a future they would have dismissed as impossible. They knew only what was good for them. Thus secured, they followed: they approved his show of riches and his skill in battle. Alfred, seeing their shallowness, kept his own counsel and led his followers silently toward the future that he could see and they could not.

Had she wished to set forth a similar display in their fortress life in London, Ethelred would have consented. It would hardly have touched him though, for he kept his own discipline. There was good reason to keep display to a minimum. London might well look to Ethelred as if he were their king, it mattered not to him. His loyalties lay elsewhere and no one of his house would claim the rule while he was alive. It would not do to set one's self higher than the King who took him in.

She set the cup down abruptly. "It is better that we are bound my military discipline than by the manners of the Court at Wessex."

"London will not be Mercian forever."

"Ethelred does not delude himself that it will."

"The throne of Mercia is empty now. Burhred is dead and his queen sleeps at Pavia." Werferth eyed her thoughtfully. "You are of Mercian descent through the line of Offa."

"I will not set myself against the King for the sake of a throne!" Where Heahstan had directed his enquiries toward Ethelred's ambition, Werferth questioned hers. It crossed her mind that though these men allied themselves with the West Saxon King, they were also Mercians with Mercian loyalties. Since she had been in London, twice had she been reminded that she was of Offa's line through her mother. "Mercia cannot survive separately and must be under one rule," she did not say aloud 'with Wessex', "and that will not be soon. If you seek assurance, Werferth, you have it. For now, Mercia belongs to the Mercians, and we will keep it that way!"

"We?" The Bishop raised his shaggy eyebrows ever so slightly.

"We," she repeated firmly. "Ethelred and myself, with your help and blessing."

"And what of your brother, Edward?" Werferth refilled her cup from a silver flagon on his writing table. "What are Edward's ambitions for the kingdom?"

She understood his concern. Would Edward be content to wait, or was he eager for power and willing to plunge them into civil war? It was not an impertinent question, even in so close a family as theirs, perhaps especially in so close a family. It happened before: grandfather Ethelwulf supplanted by his greedy son Ethelbald. She smiled at the Bishop, understanding, but shaking her head.

"I apologize, Lady. I had not meant to question."

"It is not an idle concern. Past treacheries haunt us. Those that may come do not bear thinking of." She shivered slightly as the chill hand of premonition brushed her.

The fading sunlight slanted through an open window, and she noticed for the first time how cold the Bishop's chamber was. The fired had died on the stone hearth and only a few embers glowed to remind them that it was growing dark and Evensong was approaching. Werferth appeared not to notice the chill. Here, in his own chambers he wore his coarsely spun abbot's robe and cowl. A rough cord was knotted about his waist, and she suspected that the simple garb was a means of compensating his spirit for the privileges heaped upon him by the King.

"Rest easy," she said at last. "Edward is young and perhaps a bit headstrong, but you need not doubt that he is his father's son. For now, the King wishes Mercia to be ruled by a Mercian. It is Edward's wish as well." She did not need to remind the Bishop who it was that freed London from the Danes in the first place, and placed Ethelred, a native son, as its ruler. She smiled suddenly. "You may ask Edward. He arrives shortly with Ecgwin. I will be attending her with her first birthing."

She had already offered many prayers for Ecgwin, suffering quietly through her first pregnancy. Her own loss sharpened her concern for her sister-in-law. Werferth, noticing, laid his hand gently on her arm. "My child," his voice was quiet, "your loss will grieve you forever. No, you must listen." He sensed her withdrawal from him, "You must give your loss a chance to strengthen you. You cannot spend all day in chapel, praying for the dead as your mother does. You are called to work in the world, as I am. Our duty is clearly marked. For myself, it is outside the Abbey walls; for you, it is not yet clear. Only one thing is certain: you are called upon to do other things." She turned her head so Werferth would not see the tears.

"Look at me!" he commanded firmly. "It is not given to you to bear another child. Accept what God has chosen for you, and He will see to it that you do vastly more than any queen might do. Our hearts might wish otherwise, but we cannot set aside God's choice for us. If you but accept, the will of God becomes your own!"

His solitary meditations have taught him much, she thought, as they walked in silence to the chapel for Evensong. She had seen Werferth as bishop and abbot this past year, helping with the fortification of his city. She had seen him as a busy scholar in her father's court, rendering Gregory's great works into English for the sake of a clergy barely able to read and write their native tongue. She had seen the able Churchman as a skilled tradesman, ministering to the material necessities of his great impoverished See. It did not surprise her now to see him as truly a man of God, as so many of his fellows were not, dedicated to a will other than his own. She had thought him worldly and found instead a spirit free of the world, one who used the gifts bestowed on him for a single purpose. Her father thought God called men only to monastic life. He was wrong. God called people into the world, gave them wealth, power, skill, and influence, and expected them to use these gifts wisely. To such as Werferth, God gave another gift: total detachment from the trappings of the wealth and power bestowed on him.

As Werferth intoned the opening prayers of the Evening Office, filling the chapel with his resonant Latin, it occurred to her that this worldly bishop was in close touch with the God to whom these words were addressed. The monks who clustered about him, reciting the Responsory as one voice, openly signified their contemplative ambitions by their studied simplicity of life. Werferth deliberately hid his mind and spirit beneath the gold-encrusted miter, the richly decorated cope. The carved and gilded staff he wielded with such authority meant only the humblest service to him. His monks, his people, his King, and above all, his Church, these were his masters, and he had vowed obedience to their needs as if they were his own. The marvelous color and ceremony of this faith, so unlike that of her ancestors, captivated the imagination so thoroughly, she mused, that one often never got beyond the observance of it. The peasants shrugged and followed the one openly for the King's sake, the other secretly for their own sake. All gods to them were equally to be propitiated.

Nevertheless, here was Werferth, speaking as a trusted thane to a well-loved Lord, to a person whose life he shared intimately. A far cry from the pitiless *Tir* and *Frei,* who must be propitiated from a careful distance. This new belief was surely better than the old, but it took some getting used to, and some other turn of mind than that to which she was accustomed.

Still it had comforts and rewards for those who came through the hardships of life with courage and faith. The old gods, too, had expected courage and faith, but had not offered half as much in return. Indeed, they appeared cold-hearted, unbending, and implacable when set alongside God's *Haelend.* All the old ones offered was the glory that one might leave behind when one died, but about a life afterwards, a *Valhalla,* their own words were vague. One set out in one's burial ship, like *Scyld Scefing,* to meet more fighting, perhaps. One could tire of that, even in death. So if the new belief offered a safe haven and light and warmth eternal as an end to this dark, cold world, one could overlook its minor points for the sake of more important ones. Besides, it was not likely that old customs would be abandoned too quickly, not for promises of future good. She knew her countrymen well. The struggle to survive occupied them fully to the exclusion of the future; and if the new faith failed them, well, the old gods might look the other way as long as certain observances were kept.

She closed her eyes and let the rhythmic cadences of the Evening Office wash through the weariness of the old grief, which, she realized with a sudden pang of regret, had become a burden to her. She clung to it, almost guiltily, yet she was tired of it. The insight cleansed her thoughts, lightening the submerged misery she had borne silently and without awareness these past months. She opened her hands, without thinking, as if to relinquish from her grasp the persistent vision of the tiny headstone she had guarded jealously in the back of her mind. Looking inward now she saw it again, lonely and grey, rain streaking over its little mound, marking a human life gone down into the frozen earth. She watched it, aching afresh. It flickered and wavered before her eyes, like swirling fog haunting a *mere,* and through it she saw the face of human suffering, wreathed with the thorns of life. The words of the ancient poem trembled in her mind:

I was all with sorrow troubled,
I was afraid at the fair sight,
I saw the flickering beacon
Change apparel and color;
For a while it was with moisture soaked,
Drenched with the flow of blood,
And sometimes with treasures adorned....

As quickly as it came, the insight vanished, leaving a restful darkness upon her spirit: it was as if a door had opened in her heart and all feeling had slipped quietly through it, leaving her free at last of the manacles of her loss and the unwanted emotions that had bound it to her. The poet captured what she had seen in her mind: behind the blood-drenched symbol of suffering, the blood that daily drenched their lives, one could see the treasure glinting through. It was there, but only obscurely seen.

Her eyes met the Bishop's momentarily as she rose exhausted from her prayers. The chapel was silent and deserted, save for Werferth, who stood apart, waiting for her with understanding on his face. She wished to speak, but as he helped her to her feet, she became aware of the deep and awful silence that surrounds each life born into this world, separating and uniting them at the same time.

Edward arrived, and with him Ecgwin, to prepare for her lying-in. Despite her cheerful appearance and happy chatter about the court at Winchester, Aethelflaed saw the dark circles beneath her sister-in-law's eyes and surmised correctly that carrying Edward's robust child had been a strain on her delicate constitution. Ecgwin, momentarily betraying her surface brightness, gripped Aethelflaed's hand as if for strength.

"Take her to our chambers," she ordered Edward peremptorily. He obeyed with astonishing meekness. Ecgwin demurred briefly, but Ethelred intervened. "Do not waste your strength protesting, Lady. The room is made ready and is waiting for you." He smiled down at her, and then suddenly also at Edward, who was pacing the floor nervously, and brought him to a halt with an outstretched arm. "Gently, brother," he said, "all is well."

Elfwyn peeked at her uncle from the doorway, deaf to the strident whispers of the nurse from whom she had escaped. Her eye lit upon Ecgwin and before Aethelflaed could nod permission, the child shrieked with delight and threw herself into the room. Ethelred caught her before she could throw herself at Ecgwin and carried her to her aunt for a quick embrace before handing her back to her nurse. The child's energy was plainly too much for Ecgwin. Aethelflaed met Edward's eyes over his wife's head as they helped her to the chamber above and she smiled at him with a confidence she did not feel.

The wintry spring slowly yielded and the ground warmed. As the trees grew into bud under the coaxing rains, Ecgwin's burden increased. Aethelflaed and Ethelred watched over her with a concern bred of bitter experience. The girl was pale and miserable, but she said nothing. Aethelflaed insisted that Edward accompany her as she continued her duties in the market and the borough courts, for she knew Ecgwin would prefer to be left to her women.

"You must keep Edward's thoughts busy with other matters," Aethelflaed whispered into her husband's ear as they rested in the close darkness of the night. The stone fort was sparsely furnished and voices carried well at night, well enough to be heard through the open window arches.

"There is enough news of the Dane's success among the Franks to keep him concerned," Ethelred replied a bit grimly. "While they lay waste the land of the Franks, we are safe, but only for a while. Whether they succeed or fail, they will be back. If they fail, they will rejoin their kinsmen while they lick their wounds. If they succeed, it will embolden them."

Guthrum had died over a year ago, and his kinsmen ravaged Burgundy and Aquitaine. Worse, they had marched on Paris and forced the bitterly humiliated Franks to ransom their own city; but not before they had wreaked bloody havoc on the helpless citizens of Paris and taken the best of their young men and women to Kiev on the Dnieper, where they would bring high prices at the slave market.

Word had come back from travelers into Frankia and the countries eastward that the host had ravaged into the land of the Slavs and had there raised up at least two great cities, Novgorod and Kiev. These were built on the labor of the peasant Slavs under the whips of their Scandinavian overlords, who called themselves the *Rus*.

The *Rus,* Ethelred's informants whispered, grew fat with money from the Moslem slave-buyers, and it was even rumored that English thralls who survived the rigors of the trip to Kiev then found themselves shipped by river either to Constantinople or to the Arabian Caliphate. That is, if they were fortunate. Otherwise the ruling *Rus* might take a fancy to a slave girl and keep her. Many preferred instant death, but those with the courage to stay alive were abused beyond Aethelflaed's power of belief when she first heard the tales. She found they were true. Strange beliefs these Northmen possessed, for when a *Rus* died, his favorite slave girl would be shared out to all the relatives of the dead man, as a mark of respect—she grimaced in the dark—and then would be burned on her master's funeral pyre. There only, at the last, were they merciful: they slit her throat before the fires were lit.

She shuddered involuntarily and Ethelred pulled her close, knowing the direction of her thoughts, and comforted her. "Has Edward heard these tales?" she asked. His arms tightened around her and she could feel him nod. "And he believes them, too?"

Ethelred laughed shortly and bitterly. "We have seen too much of Viking courtesy on our fields of battle to doubt the tales of the *Rus."* He frowned into the darkness. "Indeed, we have heard the same from the Moors who come to London. They have sailed the Dnieper, and the Volga, too. They tell the same stories of the thrall markets among themselves and of the terrible customs of the Vikings." He paused, thinking. "I know these Moors are wrong-headed. They do not believe the true faith, but they also are filled with loathing for the Vikings, as much as we. It does not seem they would lie about that."

"Then we must keep Edward's mind busy with plans against the host. He frets himself overmuch and cannot understand his wife's sickness. He will be in the way, and a trouble, too, if urges her to too much exertion. He thinks everyone to be as strong as himself."

"He is a soldier above all else. It will not be hard to divert his thoughts."

She smiled. "Are you not also?" she chided gently, teasing. She heard his answering chuckle. "Before I married you," he said against her hair, "I was only a soldier. But we have seen much these few years together." They were both silent for a while. "I have no skill with words, but it is hard now to imagine being only a soldier, as I was, and alone, and not a husband, too."

A twinge of remorse assailed her. For Ethelred, being a husband had meant suffering her withdrawal from him for a while after the loss of their son and her illness. She had not been much of a wife, for her grief, anger, and resentment held back her response. Ethelred bore it patiently. She had not denied him, but she found herself unable to meet him on old terms. For a while, she feared she would never feel the warmth of response again. She was wrong. It came back as soon as she let go of her anger, her sense of loss. One cannot brood without resentment. If one resents one's fate, then one resents one's life, the good and the bad alike. Yet Ethelred was softly telling her he could no longer imagine being alone, not being her husband, not living with her griefs, her moods, herself. She kissed him, thankful. "Do you not," he whispered, guessing her thoughts, "bear with my care-lessness, my tempers, my humors as well?" He returned her kiss. "Do not moments such as these," he murmured, "right the balance?" She closed her eyes, smiling. After all those months of sadness, she came back to herself and found Ethelred waiting.

It seemed only moments after they had drifted into sleep that she woke, startled. She sat up groggily, uncomprehending. Ecgwin's servant stood by the bedside, a guttering candle in her hand. "Forgive me," the distracted woman whispered. "Lady Ecgwin calls for you. The pains are upon her." Aethelflaed rose quickly and struggled into her robe.

"Quiet," she cautioned the woman, as she knotted the sash about her waist. "Do not wake my Lord, nor Edward, either. Have you sent for the midwife?" The woman bobbed her head wordlessly. "Are they awake in the kitchen also?" They hurried along the passageway to Ecgwin's chambers. "Good. Send David to fetch Bishop Heahstan quickly." The woman's face contorted with fear. Aethelflaed hastened to explain. "It is not what you think. My sister gives birth to an heir to Wessex. His Lordship must witness this child's birth and baptize him immediately."

Aethelflaed held Ecgwin's hand firmly throughout the difficult birth, loosening her grip only to offer sips of herb infusions from a wooden spoon. The midwife shook her head grimly and muttered to herself as she worked over the fainting girl. "She is very small," she whispered fearfully. Ecgwin's labor was intense and each time the pains bore in upon her, she gasped and bit deeply into the piece of wood the midwife had placed in her mouth.

"Unction," Aethelflaed said tersely to Heahstan, who was already preparing to administer it. "Fetch Edward" she ordered David, without looking up.

"He is here," said Ethelred, behind her.

The midwife at last uttered an exultant cry and held up the babe. She wiped the phlegm from his tiny and mouth and shook him gently, for he needed no more than that after the harshness of his birth. He drew in his first deep breath and screamed. She gave him to the waiting nurse for bathing, frowning at Edward, who reached for his son. "Shortly, My Lord, shortly." She turned back to the unconscious mother.

"She lives," Heahstan whispered to Edward, "but it is by God's grace, alone." Edward's eyes were dark with fear. He held Ecgwin's hand and stroked it, watching her unconscious face anxiously. Aethelflaed met her husband's eyes over Edward's bent head. Edward was no stranger to the gore of the battlefield, but the ritual of so hard a birth was terrifying to him.

Heahstan retrieved the lustily bawling child from the nurse, anointed him with baptismal chrism, and sprinkled him with the warm, blessed water. He loosened the ceremonial chrism-cloth tied around the baby's arm. "The child's name," he demanded of Edward. The Atheling's whisper was barely audible. Heahstan laid his hands on the baby's head, intoning in Latin the words of baptism, and confirming the squalling heir by removing the chrism-cloth from his arm. He handed the babe to Edward, who held him close against his chest. His face relaxed. Ecgwin was breathing easily now, and sleeping.

Ethelred turned to David. "Prepare yourself for a journey to Winchester. Tell the King that he may rejoice in the birth of his grandson, whom Edward has named Athelstan in honor of the King's oldest brother."

Ecgwin's forehead was feverish under Aethelflaed's hand, but she was rallying and would live. Athelstan was husky and strong, even now resembling Edward about the jaw. She wondered how many of Edward's sturdy children her sister's delicate frame would tolerate, and saw her fears reflected in Ethelred's eyes as he stood protectively by Edward's shoulder.

She took the infant from Edward and rocked him gently, smiling to herself as he drew a long, shuddering breath and relaxed deeply into the peaceful sleep known only to the newborn. Much would rest on his tiny shoulders.

Ethelred touched her arm softly so as not to wake the babe. "We are most blessed. We have a King of Wessex, native born to Mercia." She smiled again. Athelstan was a vital link in the chain that she, Edward, and Ethelred were forging. With God's help, Alfred's dream of a united land of the Angles and Saxons might one day be accomplished by them together: this wee, slumbering soul, begotten of the line of Cerdic, and of Offa, would inherit it.

CHAPTER THIRTEEN

(892)

*E*alhswith stood in the garden, the moonlight pale on her face. The dark stone of the fortress wall loomed behind her, casting its dark shadow over her. The Queen was ageing fast, and suffering again from dreams and depressions. Had Ealhswith not made a sudden movement to pull her cloak more closely around her, Aethelflaed, who had come outside for a quiet breath of air, might not have seen her. The Queen was worn from a lifetime of living on the dread edge of ill tidings. While her husband campaigned, she prayed and lived in fear of his death and defeat. If he were at home, she prayed and feared for Edward, who would then be fighting in his father's stead, and also for Ethelred. The strain of years showed on her face. Aethelflaed called softly to her, not wishing to frighten her.

The Queen, though she heard her, did not turn her head, but continued to stare up at the sky.

"Lady Mother," Aethelflaed repeated softly, but was interrupted by the Queen's sibilant whisper, "See you the sign?"

She looked upward as the Queen raised a jeweled finger to the sky. "The long-haired star!" Her voice shook. "It is an omen. I fear for Ecgwin's child."

"Nonsense." Aethelflaed chided the Queen and put her arm around the delicate shoulders. "Athelstan has passed his first year safely. He is a strong child."

Ealhswith shivered. "Not the Atheling. Know you not that Edward's wife is with child again?" Aethelflaed shook her head. "She has not told me, but I see all the signs," Ealhswith whispered. "She is in her chambers ill most of the day." She looked up at Aethelflaed and gripped her hand tightly. "It is an omen," she repeated with resignation.

"Perhaps not for us, Lady Mother."

"Someone will die." Ealhswith was emphatic.

Aethelflaed smiled grimly to herself. "That much is always certain." She took the Queen by the arm and walked her back to the fortress gates. "You must rest now. Tell Ecgwin I will come to see her in the morning."

She stood at the gate for a while after Ealhswith left, watching the autumn sky. The comet shone down at her, unblinking and remote, its long tail streaming palely behind it. Perhaps the Queen was right, perhaps the firedrake was truly the finger of God, writing out across the sky its fateful message. Celestial events spoke clearly to her mother. The word of God was always manifest to Ealhswith, as it was to Elgiva. They wrapped themselves in the life of the spirit and the supernatural in a way she could not, even though that world had touched her briefly once. It was strange to her, and she had no desire to remain there overlong. Werferth had taken her measure accurately. She belonged to the world of flesh and blood, even though that world included a heart-breaking war that dragged on for many lifetimes, a world in which the span of time was measured from one battle to the next.

For her, the bells of Prime and Compline only marked the dividing line between night and day, telling her when to go about her worldly tasks and when to rest from them. To the Queen and Abbess Elgiva, the firedrake, now spreading its filmy, star-sprinkled tail flamboyantly across the chilly sky, would be a sign, an answer to a prayer, or a portent, to be read only by those who dwelled deeply in the spirit. If indeed it had a message, it would not be read by such as herself, she thought, with something akin to relief.

The council chamber flickered with shadows in the candlelight. Ethelred looked up and smiled as she took her place beside him at the table. She glanced briefly at the silent faces of the men, noting the tension that carved deep lines on their foreheads and tucked the corners of their mouths down behind the edges of their beards. Ethelred's look of welcome had given away to a look of thoughtful concentration. Edward's eyes were grimly downcast. The King was poring over a crudely drawn map in front of him, and a fourth man stood with his back to her, studying the tapestries on the wall. She recognized him barely an instant before he turned to greet her, and then only because of his robes.

"My Lord Archbishop!" She rose and greeted Pleymund warmly. He no longer wore the monk's black robe that had marked him as the hermit priest of Cheshire. At Alfred's insistence, he had vested himself in the Archbishop's robes, though he clearly felt ill at ease in such unaccustomed garments.

"My dear Lady," a smile flickered at the corners of his mouth, "it is plain you do not recognize your old friend in such finery."

"You do it great honor, My Lord."

Pleymund eased his tall, gaunt frame onto a small bench. Even sitting, Pleymund's physical presence could dominate a room. Ethelred handed her a roll of parchment, which she unrolled silently and read. The words were no surprise to her. At the bottom of the writ were the signatures, Alfredus Rex, Edwardus, and Ethelred's scrawling hand, that attested to her Overlordship of London in Ethelred's absence. She opened her mouth, as if to protest, though she knew it was futile to do so. Pleymund raised his hand to forestall her.

"There is no one so fit as yourself. Ethelred informs us that you have personally visited every borough court in London and passed judgment yourself in many complaints. It is doubtful that your husband knows as much as you do about the people of London and their problems. "No," he raised his hand again to stay her as she sought to speak. "If you say us nay we shall order you to take the command."

She smiled wryly. "I am aware of the necessity that compels this action. As you so will, my Lord Archbishop, I must accept. Your faith knows no bounds."

The King handed her the map he had been studying. "The Danes are gathering at Boulogne across the channel from Appledor." She understood. That accounted for Edward's stern expression and for the Archbishop's presence at the Council. The Kentishmen would be assembling under Pleymund's leadership for the defense of Sussex. "You will remain in London, my Lord Archbishop?" she asked. Pleymund nodded.

"Good. It will be safer here than at Canterbury."

Edward at last raised his head. "The King and I will leave for Northumbria tomorrow to obtain oaths and hostages from King Guthfrith and from the East Anglian Danes as well. They are baptized, but we must be certain that their sympathy for their heathen countrymen does not tempt them. We will return as quickly as we can."

"And Ethelred?"

"I will take part of the garrison from London out to the villages. The harvest is almost ready and it must be brought in safely."

"Aye, that is necessary. She turned to Pleymund. "I will be left with half a garrison. That will not be enough to defend London should the Danes get past the defenses in Sussex, as they surely will."

Alfred agreed. "You are right, daughter. We have earthworks at Wareham and Cricklade, but those in Kent are barely underway. The people are tired of war and too hungry to work willingly."

"Then I must have a division of Kentishmen," she said firmly.

Pleymund stared at her astonished. "But surely, My Lady, they must defend the Kentish coast."

"The Kentish coast cannot be held," she declared crisply. "The Kentishmen cannot defend forts that are not built, and if they fight out in the open, they will surely be slaughtered. We cannot afford such losses." She turned to her father. "Can we not let such peasants as are willing work on the forts until the host appears."

The King nodded, understanding her line of thought. "Then we let them abandon the forts at the first sighting of the Danes?"

She turned back to Pleymund. "The people will be safe in the forests. Leave only a few men wearing peasant's dress. They shall ride to London as soon as the host lands. When they reach London, we will be prepared."

"By that time," Edward interposed, "Father and I will be back with hostages from Guthfrith." He rose suddenly. "I must see my wife before I leave. She is not well." Alfred signed dismissal. Aethelflaed caught Edward's hand as he passed by her bench. "Do not worry, Edward, I will look after her while you are gone." He gave her a grateful look and left. Pleymund left also to join the monks at chapel. Ethelred sat silently, studying the maps intently. She watched the King's face in the guttering candlelight. He was suffering old ailments again and the lines on his face had deepened during the past year. The long ride north through the countryside might do him good, even though his errand was grim.

"You spend too much time with your books, father," she scolded mildly.

His face was pensive. "I have done much writing these past two years. It suits me better than war." He looked up at the ceiling, in the direction of the Queen's chambers. "It is better for your mother, too, that I spend time with my books. I have been away too much and was never here to comfort her." He lapsed into silence, staring at the candle burning low in front of him. It was one of his own inventions, marked at intervals to show the passing of each hour as the flame consumed its way through the wax. "See," he said softly, to no one in particular, "it has not many marks to go, nor have I." He saw the look on her face. "You must not be shocked. I am tired and death does not frighten me." He took her hand and held it. "Edward has much ahead of him, daughter. He is brave but he needs tempering. Ethelred's training has carried Edward through the bad times." He glanced upward again to where Edward was now comforting his wife. "Of the two of you, you have the cooler head. He listens to you as he does to no one else."

He smiled. "Except myself, and there he has little choice." He smiled again, wryly. "And I am happy that he attends out of love and not merely honor. But," he continued, "I shall not be with you forever, and when I am gone Edward will have to finish what I have begun." His expression was sad. "I wanted to leave peace behind me, but that will be up to Edward, and to you and Ethelred."

Ethelred had laid down the map and was watching the King unwaveringly. He touched Aethelflaed's shoulder to silence her, for he could see she was about to protest. "We shall serve and advise Edward with the same love and honor with which we have served you, My Lord."

Alfred accepted this gravely, then turned back to Aethelflaed. "You and Ethelred have done well with London. Now it is necessary that you command it alone sometimes. Ethelred must ride out with Edward soon and you must accustom yourself to rule alone."

"You have many years left!"

Alfred leaned across the table, holding her hand all the more firmly. "Perhaps. And I shall ride with Ethelred and Edward as long as necessary, but I have other work to do. You must surely see that Wessex and Mercia together, with Danes on every border, could easily be too much for one man, even such as Edward. You must accept what the rest of us already know, that there is not one Mercian alive but that he would lay down his life for you."

She stood at the window of their chamber after they had blown out the last candle and sent the servants to bed. The comet still hung in the sky, a few stray stars winking through its tail. Ethelred put his arms around her. "My mother fears this star," she said finally. "Do you?"

He shrugged slightly. "Perhaps. I do not think much about such things."

She shivered and Ethelred pulled her closer. "Are you afraid?"

"Yes." She glanced at the comet again. "But not of the firedrake. You have placed much in my hands. It is you that should command London, not I."

He lifted her chin and stared thoughtfully into her eyes. "The King shows his age. He takes to the field only of necessity, but his heart-thoughts lie elsewhere."

"Aye." Her voice was soft with sadness.

"I must support Edward as I have supported your father. I shall be away too much. The King is right: there is no other so well-prepared as yourself to command a garrison."

She fell asleep at last, knowing in her heart that what he said was true. She slept fitfully, dreaming of the long-haired star. She saw her mother standing before her, laughing holding the comet in her hand. She struggled for consciousness, but the dream held her back. She looked again and saw the figure now had Ecgwin's smiling face. Aethelflaed reached out to her, but the comet burned more brightly than ever in the palm of her hand, and its blinding light obscured the face of the woman in the dream. She wrenched herself awake, and for a moment the flickering light of dawn frightened her. Ethelred was gone, and the eager, fretful pawing of hooves in the yard below her window told her that Edward and the King were leaving for Northumbria.

She dressed quickly and went to Ecgwin's rooms for breakfast. The servant at the door handed her a steaming bowl. Ecgwin lay propped up on her couch, pale from morning sickness, but cheerful. Her woman tucked a fur rug securely around her, and settled an embroidered mantle around her shoulders before Aethelflaed dismissed her.

"Chamomile infusion." Aethelflaed sat down on the edge of the couch. "You will feel better shortly." She hoped she sounded convincing. Edward's wife looked so fragile, so ethereal wrapped in her heavy rug. Ah, well, she mused, if she loses this child early, it may be as well. Perhaps, she thought, furrowing her brow slightly, we can make her stronger for the next one. Ecgwin, however, was determined to live up to Edward's rugged manner of life and had too soon subjected herself to the jolting, bone-rattling ride back to Winchester with Edward, to Aethelflaed's great dismay. "She will be ill for months after," she muttered darkly to Ethelred. He merely shrugged, saying mildly, "It is her own choice, my dearling." Which of course, it was.

"You worry too much, sister," Ecgwin said, jarring her back to the room. Ecgwin put the bowl down. "Truly, I feel much stronger with this one. She picked up the bowl again and sipped the hot brew. "I never knew my own mother," she said softly, almost to herself. She smiled suddenly. "The Queen worries about me far more than you do."

"We must make allowance for her. Age makes her anxious."

"Ah!" Ecgwin's eyes twinkled. "She has spoken her fears to you?" Aethelflaed half-started from the couch in quick anger with the Queen. "Be still, sister." Ecgwin raised her hand as if to soothe, "Her own sadness increases her fears for me, just as it did for you. I am not afraid. Edward will have another strong child. Leave the Queen to me and her grandson." The chamomile began its soothing magic and Ecgwin yawned widely, murmuring half-heartedly that Aethelflaed must not leave, though when Aethelflaed went to fetch her woman, they returned to find Ecgwin soundly asleep.

Ecgwin was right about Ealhswith. The Queen smiled only in Athelstan's presence. Most understandable, for the child lit every room he entered. He was tall for his age, which was barely over a year, and he had begun to talk precociously early. To the King's great joy he was robust and as energetic as Edward, yet he displayed a disposition that could have come only from his mother. The four-year-old Elfwyn was his inseparable companion, and they were more like brother and sister than cousins. Elfwyn ruled the nursery with an iron hand and he took orders from her cheerfully.

They were often too much for their nurse, so Aethelflaed arranged to take her charges with her to inspect the city walls and the garrison. Elfwyn sat her horse well and proudly under her mother's watchful eye, while Athelstan shared the saddle with his aunt. Outside the nursery, discipline of the garrison prevailed. A few unalterable injunctions were always issued at the beginning of such expeditions and were not on any account to be ignored. Accordingly, their behavior was painstakingly exact, their round faces as properly expressionless as they could bear to make them. Only the two pairs of lively eyes twinkling with curiosity, darting here and there, missing nothing, betrayed their excitement.

The walls were in good repair, she noted with satisfaction. The soldiers who were off military duty were now busy with fortification duty and were repairing the weak spots in the Roman foundations of the wall. New height had been added also to the wall, with rubble stone and mortar. Pleymund's Kentish division, dispatched to London by the Archbishop, were set to building walls, which was not to their hot-tempered liking. She noted the laxity of their discipline with some severity and ordered the best of her swordsmen to take the Kentishmen in hand. They would doubtless grumble among themselves at the seeming harshness of the order, but the sooner they became accustomed to firm rule and Ethelred's relentless discipline, the better they would be able to defend the city. London was no longer a lazy, open trading port. There was great wealth stored along the dockside and more pouring in daily. Haesten, biding his time in Boulogne, would be dreaming covetously of London's gold and goods and English thralls for the taking. More than that, the bustling city, hugging the banks of the Thames, was the gateway to the grain-laden fields of Wessex and Mercia, whose hillsides had ripened into amber temptation under the autumn sun.

But Haesten was waiting in Boulogne no longer. Alfred and Edward had barely dismounted from the hard ride back to London when riders from Kent clattered into the courtyard, arousing the garrison to instant activity. Alfred, still weary from the journey, sat in council, listening intently.

"My Lord King," the messenger gasped, near collapse from his frantic ride, "Haesten has landed with eighty ships and has taken the Royal village of Milton!" The village commanded the head of a creek that opened into the channel between the isle of Sheppey and the mainland. "Appledor is taken also, by two hundred and fifty ships that sailed into the Lympne."

Alfred nodded, almost absently. "There was no resistance?"

"None, my Lord." The messenger glanced at Aethelflaed briefly, accusation in his eyes. "The Kentish division is here in London." She stared back at him, stonily silent. He looked down at the floor and reddened.

"There were no losses then?" the King asked quietly.

"No, My Lord, the villagers fled."

"Good." Alfred dismissed the messenger, who mumbled incoherently and fled. He turned to Edward. "You and I will leave at dawn." He glanced at Aethelflaed. "Can you give me a few of Pleymund's men as guides?" She nodded. He pondered the map. "We cannot allow them to join forces." He put his finger of the map, halfway between Milton and Appledor. "We will make camp here."

"What of Northumbria's oaths?" Edward's tone was impatient. "Are we to trust that they will not attack from the north?"

"We must honor their Christian oath," Alfred reproved him mildly. Edward scowled. "Nevertheless," the King continued, "Ethelred will remain north of London near the Lea while the harvest is brought in." He looked up at Edward. "I myself am inclined to agree with you. Guthfrith will most probably break his oath and join with the East Anglians." Edward swore softly and brought his fist down on the table with a hard crack. Alfred ignored him and continued mildly, "Their kinsmen overseas have suffered great losses and return in desperation. Guthfrith's faith is not so firm that he can yet deny his own kinsmen. That test is too severe."

"Then why did we ask for oaths and hostages if you expect him to break with his own honor when the time comes?"

Alfred smiled at Edward, wearily, "My son, if nothing else, it will slow him down, and we need time. He may mean to keep the oath, but he is a Dane, living among Danes, and he is bound to his kin as deeply as we are bound to ours. Even so, he will give oath-breaking much thought. First he will think one way, then the other. While he argues with himself, we will use the time he gives us as best we can."

"Why are you so certain he will break his oath at the last? Even our own kin have turned against us in the past. Can he not do the same with his?"

Alfred leaned back on the settle and studied his heir for a moment. "Listen well, children," he said softly. "Much as honor is spoken of and valued by all, it is not often to be found. The Danes make much of honor and talk at great length about it, but this much is plain: the more it is spoken of, the less it is practiced. Would we require oaths if men were as honorable as their words? I think not. The words are to bind the man, to give him thought, for without the words given aloud for all to hear, there is no dishonor. Believe me, in either case, there will be dishonor, for if Guthfrith honors his oath to me, Haesten will attack him. Haesten is desperate and has nowhere to go, as Guthfrith knows well. He has no choice, he must help them. But the oath, the oath," he repeated, "gives us a little more time. They shall not find us so ill-prepared as they found us in the past!" His eyes betrayed a glimmer of satisfaction.

Edward left first, just before dawn, taking the Kentishmen with him. Aethelflaed embraced him briefly. "They are good fellows, brother, but discipline is not to their liking." He nodded understanding. "They will find me no easier than yourself."

The weeks passed uneasily and much too quietly. Ethelred returned for a short while when the last of the harvest was safely stored. Edward returned twice for provisions and fumed privately to Aethelflaed that the King would not attack.

"Be glad he is wise enough not to make a move."

Edward stopped pacing and looked at her with a grimace of surprise. "But we must drive them out!"

"And if the King attacks one camp, the other would move immediately. All of Sussex would be open to them." She pulled Edward to the window. "Look!" She pointed to the moon, glowing inside a haze of light. Edward stared, uncomprehending, his mind elsewhere. "A snow-ring," she prodded him gently. "Winter is almost here. Be patient, Edward. There is little the host can do with winter approaching. They are only human. If they are to fight, they must eat, and they have no provisions at Appledor."

The King's judgment was right, as Edward grudgingly conceded. As the first lazy flakes swirled to the ground, Haesten gave in. Pleymund baptized the Danish jarl and his family, part of the terms of Alfred's treaty, and Alfred gave them safe conduct to Benfleet. It was now too late for the remaining host at Appledor to move. Edward returned to London with the news that Appledor was silent for the winter, and stayed restlessly in London, watching over the silent menace at Appledor. Ecgwin, in spite of her growing burden, teased him into a semblance of jollity during Christmas. Nevertheless, Aethelflaed watched her with growing concern.

They had little time to fret. In early spring of 893, the Danes at Appledor confirmed Edward's suspicions. With no warning, they marched out westward across Kent toward Hampshire and Berkshire. It was certain that Winchester was their goal, but when they found that Alfred was in Wessex, not in London, they bore eastward again.

"This time," Ethelred said grimly, "they will surely try to join Haesten." Aethelflaed sent two of her best riders to Winchester to warn the King, while Edward, refusing to wait for word from his father, rode out with a full division of Kentishmen and part of the London garrison as well. They had not long to wait in London for news. Edward's impatience had served them well.

The riders returned from Winchester by way of Farnham, and Aethelflaed received them in the council chamber. They were tired, having ridden due east into the fray at Farnham before returning to London. They were also exultant, and it was clear that Edward had earned their devotion.

"He is terrible, Lady." Their broad smiles spoke of victory. She held up her hand for silence as one shouted with laughter.

"He intercepted them, then?"

"Aye, My Lady, and hounded them for twenty miles north to the Thames, on their heels like a terrier all the way!" He broke off, unable to contain himself. "By God, he is good." He started at the look in her eye, and continued. "Had they not moved as fast as they did, he'd have made bloody work of them. Lord Edward is not one to hold back with the sword!"

She breathed a sigh of relief. "Where are they now?"

"At Thorney, what's left of them."

"At Thorney?" She was incredulous. "But there's no ford at Thorney!"

"No, My Lady, none at all." He guffawed with unholy glee and mopped his brow. "Such as was left swam for it."

"Across the Thames?" Her tone was disbelieving. Edward must indeed have terrified them, for the Thames was too deep for fording at Thorney.

"Aye. Not many made it, and their heathen king is wounded sore besides." His eyes sparkled with admiration. "His Lordship is a right fierce man, Lady. I'd not care to fight against him."

She looked up at Ethelred and found his eyes mirroring the satisfaction of the messengers. She turned back to the messenger. "Where is my father now?"

"The King turned back halfway, Lady. The Northumbrians sneaked across the midlands and attacked Exeter from the other side."

Ethelred's face darkened. "Guthfrith!" he exclaimed angrily. "Edward was right."

She agreed. "Edward is always right when he tells the King not to trust. The King expected Guthfrith to break his oath, but I do not think he expected him to march to attack himself. We thought he would send the Danish army into East Anglia to help Haesten."

Ethelred left early for Thorney, taking only a few men with him. She urged him to take more.

"I dare not. Haesten sits at Benfleet, well rested. Now that Guthfrith has broken his oath, the East Anglians will break theirs also." He shook his head. "I doubt we shall dislodge them at Thorney. We have not enough men for that, but we can keep them from running over Buckingham."

He left. The comet burned brighter than ever in the sky, shining down on Ecgwin, who was laboring hard and early. Aethelflaed sat with her, wiping her face, murmuring to her, and holding her hand through her periods of wakefulness. She had her meals sent to the lying-in chamber and ate only while Ecgwin slept. The labor was going badly with Edward's wife and she feared to leave her for a moment.

Early in the second morning, Ecgwin opened her eyes and stared blankly out the window. The firedrake gleamed down at her in the half-light of dawn. She looked at Aethelflaed and moved her lips, but all that Aethelflaed could catch as she bent her head to the girl's pale lips was "Edward," whispered faintly. The final birth pangs began in earnest, as if the firedrake had breathed its secret message to her, urging her to get on with it. The midwives moved in, and the child came slowly, with great work into the cold morning. Long before it was over, Aethelflaed knew what the firedrake had spoken to Ecgwin, and she sent for Heahstan.

Ethelred returned finally, exhausted. They had been forced to treat with the Danes and to let them rejoin Haesten at Benfleet. They were no longer a force to be as greatly feared as before; nevertheless, he and Edward were not yet strong enough to dislodge them.

"Where is Edward?" she asked sadly.

"He escorts them to the border to see they do no harm."

She let the tears go at last, for she had not cried, not even when Ecgwin smiled her last sweet smile. Ethelred took her in his arms, bewildered as she choked out the words. The comet in her dream had indeed borne down heavily on the family. But Ealhswith was wrong. The child had survived the birth and flourished. The firedrake, in its star-spattered, burning fingers, had carried off Edward's fragile wife.

CHAPTER FOURTEEN

(893)

*E*dward read the King's letter with disbelief. He nodded curtly to the messenger, who withdrew, and Aethelflaed saw a flush of repressed anger on his face. The summer campaigns and the loss of his wife sat heavily on his features, etching deep furrows on either side of his nose and pulling down the corners of his mouth. He looked older than his twenty-one years.

He read the letter again and looked up, his blue eyes dark with anger in his tanned face. "He let them go!"

"I expected as much." Ethelred shrugged. "After all, one of the sons was Alfred's godson, the other was mine. Your father always honors his pledges."

No sooner had Edward returned from escorting the refugees under heavy guard from Thorney to Essex, than the ships riding anchor at Appledor and Milton set sail for Benfleet. There was nothing to be gained in Sussex and return to the Frankish kingdom that had driven them out was impossible. Had Thorney been a victory and not a bitter stalemate, the edge of Edward's grief might have been blunted a little. Instead, after the first shock of Ecgwin's death, the grief hardened bitterly within him. He longed to grind underfoot the enemy who had dragged him from his wife's side when she needed him most. He felt, irrationally, that his presence at her side might have saved her life and guilt consumed him.

He saw rightly that Haesten and Guthfrith and their broken oaths had caused his absence, but Aethelflaed could not convince him that his wife's death had naught to do with his absence. It relieved her when his guilt was turned to wrath at the host for having forced him away. No one can tolerate self-inflicted remorse and neither she nor Ethelred nor the combined forces of Wessex and Mercia could safely tolerate Edward's loss of spirit.

That he had seriously thwarted the enemy's plans at Farnham and Thorney was no comfort to Edward. His guilt turned around, his sorrow hardened into wrath, and his wrath ignited a burning hatred. So violently did his emotions turn within his anguished heart that he swore to Aethelflaed that did he but lay hands on him, he would do a Viking vengeance and carve the blood-eagle himself on Haesten's back.

"God, brother," she breathed, her throat burning acidly at the thought. She had not, thank Christ, seen it herself, but she had heard ghastly descriptions of the Viking practice of wrenching the victim's ribs away from his backbone and spreading his lungs out upon his back, like wings, fluttering with each dying gasp.

Beyond that one outburst he endured his personal loss with a stoicism that astonished her. He had looked upon his daughter, Edytha, briefly when Aethelflaed brought her to him, then turned away with no display of emotion. Only his eyes betrayed him with a momentary glistening before he wheeled about and strode from the room.

Within a fortnight of his return from Essex, he persuaded Ethelred to march with him against Benfleet. The concentration of Danish strength there was insupportable to them. War served its purpose with Edward, she reflected, as she watched the anger play in his eyes, then swiftly fade. He would not allow grief to paralyze him as it once had her. In small ways it coarsened him, for he could not give vent to his feelings. In other, larger, ways it changed Edward into a fierce and violent soldier. He was not introspective by nature, and nothing would diminish that intense energy. He bore his grief silently enough among his family, but the whole repressed fury of it he unleashed against the enemy. Had Haesten but known of Edward's lonely, wrathful anguish, he would never have left Benfleet to raid the villages of Mercia.

Edward and Ethelred struck swiftly and fiercely. Surely the name of Edward, who had proved himself well at Farnham, struck terror into the hearts of the Danes at Benfleet, for they abandoned their ships and fled. Benfleet fell quickly and among the hostages were Haesten's wife and sons. Ethelred dispatched them under guard to Alfred at Exeter. The King, to the angry bafflement of his heir, restored them to Haesten.

Edward now shook his head, puzzled. "Haesten has already made camp at Shoebury, near Benfleet. The Northumbrians are joining him. I fear he will take the King's mercy as a sign of weakness."

She had thought of that, too, and wondered briefly of the wisdom of her father's gesture. The letter had been borne to Edward by Ethelhelm, the battle-hardened Ealdorman of Wiltshire, and it had not been unnoticed by herself and Edward that he had brought with him Ethelnoth, the Ealdorman of Somerset, and every thane in Wessex east of the Parret River. Clearly Alfred knew what he could expect of Haesten, despite his generosity toward the Dane's family. Edward still considered his father an innocent in dealing with the host. It was Ethelred who now stepped in and regarded Edward with unusual sternness.

"You misjudge the King." He spoke softly, but his voice held a note of warning. Edward flushed at the reproof, but made no reply.

"I shall not," Ethelred went on just as quietly, "point out the King's many battles and successes for you know them as well as I. We have both been with him long enough to know that his wisdom tells in the end."

"Surely Haesten will move again. This," Edward waved the letter impatiently, "will encourage him."

"Haesten has no choice but to move again. It makes no difference whether he has his family or not."

Edward looked at him blankly. Ethelred picked up a goblet and filled it from a jug on the table. "There is no value in vengeance on the helpless," he said, handing the goblet to Edward. "The King's weakness is a strength you are too young to know yet. I have been with him a long time." He was silent, and Aethelflaed, watching him, was startled to see that his face was beginning to show a few lines other than those carved by hours of wind and sun. He was lost in memories that excluded her and Edward. She had forgotten in the years of their closeness that he was ten years older than herself. Ethelred, the Mercian Overlord, serving the King of Wessex, was a part of their childhood that they took for granted. The expression on his face isolated him from them now, and Aethelflaed could neither penetrate his recollections nor sense the emotions that they evoked in him. Had she been able to, she would have understood. The seasoned soldier, after years of fighting to hold his sprawling land and people together, was tiring of bloodshed and violence.

Ethelred could appreciate a man of Alfred's nature, who behaved always with civility, even to a crude and savage enemy. Brutality only led to more brutality, as Ethelred could attest to, having forestalled many orgies of bloodlust and rapine among his own men. They went into battle screaming, to bolster their own ferocity and to frighten the enemy. If they lost the place of battle, the sting of defeat drove them to any atrocity they could imagine if they stumbled across a stray Viking, and sometimes, even if they did not. If victory was their lot, the fact thrummed in their veins. It was as if the smell of blood on the slippery field of battle stung their nostrils and maddened their brains. Only a few had the sense to be sick.

But then, the Vikings were no different; in fact, it was a grim credit to the English that their imagination was not quite so ghastly as that of the Vikings. Alfred's love of God had tempered the English somewhat. They had taken their first stumbling steps toward fulfilling Alfred's vision, unbeknownst to them. Edward would learn that returning violence for violence accomplished nothing. If the host chose to think this king a weakling that was no concern of theirs. It was better, perhaps, that they underestimate him.

"You serve the King well!" Edward laid his hand on Ethelred's shoulder, his eyes begging his brother's pardon.

"I shall serve his son as well, God willing." Ethelred returned Edward's gaze steadily.

Edward sighed heavily, but his face relaxed. "You serve me well now by telling me what I need to hear, whether I will hear it or no, and I am grateful. I hope you will always do as much." His eyes gleamed with sudden wry amusement. "If you do not, I swear my sister will not forbear to speak!"

Hasten did not remain at Shoebury for long. The ripening fields of Mercia waved their golden invitation and the Danes responded boldly. The dwindling supplies in Essex could not long support Haesten and the Northumbrian and East Anglian armies as well. The raid began in early June, first along the Thames valley, then quickly reached the Severn. Edward, who kept uneasy watch on Haesten, rode to Winchester at the first sign of movement out of Shoebury. Alfred was still battling Guthfrith's Northumbrians, who occupied Exeter, and there was no doubt that Haesten, unable to unseat the English in London, had decided to content himself with Winchester instead. Ethelred, Ethelhelm, and Ethelnoth set out after Haesten, who had veered northward into the Vale of Gloucester soon after Edward reached the capitol of Wessex.

She had sent David along with Ethelred and anxiously awaited his return. He would bring news of the hard pursuit into the fastnesses of Mercia, and when at last he clattered into the courtyard, he demanded, with a boldness born of exhaustion, immediate audience with the Lady of London. The relief in his tired face was evident, but she refused to let him speak until the servants brought wine and goblets, and cold roast fowl. His eyes widened when he saw the fowl placed before him on a wooden platter.

Lord Ethelred, he told her, between gulps of food, and Ethelhelm had overtaken the Danes north of Welshpool at Buttington, forced them onto an island in the Severn and surrounded them. The siege, if he was any judge, would last for many weeks.

"And the Welsh?" she prompted.

He took a long pull from the goblet, gulping thirstily. "Aye, they joined the siege," he responded laconically.

Aethelflaed smiled in spite of herself. There was no love lost between the Welsh and her husband. Border skirmishes between the Mercians and the Welsh had not often been interrupted by other wars.

David acknowledged her smile with a sudden grin. "This time it was too much for them." He smiled lamely. "Ah, but I am English, too. Anyhow," he continued, leaning back wearily, "they saw for themselves what the enemy did to the valley. It was not hard to persuade them that the Danes were more dangerous than the English."

"And...?"

He spread his hands in a gesture of uncertainty. "I would not care, myself, even if I were as fierce as a Dane, to be sitting on an island surrounded by Mercians, West Saxons, and," his eyes glinted, "Welshmen." He nodded, smiling to himself with satisfaction, enjoying some grim and private joke. "Indeed, they will find the Welsh no small trouble. But they will have an island to themselves, a very small one, and they can dig roots and eat wild fowl, if there be any, and fish."

"Their food will soon be gone...."

He smiled with grim pleasure. "It will but my Lord Ethelred will still be there when it is gone."

She eyed David thoughtfully. "You have done well for your English masters, David."

He stood up, obviously uncomfortable sitting in her presence. "I was a thrall in the Queen's household before you took me. I had no name, I could not read nor write. It is you who have been good to me, Lady."

"But does your heart, like Asser's, lie in the Welsh hills beyond Welshdyke?"

He looked at her strangely. "Surely you do not think of sending me to Wales?"

"No, no," she reassured him quickly. "I have great need of you. I thought perhaps the sight of your countrymen might have moved your heart to find your mother's people."

His eyes darkened with thought. "No," he said finally and slowly. "My blood is only part Welsh, and though I am proud of it, this household," he waved his arm in a sweeping gesture, "is my family. I was born in your mother's kitchen, not in Wales." She said no more for she could see the thought of leaving disturbed him and she had no intention of sending him away. She had another thought in mind, but it could wait.

David rested a few days, then returned to the Welsh border with food, clothes, herbs, and medicinals of all kinds. June grew hot and passed into July under skies of clearest shimmering blue. Edward stayed at Winchester while the King camped outside Exeter's gates, waiting and watching. Guthfrith and his men had taken to their ships and were waiting off the Devon coast for Alfred to leave. It would be six months all told before Alfred would be able to do that, and the better part of two years before he would be able to relieve Exeter of the long siege.

July ripened into August and Ethelred finally came home from the reaches of Wales and Mercia, grim, haggard, and wounded from the long siege. A gash on his arm had festered and left him feverish. She forgot everything else and tended to Ethelred's wound, wrapping it with poultices to draw off the poison. He endured them silently, though his eyes glazed with pain if each fresh poultice was not cooled enough before she laid it on the infected arm. Fortunately, the cut had been a fairly clean stroke, like that made by a scramasax, and was not deep enough to expose the bone.

He told her about the Danes' escape from the siege as she worked over his arm. "They surprised us completely." He gasped involuntarily as the poultice touched the raw wound. "We were certain they could hold out no longer. They stripped the island of berries and game, then killed their horses and ate them." He took a deep breath and sighed as the poultice on his arm cooled and the pain of the infection eased. "They cut through our guards at night, each one carrying only a scramasax."

They swam the river, he went on, as they had done at Thorney. Most of them were able to steal quietly through the English, who were lined along the east bank of the river. Some were caught and fought like demons, cutting their way through the English. The rest slipped through unnoticed. Enough to be counted as a small army, but not before they had been severely mauled by the Welsh and English. They returned quickly to Shoebury among their kinsmen to lick their wounds.

Ethelred shook his head admiringly. "I have never seen men put up such a fight. They are a fierce breed." He smiled, wryly. "The Welsh, I mean." She knew better than to ask how they disposed of the men they captured. He read the distress on her face and pulled her to his side with his good hand. "It is not always possible to stop the men. You did not see the Mercian villages the Vikings left behind them." The eyes he turned on her were filled with a mixture of bafflement and guilt. "I saw the villages; I dare not describe it." He looked down at the floor as if he were unable to meet her eyes any longer. "I did not try to stop them. I could barely keep from joining them."

He sat on the edge of the settle, weary and disheartened. His conscience preyed on him. He had always decried so strongly the violence, vengeance, and bloodlust of the men he commanded, having been well schooled by Alfred. Now he had tasted for himself their hatred. Can one ever, she wondered, see such ugliness and not hate those who inflicted it? How vengeance explodes in the mind when one sees the cruelty done to those whom one loves best; Ethelred's land and his people. How does one not hate? She had asked her father this question many years ago. For answer she had received the same look she saw now on her husband's face. He raised his eyes, misreading her silence, thinking her ashamed of him. There was nothing she could say to ease the guilt. She kissed him and pulled his head against her breast, comforting him as if he were a child.

The arm healed quickly, and while it did, the host in Shoebury stirred again. Without warning, silently by night and day, the Northumbrian and East Anglian Danes set out again on a forced march that took Ethelred completely by surprise. By the time the exhausted messengers rode into London, their horses lathered from the hard ride, Chester had fallen.

It had fallen because there was no one there to defend it but the ghosts of the Romans who had built the great city of *Deva Victrix,* camp of the Legions. The walls were crumbling and the enclosure, with its grid of streets and its outlying amphitheatre were overgrown with brush and weeds and hidden by the debris of centuries. The River Dee flowed quietly by, waiting for no one in particular. A perfect spot for the host, she reflected bitterly, a ready-made fort from which they might control all of English Mercia. The borders of Danish Mercia were not far to the east of Chester, linking the Norsemen to their kinsmen in the Danelaw. Worse, the Rivers Dee and Mersey promised good communication with the Vikings in Dublin across the Irish Sea. It was a temptation of water that no sailor could resist, and easy sport for men whose seaworthiness had been tried on the deep and treacherous fjords of the far north.

The invaders of Ireland were the tall, fair-haired, blue-eyed Vikings, not the stocky, dark-haired, dark-eyed Danes from Jutland. These Irish Norse were big, majestic men from Norway and Iceland, with a reputation for bloodthirstiness that far outstripped that earned by the Danes: men who took to the open sea and sailed northward and westward from Iceland to unknown places. Mercia and Wessex, beleaguered from the east, were now to be pressured from the west.

"Oh, God," she said aloud, wearily, "is there to be no peace in this lifetime?" and realized dimly that when peace might eventually come, she would not see it. The Danish menace had not been overcome and there was now another evil to contend with. The Irish Norse would be no less tenacious and aggressive in their pursuit of lands and riches than were their Danish cousins. She and Ethelred had their future laid out for them. The Danish Norse and the Irish Norse between them might join forces at Chester, and from there they would squeeze the life out of Mercia. No quarter dared be given now. The Viking threat was more deadly than ever.

Ethelred ordered every thane and every *fyrd* in Mercia out and sent word to Edward to remain in Winchester. He tested his wooden shield on his arm and was satisfied that it was strong enough to hold it. David polished the bosses on Ethelred's shield until they glowed and shone like pale gold in the sunlight, and sharpened and polished swords until the steel glittered at the slightest movement.

"There is no pain in the arm," Ethelred assured her, "and it is as strong as ever." She nodded mutely and embraced him, laying her cheek against the ring mail covering the leather byrnie on his chest. The tone of his voice betrayed a hint of weariness, but the arm was well healed. She had seen to that herself. Twenty years of fighting had left him strong and sinewy, capable of throwing off battle wounds and small illnesses. Even so, there was an edge to his voice that told her his spirit wearied of war. A young lad, he often told her, needed the excitement of battle to let off high spirits and to temper the will. All very well for green lads in battle, but Ethelred was no green lad. He was thirty-three now and soldiering was an ingrained discipline, not a relief for high spirits. Sooner or later, the mind grows weary of killing. She kissed him and stroked his cheek, repressing a small shiver of foreboding and reluctantly let him go. This would be a bitter campaign.

The force that rode out of the garrison at London behind Ethelred and Ethelhelm was formidable. Aethelflaed's remaining troops were few, but since the Danes had left only women and children in East Anglia, there was no need for a large defensive *fyrd* at London. All the Danish ships and booty were there in East Anglia, too, but Edward was in Winchester, Alfred was still at Exeter, and Guthfrith remained off the coast of Devon. There was nothing the English could do about the rich horde waiting unattended in Danish Essex. Virtually every able-bodied Dane, now occupied Chester, and Ethelred meant to see them out of the ancient walled fort. "One way or another," he said, his voice grating with unusual harshness. She had seen the same look on her father's face once before, when he marched on London, burning everything in his path.

She watched them from her window until they disappeared into the forested hills as they moved swiftly north. David went with them, under Aethelflaed's orders, to help Ethelred deal with the Welsh, since few of the English could speak Welsh. She silently blessed Asser, who with unwitting foresight, had taught David to speak his mother's language.

It would be a bitter siege. Winter was close upon them and there was only one thing that would dislodge the enemy from the rich cornfields of Mercia. It would be the siege of London all over again.

"See to it," she said sternly to David, "that you are with my husband when they set the torches. See to it that the weak arm suffers no unnecessary burden." But it was not the arm she was worried about.

"I will lay the fires myself," he promised, understanding her unspoken thought. They both knew the promise was empty. Ethelred would never allow another the burden of his own duty.

It must have pained David's heart cruelly when the Danes, whom he helped to starve out of Chester, escaped into Wales the following spring. The messengers rode back weekly with reports. The Danes left Chester early in 894, and having nowhere to go, ravaged Wales from the northern shores to the Bristol Channel. Westward of King Offa's earthwork dyke, built to defend the Mercians from the fierce Welsh hill people, the host vented its fury with the English on their Welsh neighbors. Aethelflaed's rage grew beneath her calm, her own hatred flared, and the look in her husband's eyes when he returned to London briefly midwinter did nothing to allay her anger. What she had feared earlier, she saw now, mixed with a rage deadlier than her own.

Winter came as a relief to the bitterness of summer. Edward went to Chester and stayed there: Ethelhelm took his place at Winchester and Ethelred returned to London. The fighting would stop for a few months and the English forces surrounding Chester would prevent the Danish from moving until spring, though none had expected them to rampage over Wales when they at last fled Chester. As winter laid in upon them, Ethelred grew silent and kept to himself. For a while she forbore to say anything, for the summer's battles had drained him and he needed rest. She left him to his silence for a few weeks, then approached him gently.

"They are starving," he said almost to himself when she questioned him. "At my hands, my own people are starving." The look in his eyes was the same look she had seen in her father's eyes after the siege of London. She put her arms around him and held him, but he pushed her away and would not be comforted.

CHAPTER FIFTEEN

(894)

Spring came, and when the host finished their depredation of Wales, they returned north and stealthily moved eastward into Northumbria, and then returned to East Anglia. They sailed to the estuary of the Thames, to Mersey Isle and made camp for the summer, quietly and without incident.

Aethelflaed lay silently awake by Ethelred's side as he tossed in his sleep. He cried out about the fires and she thought back to London of the fall of 886. Each night she let his dreams go on until she could stand his suffering no more. She felt compelled to wake him and soothe him. If she did not, he soon started out of sleep and wept. She held him and comforted him until he slept again.

They had seen these things before; did one ever grow accustomed to them? So many of the nobility took pleasure in these awful acts, and the peasants had seen so much from both sides their eyes grew dim. Ethelred did not take pleasure in the business of war, despite occasional lapses into rage. He defended his mind against the ravages of war by opposing his feelings with a disciplined will and an inflexible intention to restore English lands to the English. For the most part, will and intention did their work, but every person has a breaking point. The sight of the fields and granaries of Chester in flames, the dread knowledge of the coming winter's toll of starvation and death overcame his will and discipline. His pity could stand no more. He left the garrison only occasionally; he rarely spoke, and though his erect carriage gave no hint of his mind, his eyes looked past everything, seeing little.

David stayed anxiously close to him. "I know well the thoughts he veils from us," he said to Aethelflaed. "I saw them, too. Guilt has stopped his reason, not just because of the happenings at Chester, but because of all that he has ever seen and had to do. All these eat at his mind."

David's figure of speech was far too apt. Memories, long held back, swallow the mind in huge gulps until reason is no longer possible. One feels only anguish and emptiness. But the spirit will sooner or later protect itself and heal. There was naught to do but wait. The time would come when he would not be able to ignore duty; it was too strong a habit with him. The voices would one day die down; he would awake from his long nightmare.

His distress remained the entire winter and lifted occasionally in the presence of Elfwyn, who was as fiercely devoted to her father as Athelstan was now to his aunt. When the countryside warmed, Ethelred sought his wife's counsel as it was time to ride out and inspect his holdings. She searched his eyes for shadows; they were there, but abating. The sorrow would never go, perhaps, but he had come to some agreement with himself. He got to the point quickly. "She is almost six now, and hardy enough for the ride."

Aethelflaed looked at her daughter fondly and it seemed as if she studied a mirror, Elfwyn's features were so much like her own. The child was tall for her age and sturdily built, like Ethelred. Her small face was flushed with excitement at the prospect of attending her father, but Aethelflaed had a twinge of misgiving. Ethelred's duties would be strenuous; overseeing the rebuilding of devastated villages, and supervising the food-rents to see that the King's share was not withheld. And there was the repairing of bridges that never seemed to withstand either the winter or the onslaughts of invasions. Worst of all, the child would see the hunger and privation everywhere she went.

"She must learn of these things sooner or later." Ethelred read her hesitation accurately. "It would comfort me to have her along." She gave in, unable to refuse, but the maternal misgiving remained long after her husband and daughter were gone.

Athelstan sorely missed his playmate, but Edward's unexpected visit brought some brightness to his face that even the prospect of hawking with his aunt in the forest north of the fortress could not surpass. Edward was his father and belonged to him.

Edward's temper had grown formidable over the past year and reports of frequent outbursts reached Aethelflaed from the palace at Winchester. The Queen's fits of depression did nothing to ease Edward's loneliness, and she could only suppose that Ealhswith's attempts to sooth him irritated him beyond endurance. So she was not surprised to see him. He was as proud and angry as the raw edges of a wound, and his eyes held no softness. Even as supper was placed in front of him, she saw the wrinkle of distaste on his brow.

She signaled the thrall to remove the food and ordered him to bring the wine jug instead. There would be time enough for food later. Edward drained the cup impatiently and sat moodily withdrawn.

"Edward," she prompted, "you must go to the children this time. You cannot put it off forever. Athelstan grieves for loneliness of you."

"They are not well?"

"They are in health."

He refilled his cup. "Then I see no need."

"Their bodies are well, but they ache inside." She tapped her chest. Edward stared haughtily at her and she saw the warning in his eyes. She continued relentlessly. "Athelstan has talked of nothing else for days." A slow flush of temper stained Edward's cheekbones and his eyes glinted with anger. "Edytha," she persisted doggedly, "does not know her own father."

Edward stood up, towering, the hotness of anger gone, his face frozen with hostility. Edytha, now turned one year, was the image of her mother and Aethelflaed was well aware that this was the reason for Edward's avoidance of her. She took a deep breath and stared unflinchingly at her brother. This was part of the obligation she owed him, if she had understood her father rightly. Edward needed help in taming the sorrow that festered inside him. She sighed inwardly. Ethelred's brooding sorrow had been hard to bear; her brother's adamantine grief was beyond bearing. She studied his averted face with pity. She would even risk their closeness to rid him of this poisonous melancholy, and unerringly, she chose the most potent weapon at her command.

"Go to the children," she insisted, softly. "If ever you loved their mother, you cannot now turn your back on her children. They are all you have left of her." He was so tightly wrapped in grief compounded with guilt that he could not bear the sight of his own children, though they were fair enough to melt harder hearts than his. Grief could turn good men to ice, and she was resolved to crack this exterior, to force a thaw. "Go to your children," she repeated. Edward angrily smashed the cup on the floor and strode from the room. She watched the wine trickling among the stones of the floor, seeping into the packed earth around the stones, the shards of broken pottery scattered about, then signaled the frightened thrall, huddling in the corner.

"You may bring my supper now," she said calmly. It was not what she had hoped for. Edward's horse clattered in the courtyard. She listened as the pounding hooves receded out of hearing. He did not come back for several days, and when he did, the cold and distant look in his eyes told her that for the present, the closeness she had risked was gone.

Ethelred returned in late summer with a tanned and taller Elfwyn. Aethelflaed hugged her and quickly sent for Athelstan. Ethelred looked refreshed and the haunted look was gone. The work of rebuilding had replace his feelings of guilt with healthier thoughts. There was nothing so effective as work, especially the work of rebuilding to banish sadness.

Watching something take shape under the work of one's own hands drove out all other thoughts. Athelstan appeared, looking morose, but the sight of his cousin brought a half-hearted smile to his face.

Ethelred was surprised to find out that Edward had returned to Winchester. "I should have thought he would stay here." He released her from his embrace and looked at her sharply. "Is something wrong?"

"I'm afraid he went back to escape my meddling." She told him how she had incurred Edward's displeasure.

He put his arm around her shoulders. He understood these two, these different expressions of the same mind. It would secretly distress them both, more than either would admit, to be at odds, though neither would give in easily. They would come to terms soon enough. Occasionally their closeness caused him a twinge of jealousy. Had he not been Alfred's adopted son, he might have resented all these ties of kinship. But he had been a part of this family too long to misunderstand; it was close and tightly bonded. A man of lesser strength of mind than Ethelred's could not have made his own place in this family of intense and strong-willed people. Alfred had sired a brood of eagles, cunning and quick-witted, and Ethelred was gratified to have been accepted in the same spirit. Whatever twinges he had were swallowed up in pride. "Where Edward is concerned you will always meddle. If you were not so even-tempered, he would find it better sport to do the same with you." He frowned slightly. "I cannot scold you for trying to do something. He cannot let his feelings interfere with his duties any more than I can. We must call him back. My messengers tell me the enemy has set sail from Mersey Isle, off Essex. They are headed for the Thames." He kissed her firmly with something of his old spirit. "He will come to his senses."

Before Edward arrived, the Danes sailed into the Thames to the mouth of the Lea. From there they towed their boats upriver and made camp twenty miles north of London. Ethelred met Edward north of the city and together they rode out with the levies to protect the harvest. An engagement was not likely. The defeat at Chester had been too hard on both sides and neither wished to risk their weakened armies. Ethelred's eyes snapped with frustration when he and Edward returned barely ahead of the first frost. They had not been strong enough to force the Danes back to East Anglia, so there they sat, biding their time patiently.

Edward's annoyance with her had subsided somewhat, for he greeted her with shame-faced warmth, though his eyes were wary. She held her peace and ignored his temper, which still flared unpredictably. She chose to act as if nothing had happened and that had the desired effect. He relaxed a little and became slightly more affable, though he still made no attempt to see Athelstan and Edytha. She said nothing further about it, but on no account did she intend to let the matter drop. She would, when the right time arrived, again call it to his attention, and she bent her thoughts to finding a more effective way to do it.

"My Lady," David interrupted her quietly, for he could see she was not aware that he had come in. "Lord Ethelhelm begs permission to speak with you." She nodded and rose to greet Ethelhelm, who was hovering in the doorway with an expression of mild concern on his face.

"Dear friend, it is my pleasure!" She was genuinely glad to see him.

"I have a favor to ask, Lady. My daughter Elfled wishes to visit in London."

Aethelflaed looked at him puzzled. "She is free to come anytime she wishes."

Ethelhelm shifted his feet uncomfortably. "She especially wishes your permission and good will. She fears you are displeased with her." He wiped his brow nervously.

"Sit down, Ethelhelm, you are tired." He dropped heavily to the bench she offered, wincing as he did so. "It is nothing," he said at her look of concern.

"I am not displeased with your daughter," she reassured him. His face relaxed behind the grizzled beard. "We have disagreed though," she added.

His eyes glinted with mixed annoyance and puzzlement. "She is a hot-headed one, more like to her mother than to me." He looked up. "She has not offended you, I hope. If she has, I shall soon settle with her." He looked so grim that she hastened to reassure him.

"No, no," she interposed before he could say more. "Bid her come quickly and assure her of my welcome."

He rose and stomped heavily to the door, pressing each stone underfoot firmly into place. He paused at the doorway. "Do you mind telling an old man what you disagreed about?"

"I believe," she responded, with a show of disinterest, "it had something to do with Edward."

The old man's eyes glinted with amusement. "I thought as much," he said, and left without further comment. Within the week, Elfled presented herself to Aethelflaed.

"Your father is one of our oldest friends. His daughter is most welcome," she said to Elgiva when the girl presented herself. She noticed that the day that Elfled arrived Edward had put off his rough soldier's tunic for a long robe of fine woolen stuff, and an embroidered cloak. She restrained a smile, lest Elfled misinterpret it.

Elfled was now about twenty and was handsome, with softly waving chestnut hair and snapping hazel eyes. Good-looking enough, she decided, to attract some attention from Edward. It was not likely that he would notice the slightly waspish expression about the eyes, nor that her lips were a trifle thin and compressed at the corners. If she helped to lighten Edward's grief and helped to bring him back to himself, Aethelflaed thought, she will find me well pleased.

Elfled stood before her now, looking uncertain. "I thought you might be displeased with me."

"Our disagreements were long ago, and that is past. I am pleased that my brother is obviously cheered by your presence."

"I hope you have no objection, Lady."

"None at all." Aethelflaed put her arm around the girl's shoulder and felt her stiffen slightly; all was not as well as she had hoped. Old grudges were not easily forgotten.

Nevertheless, as Edward's spirits rose and he slowly returned to something of his former disposition, Aethelflaed could see that Elfled was having a good effect on him and warmed toward her.

One thing yet remained and Aethelflaed, having devised her plan, was determined to see it done. The royal grandchildren were outfitted, for she planned to bring them out into public over the Christmas celebrations. Had she not pursued her plan, Elfled might have softened further toward her, but as it was, Elfled left shortly after Christmas, convinced that Edward's sister was set against her. Nothing was further from the truth. What really mattered, Aethelflaed reflected, was that Edward might be induced to let go of his grief.

The feast in the Great Hall of the garrison was in its early stages when Aethelflaed signaled the nurse, who parted the curtain at the entrance to the hall. The children stepped in hesitantly, dressed in their embroidered robes. Tiny Edytha, on her newly discovered legs, her gold-encrusted blue robe trailing behind her, toddled confidently toward her father, though she could not possibly have remembered him. Her golden curls tumbled about her shoulders, her guileless face turned up to meet her father's eyes. Aethelflaed caught her breath. The child was the very image of Ecgwin, and Edward, taken by surprise, was undone. Since he would not go to them, Aethelflaed had brought them to him.

He stared at his daughter, long and hard, and at Athelstan, and the coldness dropped from his eyes. The pain behind the cool mask was bared, and his tears at last flowed. He lifted Edytha to his lap and with his free hand, he reached out to embrace Athelstan, who was standing eloquently silent by his side. Edward wept without shame in front of his family, hugging his children. The King's eyes rested briefly on Aethelflaed's before he rose and raised his wine cup in a toast to his son and grandson, his heirs.

Elfled raised her cup, but her eyes glistened hotly as she met Aethelflaed's glance. She could not bear to be reminded of Edward's dead wife.

There was no dissuading her later, as she angrily prepared to leave. Edward was devoting himself to the children he had neglected and for the moment there was no time for Elfled.

"Don't you see?" Aethelflaed explained urgently. "You have helped him. For the time you must be second. It will change, and he will soon share his time between you and the children."

"You have done this deliberately!" Elfled's voice trembled with rage. "You have never liked me."

Aethelflaed sighed. "Edward has not forgotten, you will see. But if you have forgotten that Athelstan is heir to this kingdom, I have not. He needs the companionship of the man who can show him what it means to be a king. No one," she said slowly, emphasizing each word, "no one in this family puts his own wishes ahead of the needs of the kingdom. If you wish to marry Edward, you will do well to remember that." Elfled's face whitened, and she might have indulged her over-quick tongue had not a glint in Aethelflaed's gray eyes stopped the words in her throat.

Elfled left London without further words, and Edward was too busy with his children to notice. Ethelhelm, correctly guessing the cause of his daughter's sudden departure, apologized to Aethelflaed and grumbled that his daughter had retired to St. Mary's until spring.

It was a relief that Elfled had secluded herself, for Alfred insisted that Aethelflaed and Edward return briefly to Winchester. Ethelhelm and Ethelred stayed in London to keep an eye on the Danes camped on the Lea. There was a special reason for the journey to Winchester. The King had spoken fondly of his own investiture as a child, and now, he explained urgently to Edward and Aethelflaed, it was time for his grandson to be likewise honored, for there must be no mistaking the succession. She wondered idly if he now had come to distrust Ethelwold, but the King indicated nothing.

In early spring of 895 Alfred presented his grandson to Bishop Denewulf in the Minster at Winchester. Athelstan, unblinkingly, received the Bishop's blessing and anointing as the future king. Edward stood beside his son as the King took from Denewulf a sword, its golden, gem-studded hilt glistening with intricate patterns, and laid it on Athelstan's small outstretched hands. From the look in the King's eyes, it was clear that the responsibility he was handing over to his son and grandson was one he no longer wished to bear.

The solitary bell in St. Martin's tower tolled as the ceremony concluded, and they proceeded out of the huge doors and stood for a moment at the stone cross that marked Bishop Swithin's grave. It was too brief a respite from war, for Alfred was already preparing to return to Exeter on the morrow. Aethelflaed glanced quickly toward the tiny windows of St. Mary's, wondering if Elfled, in spite of herself had watched the brightly dressed royal party, their jewels and gold cloisonné sparkling in the sun. Certainly she must understand the intent beneath all that glitter.

The sun shone warmly on the procession as it wended its way back to the palace. Athelstan's face glowed with excitement as the King escorted him through the gates. Edward, jumping lightly from his horse, reached up to hand Aethelflaed down. The firm pressure of his hand as he helped her to dismount, the look in his eyes as he met her eyes when he set her on her feet, assured her of his gratitude. They would never again be divided in spirit.

CHAPTER SIXTEEN

(895)

*T*he London garrison breathed a sigh of relief when the Danes reluctantly broke camp on the Lea and left. They were not induced to do so until autumn in the year 895 when a cunning greater than their own forced them out.

Edward and Ethelred spent the summer pacing the council chamber, unable to prevent the Danish ships from being towed upriver. All the while, English forces were dwindling. Many of the ceorls and thanes had completed their fyrd service and were anxious to go home. Ethelred could not prevent them from returning to their lands and villages. The ceorls must put in crops, and the thanes had to collect their rents and repair bridges and fortifications. The war-weary peasants were bickering among themselves and needed authority and direction. The shire courts were crowded with thievery cases and with food scarce, violations of the royal hunting preserves abounded.

The situation was precarious, for the garrison was now undermanned. In spite of constant war, the city teemed with trade and wealth, more than ever a handsome prize. Summer progressed, the Thames valley renewed itself from war, and the Danes stayed on, twenty miles upstream on the Lea. London was intended by them to be under siege again, this time by the host. Aethelflaed prayed fervently that fate would be on the side of West Saxons and the Mercians.

There was no need for fateful intervention. Divine providence in the form of King Alfred was on their side. She wrote her father, in desperate terms, of the plight of her beloved city. She mused, as she broke the seal on the King's reply, that the affection she bore her adopted city and her husband's sprawling county was so great.

She smoothed the parchment with her fingers. Exeter, the King wrote, was free of invaders at last. Guthfrith of Northumbria had died and his army left Exeter to defend York. Sigfrid, the pirate, heard of Guthfrith's death and sailed back to Northumbria. He was certainly looking to be king. In 893 he had sailed to Ireland, hoping to overcome Sigtryggr, son of Ivarr the Boneless, King of Dublin. He was foolish to think he could do so, Alfred went on, for a man such as Sigtryggr, who had killed his own brother for the throne, would not be easily dislodged. Sigtryggr was not dislodged and angrily set out from Dublin to pursue Sigfrid across northernmost England back to Northumbria. The Northumbrians disliked Sigfrid: his reputation as a pirate had preceded him and he was not warmly received. He then set sail for the coast of Devon, waiting for either Alfred or Guthfrith's men to prevail at Exeter. He would move in on either for the sake of the spoils. Instead, Guthfrith died, his men marched home to defend their leaderless city, and Sigfrid was hot on their heels.

Thus Exeter was at last free of the siege and Alfred would shortly be on his way to London with the levies of Wessex. "Dearest Daughter," he wrote, "your fears for London are well founded, but you must place your faith in God, who has so frequently of late delivered us. Trust," the little strokes that plodded across the parchment assured her, "and you will see. The city shall remain yours." He was undoubtedly right, as so often he was. Tears of relief stung her eyelids; Alfred's optimism and faith pervaded the letter, even seeming to warm her fingers as she held the missive. Her faith was in him, the King, and in her husband and her energetic brother. She might implore the Lord for help, and thank Him heartily when it was forthcoming, but the help he sent invariably arrived in the form of Alfred, Ethelred, or Edward. "Even so," she murmured, "God be thanked for that."

She ordered a Mass of Thanksgiving to be offered at St. Paul's for the relieving of Exeter. Heahstan, aged and weak, lifted his hands high in blessing. It was only as he turned to leave the Sanctuary that Aethelflaed noticed how Werferth stood close by to help support his fellow bishop.

Later she sent for David; she had business with him. He stood, silent and perplexed before her. He had been the Queen's wedding gift to her daughter. He had gone to London with her and served her and her husband with devoted good cheer for nearly nine years. Now she was sitting at her work table, studying him quizzically.

He flushed, aware that she had asked him something.

"I asked if you were happy being a thrall?"

"Who would not be, under your key? You have given me everything."

"But have you not thought to marry and raise your own children, perhaps farm a small plot. And above all to be your own man?"

A sudden fear gripped him but instead of voicing it, he answered, "I have thought of it, my Lady, for such is always a thrall's hope. But to live such a life would be to give up your service. In your service I have been taught to read and write, I am fed and clothed well, and I have done things that many freedmen may yet not do. I still have the half-penny you gave me years ago. I have earned enough to buy my freedom since then."

"Then why do you not buy it?"

"Where would I go?" he said simply. "Where should I be half so free as I am as a thrall in your household?"

His loyalty was no secret to her. He had watched faithfully over her and Ethelred's least need as if his life depended on fulfilling them. He had cared for Ethelred at Chester, bringing him home safely, tending his wounds, guarding him in his sorrow. Aethelflaed had long intended to reward him and Ethelred agreed. David was in all but fact, free, and this last she would give him.

She unrolled the parchment on the table between them. "Read this," she commanded softly. He hesitated before reaching out with trembling fingers to pick up the document. He knew what it would say. A good thrall was rewarded for faithful service with freedom, but freedom was not what he wanted. He read as commanded, then looked up, stricken.

"Where would you have me go?" he asked, trying not to betray his distress. "I do not know farming, and I have always liked my life here."

"But you are not free! Does that not matter?"

He sighed heavily. Not after all these years of belonging to and being part of a family such as this could he leave, not even for the sake of a freedom he had never known. "Not as much as you might think," he replied finally. "I would not be truly free without a family or a Lord. A free wanderer is a dreadful, sorry man in this world. No one is more alone than one who has lost his Lord."

She looked at him in surprise. She had not realized what he had supposed her to be doing. "David, I shall not free you to be alone. Read on!" She tapped the parchment, and he forced his eyes back to it, hearing her next words as if from a great distance. "You are free. This is your Writ of Manumission, but you are released into free service under my own Lordship. You will be my own steward and you will see to my household, though you will now see to the freedmen as well as the thralls. You will have lands of your own, which you may rent out if you wish. I am your Lord now, not your thrall master, and you shall swear fealty to me as does any freedman to his Lord."

He was stunned, reading the document again and again, and not until the next day, when Ethelred witnessed and attested to the Writ with his own hand, and Wulfsy stood beside him as he gave his solemn oath of fealty to his Lord and protector, Lady Aethelflaed of London, did he realize what had happened to him.

The King arrived in London with Ealdorman Ethelnoth of Somerset and promptly called for Ethelred, Edward, and Aethelflaed to attend him in council chambers. "I do not know," he began without preface, "who Guthfrith's successor will be. For the moment, Archbishop Wulfhere controls the city of York and wields great influence. And," the King added, gazing with bland significance at Edward, who was already beginning to fume, "he is greatly respected here."

That was certainly true. Archbishop Wulfhere had lived in Mercia for a while under the protection of King Burhred. Egbert, who was then the Danish-appointed King of York, had been driven out by the Northumbrians and he and his Archbishop had sought shelter in Burhred's Mercia. That had been some twenty-three years ago. Those had been turbulent times in Northumbria, and Wulfhere had been forced to make many compromises to keep his great See of York going in spite of the Vikings. Added to this was the threat from the Scandinavian Vikings.

In those days the brothers Ivarr the Boneless and Halfdan had divided England between them. Halfdan fought against King Aethelred and his younger brother, Alfred. Ivarr rampaged over Ireland. Then in 894 he came to England and overthrew Northumbria in a fierce battle at York. He feared no Gods but his own, which he demonstrated by sacrificing Aella, King of Northumbria to the pagan God *Odinn.* He then set himself up as King of York. When he died, his brother Halfdan stepped in and claimed Northumbria. He parceled out land to his men, who took quickly to farming: still he was not satisfied. He wished for war, his men wished to farm in peace. When Halfdan neglected the fields of Northumbria, letting the crops rot for the sake of fighting, they drove him out. He was finally slain by his Norwegian enemies.

Wulfhere survived all this, thinking only of the safety of his church. For that Alfred respected and admired him.

In spite of Alfred's glance, Edward burst out, "But Wulfhere buried Guthfrith in York Minster!"

"So he did," returned Alfred mildly.

"But he was an oath breaker!"

"We saw him as such. But he was baptized and a king. As far as I know, he never interfered with the Church. He must have appeared to his Archbishop to be a devout believer." Edward glowered. "I am not here," Alfred continued, "to concern myself with Guthfrith's worth. I am concerned about a greater necessity. Northumbria is without a leader other than Wulfhere, and he is, perhaps, a friend. He was welcomed in Mercia with respect and honor. We do not wish him to turn to Sigtryggr Ivarsson in Dublin for friendship. An alliance of Dublin and York must not be allowed to happen. Let us not worry about the purity of Guthfrith's faith, nor about the loyalty of the Archbishop to his anointed king."

Edward subsided, sufficiently rebuked. Aethelflaed had secretly agreed with Edward, but said instead, "What do you think of doing to prevent this alliance?"

Alfred looked at Ethelnoth. "That is why I have brought the Ealdorman with me. He knows many Northumbrians from the recent campaigns. He will go to York and discuss with Wulfhere a treaty to end the battles with us. Pleymund has spoken to me his sorrow that the great Sees of York and Canterbury are separated by warring leaders. And," he added, "it grieves me that two great men of God must be separated by their loyalties to their own kings."

Edward agreed. "I dearly hope it may work well for all of us. But I fear it may not."

A wry smile curled Alfred's lips. "I fear it may not either, and no doubt we will both be right on that. But Sigfrid is sailing north and we must do what we can before he reaches York."

Ethelnoth left for York the next day; Alfred, without further delay, addressed himself to the Danes camped on the Lea. He set his men out to guard the harvest, and took a position on the Lea downstream of the Danish camp. Quickly, he threw a dam across the river, and when that was up, the levies crossed the dam and built small forts on either side of the river at the ends of the dam.

Edward shook his head in admiration. Aethelflaed, noting the thoughtful look on her husband's face, observed, "He learns from the enemy, does he not? We have built only a few, and only when we are threatened."

"Wherever they settle," Ethelred picked up her train of thought, "they build a fortress as a matter of course. Your father this time has used their own plan against them."

The trapped Danes left quickly, for their position was now hazardous. They fled westward across the midlands to the Severn, abandoning their ships to Alfred, who took great interest in them. The Danes wintered at Bridgnorth, high on its rock above the river.

Ethelred grumbled wearily. He had hoped to spend the winter at home in London. Instead he and Edward followed the Danes to Bridgnorth and surrounded the village and kept an eye on the movements of the host.

In spring, Ethelnoth returned, having spent most of the winter trying to convince the Northumbrians of the advantages of peace. He had almost convinced Wulfhere, but fate intervened. Before Ethelnoth could get a formal agreement, Wulfhere died. The great See was left without a leader and the city was left without governance. Sigfrid was waiting. With Wulfhere's death, opposition to Sigfrid's rule crumbled, and very shortly thereafter, the York mint issued a silver penny bearing the inscription *SIEFREDUS REX*.

Ethelnoth brought a handful of these with him and dumped them, with great disgust, on the table in front of the King. "I tried to show him it was better to treat with us than to fight with us. He begged me to stay to consider the matter further. I don't believe he ever intended to consider a treaty at all."

"Then he did not have the Church's blessing on his crowning?"

"The Archbishop was dead. Sigfrid would not be king otherwise."

"Has he chosen his new Archbishop?"

"No." Ethelnoth stroked his beard thoughtfully. "Though I've no doubt it will be Bishop Ethelbald, if he does not object to Sigfrid's pirate ways. Mark you well," he said darkly, "Sigfrid is no more a king than I am. He will remain a pirate and will not be content to be only a king."

"Ah!" Alfred leaned forward, interested. "Did you see anything while you were there?"

"Nothing, my Lord. I tried, but Sigfrid kept me under close watch, so I have no doubt he had plans. That may be why he refused to treat with us."

It was not until summer that the Danes camped at Bridgnorth gave up. Some went back to East Anglia or Northumbria, some went back to Danish Mercia, and some, perhaps fearing the plagues and murrains that had fallen on man and beast alike for the past three years, went overseas to Frankia. London received the news thankfully and Edward and Ethelred returned home safely.

Alfred returned to Winchester, taking Werferth with him. He was devoting more and more of his time to writing. It was, this time, an extremely brief respite. The Northumbrian pirate, as Ethelnoth predicted, had plans; Sigfrid and the East Anglian Danes together took to their ships and began raiding off the coast of Wessex.

The Mercian levies brought one bit of welcome news from the midlands. It had come by way of Irish settlers moving into the area in their desperate attempts to get away from their Norse rulers: Sigtryggr Ivarsson, who had come to the throne of Dublin by fratricide, was murdered by other Norsemen. With Sigtryggr's death, uprisings abounded in Ireland. It was a happy stroke of fortune that kept the Irish Norse boiling amongst themselves, for it appeared that the West Saxons must now deal with *SIEFREDUS REX,* the pirate king of Northumbria.

Alfred put aside his poems and meditations long enough to call Edward to Winchester. When Edward returned to London, he was in high spirits and called Aethelflaed to his chambers to show her the sketches and drawings he had brought back with him.

"He is building ships!" He pointed to a rough sketch that the King had sent with him. "They are twice as large as any the Danish have."

It was a stroke of genius. If they were not entirely successful, they were effective enough to persuade Sigfrid to retire to York to think of other things for a while. Six of the Northumbrian and East Anglian ships sailed to the Isle of Wight and wreaked havoc there, and from Wight, they raided the coast of Devon, doing more damage. Alfred ordered nine of his new ships to blockade the Isle of Wight from the seaward side to prevent the Danes from escaping. Several of Alfred's ships ran aground: the sixty-oar ships were difficult to handle and the Frisian and Saxon sailors were not used to the clumsy size of the ships.

In spite of the difficulties, only a few of the Danish ships escaped, but they were so crippled from their encounter with Alfred's warships that they could not row past the Sussex coast. The tide dragged heavily at them and brought them to shore. One of them barely managed to escape back to East Anglia. Two of the ships were seized at the entrance to the estuary and the men on board were killed. Some beached at Poole Harbor and the men went off inland. They were rounded up, taken prisoner and sent to Winchester.

It was a good beginning and Edward later wrote her an account of the events. It was just as well, she later told Ethelred, that one of the ships had escaped. The wounded Danes in their crippled dragon-prow would have some dire warnings about sending men against the powerful king of the West Saxons.

The coastal waters grew quiet, Alfred went back to his writing and meditating, and, as Edward noted with satisfaction toward the end of his letter, the captives who had been sent to Winchester were summarily hung by the King: another sign to the pirate king that the King of Wessex would not deal gently with one of Sigfrid's ilk.

CHAPTER SEVENTEEN

(898)

"My Lord Archbishop!" Aethelflaed extended both hands to Pleymund, whose arrival they had all awaited. He turned to the others in the council chamber: Heahstan, Werferth, Wulfsy, and Ethelnoth, greeting them and calling each by name. A roaring fire had been built in the fireplace and Aethelflaed found it stifling. In spite of the heat Heahstan was shivering.

Pleymund removed his long cape, lightly shaking snow from the bottom of it. "Now, Aethelflaed," he said, rubbing his hands, still stiff from the outdoor chill, "What is this letter you spoke of with such mystery? It is not the King's habit to be obscure."

"I did not mean to let you think so. He has a request that concerns all of you, including," she nodded at Ethelnoth, "the Ealdorman." Pleymund studied Ethelnoth attentively, knowing of his efforts to treat with Sigfrid. "Sigfrid, until lately our enemy," she continued, her voice heavy with sarcasm, "has now seen fit to approach us for a favor. He requests that his Archbishop, Ethelbald, be consecrated in London." Pleymund nodded assent. "I would consider it fitting," she went on, "that the new Archbishop of York be consecrated by yourself, Heahstan, and Werferth."

Pleymund cleared his throat, repressing the smile that quivered at the corners of his mouth. "Lady Aethelflaed, King Sigfrid's request is entirely proper and shows him to be a man with great respect for the Church."

"Indeed," she replied, somewhat haughtily. She caught Werferth's eye and her face relaxed into a smile. "Your feelings, my Lord Archbishop, are as they ought to be. However I suspect that Sigfrid fears for the stability of his throne if his Archbishop is not properly anointed."

"I must agree with you, Aethelflaed, but under the circumstances, it would be far better to consecrate Ethelbald here, with the proper authority and conditions than to allow the Church of Northumbria to be under questionable leadership."

She laughed, somewhat ruefully. "You are always right. It is of course as you say. Sigfrid's worth is not in question." She looked around the table at the four ecclesiastics and the Ealdorman of Somerset. "I have called you here to lay the matter before you. I shall abide by whatever you decide, and will help with whatever plans you make. I am myself in favor of the matter, though not for the same reasons as yourselves. I wish to know more of Ethelbald and what nature of man he is, as I assume you are also. Above all, I wish to know if he would choose peace between us. My father has asked Ethelnoth to carry our consent to Northumbria and to give Ethelbald safe passage on his journey to London. The Ealdorman is also a clever soldier; his information on the state of the kingdom that he sees there will be useful. I must be about other matters and I leave the health of the Church to you."

Pleymund turned to Ethelnoth. "Are you willing to take this upon yourself?" Ethelnoth waved his hand impatiently, as if he were ready to leave on the instant. "You know," Pleymund continued, "that perhaps Sigfrid may have other plans for you? He may hope instead to gain information from you. Not, of course," he added blandly, "that we would accuse him of dishonorable behavior. But, it is always better to careful."

"I understand you well, my Lord. I have the same thoughts myself." Ethelnoth smiled wryly. "You are a fighting man yourself and you would also like to know what fills Sigfrid's thoughts."

Since it was agreed, Ethelnoth begged leave to prepare for his journey north. Aethelflaed left the room with him. "How does my father?" she asked when they were alone.

"He is an old man, Lady and he has never been free of complaints," was Ethelnoth's blunt reply.

She took a deep breath. "He is not well, then?"

"No, but he does not complain. He writes and he prays." His eyes were full of concern. "I cannot say how long he has, for he grows old quickly and one can see a longing in his eyes. It would be well if you kept yourself in readiness."

She gave him her hand. "Ethelnoth, one could not ask for a truer friend. You tell me only what I have seen for myself, and what I already believe to be the truth of the matter. Godspeed you on this journey. Be wary of Sigfrid, and send us the messages we have agreed upon."

She hoped the negotiations would move quickly, for Heahstan was growing ill rapidly. When Ethelnoth's messages arrived, she learned that Sigfrid had not changed his vacillating ways. One day he would be resolved to send Ethelbald to London, the next day, he would not. There was no apparent reason for his whimsy.

In the end, it did not matter, for Heahstan was not destined to see the Archbishop anointed. In late spring he took to his pallet with a hacking cough that grew rapidly worse. When she went to visit him, she was shocked. Werferth had called the ageing Wulfsy to him also that he might lay hands on him and bless him as his successor. Wulfsy shook his head sadly. "It is a mistake, my Lord. I shall not be long in following him."

Wulfsy retired to prepare himself with prayer and fasting for the honor which he felt was being bestowed on the wrong person. He called to him a young monk, faithful and devout, and an excellent scholar. "My dear Theodred," he said wearily to the young man, "I can be of use in this high office for whatever small time remains to me only if I have your service."

"My life is yours, my Lord Bishop."

"Then you will prepare yourself for Holy Orders. You will begin by serving as my Mass-priest and learning everything you can about this See in the next six months. You may not have more time that that."

"My Lord Bishop...." Wulfsy cut him off with a weary wave of his hand. "I do not have the time. I am commanded by both King and Archbishop to assume a position for which I feel not the slightest qualification. You are under vows of obedience, even as I am. You must do as I ask," his voice was now urgent, "for the time is short."

Aethelflaed had cause to be grateful to Wulfsy, though she was not to know to what extent until after he died. During the few months that he was Bishop of London, he did indeed prepare for the future. With uncommon and deliberate foresight, he had chosen a man ideally suited to be mentor to a future king.

Heahstan opened his eyes briefly as Werferth read the last rites over him, and the old Bishop's eyes closed forever on the harshness of life. She wept as Heahstan's features relaxed into the tranquility of death.

She felt his loss keenly. Wulfsy's young assistant, Theodred, now took Heahstan's place as she continued her duties in the borough courts. Ethelred offered silent support, since the shire and borough courts were filled, but he had spring duties to attend to and could not spend the time in London.

Theodred was quick and intelligent and listened quietly to her with understanding as she remembered aloud to him Heahstan's wisdom. Heahstan had helped minister to the problems of the city, pondering gravely each complaint that was presented. His advice was always a mixture of mercy and justice that tempered the harshness of the law with his own compassion. It would not be easy to replace such a man.

"I hope," she said, looking at Theodred's youthful face, "that you and Lord Wulfsy can bring the same manner of understanding to the people. We are sorely in need of more than the letter of the law, for in such times as these, the letter of the law does not suffice."

She mentioned Theodred's age to Wulfsy. She did not object to it, but she feared he might be lacking in experience.

"That he might be," Wulfsy agreed, "though he will not be for long. It is for that reason that I sent him with you in my place."

"I do believe you had some other thoughts when you sent him along." She eyed him quizzically.

He inclined his head, smiling. "I did indeed, my Lady. I shall speak it straight forth. It is not practical for an old man, such as myself, to prepare for a See I shall not live long enough to serve. I should not have accepted had I not been ordered to do otherwise. This young man will serve you well." He paused, thinking. "He will have an excellent example in the Bishop of Worcester."

"Most certainly," she agreed. "But Werferth has gone to Winchester to assist the King. Athelstan is without a tutor, now. Do you have something in mind?" She raised an eyebrow.

Wulfsy rose painfully. "I had hoped you would ask. It would be a good thing for a future king to know his bishops well as do you and your father."

"Then it is settled. I trust your judgment." The young heir's education had long since begun. He could read and write his own language, and Werferth had started him on Latin, but there were many other things that Athelstan would need to know.

She had hoped that Athelstan could have spent more time with the King, for his very companionship was instructive. But the King was wrapped up in his writing and translating; Boethius presently occupied his thoughts. *The Consolation of Philosophy* suited him well, for though he had not suffered the same reverses of fortune that the great Roman had, he had certainly been embattled enough during his life to understand that worldly fame could hang on trivia, and a man could be thrown into despair by events beyond his control. It was best to keep the affairs of the world in perspective. Boethius eased his mind and provided him with landscapes of meditation wherein he could wander to his heart's content. Where he presently wandered, though, a small boy could not easily follow.

Wulfsy interrupted her thoughts. "May I suggest that your daughter's lessons be joined with Athelstan's, that when the time comes, they may both understand beyond doubt in whom the overlordship resides."

She smiled ruefully, knowing this to be a wise suggestion. "You are a worthy successor to Heahstan, and it is my wish that your premonitions about yourself are wasted. I will pray that your wisdom and counsel will be ours for many years to come."

He smiled his thanks but said nothing, and to her sorrow, he was right. He was not to see another year. Theodred, by Christmas, occupied the Bishop's chair at London. True to the old Bishop's predictions, he had learned quickly and well, and she knew that Athelstan would prosper under his tutelage.

About Elfwyn she had second thoughts, for the girl, now ten years old, was strong-willed. She trusted that Theodred would find the right way to instill in her the understanding that her younger cousin, whom she treated with some disdain, would one day claim her fealty, and not the other way around.

Before Wulfsy fared forth on his last journey, another trusted soul left. When David brought her the sealed parchment, she knew a moment's dread, for Ethelnoth's warning hung in her mind. She broke the seal with trembling fingers and saw, with great relief, the King's own hand. The message was grief-laden. Ethelhelm of Wiltshire, the King's dear friend, was dead. Alfred mused sadly on the loss, and she read in the grief-stricken words, a hidden longing for his own death. Ah, she thought, that was the why of the Boethius; the King read and translated to prepare his own soul, for he was weary of the world and its bitter struggle. A warm place and blessed conversation with ancient sages, that was all he craved.

She turned back to the letter. Ethelhelm's daughter was alone, without relatives, without protection. She had inherited Ethelhelm's vast estates and fortune and there were many who were all too willing to relieve her of it, if not by marriage, then by other means, regardless of the law. Marriage offers she had aplenty, and many of them from men of good position. She would have none. Aethelflaed smiled. Of course she would have none. She had never loved any but Edward. Elfled was, the King wrote, distracted and beset by those who were too interested in her large inheritance. Would Aethelflaed oblige her father, and for the sake of their dear friend, Ethelhelm, receive his daughter under her protection at London?

"Send her to me," she said to David. "I trust the King felt no need to wait upon my consent, for he has it."

David bowed, his smile stretched from ear to ear. "Indeed not. The Ealdorman's daughter was sent by the King with his letter."

When Elfled was brought to her, she reached out and took the girl's hand in both her own. "Elfled, you are welcome to my household. Your father has done us great service and we owe him much. For his sake, let us be friends." She could see the loss of her father grieved Elfled greatly.

Elfled's eyes met her briefly and Aethelflaed saw that she wished to accept the offer. "I have great need of your protection, Lady Aethelflaed." She faltered but went on, "I am in your debt."

It was just as well she had come to London. The King seemed not to have considered any of Elfled's suitors to be a good match for his friend's daughter. Perhaps the King might be considering his own son as the proper match? She glanced thoughtfully at Elfled, who had barely touched the food that David had brought for her. She possessed a spirit almost as fierce as Edward's, and flinching inwardly, Aethelflaed imagined that any disagreement between two such natures would be marvelous to behold.

Edward was tough and resilient and was daily becoming more imperious. He had not inherited Alfred's slenderness. He was heavier and at least half a head taller than his father. His physical presence alone was commanding, and if that did not suffice, the sternness of his face would draw attention to himself. It was not that he tried to draw attention to himself. If anything he was taciturn in the presence of others, but he was demanding and forceful. It would take courage to stand up to him.

She smiled at Elfled, seeing her in a new light. "Come, if you are finished I will take you to your chambers. You are surely tired and wish to rest."

"I would be grateful, Lady, if you would excuse me this evening. I would like to rest."

"No." Aethelflaed's tone was firm. "I shall not excuse you, mourning or no. I shall expect you in the Great Hall. You may come in mourning garb, but we will go down together."

Aethelflaed ignored her protests. Edward was back, though Elfled did not know it. If this was the King's judgment, she was not unwilling to give the matter some attention.

CHAPTER EIGHTEEN

(899)

*T*he track wound southward through the forest and up the back of the escarpment. They rode slowly along the twisting path. It was near sundown when they reached the edge of the village, where they stopped and looked up at the palisaded wall of the burh, looming darkly over them in the lengthening shadows. Instead of entering the north gate, they rode around the banked earth at the foot of the palisade on the western spur of the hill. In the fading sunlight, the Vale of Blackmoor spread itself more than seven-hundred feet below them in the chill October dusk, the evening mists already collecting in the hollows beneath the spur.

Aethelflaed had brought with her to Shaftesbury only one thane, Eadred, one of Ethelred's best men. She called to the guard and when the heavy wooden doors swung open, Eadred dismounted and led their horses into the village.

"Tell the Abbess," she said to the gatekeeper, "that her sister is here. I have come from King Edward."

The man stepped backward, his face showing his dismay. "King Alfred is dead, then?"

"Four days ago," she replied, "and his son Edward, by the will of the Witan, is King."

Alfred's health had failed rapidly throughout the past year, and though they lived in constant expectation of his death, the blow fell heavily when it came. She had packed Athelstan quickly to Winchester, leaving Ethelred and Elfwyn in London. She was none too soon, for it was only two days after her arrival that Alfred died, regretting sadly that his work was not yet over.

When the King saw Edward silent and pale, kneeling at his bedside with his arm clasped around his son, Athelstan, he rallied enough to stretch out a weak hand to bless them, touching first his son's head and then his grandson's. Athelstan looked into his grandfather's clouded eyes, his own young face stricken with bewilderment. Edward bowed his head and took his father's hand firmly in his own. There it stayed while Denewulf chanted Last Rites over the King, and there it stayed throughout the night until early the next morning.

It was October the twenty-sixth and the air was chilly, the dawn, grey. Alfred opened his eyes for the last time and smiled upon his weeping wife, who like Edward, had not left him. She bent over him and kissed him good-bye. He had not the strength to speak to his son, but Edward could see, as he looked into his father's eyes for the last time, that the old King was well content with his son.

Ealhswith, regarding her son through eyes blurred with gathering tears, saw the look on Edward's face and remembered as if it had been only yesterday, the expression she saw there, so like Alfred's. She saw the invisible burden descend upon Edward as it had upon his father. She understood the changes that were even now working in his soul.

Aethelflaed found them there after Mass. Denewulf had already informed her of the King's death. Edward was unaware of her presence until she knelt before him and he looked up blankly and rose to his feet. He held out his hands to draw her to her feet, but instead she laid her hands in his in the gesture of fealty. His blank look faded as he realized what she was doing. "You are the first," he whispered, "and by God, the most important. I cannot carry out the King's will without your help."

"The Witan is meeting now and will give you their decision shortly. You must go make yourself ready for them." She kissed her mother and smoothed her hair, but did not stay. She had bidden the King goodbye the night before; she would remember him as he was in life, not as he lay in death. Father and daughter had looked wordlessly at each other, both conscious of how much was left unsaid, and would remain unsaid forever.

The will of the Witan was swiftly made known and came as a surprise to one person only. Ethelwold's face paled first with shock, then reddened with anger. He remained in his own quarters until the reading of Alfred's will the following day, and was the last to swear fealty to Edward. It was done unwillingly, and while Edward's face showed nothing as he looked down at the kneeling Ethelwold, Aethelflaed saw suspicion in her brother's icy blue eyes.

Other than the knowing look in his eyes, Edward accepted his cousin's pledge in the same manner that he had accepted pledges from his friends. Aethelflaed saw the old Edward, the hot-heading Atheling, quickly being submerged in the new role of Edward the King. She saw also the closed look on her cousin's face and the cool disinterest displayed by her brother and knew at once that the Witan had not really settled the matter. Edward and Ethelwold, both sons of illustrious kings, would have it out in their own good time.

Ethelred arrived from London with Elfwyn for the reading of the will. There were no surprises, for Alfred had informed everyone long since of their portions. Edward received most of the King's private lands as well as all of the charter lands, though Alfred wished the village and community at Cheddar choose their overlord for themselves. All of Alfred's children received portions of the lands passed down from Ethelwulf, but Alfred pointed out in his will that Ethelwulf had left only to the spear-half of the family and not to the spindle-half. *Therefore,* Alfred continued, *if I have given anything to the spindle-half of what he, Ethelwulf acquired, then let my kinsmen redeem it if they wish to have it in their lifetime; otherwise it will go, after the female inheritors, to those begotten of the male line, as Ethelwulf dictated in his will.* Alfred bequeathed to male and female heirs both, for, he asserted, *I may leave the properties however I wish.* If those of the male line wished to take possession of the property sooner than the death of the holder, they must pay for it. It was a wise provision. There were some who would not leave the female heirs in peace about their portions, nor would they hesitate to divest them of it by force.

Ethelwold received properties; the manors at Godalming, Guildford, and Steyning, and all the lands that went with them. Aethelflaed glanced at her cousin, but the gift of these excellent properties did not appear to placate him.

Certain monies were apportioned among Alfred's children, Edward and Ethelweard receiving five hundred pounds each, and Aethelflaed and her sisters and mother each receiving one hundred pounds. All of the ealdormen received one hundred gold mancuses each and Ethelred, in addition, received a sword of Alfred's worth one hundred and twenty gold mancuses. Aethelflaed caught her breath, for the sword, with it worked-gold hilt and jeweled inlay, was a magnificent gift, one that proclaimed to all present the high regard which Alfred bore his son-in-law.

When the reading was over, Aethelflaed and Ethelred retired to Edward's chambers as he had requested. Edward called a steward waiting by the door and sent him for food, since it was nigh onto afternoon and none of them had eaten. He sat silently, and ate silently when the food was placed in front of him. When he finished he turned to Aethelflaed and said, "Sister, I would that you deliver the news of the King's death and will to Elgiva yourself, since she could not be with us." She was surprised but consented. "Arrange with her for Edytha's future," he went on.

"I hope that you do not bind her to the Abbey because of her mother's death," she replied, after thinking about it. His tired face looked grim and she thought for a moment that she had offended him. "I'm sorry," she said simply.

"No cause, Ae'lflaed," he replied, patting her hand awkwardly. "It was a just observation." He rubbed his eyes wearily. "No, I see in Edytha the same unworldliness that her mother had. Abbey life may suit her. Speak to Elgiva about her and send Edytha to her if she so wills. Let Elgiva make the decision. She will know if it is ordained. But I dare not deprive you of my son," he continued thoughtfully. "His education is still in your hands and Ethelred's. He must stay with you as long as you see fit."

Athelstan had become to her as the son she had lost in Worcester. She had raised him and Edytha as her own children. They knew Edward was their father, but they stood greatly in awe of him, looking more on Ethelred as their father.

"He must learn with all speed," said Edward, interrupting her thoughts, "and he must come to know the people of Mercia."

"When he is old enough to fight, he will wish to go with you."

Edward shrugged impatiently. "That cannot be often. He must go with Ethelred or yourself. Mercia must come to accept him as their own, and they will not do so unless they see him as an heir to Ethelred and yourself."

"The Mercians have cause to be grateful to you, Edward," Ethelred reminded him. "Chester. There was Chester, and Bridgnorth, and Buttington. These past ten years, Alfred has spent much time in Wessex, but you have devoted yourself to the defense of Mercia."

"Nevertheless," Edward's voice was firm, "I will be seen as the King of Wessex. Athelstan must be shown to Mercia as one of their own. There must be no misunderstanding when the time comes."

Aethelflaed and Ethelred glanced quickly at each other, but Edward was absorbed in his own thoughts.

"Mercia will be brought again under English rule, as will Northumbria. If we cannot drive the Vikings out, then they must be brought to submit to English rule."

She stared at her brother. His ambitions, she was certain, exceeded Alfred's. To Alfred, "all England" had not included Northumbria. England was too open to invasion. Unless it could be united under a single rule, there would be no peace or security.

"What of Elfwyn?" Edward suddenly asked.

She brought her mind back. "Theodred instructs her. She does not consider herself the heir to Mercia."

"Perhaps not," Edward responded, "but the Mercians will."

She turned to her husband, seeking his feelings. He was silent for a long time before answering the unasked question. Edward's eyes were carefully blank, and Aethelflaed's face reflected her inner struggle with the unhappy fact that she must disinherit her daughter if she were to remain loyal to her brother. She and Ethelred had known all along that this moment would come.

It was clear to Aethelflaed that whether she liked it or not, she must begin to favor Athelstan as he approached manhood over Elfwyn so that he would be associated with the overlordship.

"There is no other way," Ethelred finally said aloud. "We cannot risk quarreling among ourselves. It was settled years ago that the thrones of Wessex and Mercia must be united. We cannot fight among ourselves and fight the host as well. She will understand, I'm sure. She would not oppose us," he assured Edward. It did not cross their minds, as it had Edward's that Elfwyn might see the matter differently.

Aethelflaed saw the fatigue and grief on Edward's face and realized the loneliness he would experience without Alfred's guiding hand in his life. He had no family other than themselves to support him now. In empathy, she transferred Edward's plight to herself: one day Ethelred would be gone, and she would be alone. Somehow she had refused to believe that anything would overcome him, an injury perhaps, but never death. She could not at the moment imagine how she would ever live without him.

As she lay beside him later in the darkness of their chamber, thinking of the shortness of their lives, she drew a long shuddering breath. Ethelred, hearing and guessing her thoughts, reached out in the dark and drew her close, stroking her hair and comforting her in the way he knew best. They fell asleep with their arms locked around each other.

Now inside the palisade at Shaftesbury, she and Eadred stood a moment, listening to the thud of the bolt sliding across the heavy wood of the door. She left Eadred at the traveler's quarters and went to Elgiva's chambers. She sat down at a heavy oaken table near the fire and yawned. "Can you bring me some supper? I have ridden all day with little to eat," she said to the nun who had greeted her at the door. The nun glided quietly away.

Aethelflaed removed her mantle, sat down at the table, and put her head down on her arms. A few days in this quiet place atop its hill, isolated from the world, would refresh her. Contemplating the prospect, she drifted into sleep.

When she awoke it was dark. A single candle guttered in a wall sconce and a fire had been kindled in the hearth. She stared at the shadows flickering against the dark stone walls, struggling against fatigue to recall her surroundings.

"You have come to tell me that the King, our father, is dead." The words drifted into her sleep-laden mind, but Elgiva's voice was quiet and full of acceptance. Her mind cleared abruptly and she sat up. The Abbess, seated at the other end of the table, signaled the nun, who disappeared briefly and returned with the food Aethelflaed had requested several hours earlier. Aethelflaed rubbed her neck to bring the circulation back and watched the nun as she set the wooden dishes on the table in front of her. She nodded wordlessly in thanks, and ate silently.

"My dearest Elgiva, she said, pushing the plate away from her when she had finished, "I come here on matters other than our father's death. Edward wishes Edytha to be given into your hands for training. Is this agreeable with you?"

"Only if he is not trying to escape Ecgwin's image."

"No," Aethelflaed responded, thoughtfully. "I am certain he is not. That truly is behind him."

"Then send her to me and we will see if she is called to this life." Elgiva studied her quietly for a moment. "And what other matter?"

"Myself. I am tired of the world for the moment. I have been too burdened and Edward expects so much of me, much more than before. I need to refresh myself."

"You shall do so." Elgiva leaned forward. "I have expected you, for I know your duties are heavy." Her eyes showed her concern and the gaze she turned on her sister held hints of the future. "Your hardest tasks are ahead of you." Aethelflaed started uneasily. "No," Elgiva reassured her, "I have not inherited the Queen's fancy for signs and omens. But your fate now comes full circle."

"But Edward and Ethelred...."

Elgiva waved her hand impatiently. "Athelstan will be in your charge, will he not? Edward will not take the boy back?" Aethelflaed shook her head. "He is wise. You will raise him better than Edward could. Our brother has not inherited his father's level-headedness."

"He will have to learn," replied Aethelflaed, wearily.

"No, he will not have to learn. He has you. He will fight. That is his nature and his first love. Mark me well, you will plan and you will even fight when the need arises."

"Elgiva, you confront me with burdens I am not yet prepared for. I came here to refresh myself and you are already placing new weights on my shoulders."

"You shall rest, but you cannot expect to find escape."

"Where else if not here?"

Elgiva laughed aloud, then checked herself. "You may escape the world and its problems for a little while here. You have left all your cares at the gate outside and they will still be there when you are ready to take them up again. But you have brought yourself in with you. That is where your hardships begin. In here the busyness of the world no longer stands between yourself and God. Here you can see yourself just as you are. That is why so many cannot tolerate this life. It is very hard on the spirit. It is easier to dissipate one's energies and discontents in battles and intrigues."

Aethelflaed eyed her sister with some surprise. Elgiva ran her own affairs with little interference from anyone. She held the power of Absolution over men whose wealth was great. Yet their wealth did not surpass the Abbey's holdings. The Abbess ruled the village, which was in her overlordship, controlled its markets and received its food rents owed to the King, now her brother, the same duties as any thane or bishop.

However there was no personal wealth displayed here. Elgiva shunned such pretensions, for unlike many well-born ladies, she had taken her vows because she believed this to be her true calling.

"Come," said Elgiva, "you are too tired to talk. You must rest."

The wooden cot was narrow and hard, but the straw pallet on it was fresh and sweet-smelling. Elgiva had chosen a small cell for her this time, since Aethelflaed wished to stay apart. She pulled her woolen mantle over her and prepared her mind for sleep, which, tired as she was, should have come quickly. Instead her eyes remained obstinately open. "Live as one of my nuns for a week," Elgiva had said, throwing out a gentle challenge. "Forget you are the Lady of London for a while and live the life of my Abbey and my village." Aethelflaed inhaled deeply and drifted slowly into fitful sleep.

At dawn she awoke for Matins. The priest arrived as soon as Matins ended and chanted Mass. After the morning Offices she had planned on going down the steep road to the village, to see the market, but fate intervened. She returned to Elgiva's chambers to prepare for her outing, and went in without knocking, as the nun at the door signaled her to do, and found Eadred in earnest conversation with the Abbess. They both looked up as she entered, their faces somber. She stopped abruptly inside the door and waited; something was dreadfully amiss. Eadred jumped to his feet, his agitation showing in tense movements as he crossed the space between them.

"My Lady," he exclaimed, breathless with anger, "Ethelwold has challenged King Edward. He has captured the manor at Wimborne and all who live in it."

"Our cousin Ethelwold has also," said Elgiva, her voice edged with ice, "abducted a professed nun and holds her prisoner there." The Abbess studied Aethelflaed's face for she realized her sister was controlling her anger with great difficulty.

"I am not surprised," Aethelflaed said, when she had regained her composure. "He has ever envied Edward's position and was certain that the Witan would choose him!" She turned to Eadred. "My brother?"

"Has gone to Badbury," finished Eadred.

She sighed. There was to be no week of rest, no respite to feel and examine her grief and come to terms with it. She was, at least, a little refreshed, and five minutes of anger had given her body new tone and vigor.

"We will leave for Winchester within the hour," she said to Eadred. She turned away to leave, and he opened the door, smiling grimly.

"I am ready now," he said.

PART THREE

THE LATER YEARS:
THE FORTRESS-BUILDERS

Historical Notes

In the fall of 905, a comet appeared. Ethelwold led the Danish army in attacks across English Mercia.

Early in the year of 918, Aethelflaed took possession of Leicester peacefully. The Danish forces there gave her their allegiance and became her subjects.

PART THREE

ÆTHELFLÆD'S & EDWARD'S
FORTIFICATIONS

■ ÆTHELFLÆD
    SITES UNKNOWN:
BREMESBYRIG, SCERGEAT,
    WEARDBURH

▲ EDWARD
    SITES UNKNOWN:
    WIGINGAMERE

CORBRIDGE

NORTHUMBRIA

○ YORK

0   40
MILES

R. TRENT

■ RUNCORN
■ EDDISBURY
■ CHESTER

DERBY ○

○ LINCOLN

○ NOTTINGHAM

■ STAFFORD
TAMWORTH

TETTENHALL

BRIDGNORTH

■ LEICESTER

R. WELLAND

▲ STAMFORD

CHIRBURY ■

WARWICK ■

TOWCESTER ▲

HUNTINGDON ▲

▲ BEDFORD

WORCESTER ■
(ÆTHELFLÆD &
ETHELRED 889)

BUCKINGHAM ▲

HERTFORD ▲

COLCHESTER ▲
WITHAM ▲
MALDON ▲

The Later Years; The Fortress Builders

CHAPTER NINETEEN

(899)

*E*thelnoth of Somerset laid his drinking horn on the table, a great weariness underlining each movement. Success had eluded him, for Sigfrid had played cat and mouse with him and with the Northumbrian Church for four long years. Ethelbald was still unconsecrated, Sigfrid having found one pretext after another to refuse Ethelbald's consecration by Pleymund.

Aethelflaed broke the uneasy silence. "What advantages had he expected by waiting? Is Ethelbald strong enough to oppose him openly?"

Ethelnoth drummed his fingers on the table, thinking absently. He turned his head and met her gaze, smiling faintly. "He might have been consecrated, for the Northumbrian folk respect an anointed monk more than an anointed king. They still call Sigfrid 'the pirate' and it galls him bitterly. If Pleymund gives Ethelbald his blessing, Sigfrid would lose what little influence he has. The Northumbrians might be persuaded to follow their archbishop instead of their king."

She eyed him thoughtfully. "And he was doubtless waiting for my father to die!"

"Aye, he was. Methinks he meant to attack again and add the West Saxons to his rule, and Kent as well."

"Christ be thanked Sigfrid died first, even by a few days!"

"Had he not, Lady, I would not be here. I might as well have been his hostage, for the steward he gave me was a guard and everything I wrote was intercepted."

Ethelred stifled a weary yawn. "We thought as much. Ah, well, we are spared. It is enough that we have treachery within our own house; Sigfrid would have made much of that." He stood up and stretched. "We must all sleep, especially yourself." When Ethelnoth had gone, Aethelflaed looked up at her husband, concern wrinkling her brow.

"Edward must be told immediately. It is as dangerous to have the throne of Northumbria empty as it was to have it filled by Sigfrid. We must bring Ethelbald here as quickly as possible lest someone unfriendly takes the throne by force and again prevents him from coming."

Ethelred pulled her to her feet. "As soon as Ethelnoth is rested we will send him back for Ethelbald. I will send Eadred to Edward in the morning. There is nothing to be done here now."

She fell into a deep sleep of exhaustion and woke late the next morning astonished that she had slept well past sunup. Eadred had already been dispatched to Badbury and, when she joined them, Ethelred and Ethelnoth were deep in plans.

"I will leave tomorrow," Ethelnoth said, ignoring the protest he saw on her face. I must bring the Archbishop-elect back secretly, if need be. There are many who would prefer a Churchman not anointed by Pleymund. They are envious of the high estate of Canterbury."

"They will have no pallium from Rome unless Pleymund lays hands on Ethelbald."

"They are not overly concerned about His Holiness' wishes in Northumbria," Ethelnoth replied drily.

Eadred returned the following day to report that Edward was still camped at Badbury Rings, near Wimborne, with his levies, Ethelwold and John were still in possession of the manor at Wimborne, and the hamlet of Christchurch was now seized by them also, and without Edward's consent. Ethelwold sent word out to Edward that he meant to stay there alive or dead: Edward would not take him, he declared.

Ethelred pondered this silently and at last voiced his doubts. "He will not keep Edward there long," he prophesied. "His words mean nothing, and it is unlikely that Edward believes he will stay."

He was right. Nothing happened for a week, during which time Aethelflaed was able to find out that the nun Ethelwold took with him came from Nunnaminster in Winchester. Ealhswith, who was spending her mourning period in the Abbey she had founded, was sought out of solitude by her daughter and plied with questions.

"It was too much for him. I saw his envy and hoped he might overcome it before it destroyed him," the Queen said sadly.

"His envy may not destroy him, but Edward certainly will now," Aethelflaed responded sourly. Edward had not shown the tendency to forgive his enemies as his father had, nor was she surprised that he did not. The had both seen that Alfred's beaten and forgiven foes had returned again and again to torment him with war. Edward had endured his father's generosity with his enemies wordlessly, to his father, though not to Aethelflaed or Ethelred. If Ethelwold had gained even the slightest knowledge of his cousin over the years he would know that Edward, with the reins now in his hands, would show little tendency toward mercy. "I would waste no sympathy on him, Lady Mother. He gave Edward his vows of loyalty and he deserves his fate."

The Queen's face was unhappy. "He could do naught else. But he has done another thing as well. He has taken with him a young girl who was professed, and against her will."

"Had she wealth?"

Ealhswith lips were a firm line of disapproval. "She did. Not great, but enough to be a temptation to such as Ethelwold. He knew her before her uncle brought her here."

"But how," protested Aethelflaed, "did he get in to speak to her?"

The Queen knit her brows. "He did not, himself. He sent his man, dressed as a monk, to speak to her. The Abbess did not know the man was lying."

Aethelflaed leaned forward, anger reddening her cheeks. "A tall man, Lady Mother? Dark?" The Queen inclined her head. "John!" Aethelflaed barely breathed the name aloud, but her voice was filled with loathing. Lest she be pressed to explain, she begged her mother's leave.

In spite of Edward's watchfulness, Ethelwold and John escaped, leaving Wimborne by night. When Edward discovered the trick, he followed them, after storming the manors at Wimborne and Christchurch. They gave in without a fight, since the quarry had fled, and though Edward had ordered pursuit, he was too late. Ethelwold, within days, arrived safely in Northumbria.

Aethelflaed was beside herself with anger. She paced the floor in her chamber, cursing John with every imprecation she had learned in the garrison at London. She finally ran out of words and sat down. Edward, who had disposed himself full-length on a bench, listened while she raged, his eyes closed, an expression of interest on his face. She stopped to catch her breath and he yawned and sat up.

"Do you not care?" she asked, still breathless.

He raised an eyebrow at her. "Sister, you have learned much from life in a garrison. Yes, I care, but at the moment he can do me no harm. He is out of Wessex and he has shown himself openly the traitor we had always believed him to be." His face hardened. "We will deal with him when the time comes. It will not surprise you that he left the girl behind." He was mistaken: she was quite surprised. "An abducted nun," Edward explained, "would not be acceptable to the Church of Northumbria."

"What do you mean? Why should they care? Abducted nuns are not an uncommon matter."

"I mean that he intends to take the throne of Northumbria, since he cannot have the throne of Wessex, and he cannot do that with a nun as his bride!"

She stared at him, speechless, her anger against both Ethelwold and John rekindling. Then she remembered. "My God," she exclaimed, thunderstruck. "Ethelnoth! With Ethelwold in York, he will not get out alive!"

Edward's grim face relaxed into a smile. "Peace, sister. Ethelnoth is in London with your husband. He has brought Ethelbald with him." He reached under his mantle and pulled out a roll of parchment. "I have this from Ethelred only this morning."

"And what about the girl?"

Edward's face hardened again. "They had not expected to find her already professed. She was young and easily swayed by Ethelwold. John thought she might be persuaded to turn her wealth over to Ethelwold. They planned to raise an army inside Wessex and they needed gold to buy it. Ethelwold has only what the King left him, and it was not enough. He promised the girl she would be Queen of Wessex if she found a way to help him." He shrugged, his face dark with anger. "She was barely more than a child, and her kinsmen shut her up in a convent to be rid of her, hoping to use her wealth themselves. It was not hard for Ethelwold to convince her that they could free her from the convent." There was a hint of pity in his eyes. "When they could not put an army together, even with a little gold, they disguised themselves as peasants. Someone left horses for them in the woods near Wimborne and the two of them escaped. The girl was no more use to them so they left her behind." He paused and looked at his sister sideways. "I brought the rest back here," he said, indifferently.

She did not ask further about the handful of traitors Ethelwold left behind him. "What about the nun?" she asked instead.

"She is young and silly. I have placed her under guard and given her into the Abbess' supervision. Her fortune has been removed from her family and given to the Church."

Aethelflaed smiled her approval. Edward looked glum at the fate of the girl. "She is fortunate to be alive," she said, but asked no further.

The last few weeks of the year passed uneventfully, and after a brief stay in London, Aethelflaed, Ethelred, and all the children returned to Winchester for Christmas. They kept the twelve days' celebration that Alfred had established some years earlier but the capitol of Wessex was still in mourning, as ordered by Edward.

The news that came from Northumbria that chill December surprised no one and so hardly affected their Christmas mood: Ethelwold had been accepted as head of the Northumbrian army and from there it was a small jump to the throne. Ethelwold, so persuasive, had no difficulty in convincing the leaderless Northumbrians that he had as good a claim as any to the vacant throne of York. "They are short," Edward observed sourly, "of royal blood. Athelings of the House of Wessex, treacherous or no, will do as well as any!" Ethelred glared blackly, but Edward only shrugged, threw aside carelessly the missive detailing Ethelwold's further perfidy, and said, "We will see." His eyes glinted icily despite his apparent indifference.

Aethelflaed had brought Elfled back to Winchester with her as a companion, then left her at liberty with no duties to confine her. While Elfled had no objection to this, it was clear that she did not understand that Aethelflaed was quietly giving her consent to a renewed friendship with Edward. Despite Aethelflaed's best efforts, she could see that Elfled still distrusted her. Aethelflaed sighed but made up her mind to accept Elfled's wariness as best she could. "People cannot help being what they are," she observed to Ethelred in the darkened privacy of their quarters, "and she has always been jealous."

"She had best get over it if she will be Edward's wife," Ethelred said dispassionately. "Edward has never lacked for admiring women, and there will be plenty now trying to catch his eye." He broke off because she was chuckling to herself. "You find that funny?"

She was thinking of the lures she had seen thrown out to Edward, who appreciated them, but deftly avoided them. "Yes, but Elfled, no. That is not funny for her. She will never master her jealousy, but if she learns not to show it, they will manage. Edward will still mislike a snappish tongue and I expect they will fight more than a little."

Ethelred raised himself on his elbow and stared hard at her in the dark. "If that is what you think, why to you encourage this? Surely you wish him some peace in life. If you were a quarrelsome nag, I should be grievously tempted to beat you." She smiled to herself, for as he threatened, he leaned over and rubbed his cheek against hers. She turned on her side to face him. "You are a peaceful man, Eth'red, but Edward enjoys a good fight, be it on the battlefield or in his own palace. She has a temper to match his own and he will never intimidate her or get the best of her." She was quiet for a long time, so long that Ethelred thought she had fallen asleep. Finally she said, "She truly loves him."

Ethelred nodded into the dark. "Aye, she does. No one could miss that. But that is not so important for a king."

"Not if the king is Edward! She will argue with him, but she will never betray him. She will strive for his interests with all her strength. And you may not consider love important," she gave him a sturdy poke in the ribs, "but Edward must have it. He is not a gentle man, and even if he is my brother, I must say that without his needs be fulfilled, he could be a brutal man. He needs Elfled's love to take the hard edges from him. He does not always set a limit to his actions, as you do, for he does not much care to look into his heart."

"He cannot." Ethelred's voice was edged with regret. "We have no need for dreamers on the battlefield. Edward must be cunning and swift and he cannot fret himself overmuch about misgivings. Such niceness of mind tormented your father all his life. It is good for all of us that Edward inherited Alfred's will and courage and only half his conscience." He reached out and pulled her close. "I did not mean that love is not important. I only meant that with Edward, as with most, it cannot be the first consideration. We are fortunate." He said no more. They had been fond of each other at the beginning; now they loved each other with silent devotion and shared their demanding life and responsibilities. Elfled would become Queen of Wessex, but she would wield no power, for Queens of Wessex, as Asser lamented, were wives of kings only. Someday, she thought drowsily, when Edward is accepted in Mercia, Elfled can be Queen of Wessex and Mercia both. The thought brought her fully awake, since that would happen only at her death. She put the thought out of her mind and fell asleep.

The consecration of Ethelbald took place during Epiphany of the year 900. The pallium would be sent later; Pleymund had written Rome and explained the urgency of the matter, though he doubted he would be understood. Rome was too remote from English affairs and even though he was informed of the state of the Western Isles, His Holiness failed to comprehend that his wishes there were not paramount. He wished them to cease contending with each other and was baffled that his request was ignored. The Saxons, prevented from fighting each other by the necessity of uniting against the invader, were fortunate to have found one amongst them, Edward, whom they would follow. It was a gracious happenstance that the southern and western Saxons were united under one man. It was too much to ask that they try to unite with the northern Anglians. Besides, his Holiness did not understand that the northerners were as much Danish as English now, and each wished to rule the other. It was not a question of union, not yet at least. Besides, neither would consider the dictates of a foreigner, and His Holiness was such, about whom they knew and cared little.

Aethelflaed, Edward, and Ethelred had lately begun to accept that the invader would never be persuaded to leave, and the new Archbishop of York, in his own way, was partly responsible for that. Pleymund saw all the faithful united under one spiritual authority: that authority was Rome. He must have forgotten that her father had practiced, though not pronounced openly, that the King was the head of the Church, and from the King did the spiritual order derive its lands, its revenues, and its worldly well-being. Thus to the King did the Church owe worldly service in return for favors granted. Pleymund seemed unaware of any division between the aims of the King and the aims of the Church. But then, he had not talked with Ethelbald about his flock, the Danish-English mixed people of Northumbria.

It was unfortunate, Aethelflaed reflected, that Pleymund, whose hermit background made a great Churchman out of him, had lost, by his continuing isolation, the bond that connected him with his countrymen. He felt himself concerned with needs greater than the worldly aims of his flock. A sincere and honest compulsion for matters of the spirit burned within him.

Had he been more attentive to Ethelbald's quiet words, he would have spared himself later disappointment. When Pleymund laid his hands on Ethelbald's head, anointed him and crowned him Archbishop of York, he fully expected Ethelbald to conform to the wishes of the See of Canterbury which had bestowed on him the spiritual authority he needed to manage his northern flock. He was mistaken, and that Aethelflaed saw with an inner eye surprisingly undimmed by her own strong family loyalty.

Ethelbald spoke softly but bluntly about the needs of his flock when Pleymund later brought up the matter.

"They are Danes, they are invaders on Saxon lands," Pleymund objected, expecting his opinion to carry more weight than it did.

"Ah," replied the soft-spoken Ethelbald, "but it is their land, too. After all we are of Danish blood as well as English in the north, and of near two-hundred year's breeding." Pleymund looked discomposed. "I myself," Ethelbald went on, "have as much of the invader's blood in me as I have of Saxon." He smiled apologetically. "It is, after all, no crime to be a half-Dane in Northumbria."

"But you can see," Pleymund waved his hand with an air of finality, "that they must not move against their southern brothers in faith, from whom you received your authority. They have taken Christian oaths with us and broken them. This is a serious matter. This endangers their souls."

Ethelbald smiled patiently at Pleymund. "We must see to their other needs as well as to their souls. My people have worked these lands as hard as any Saxon, and did not the Saxons drive out their Roman overlords from these very lands they claim as theirs? My Danes are good farmers and they have even moved against a king of their own blood when he pressed war upon them too often. Halfdan was a great warrior, but he was mad for slaughter. His soldiers were content to farm, he was not. So they drove him out." He shook his head. "They have earned their right to stay. One cannot ignore their claims."

Aethelflaed could see, watching the two faces, that they were as different as fire and earth. Pleymund burned with the spirit; Ethelbald was a man with the blood of Danish farmers in his veins. She had studied him with undisguised curiosity, for he was so unlike his fierce and bloody war-rior countrymen. He bore no resemblance in disposition to the fearsome Halfdan, who fought her father and uncle, nor to Halfdan's brother, Ivarr the Boneless, ruler of Northumbria and butcher of the east Anglians. This man had the same stocky build as his Jutland ancestors, the same dark eyes. But his eyes had a kindly sparkle and the face was gentle, though she doubted not that he was as quick to anger as his forebears. His name showed that there ran in his veins also the blood of Saxon nobility, yet this man plainly cared little for that. The material needs of his diocese con-cerned him, and their complaints about the harshness of their daily lives were heard.

She admired him instantly; one could not fail to give proper due to such a man. She also knew he could not be counted on to uphold the claims of Wessex or Mercia simply because Pleymund had anointed him. He would accept the spiritual authority that Canterbury invested in him but he would be loyal to his own kin, not to the house of Wessex.

She had been given one chance to speak to the Archbishop alone after Pleymund left them. Ethelbald smiled his eternal smile after Pleymund's retreating back and said only, "He is a most devout man, and exactly the man I would have expected the late King, your father, to have chosen."

"He does not share your views of your loyalties," Aethelflaed said bluntly, "nor your views on the needs of your people."

"My dear Lady," he replied, still smiling, "there are many ways to attend either to one's flock or one's loyalties."

"My father would have understood your thoughts. You remember only Alfred's devotion to the Church. Did you know also that seeing his people starve at the hands of your countrymen moved him to tears?"

Ethelbald's face lost its benign smile. "I crave your pardon, Lady, for that I did not know. The Church makes much of spirit, little of the body, so that its shepherds are often led to overlook the physical sufferings of their flocks. One forgets how much the state of the body influences the state of the spirit."

"There are those among you who add treachery to perfidy, my Lord Archbishop. I understand fully your feeling for the needs of your people but it is likely to conflict with your duty as a Churchman."

Ethelbald lowered his gaze and studied his hands. "You mean your unfortunate cousin Ethelwold, who is now our king"

"Not only our cousin, but his thane, John."

Ethelbald nodded. "He is a fierce man. What of him? I see no harm in a good soldier," he grinned suddenly, "even if he is a West Saxon."

"He is not a West Saxon," she snapped, "he is John, known as the Old Saxon, and he is a professed monk, priest, and abbot. He was Abbot of Athelney, and so cruel a man that his brothers attempted to murder him." The Archbishop's face blanched. "Aye," she agreed, "'tis dreadful, but true. Revenge against us eats at him. He encouraged Ethelwold to break his vows to Edward. This was not enough for him; he aided Ethelwold in abducting a nun and did not prevent him from defiling her that they might use her to attain their own ends. He has lived in the world these many years now, and while it is no crime for an abbot to bear arms, I pray you consider his lapses. Will you tolerate such a man in your midst? I cannot beg your interest in West Saxon or Mercian matters over Northumbrian, but I would beg you to have a care to this man. I am shamed to have so treacherous a relative as Ethelwold; the Church must be shamed by so treacherous a priest as John."

The Archbishop's face had become grave during her angry speech. Now he stammered, "I...I am grievously sorry. Again I beg pardon." She was secretly glad to see his composure shaken. She sympathized with his compassion for his countrymen. But treachery had been done, and one could not be perfidious in the world and remain honest in the spirit. All she said, though, was "Lying is lying and treason cannot be left unchallenged by either King or Church."

Both she and Ethelbald were saved the necessity of action on their convictions, for Knutr the Dane chose the unlikely month of February to sail the icy North Sea. He landed on Scarborough beach where Ethelwold's hastily collected levies opposed him futilely. Knutr marched swiftly on York. Ethelwold and John fled overseas; Knutr settled into the rule of Northumbria, and, like Sigfrid before him, began to mint coins in his own likeness, lest any be in doubt of his kingship. With *CNUT REX* on his coinage, Northumbria settled quietly back to its own affairs after Ethelwold's short and unsavory kingship.

Privately chastened by Aethelflaed's forthright discussion, Ethelbald, on leaving London, had forestalled her formal bow of parting. He had taken her hand instead and said to her, "I dislike conflict over unsolvable problems as greatly as you do, Lady Aethelflaed. I shall consider your words seriously." He had apparently done so, considering the smoothness with which the great See of York returned to a semblance of peace. It seemed obvious to her that although Knutr ruled Northumbria, a firm hand ruled Knutr.

CHAPTER TWENTY

(901)

*E*dward's wedding in the old minster was splendid. Grimbald persuaded Edward to build a new minster abutting onto the old one and wistfully entreated Edward to delay his wedding a year or two until the New Minster be ready, saying how fit it would be to follow the consecration of the Church with a royal wedding.

"God's bones," Edward exclaimed to his sister, "does he think I shall make the intended Queen my mistress until then?"

Aethelflaed wiped tears of laughter from her face, so pleased was she to see him smiling and happy.

"The Old Minster will do well enough for me."

"Have you talked with our Lady Mother?"

"I have." Edward was puzzled. "But I could see from her face it is not to her taste."

Aethelflaed pressed her lips together firmly. Of course Ealhswith would not like it. She was still attached to Ecgwin's memory, but she could hardly expect Edward to remain celibate the rest of his life. Edward broke in on her thoughts. "She says Elfled likes you not. Is this so?"

"Ah!" Her tone was careless. "It looks that way, but it is not true. Don't listen to her."

Edward strode across the room and put his hands on her shoulders. "Tell me," he commanded, giving her a light shake. "Is it so?"

"She has not liked me in the past, but that is over."

"Why?"

"Oh, she has been fond of you since we were children, but you did not take to her then. I think she had hoped I might intervene on her behalf, but I did not." Edward said nothing. "Well, you see," she stammered, unnerved by his silence, "it is different now." He glared at her. She tried to back off, but he held her shoulders firmly.

"How long, dear sister," he said, frowning, "have you been managing my life?"

"Now, Edward!" She was genuinely distressed, for only once had he been angry with her, and it was for meddling in his life.

He threw back his head and shouted with laughter. She punched him in the ribs, as if they were still children, but his amusement relieved her. He straightened up and threw his arms around her, smothering her in a bearish embrace. "I have always known you ran my life," he laughed. "You have considered it your privilege from the moment I was born." He let her go, but retained her hand. More soberly, he said, "I expect Elfled knows that. You will always have my ear and she knows that also." He led her to a bench and sat her down on it, seating himself beside her. "Tell me truthfully, Aethelflaed, how say you to this marriage, knowing my bride is not fond of you?"

"She loves you dearly, Edward. That is what matters. But," she looked up at him, "have you not always known of her feelings and jealousies?"

"Aye," he agreed, "I have. It will not be easy, but I do care for her. Can I be sure you will take nothing amiss?"

"Edward, I encouraged her." She thought he would at least show surprise but he did not respond.

"She will tolerate my failings well," he said suddenly, grinning. "And if she does not, I shall remind her she has a few of her own." Aethelflaed only grimaced by way of reply. He would find out the unwisdom of reminding Elfled of her shortcomings. On the other hand, Elfled would discover the unwisdom of treating Edward to a pettish whim when he was not in the mood for it. She kissed Edward on the forehead and rose to leave. His way of life with Elfled would certainly be much different from hers and Ethelred's, but she did not doubt that they would manage better than most if they survived their honeymoon.

After the wedding, Aethelflaed took Edytha, who came from Shaftesbury to see her father, to London with Athelstan and Elfwyn. Edward was still firm in his decision: Elfled should not have the raising of his first wife's children. One glance at Edytha and she understood. The child resembled her mother more every day. So she kept her out of the new Queen's sight.

The child had barely left for Shaftesbury when Edward and Elfled returned from Cheddar, not as she had half expected, in bad humor with each other, but glowing and happy. "Thank God," she breathed softly to Ethelred when she saw their faces, "this bodes well." She embraced Elfled heartily and found the embrace returned.

The summer passed quietly, marred only by two events. Ealhswith's brother died. He was the last of her family from Mercia and he had been her companion after Alfred's death. She became more inward than ever, fixed upon the family that had fared forth long since, and, Aethelflaed suspected sadly, longing more to be with them than with those who were left. Grimbald died also, sad that the new Minster he had persuaded Edward to build had not been completed.

It was a hot July, hotter than most, and the long Requiems tired every-one, especially Elfled, whom Aethelflaed noticed mopping her forehead surreptitiously. As quickly and quietly as she could, she slipped her arm around Elfled and removed her outside into the fresh air.

"You goose," she chided her in the privacy of her apartments. Elfled sipped the tea David brought and the color came back to her face. "You need not have attended, you know," said Aethelflaed. She had rightly guessed that Elfled was with child and was gratified at the glow of fulfill-ment on the younger woman's face. How Edward must be looking forward to this child after so many years!

Their tranquil summer was disturbed again, this time by Ethelwold, returning from overseas with an army of Frankish Danes whom he had convinced of the rightness of his cause. Long had these Frankish Northmen coveted the rich and rolling lands of Alfred, described to them by Ethel-wold as his own birthright. Essex submitted, even capitulated willingly, for none had ever risen to lead them since Guthrum's death. Here was one of the enemy's own, God-given, to them. It was not long before the word spread to the East Anglians that Ethelwold of the House of Wessex, whose father, King Aethelred, had fought and bested the mighty Halfdan, was back with an army of Franks and Essex Danes. The East Anglians joined him enthusiastically.

The raids began, first in Mercia, then into northern Wessex. Edward marched out and raided back, since the Danes could not be raiding Mercia and protecting their own villages at the same time. Elfled increased and Aethelflaed fretted quietly: it was as if the years had maliciously rolled back to play their mischief all over again.

She was mistaken. Edward knew Elfled to be strong as a horse and wasted no time in undue worry. He came home between raids, surveyed his wife's progress, and took her to bed. Where he had been fearful as a man walking on eggs with his first wife, he appeared almost careless of Elfled's health. She thrived on it. She increased and took no pains to hide the size of her belly. Aethelflaed watched them both with amused bewilderment, but all she would say to Ethelred was, "Heaven be praised, they are a bet-ter match than we dreamed!" She had never seen Elfled happier nor Edward more content.

Their son was born on one of Edward's brief sojourns at home. They named him Aelfweard and he was a sunny child from the moment he entered the world. Edward doted on the infant, showered his wife with attention, and all was well, except for Athelstan.

Athelstan saw the pride and joy on his father's face as he played with his new son, and he could not conceal the pain in his eyes as he remem-bered his own rejection. Aethelflaed, watching him, felt his distress, for

Edward had never been so freely affectionate with his heir. He stood off from Athelstan, for the boy carried himself, unconsciously, like his grandfather. Edward had always been in awe of his father, and the image of his father on his heir's face discomfited him. Even so she could not feel sorry for Athelstan. She and Ethelred loved him inordinately and he had never lacked for affection from either of them. He had, as a child, equal access with Elfwyn to Ethelred's lap, and without Aethelflaed he would have forgotten a mother's touch, so young had he been when Ecgwin died.

Aethelflaed laid her hand on his shoulder now, and reminded him that he need not envy Aelfweard.

"I know, Lady Mother." He sighed. "He is happy, is he not?" he asked wistfully.

"Happier than I have ever seen him," she answered truthfully. "He loved your mother desperately, but fate chose otherwise for him. Do not begrudge your father a share of happiness. He has waited a long time to love again."

She laid her arm lightly around his shoulders. She looked at Edward again as she tried to frame what she wised to say to Athelstan.

"There are different ways of loving people. Your father has not stopped loving your mother. But he loves Elfled differently. When I outgrew being a child, I loved Lord Ethelred differently. Most people do not know when that happens. I did, for a life was handed back to me." She looked over at Edward and smiled, enjoying his pleasure. "I did not have to wait so many years to be happy."

Athelstan glanced at his father and stepbrother. He looked back into his aunt's face and saw it glowing with affection, which he knew to be for himself. "You said a life was handed back to you. What meant you by that?" He could not mistake the tears that suddenly glistened on her eyelashes.

"My son," she said pausing, and he thought she was speaking to him, but she was looking straight ahead, past Edward, through the stone walls, northward, back through the years. "My son," she repeated, "is buried in Worcester. Lord Ethelred suffered that death with me more than I knew. When I understood his sorrow to be as great as my own, I stopped loving as a child. We both changed and loved each other the more for it. Then your mother died and Edward gave you to us, because you must be taught to be a Mercian. I do not think of that as a duty, but as an honor and a great pleasure. When Edward gave you to me," she turned her tear-sparkled gaze to Athelstan's grave blue eyes, "he gave me back my son. We love you as our own, freely and willingly. You do not need to envy Elfled's child, Athelstan. Your father enjoys now what Providence denied him before. But everything he works for all his life, everything he does will be for you, not Aelfweard. Believe me, it is your future that fills his thoughts."

Athelstan smiled finally, then walked across the room to his father, smiled at him, and held out his hands for his half-brother.

The harrying did not cease for the birth of Edward's son. Ethelwold worked his way westward across English Mercia, raiding villages, killing, and stealing all he could find. "His own countrymen and kin," Ethelred exclaimed, outraged, "men who have fought by his side." Edward's face grew grim, then grimmer. Ethelwold went as far as Cricklade, ravaged the surrounding land, and returned to East Anglia. Edward was astonished and outraged by turns, but his own punitive raids into East Anglia did not deflect Ethelwold from his apparent attempt.

"He had not the strength to hold onto York," shouted Edward, throwing himself into the Great Hall at London and refusing the drinking horn Aethelflaed held out to him. "How does he think to take Mercia and Wessex from us?"

"It is obvious," Aethelflaed replied sourly, "that he expects he will do so one way or another."

"Then he will be stopped," snapped Edward, furious. He turned to Ethelred. "What levies can you give me?"

"There are Aethelfrith's men and the Kentishmen."

"Good. I'll have them."

Ethelred looked up at him, hesitant. "The Kentish are better than they once were, but their discipline is still not that of the Wessex or Mercian levies."

"How do they fight?"

"Fierce and well. Ealdorman Sigewulf and his son Sigeberht can harry as well as the Dane. Once they have sunk their teeth into the host they would rather die than let go."

Edward sat down and took the drinking horn he had refused earlier "I will take them. We will go at dawn." He pulled a battered parchment from his girdle and handed it to Ethelred. "I have it from Asser at Sherborne news of trouble in Wales. If it is true, it does not bode well." He smote the table angrily with his fist. "It is ill-timed for us."

Aethelflaed, who had been sitting on the bench with her back to Edward and staring moodily into the great fireplace, swung partway around to face him. "He cannot see it that way. I think he truly believes to take Mercia and Wessex and then march on Knutr at York." She looked up at Edward, who was shaking his head at the impossibility of it. "Nor do I believe, Edward, that he can succeed. He is wood-wild, bewitched enough to try." She turned to Ethelred. "But what is Asser's news?"

"Ireland," he said, cryptically. "Dublin had been delivered of Ivarr the Boneless, son of Sigtryggr, by the Leinstermen. Some of the Northmen have gone to Galloway and the islands with Ivarr and Ragnall." Edward retrieved the parchment from Ethelred. "Some of them have gone into Wales," continued Ethelred, "along with their Irish friends who were driven out with them."

"I cannot imagine, said Aethelflaed, making a wry face, "that the Welsh will give them leave to stay overlong."

"Nor can I," agreed Ethelred quietly but with such urgency that she raised her head sharply to look at him directly. She read his expression correctly and was silent, knowing that her husband had memories that still haunted him.

"I suppose you mean Chester," she said at last, staring again into the crackling fire.

CHAPTER TWENTY-ONE

(905)

*A*ethelfrith waited upon Aethelflaed in her chambers. She had some inkling of what possessed his thoughts and why he desired her counsel. She was pleased. She surveyed his broad, tunic-clad back and muscular frame with approval. He reminded her of Ethelred, for he was now a little past Ethelred's age when he had thrown in his lot with her father. She was inclined to regard this stalwart young man with approval; all signs augured well. She smiled and cleared her throat. Aethelfrith turned with a start and stammered his apologies, which she forestalled with an upraised hand.

"You must sit." She urged him to a bench and nodded to David, who served them wine in cloudy-blue tinted tumblers. He sipped nervously and covertly regarded Aethelflaed over the rim of his tumbler, then drew a deep breath.

"I have approached Lord Ethelred," he began, then faltered. Aethelflaed repressed a smile curling at the corners of her mouth, and nodded to him to continue.

The young man opened his mouth, closed it, then blurted out "I have asked Lord Ethelred for your daughter Elfwyn to be my wife. He says I must seek your approval before he gives his." The words came out in a great rush, and then he fell silent.

Aethelflaed signaled David to refill his tumbler. "Now Ae'lfrith, surely you did not take that to mean that I might be against the match?" she said, now smiling with amusement. She had never been a beauty, but at thirty-four, a busy life had ripened her into a handsome woman. The mouth and chin were firm and full of purpose, the complexion clear and fresh, a healthy ruddiness on the cheek. Her curling hair, pulled back and fastened at the nape of her neck, had darkened from its youthful honey color, and a few premature streaks of grey in it only served to emphasize the youthful face.

He relaxed and smiled broadly. "No, Lady, Lord Ethelred did no such thing. He felt you would be...sympathetic." His look was hopeful and entreating.

She laughed with delight. Elfwyn was fortunate to have such a treasure seeking her hand. "I am indeed sympathetic. You have served us well.

Your bravery and courage are known to all, and your lands thrive under your care. I cannot fail to be pleased." She reached out and patted his arm maternally. "Now you must seek to please my daughter, for I wish her to marry to please her heart. I shall not force her to marry against her inclinations."

Aethelfrith relaxed and smiled with relief that she had not made him stagger through a long speech of request, and also because it was his own wish to marry for love, and Elfwyn had caught his fancy. Aethelflaed saw that he was by no means hopelessly in love with her daughter, though certainly attracted by her liveliness, and as he hurried off to plan his campaign for Elfwyn's affections, she considered that it was perhaps as well.

Elfwyn was headstrong, stubborn, and inclined to believe her every whim a royal mandate. She managed to coax, wheedle, or outright demand her own way with everyone, except her cousin Athelstan; he was used to her and was already bored with her imperious ways. Nevertheless, this young man, if he was not head-over-heels in love, would stand a better chance of getting her attention than one drowned in lovesickness.

She saw him later in the Great Hall below and he had at least captured Elfwyn's interest, for she was regarding him attentively, her eyes sparkling in the firelight. They moved around to the other side of the central fire, which was ringed around with containing stones and vented upward through a slot in the roof of the Hall. She was glad they moved. She did not want her daughter to find her watching them with such hope and interest.

She brushed her thoughts away as Edward and Athelstan approached her table and sat down opposite her. Edward, following her gaze through the flames, slapped his thigh and exclaimed, "Ah, that is a hearty young fellow. I am glad he is to ride with me tomorrow."

Athelstan looked worshipfully at his father. "Please, father, may I come, too? I am old enough and truly, I know how to handle my shield and sword." He turned a beseeching look on his aunt, knowing as he spoke what would be Edward's response.

Aethelflaed turned a winning look on Edward, because his face had become stern as he framed his refusal in his mind, and she wished to woo him away from being too kingly with his son. Edward's face relaxed and he threw an affectionate arm around Athelstan's shoulders.

Aethelflaed laughed. "Edward, you were the same age and chafed mightily when you were refused. Your son has better manners, though, for you would sulk for days when refused."

Edward grinned ruefully. "She speaks truthfully, Athelstan. Your temper is by far the better of mine. How say you to this, then? If you cannot go with me, will you accompany your Lady to Chester?"

Athelstan looked at Aethelflaed, puzzlement mingled with disappointment on his face. "To Chester? But there is very little there!" His tone reflected a polite disbelief that there could be anything of importance at that desolate, neglected outpost and hardly significant when compared with his father's forthcoming campaign into the fens of Cambridgeshire. This last he had not been told by Edward, but since he loitered frequently around the buildings surrounding the garrison, he heard and pieced together the rumors that reached his ears. He connected the gossip with the exercises and preparations he could observe for himself. He knew the King to be preparing for a raid deep into Danish Mercia. It would be exciting and eventful; a trip to the deserted wilds of the Wirral could hardly be expected to have the same appeal.

Aethelflaed understood his unspoken dismay, "I think I would rather be with Edward, myself," she agreed, thinking of Ethelwold. Edward frowned, as if reading her thoughts. "But," she continued, "We have work to do in Chester and it is important to your father that it be done. The Irish of Dublin and their Norse masters have been driven across the Irish Sea into Wales and are harrying Clydog ap Cadell these two years now. They shall some day cross the border into Cheshire. We cannot permit them to harry us as well."

Athelstan was puzzled. "Shall not my uncle go with you?" he asked.

A spasm of worry crossed Aethelflaed's face and she looked away from Athelstan to see her own concern reflected in Edward's eyes. "He cannot go right now," was all she would say about it. Ethelred, as everyone had noticed, was not in the Hall tonight. He had awakened two days back, his eyes bright with fever, insisting he was fit. But he had been awake most of the night, thrashing hotly beside her. For once, her will prevailed, for the brightness of his eyes frightened her and she insisted firmly. He laid back on his pillow, thankfully, and she noticed that his face was thinner. I must have seen it before, she thought. One did not grow thinner overnight. She called David, who knew how to soothe Ethelred, to attend to him. No one else would be able to tolerate Ethelred's irascibility, for so he was when he was confined to bed.

She turned back to Athelstan. "You will come with me in his place." Athelstan's serious face broke into a wide smile; his presence at his aunt's side was now a great responsibility, no matter how dull Chester might prove.

Elfwyn, who had come around to the other side of the fire with Aethelfrith, stiffened imperceptibly as she watched the group as they sat in intimate discussion, unaware of her scrutiny. She edged closer to them in time to hear her mother's last words and flushed angrily, but the glow of the fire hid the brightness of anger on her face. She sat down beside her uncle, who fondly put an arm around her, hugged her, and winked broadly at Aethelfrith. She returned the hug briefly, and when she had mastered her annoyance, raised her eyes to her mother.

"You are taking Athelstan?"

Aethelflaed realized with a start that her daughter had been planning to ride with her. Uneasily, she replied, "I must," and did not explain further. "Your father is still ruling London and he will need your assistance to carry out his duties for as long as he is confined. Theodred will advise you in all things." Elfwyn's face had lightened as Aethelflaed outlined her duties, but as her mother finished, Elfwyn frowned.

"I do not like the Bishop's advice. He is an old man."

Aethelflaed smiled faintly, deciding to accept this as humor. Theodred was young and able. He was an old man to Elfwyn because her cajoling and imperious manner touched him not. With her father keeping to his room, Elfwyn would surely extend her overbearing manners beyond the garrison walls. If she must sit in upon the courts, it would benefit them all if she were under a firm hand. Her annoyance at this showed plainly. Aethelflaed continued to smile pleasantly at her. "Nevertheless, I charge you, attend to him in all matters. All matters," she repeated.

She rose, suddenly weary, and Edward rose with her. She wanted to leave; she had seen her daughter a shade more clearly. She was not her mother's delightful headstrong moppet any longer, and Theodred's gentle warning of long ago now came back to her. Perhaps a parent never did see these things. She was glad that she and Ethelred had agreed that Theodred's judgment should prevail when they had talked about it earlier. She closed her eyes, thinking of Ethelred, now ill. Fate was intervening with her family, her beloved husband, her incomprehensible daughter, her two dearest people. A wave of panic assailed her. She set her teeth against it and when it had passed, she bent her head to kiss Elfwyn and smile at Aethelfrith, still standing with them, a thoughtful look on his face. Edward and Athelstan quickly moved to either side of her; Edward, because he was acutely tuned to her distress, and Athelstan, because he always followed his father's lead.

She saw her daughter's watchful eyes harden. Her two dearest people? No, it was four. Perhaps that was what Elfwyn disapproved of, the great affection she held for her brother and his son, love that Elfwyn begrudged them. Ethelred's illness filled her with panic, and Elfwyn's recalcitrance dismayed her, her brother's strength and affection as he placed a steadying hand on her arm, and Athelstan's filial devotion as he sprang to her side, sustained her. But Elfwyn could not see how she needed them.

As they left the Great Hall, Athelstan's voice cut into her silence. "Lady Mother," he said soothingly, "you must not let her bother you."

"I wish I knew what troubles her."

Athelstan smiled patiently at her, as if he were dealing with one whose wits were addled. "It is plain," he said softly, "that she is envious."

Edward brought them to a startled halt and swung his head around to stare at his son. "You impertinent cub," he barked, but Athelstan did not cower under his stern look.

"Father," he said with solemn dignity, "I am thirteen and a man. If I were still a child, I would not presume to speak so."

Edward snapped his mouth shut and threw Aethelflaed a glance pregnant with unborn mirth, but at the flickering look in her eyes, withheld his laughter. "Then we must hear your opinion," he replied with gravity.

"I believe," Athelstan continued, somewhat self-consciously, "that she wishes to be more like Lady Aethelflaed and to rule one day on her own. She does not believe Mercia will submit to one of the House of Wessex."

Aethelflaed gaped at him and stumbled. Athelstan's clear perception stunned her. Edward retained his grip on her elbow, steadying her, and gave vent to his laughter, though his son had voiced his own misgivings as well.

How long had it been, she thought, that her exuberant sprite of a daughter had been gone and this stubborn, willful young woman come to occupy her body? Athelstan, eager to comfort her was about to speak, but Edward, reading her feelings, silenced him with a wave of his hand. He put an arm around her and kissed her on the forehead.

"Come, sister, you have done the best you knew. We cannot account ourselves the keepers of the deeds and thoughts of others, even if they belong to us. Do not trouble yourself further." His voice was curt, but his eyes were soft with understanding. Thank God for Edward, she thought and smiled at him, grateful that he had not been too sympathetic. She looked at Athelstan, still watching her nervously.

"Lord Ethelred will be waiting," she said to him by way of comfort, "to hear of the tales and songs from the Hall, and he will tell us about Chester."

CHAPTER TWENTY-TWO

*D*eva Victrix, Castra Legionis, the City of the Legions, was quiet and deserted when they arrived, except for wild things that scuttled at their approach. The streets and yards were overgrown with brush and rotting timbers lying all askew. Even the stones that once faced the timbered walls and buildings lay as they had been scattered, first by her invading ancestors four hundred years back, then by the ravaging Britons, and again by the Vikings. Little more than ten years had passed since Haesten's men had camped here among the ruins while Edward and Ethelred burned the fields around them. The invader's stay was short. The fields had recovered and yielded their bounty to patient Saxon farmers.

Mud-and-wattle huts were scattered along the River Dee, but there were none so bold as to build inside the crumbling walls. Aethelflaed surveyed the ruins regretfully. Her people had an ancient dread of living in the stone buildings of the Romans. They feared that the spirits of the Romans might occupy their former dwellings and torment those who came to live in them. So the invading Saxons pulled much of them down. This rendered the spirits homeless and condemned them to wander abroad. The Saxons themselves could live in the open or in crude huts more easily than in stone buildings. But when it came to protecting themselves, all understood the need for walls.

Crumbling remains of towers marked the corners of the enclosure and one or two of these would have to be rebuilt. She picked her way silently among the ruins, Athelstan and David close behind her, not speaking, not daring to break the ancient quiet that hung over this place. It had an air of expectancy; they could feel it prickling at the hairs rising on the backs of their necks, as if the dust-crumbled bones of Briton, Roman, Saxon, and Dane, all who had invaded, built, and taken refuge here, were reinfused with the spirits that had once commanded them in the past and come back to see who came now their way and why.

They walked the inner walls, surveying the wreckage of centuries; she finally called a halt at the southwest corner among the tumbled stones and timber of what appeared to have been granaries. David left, and shortly returned with a few of the levies and set them to clearing a space for a small camp. The area was swiftly cleared, a fire laid, and two thralls came bearing a cauldron of water between them on a pole. They would have barley cakes and cheese for their meal. The water would be heated and the roasting fires set for the fresh game the men would bring in later.

"There is much here already," Athelstan ventured to say. "Perhaps it will not be long in fixing." He tried to sound more hopeful than he felt. Aethelflaed, who was lost in thought, was scratching idly in the dirt with a sharp stick, and when she did not at once reply, he watched the patterns she had drawn in the dirt and saw with surprise that they were not random. She had sketched the outline of the Roman *castra,* the camp, the major roads crossing it, the four main gates, and the path of the River Dee, flowing by the southern and western walls. He watched with growing interest.

"There is much," she agreed at last, "but not enough. See how far away from the river we are?"

He saw and looked up quizzically. "They must have had many thralls to carry water," he said, divining the direction of her thoughts.

"Aye, they had thralls, but they did not carry water here. 'Tis said the Romans had pipes to bring water in, and they must have had such here." She pointed to a heap of what appeared to be broken pots, swept up by the levies.

Athelstan shrugged. "They are only pots." He looked closer, as she said nothing, and saw they were fragments of curved tiles, some shards still large enough to show that they had once been cylindrical. He looked up, startled with the discovery, and saw his aunt smiling at him.

"That is how they brought the water in from so far away," she explained. The river was many yards from the nearest wall. "The path is overgrown now and the tiles crumbled."

"Then how shall we bring water in or store enough. It is dangerous to be so far away from water. If we should be surrounded here…."

"You are right, it is likely that we shall be, some day. But we will not bring the water to the fortress. We shall bring the fortress to the water."

He studied her with concern. "But that will take years!"

She laughed. "Look," she said, scratching in the dirt with her stick. He saw that the figure she had drawn was the old Roman fortress appearing as rectangle lying in the northeast corner of a larger rectangle. The new and larger rectangle, which would be the new fortress, was protected on its southern and western sides by the bend of the river against which it would be built. Water could then be obtained through ports in the wall, making their water supply secure. Only the northern and eastern sides needed to be heavily defended.

She went on describing how the extensions could be quickly built and palisaded, and the inner ramparts built. Slots would be left in the palisade from which spearmen could discourage wall-climbers. Even large rock fragments could be used to throw down at the invaders, and fires could be built on the stone and timber walkways to boil water in cauldrons to spill on the enemy.

"But how long will it take to do this?"

"The summer, perhaps. The stone work may take two years."

He stared at her, concerned. "But we will not stay here that long!"

She tweaked his ear. "No, we shall not. We shall go home by autumn and leave someone here to do it for us."

In later years he was to look back on this as one of the most exciting times of his young manhood, and winced as he remembered that he had wished to go with Edward instead. His remarkable aunt, whose adopted people were already calling her "The Lady of the Mercians" and openly accepting her as their Queen, showed him that there was another side to kingship, something other than blood and battle. She had watched her enemies for many years, saw them building fortresses on the edges of Danish Mercia. She had mulled it over, silently. The deserted wreckage of the Camp of the Legions had been given to her to defend, and the lessons she had learned from her enemies had turned into a plan of her own.

The land was fertile again, and lay open to the Irish Sea and undefended from the Norse and their Irish friends, still fighting the Welsh. The Norse might rage forever in Wales; the Welsh would find a way, Aethelflaed was certain, to throw the Norse out onto the Mercian doorstep. It was only a question of time, and, she hoped, time was on their side.

The Welsh and the Norse would keep each other busy while Aethelflaed built her fortress. Athelstan could see that she planned it to be the stronghold of Western Mercia, for it would command the approach from the sea, it would be a sentinel to watch the hills and mountains to the north, even as far as Strathclyde. It could also keep watch on the northern reaches of the Welsh border, for the Welsh, while no friends of the Northmen, were no friends of the Mercians, either. Great Offa's dyke along the border was still in use more than a hundred years after it was built.

One other matter did he look back on as he recalled this busy summer. It impressed him deeply and later, in his own kingship, he used the lessons here laid down. They were ringed about with enemies, which spurred a desire, a hope, and finally the actions that would bring all these diverse peoples together against a common foe.

They had not been there many weeks, with the timbering of the fort progressing rapidly, when there came by river a small boat. Five or six men disembarked, along with large and shaggy animals that they found, as the group drew near, to be the largest dogs they had ever seen. Athelstan was transported with delight and would have run to greet them but Aethelflaed's restraining arm barred him from doing so.

Work temporarily halted as the men came out to view the strange arrivals, and a score of heavily armed levies quietly closed around the Lady and the Atheling. They waited, their ring-mail chinking softly in the yawning silence as they shifted shield to arm and sword to hand. The small group halted suddenly, daunted by the well-armed levies. The woman clad in soldier's tunic and mantle, the jeweled hilt of her sword winking in the sun, and the tall youngster at her side drew their gaze.

The newcomers and the English regarded each other with curiosity and veiled hostility for what seemed hours. The leader of the group stepped forward cautiously and removed his sword belt and knife. He laid them on the ground, stepped over them and approached Aethelflaed, kneeling some distance in front of her to show that he had come upon an honorable mission and meant no harm. Aethelflaed, looking stern, bid the man approach.

His name, he said, was Niall, and he had come hence from Dublin two years ago with his Norse overlord, Hingamund. "These two years have we fought with Clydog ap Cadell," he opined, "and we shall not have the better of him. My master, jarl Hingamund cannot imagine this and he fights on. The time will come," he said, eying the guard nervously, "that we will be forced to leave Clydog's accurst country and seek refuge in yours."

Aethelflaed laughed derisively. "You cannot expect me to believe that jarl Hingamund will come peaceably. Indeed, none of the Norsemen have ever done so before, and if the tales that reach my ears be true, these fair giants that rule you are bloodier than their brethren from across the North Sea. Peace will come to them only with death, for naught else has ever stilled their bloodlust."

Athelstan watched his aunt with amazement, for he had never seen her features so carved in granite or her eyes so chill. He knew she was not a gentle woman—he had seen her in a stern mood often enough—but he had not seen this spirit of hammered steel, sheathed, like a sword, in the womanly exterior, now drawn and presented to a possible foe.

The Irishman had seen it once. He bowed the lower and exclaimed, "Your distrust is justified and I speak only what I think may happen. The day will come that Hingamund will beg your mercy and indulgence. I can speak truthfully for myself only, for I do not care for the Welsh and if I can escape with life and all my limbs whole, I will assuredly throw myself on your generosity. We cannot stay in that dreadful place," he jerked his head backward in the direction of the hills from whence he had come, "and when the time comes, I wish only a small place to grow my corn and breed my dogs in peace."

He signaled the man behind him to bring the animals forward. Immense, imposing, deep of chest and tight of belly, they appeared about the size of a small pony. Athelstan reached out and stroked the shaggy coat. The dog swung its head on its powerful neck to study him with dark, surprising gentle eyes. "He is beautiful," Athelstan breathed.

"Then he is yours," the Irishman smiled, "for this pair is my gift of peace." He brought the bitch forward and offered the rope looped around her neck to Aethelflaed. "They are my best. We call them wolf-hounds, but they are bred and trained to hunt our Irish elk. Their courage is a match for your own."

"And what do you ask in return, beside your peaceful hide of land?" A smile curved her lips as she watched Athelstan out of the corner of her eye. The dog suddenly lifted his forepaws and placed them on Athelstan's shoulders, making him stagger backwards.

Niall smiled broadly, his bright blue eyes twinkling under an almost black thatch of hair. "That I may be counted among your friends and privileged to bring news of our common…" he hesitated, "friend, Hingamund."

"I see," said Aethelflaed quietly, "you are offering to spy?"

"No, Lady. Spies are for seeking out battles. I wish to avert battles and bloodshed; peace only do I wish, for my own city of Dublin has been bathed in blood for many years. When the Norsemen are not busy killing my people for the sport of it, they kill each other in earnest. They all wish to rule Dublin. I am tired, and Hingamund will tire soon."

"Then you wish me to trust him when he comes?" Her eyes glinted.

Niall shook his head vehemently. "I did not say he was to be trusted—only that he will come in peace."

"Then," said Aethelflaed with deceptive amiability, "you would say I should continue my fortification?"

"If you did not," Niall responded softly, "I would believe you to be without cunning or wit, and I have already seen with my own eyes that such is not the truth."

Aethelflaed took the rope from his hand and gently encouraged the bitch to her side. The great, shining eyes regarded her warmly, the tongue lolled out and the open jaws showed the tips of her fangs in a canine smile. "I must accept your offer," she said to Niall, "for your ambassador is all friendship." The bitch waved her tail majestically. "But," she said, so quietly that only Niall and Athelstan heard her, "do not cross me, for I am no friend to those whose hearts are filled with perfidy. If you will be my friend and I, yours, remember that!"

Niall did not smile back at her and she was glad he took her warning solemnly. He bowed deeply before her and said, "My life is in your hands." He turned quickly and went back to his companions and his boat. She watched him go, scratching the bitch's ears absently. Athelstan saw the pensive look on her face and knowing her better now, knew that ideas were thronging behind the thoughtful eyes. Neither of them knew for certain if Niall was their friend, or if he might work with them. But out of the Irishman's visit would come a plan that would serve them well in the trials to come.

They left the timbered walls of Chester behind them at the end of the summer, along with a small force to defend them and a crew of stone workers to face the timbers according to Aethelflaed's own instruction. It had been, thought Athelstan, an arm around each great, shaggy neck, a most rewarding summer.

CHAPTER TWENTY-THREE

(905)

*E*thelwold was dead, though not by Edward's hand. Aethelflaed had expected to find him dismayed that he had not had vengeance himself. Had his cousin chosen to remain loyal, Edward would have cared little how much Ethelwold envied him the throne, but Ethelwold had moved against Edward's power. Worse, he had involved the East Anglians in his treason and the peace between Mercia and East Anglia had been dependable only until Guthrum died. Thereafter, peace was in a delicate balance, much depending on Haesten's current ambitions.

Edward's rage was against the East Anglians for ignoring Alfred's and Guthrum's treaty after the deaths of the two principals: to Edward the treaty was unaltered and firm. That the East Anglians thought otherwise aroused greater ire than Ethelwold's betrayal. Edward acted accordingly. The East Anglians bore the brunt of his raids of retribution. Edward penetrated East Anglia, deep into the Cambridgeshire fens, following roughly the paths traced by the Rivers Cam, Ouse, and Wissey, ravaging the fenland between the dykes of Cambridgeshire and the Wissey before he gave the order to withdraw. Edward retired in safety, but Ealdorman Sigewulf and his son, Sigeberht, and the Ealdorman Sigehelm, all of the Kentish levies, refused to turn back. Edward, first with growing anger, finally with a black fury, sent one messenger after another ordering them to turn back from the fens. No answer did he receive, nor did he ever, for Ethelwold's men came upon the Kentishmen and the battle was quickly joined. Sigewulf, Sigeberht, and Sigehelm were killed along with the best of the Kentish levies and their thanes.

Edward was filled with mingled anger and pity for the slaughtered Kentishmen. Independent, insubordinate, and unruly to the end, they nevertheless did him one great favor: they did not fall alone. They brought down with them the king of East Anglia and several Norse barons. They also killed Ethelwold. The Danes won the place of battle, but with the loss of their king and Ethelwold, the rebellion collapsed, drowned in the blood of both sides.

"And John?" asked Aethelflaed in a chill voice.

"He did not escape," was all Edward would say. John had been seen to fall with a spear in his shoulder. Edward did not care, as long as John troubled them no more.

Ethelred, to their great relief, was no longer confined to his couch. He had been plied with herb infusions, lathered with malodorous salves, and had drunk potions concocted from the Leech Book for his recovery. He was much improved in spite of it, and though Aethelflaed thought him uncommonly thin, her relief at seeing him alive crowded out of her mind all other considerations.

When Niall had come to her about Hingamund, she had not attempted to hide the hatred she had for the Norse. It was on Ethelred's account. His boyhood, his manhood had been spent on this greedy, relentless foe. His spirit had suffered and rebounded: his body could no longer bear the burdens. He stooped now, his hair and beard were grizzled, and his hands were becoming gnarled from illness, age, and old injuries. Worst of all the very air he breathed seemed to poison him. But the eyes still burned with a lively spirit and she could still see in the weathered lines of his face strong traces of the handsome, vital man she had married eighteen years ago.

Still, he was better. She looked on him, loved him, the more painfully for her helplessness to stop the flow of time. It ran through her fingers like sand; if she closed her fingers to stay it, it spilled over her palms and away. Ethelred's life was spilling slowly away, the time was running out and she could not stop it.

They sat in their private garden side by side; their hands locked and said little out of sheer relief at being together still. Aethelflaed saw in his eyes that he had been considering his mortality as never before. To be attacked with the flying venom, as his Leeches, his doctors, explained to him, and to survive it was a wonderful good fortune. "I cannot help but be well again," he assured her, and she rested a little easier, because she saw he was reassured and not at all frightened. Nevertheless, Bishop Theodred, whose position as a sage, being a priest, was superior to that of the Leeches, told him he must not overtax himself.

"I am not to leave London," he complained, but without bitterness, "so the burden of Chester must be yours." His eyes held a mixture of regret and relief, for he did not wish to return to Chester. His last defense of it had left an imprint on his spirit that he could not erase.

She had not had time to show him the sketches she had made. They could wait because it was important for them to sit here side by side, absorbing each other's presence. She begrudged every second away from him. They sat silently in the darkness and occasionally she sensed a strangeness in the garden, which she could now see dimly. She had seen this picture before and searched her memory for its likeness. She turned her head to study the outline of Ethelred's upturned profile and, following his upward gaze, was seized by sudden recognition.

"How long has it been there?" she whispered at last.

"Only a few nights." He did not take his eyes from the sky.

The firedrake glowed down at them steadily, moving with stately dignity along its appointed path. As we are also, she thought. We move along our ordained paths, and no more than the firedrake do we know the shape of our path until we have traveled it and look back. She closed her eyes to shut out the sight of it: the long-haired star never appeared but to speak of someone's path. A life was always connected with its brilliant appearance. She stole a fearful look at Ethelred's face, but his face was full of repose. Who, then? It was only a few days from the anniversary of Alfred's death and she straightened up abruptly. The firedrake hesitated, barely perceptibly, and sent a bright and wordless message through the cold sky into her heart. For once, she understood and was dazzled with the sorrowful knowledge.

"Eth'red," she said heavily, breaking the long silence. "I must go to Winchester tomorrow."

He turned his head slightly. "I know, he said softly, raising her hand to his lips as if to comfort her, and she realized the message had been given to him also. They were so close these days that to speak to either was to speak to both. When he took her up to their chambers and pulled her gently down to their couch, she did not demur, though she did not wish to spend his energy needlessly. "There is naught to fear," he whispered, reading her thoughts. "One cannot shorten or lengthen one's life a single whit by refusing out of fear to live it. I will not go before I am ready to go. Do not fear for me." He stopped her protest with a kiss.

She arose early and was careful not to wake him. It was strange, she thought, that his illness was pulling them closer. He was optimistic and insistent that he would get back to his old duties. She doubted it. Years of campaigning had drained him and though he was still tall, the slightly halting gait dragged at her heart, he who had always carried himself as straight as the ashen shaft of his spear.

She reached Winchester with little time to spare. She and Edward went to Nunnaminster without delay and bid their farewells to Ealhswith. Aethelflaed wept when they left her. She was such a frail wisp and called to Alfred several times as they sat with her. Even when she sighed and slipped softly away from them, they did not know if she was aware of their presence as they held her hands and spoke to her.

Aethelflaed stayed in Winchester only long enough to admire Elfled's daughter, Eadflaed. Elfled was well content with herself and her family, and was breeding again. She kissed her sister-in-law warmly, deeply grateful for Elfled's and Edward's happiness and was relieved to return to London for Christmas. She wanted to be with Ethelred; she knew he needed her and she needed him more than ever.

The new year was marred for her by a matter close to her heart. Aethelfrith courted Elfwyn patiently and persistently but was not rewarded for his perseverance. It broke Aethelflaed's heart but she dared not interfere. Her one brief talk with her daughter disclosed only that the girl's anger at being passed over in the succession had not abated.

When later she saw Aethelfrith in the Great Hall, she knew from his face that Elfwyn's hurt had been vented on him. She wished perversely that she had not given her approval in the hope that this might have driven her daughter to accept the young man. Ethelred only said, a little sadly, "That would have served no good and might have hurt Ael'frith. He is too valuable to us."

She agreed and resigned herself to it as best she could. She was leaving London and Ethelred again: the fortress-building at Chester had progressed enough that the city was ready to be fortified. Aethelfrith and his levies were chosen for the outpost. There was another reason demanding her return to Chester: the uninvited Norse in Wales. As Niall had predicted, Clydog ap Cadell had finally worn through Hingamund's ability to fight. There would be no respite for the Norsemen in Wales, and Hingamund was in no position to enter Mercia belligerently. Return to Dublin was not possible, for the Ulstermen ruled, and the few remaining Vikings had been starved into submission. Niall relayed Hingamund's request to speak with the Lady or her husband to hear their terms.

It was not unduly chill for November, but it was the edge of winter and Hingamund would certainly be entering Chester, so desperate was he. She wanted it to be on her terms that he did so. She and Aethelfrith, with a large force of levies, would go to present the necessary display of power. Athelstan would go with them. They had not been long in Chester when word came to them that their sometime Norse enemy begged audience with the Lady.

Hingamund strode into the timbered building in Chester that served as Aethelflaed's Hall and blinked at the sudden darkness. Aethelflaed stood at her table facing him, her back to the crackling fire. He blinked again, adjusting his eyes to the dark Hall, seeing only her silhouette against the flames.

The stories she had heard were true: the man before her was extremely tall, large-boned, and fair, with vivid blue eyes. His hair was pale blond, trailing shaggily over his shoulders. His beard was almost red, crisp and curling. His eyes focused on her and took in Athelstan at her left, who was studying him with undisguised curiosity, and Aethelfrith on her right, who returned the scrutiny impassively. Aethelflaed's steady, unsmiling stare did not appear to unnerve Hingamund, for he grinned broadly, bowed, and waved a hand at his retainer, who scuttled forward with a small wooden casket bound in brass and iron. He opened it and offered it to her. It was filled with silver brooches, worked with twined dragons and leaves, and buckles of silver niello, and other trinkets. She motioned him to set it on the table between them and come forward.

"I am here at your request," she said impatiently, "and though your gifts are pleasing, it is surely not these that brought you here."

He bowed again. "No, Lady, I have come to beg your indulgence."

She raised her eyebrows but made no comment. Hingamund kept his eyes on her face as he continued. "We have fought without rest for many years in Britain, but Clydog is fierce. We cannot hold out forever against him. We are tired of war and wish only to settle peaceably amongst these Britons."

She smiled sourly. "One does not live peaceably amongst the Britons. They do not live peaceably amongst themselves. You cannot hope to live in peace with the Welsh or anyone if you are trying to take their land away from them."

"But, Lady, I have heard that it is possible to live peaceably amongst your people, for it is said that in Northumbria my kinsmen and your English live in peace and dignity together."

"That is so," she agreed. "But they live under the Danelaw. Here we live under Mercian law."

"We have heard that your father was a fair and just king, who dealt most nobly with his enemies." He eyed her speculatively. "We should consider it our good fortune to treat with the daughter of so great a king."

She was unmoved by the flattery. "I do not need to be told that you wish a noble favor of me, one such as to honor my father's name," she replied drily. "What would you have me grant you?"

"We wish only to live in peace with your people."

"I have not known Northmen to come in peace and yet be satisfied with so little. What assurance do I have that you have not come to steal my people's land and food? You cannot expect trust here, for your kinsmen have betrayed their own honor and broken sacred oaths made to my father more times that I can remember."

"Alas," he replied, with show of humility, "what assurance can I give you? See how few we are amongst you. Could we hold out against your levies, so many there be, if we could not prevail against the Britons?"

There was no point in prolonging it. If she did not give permission, they would be forced to fight and she did not wish to waste her strength on this ragged band. They were no threat for the present. Her glance flicked to Niall in the shadows. He was staring impassively into the fire. She looked back at Hingamund. "Very well. You shall have land of your own, attested to by my own hand. You will abide by Mercian law here, and as your land is granted in the name of Ethelred and myself, we are your overlords. You will swear your oaths to me and you will owe all land and food rents to us. I will remit these to Ealdorman Aethelfrith, who commands this fortress. Pay your duties to him as to us."

The big Norseman bowed deeply. "I am grateful, for our weariness is beyond words."

"Good." Her tone was brusque. "Then you will leave your weapons here, not just for the swearing of oaths, but forever, for you will now plow the land and not spill blood upon it. As long as you abide our terms and remit your rents and duties, you will be protected under our law." She watched him narrowly as he bobbed his shaggy head and smiled blandly at her. "But I must warn you," she said with deceptive gentleness, "if you plan treason and oath-breaking, you will be sorry. My father was generous with his enemies. Do not think because I am a woman that I will be forgiving, either for my father's sake or my woman's heart." Hingamund stared back at her, his smile less certain. "Do you understand?" she persisted.

"I must believe you, Lady, for our own women can be more terrible than men when they are crossed."

"If what I hear of the customs of the *Vik* be true, they can scarcely be blamed. You are fortunate not to have been murdered in your beds by your wives and sisters, or strangled at birth by your mothers. Do not mistake me, Hingamund, now or ever: I do not trust you or your kin. You are a pestilential lot, without honor or Godliness, and you do not deserve the land you will be given. I will not hesitate, if you do aught amiss, to destroy you!"

He blanched under the tirade and dropped his eyes from hers against the coldness and fury he saw directed at himself for the guilt of his kinsmen's bloodlust and dishonor.

"Now leave," she ordered curtly, "and let me hear naught of you but good"

He left abruptly and she signaled Niall to come sit with her and Aethelfrith. They drank in silence. Finally Niall said, "You know he will not be content with only a few hides of land. Once he is restored to himself, he will be troublesome." He studied her anxiously.

"I am certain of it." She glanced at Aethelfrith, who ducked his head in silent agreement. "How long will it take you to finish the wall?

"A year perhaps. Less if I had more levies."

"I will send them to you, in small groups. I do not wish the Northmen to be aware of strength immediately. See you to it. It will not take him more than a harvest or two to recover." Athelstan caught her eye. "Yes?"

"Lady Mother, you did not believe him?"

"That he is tired of war? Yes. Everyone grows weary of it sooner or later, and Hingamund has the look of it about the eyes. He is a *nithing* for now; but he will till his land, feed himself, and grow greedy again. When the time comes, we will be ready. Is that not so, Ae'lfrith?"

"We will be ready," he replied, resolutely.

She turned to the Irishman across from her. "Niall, have you a mind to place yourself at my service? You have done your part well in this matter and I will give you my protection. I would be well pleased should you decide to serve Lord Ethelred and myself."

He shrugged. "I would gladly, but I am no soldier."

"I do not need a soldier. I need a man who knows his people and who listens to their desires. Do you do that well?"

His eyes glowed with quick understanding. "I do that very well, Lady."

"Ah! Do then your people wish for other friends if the Northmen prove unfaithful to their Irish ties?"

"They do, right enough. Hingamund is certain to be as untrue to his friends as he is to his enemies."

"Then," she said, smiling at him, "you must assure your countrymen that they are not without help. Though we be foreign to them, we welcome them and offer friendship and assistance. We are not oath breakers and pagans, as are the Northmen, and the God who watches over your people watches over us as well."

Niall drained his drinking horn, and David filled it again. Athelstan watched his aunt's face, delighted and fascinated with the quiet conversation with Niall. She was suggesting alliances, something Ethelnoth had earlier tried to do in Northumbria and failed. Here the Norsemen were a small group surrounded by enemies; it might be easier to come to terms. But what could a handful of bedraggled Irish, lately come unsuccessfully from Wales, add to a fortress far stronger than themselves. Aethelflaed's next words to Niall explained to them what she had in mind.

"Niall," she said thoughtfully, "have not great numbers of your countrymen been forced across the sea with the Vikings to the Isles of the north? And to Strathclyde? Do not the Vikings now fight among the Scots and Britons there?"

"Aye, they have." Niall's face darkened with anger. "They are forced against their will by their Viking overlords. The Norse jarls will kill them if they do not fight, the Scots will kill them if they do."

"The Scots and Britons cannot like the Norse who ravage the lowlands. Surely there is something we can do about it?" She raised her eyebrows quizzically.

Athelstan watched with delight. She was suggesting a treaty not merely with the Irish newcomers, but with the Welsh, the Scots, and the Mercians together against the Norse. Most astonishing would be any treaty involving these ancient enemies, the Welsh and the Mercians. But, he doubted not, she would do it. She would assist them, not protect them. The Welsh would be wary about Mercian protection, but not about Mercian assistance. Hingamund thought that he could walk in the back door of Mercia, pretending to need help, and take it away from a helpless woman. Little did he know, thought Athelstan. The Norseman might tower over his aunt by a foot or more, but was not Alfred's daughter cunning enough to be a king?

"Surely we can," Niall now responded. "I have kinsmen amongst them myself, men who have escaped their Viking masters and gone to live with the Scots."

Aethelflaed's face relaxed into a broad and satisfied smile. "Then you will know what must be done."

Niall rose and bowed to her, his eyes sparkling appreciatively. "I will leave at once, Lady."

CHAPTER TWENTY-FOUR

Summer ripened into a harvest of unparalleled bounty. Hingamund restored himself on his land outside Chester. His restlessness remained in check, and he was out of touch with his kinsmen, so there was nothing to do but farm his lands. He could make no move but what Niall knew of it.

Since the East Anglian's King Eohric and Ethelwold had fallen in the Kentishmen's ill-advised stand at Holme, all resistance had collapsed and Edward had grown more powerful. This the somewhat disorganized jarls of East Anglia had been compelled to acknowledge, and together with the Northumbrians, were willing now to treat with Edward. Ethelred's illness had so far not tempted the Vikings in northwest Mercia to any rash action, and the wife of the "King of the Saxons" was no one to trifle with. The very fact that she permitted the enemy to settle on her lands was considered proof of strength. It was a fortunate misinterpretation of the situation. She and Edward had long seen that driving out the Vikings was an impossibility: it was, however, possible to dilute the danger. To this end, Edward quietly moved English families into East Anglia, or wherever they would be peaceably accepted, to settle and live among the Danish. Aethelflaed only considered that she had done something of the same, though in reverse, with Hingamund.

It helped her in another matter: the Scots and Britons, Niall had found, were eager to ally themselves with one strong enough, daring enough to tolerate with apparently careless disregard the presence of such a one as Hingamund. They called her "Queen of the Saxons," a title she deplored but found impossible to eradicate. Was she not, Niall pointed out amiably, the wife of the Saxon King Ethelred, and was it not herself who acted in his stead rather than her brother? She could not expect newcomers to think otherwise of herself. Even the Norse respected her.

She learned from Niall that Hingamund and his kinsmen, while related to the Danes of Northumbria, came from a different kingdom, called *Norweg*. The language of the Norway Norse was similar to that of the Danes, but there the resemblance ended. The *Norweg* were very tall with bright blue eyes like those of Hingamund, and had fair skins and pale hair, a race of giants who dwarfed their Danish cousins and the Saxons. Yet they said they were cousins; and so they must be, for the kings of Dublin descended from *Ivarr inn beinlausi,* once king of Northumbria. Ivarr's sons and grandsons ruled Dublin, and his brother Halfdan was remembered as the ravager of Wessex. So blood-kin they must be, for Halfdan's name itself implied the mingling of the *Norweg* and Danish lines. Ivarr's grandsons saw all this as a valid basis for their claim to the throne of Northumbria. Now that the Leinstermen had expelled them from Dublin, Northumbria was more attractive than ever, though it had one drawback: Northumbria was under Edward's influence. Peace was ratified at Tiddingford, and Northumbria and East Anglia were no longer at war with Edward.

Sigtryggr's sons went across the Irish Sea to Strathclyde, while Hingamund sought a place for himself in Wales and Cheshire. It was an uncomfortable fact that the Scottish Isles, Galloway, and the Isle of Man were firmly under Norse control when Hingamund fled to Wales, and Ragnall, grandson of Ivarr, sailed northward to Strathclyde. It was not good; it boded ill, and while the crops ripened and Mercia flourished, Aethelflaed's concern about the Norse among them flourished.

Yet, it was quiet, a peaceful time, the type of atmosphere that precedes disaster. Ethelred was slowly worsening, to her profound distress. Elfwyn helped him govern London in Aethelflaed's absences, which were growing more frequent as she took over more of Ethelred's military duties, and Elfwyn had ceased to inveigh against Theodred's constant presence and supervision.

Aethelfrith returned periodically to London with reports of progress at Chester and each time returned to his outpost with more levies. With each trip to London, he saw more of Elfwyn's lively companion, Leofwyn, and said no more of his progress with Elfwyn. He came to Aethelflaed at last and explained, apologetically, that Elfwyn had refused him, not once, but many times. He wished to be released from their understanding. Aethelflaed readily assented. Aethelfrith was of an age when a man should have a family of his own. Aethelflaed assured him he had no further obligation to her daughter, but it saddened her. She had grown fond of the young man; moreover, Athelstan stood in awe of him and they were becoming fast friends.

She gave Leofwyn a wedding present of a gold necklace inlaid with garnet and an intricately wrought gold-wire brooch. Ethelred gave Aethelfrith a handsome gift of land for his future family. If Elfwyn was disappointed by Aethelfrith's marriage to her friend, it was not obvious. At least she had softened toward her mother, and Aethelflaed found some compensation in their mutual interest in the affairs of the city.

It was a harsh and uncompromising providence, Aethelflaed told herself, that Elfwyn had only marriage or the convent as her future, for she had Aethelflaed's ability to administer to the borough courts. Her understanding was quick and she grasped the essentials of a situation before others had barely discerned the problem. Aethelflaed mused bitterly that it was a waste, but said nothing. It was enough that they could talk eagerly and without restraint in the matter of governance. Beyond that and Ethelred's illness, they discussed no other matters.

It was fortunate for Aethelflaed that Niall sent her a message full of warning, since it successfully diverted her attention from her daughter. It was not the sort of news she wished to hear; it was what she regretfully expected to hear. When she unrolled the parchment read his terse message she sent for Aethelfrith, recently returned from his honeymoon. He, at any rate, appeared happy.

"I am distressed," she said without preamble, "that I must be the means to part you from your bride-bed for a time." She handed him the parchment, which he read, nodding thoughtfully.

"It is as we thought, is it not?" he asked. "We did not believe that Hingamund would stay forever rooted."

She motioned him to sit. She had sent for Ethelred and had no time to warn Aethelfrith that he had taken a turn for the worse. When Ethelred joined them, Aethelfrith looked away, quickly enough that Ethelred did not see his face, but Aethelflaed, who was watching for it, saw the flicker of fear in the younger man's eyes. Ethelred was thinner and more haggard, for he had been too active in his duties. Aethelfrith looked at her and noticed for the first time the dark smudges under her eyes and guessed that between Ethelred's illness and her daughter's growing haughtiness, she had spent a hard summer. Hingamund would present a needed diversion for her. This was the best that could be said for the matter.

Chester, under Aethelfrith's care, had grown rich, its market flourished and the local folk were encouraged back into the city. The enlarged enclosure provided much land not earlier inhabited by the Romans, which removed the objections of the more fearful. Aethelflaed had instructed Aethelfrith to pull down the remaining Roman ruins and clear them away. The folk returned gradually, for their goods could not be sold at markets not authorized and controlled by the overlord.

Hingamund came also to Chester to barter and sell his goods. The harvest had been indiscriminately bountiful to all. Nevertheless, it was apparent to those watching Hingamund survey the riches that abounded inside Chester, that greed was working on him and that he believed that if he desired it, then it should by right be his. Niall had noticed and reported unusual activity having to do with Hingamund's land. Uncommon numbers of visitors sought Hingamund, asking casually in Chester's markets for his whereabouts. The visitors did not trouble to conceal their accents, since the folk were becoming as much accustomed to mixed accents as to mixed blood. Even so, Niall sent his people on missions to the north and himself followed some of the visitors to Hingamund's lands. Being on good terms with Hingamund, he had even been there when some of the visitors arrived.

What he found alarmed him. They were not just from one place or the other; they were from Strathclyde and York in particular. The traffic was too regular for kinship visits alone.

"You must spend the winter at Chester," Ethelred said wearily to Aethelfrith, "for we must have someone firmly in command. If he is going to attack, it is unlikely that he will so do before spring."

Aethelfrith agreed. "The harvest is safely in and under our guard, and though theirs is in too, they could not feed so large an army for the winter."

"If you wish to leave Leofwyn here, I shall care for her as my own," Aethelflaed promised. "She will be given every privilege to show the honor in which you are held."

Aethelfrith smiled, grateful for her gesture. "Lady, your esteem is valued above all things to me, but I have already told Leofwyn that this would happen. Did we not assume from our first meeting with the man," he pointed contemptuously at the parchment, "that he begged for land not because he was so weary of battle, but because he wished to gain peaceable entry to further his own treachery?" His eyes narrowed thoughtfully. "He would wait only long enough to supply himself with food and weapons before he took what he wished."

She recalled his thoughts to his wife. "Then she wishes to winter at Chester with you?"

"She does."

It will be hard, for we will surely be attacked come spring!"

"She knows." His eyes shone with pride. "She is full of heart and insists she is no lily."

Ethelred smiled at his wife, his careworn face lighting up briefly, then looked at the young man. "You will take the best we have with you. We have called out Werferth's levies from Worcester and Gloucester. Edward has called upon the levies of Asser at Somerset, and Bishop Asser has assured us that he himself, old as he is, will undertake to speak to the Welsh if necessary to secure their peace."

Aethelflaed handed a roll of parchment to Aethelfrith. "You and your wife will use my *haga* as your home. I will join you early in the year, before the last snows are gone, and we will set our trap in advance. I must stay here until then so that Ethelred and I may work out the plan together. We will send messengers to you, and you must send them back to tell us of your needs. Everything needed for the defense of the city will be given."

"The Dublin Norse and the Danes of Northumbria," Ethelred explained, "have tried for many years to join their kingships. If they were ever allowed to do so, all of northern Mercia would be lost to us."

"Hingamund himself," interjected Aethelflaed, "is of little account; he is a *nithing*, but the leader of his Norse kin in the kingdom of the Scots is Ragnall. The son of Sigtryggr Ivarsson must not be given breathing space in Mercia."

Aethelfrith left, taking his wife with him. Aethelflaed spent the winter uneasily, fighting an immense darkness of spirit, for in this, the thirty-sixth year of her life, when she wished peace and respite, she found only trouble. She knew with unspoken certainty that her husband was sick, perhaps to death, though he constantly assured her of his increasing health. Her daughter's heart appeared set against her, and the Viking host was on her doorstep. Of her own efforts she must find a way to stave off these specters, not the least of which was the loneliness and isolation growing in her soul. She was deprived even of Athelstan and Edward's company, at this time when she needed it the most, for they had gone into East Anglia and Northumbria.

Edward and Ethelred together had decided, upon seeing the influence of the Danes settled in English Mercia, that they must somehow reverse the process. Since there was tentative peace now between Danish and English Mercia, they hit upon the plan of buying land in East Anglia and Northumbria and bringing English in to settle it. The Danish eye for trade was as sharp as their zest for war. After a few brief exchanges of intentions, Edward was invited to visit the Danish-held territories and view the lands he wished to purchase for himself and Lord Ethelred. He departed, taking Athelstan with him. Aethelflaed felt an irrational resentment against the forces that had not only burdened her with misery, but had also deprived her of comfort.

When she could stand her solitude no longer, she left the garrison and waited upon Werferth at his stone palace beside the Walbrook.

"My dearest Lady," he exclaimed, extending both hands to her, "you should have sent for me. I would have been pleased to attend you." She was silent while he sent to the kitchen for refreshment. "Now," he said, when they had disposed of their small repast, "what troubles you?" His eyes rested on her tired face. "I know your spirit is heavy for I can see it in your eyes."

She exhaled slowly and wearily, and told him, not of her burdens, which he already knew she bore, but of her loneliness in the face of it, her sore-heartedness at her daughter's plight.

"You do not speak of the enemy. Do you not fear the coming battle?"

She pondered. "No," she replied, "for we have prepared Chester well, and Aethelfrith is as strong and clever as Ethelred was in his younger days."

"As he was," said Werferth softly. "That is a hard matter to abide, is it not?"

"Aye," she agreed, tears beginning to trickle down her cheeks under the gentle probing. Compassionate and loving though he was, Werferth never failed to scald the spirit, to open and cleanse a wound. He considered it unkind to spare the truth. "Ah," she cried out, when she could speak, "he bears his suffering better than do I!"

"He must. And," he continued, "you would find it easier if your daughter were more accepting of her fate?" Aethelflaed nodded mutely. Werferth studied her with sympathy, then said suddenly, almost peremptorily, "You must forget Elfwyn for now. You can do nothing about it."

Her tears stopped, stanched by the unexpectedness of his words. "How can that be so? I have wracked my mind for ways to help, for surely there is an answer for it."

"You can do nothing," he insisted. "If there is an answer, as you believe, then it lies within the girl. She has chosen to ignore you for reasons of her own. You must not forget, my dear, that you have no ultimate control over the will of another."

"She hates me," she said bleakly.

"It is to be expected, Aethelflaed," Werferth said patiently, and with great sympathy. "Your aims have always differed. You gave your oath of fealty to Edward; you made his cause yours. Elfwyn does not understand the loyalty between you, Ethelred, and Edward. The faithfulness of the three of you to each other is remarkable, you know."

A spasm of worry touched Aethelflaed's face. "When we are gone it will go hard with her if she crosses my brother."

"She may do that," he agreed, refusing to comfort her or allay her fears with false hopes, "but it is not in your hands. Edward will not allow her to oppose him. Remember, Aethelflaed, that many years ago we spoke of your destiny?"

"Aye, we did, but I cannot see it yet." She rubbed her forehead wearily.

"You cannot see it because it is upon you now. God's will unfolds and is there for you to see."

She felt pulled too many ways at once. "I do what I do by necessity. I cannot say I would choose this life."

"Providence does not always yield to our choice. You must attend to matters that are within your power to shape and leave those that are not to others." He regarded her silently, then said, enigmatically, "Trust Edward."

He smiled and reached out to take her hand. "What you are about to set out upon was chosen for you. Your hardest work is yet to come!"

His words froze her. She was tired and overburdened. She wanted to hear that all this would soon be over and things would be right again, if they ever had been. Instead, Werferth was telling her that she had only begun. He was sympathetic, understanding, all of that, but comforting, never. Contact with the spirit of this most singular bishop was as bracing as a stiff sea breeze. He could gently scrape the feelings raw, kindly expose to view one's hidden, well-loved illusions, and though one felt the soul run blood before he had finished, the healing had begun without one's conscious awareness. He was a curious blend of toughness and compassion.

Until her strength was called upon, her acceptance was expected. She returned to the garrison, knowing that whether she accepted her difficulties or not, she could spare them no more worry. She steeled herself to deal kindly, but firmly, with Elfwyn, recognizing the truth of Werferth's words. Elfwyn's destiny was no longer in any hands but her own. She knew with unspeakable sadness that her daughter would be held in check only so long as her mother and father were alive. She winced at the realization that it would be Edward who must take her in hand.

She counseled with Ethelred and learned all he had to impart to her. He had studied the plans she had drawn for the rebuilding of Chester, which were now nearly complete, adding what details she might have overlooked. He awaited Aethelfrith's frequent dispatches as eagerly as she did herself and occasionally his eyes glistened with a familiar light.

When they were not working on battle plans, they spent quiet hours together, talking, absorbing each other's company, for neither knew how much time was left to them. Some days Ethelred was exhausted, and she put him to bed herself and plied him with herbs to help him rest. His joints ached and swelled and old scars pained him. Some nights she sat by his bedside, listening to his labored breathing until David came with hot wine and food to ease her own sleepless vigil.

Then after several days, Ethelred would be more himself again, and they would work and plan anew. When the message finally came from Aethelfrith, the one they had both awaited, they read it together, then reread it and wordlessly laid it aside.

It was time for her to go.

CHAPTER TWENTY-FIVE

(907)

Hingamund stood before her, arrogantly at ease. A year and a half of good farming and hunting had fattened him and erased the haunted look. He flashed her a mirthless smile, as though with a smile he could disarm her suspicion. He was mistaken; there was nothing to suspect. Niall had already told her the truth of him. She stared steadily at him, unyieldingly cold. His eyes flashed with quick anger that she did not unbend and welcome him, for as he told Aethelfrith earlier when he had requested her presence, he came entirely in peace. She deliberately held her tongue, waiting for him to speak.

He bowed stiffly and repeated to her his intention. "Lady Aethelflaed, I have come in peace."

"So you have said." She raised and eyebrow and saw a muscle twitch in his cheek. Otherwise, his calm was unruffled by the disbelief in her tone, and his manner exuded a confidence she knew he would not have possessed had he been alone in this venture. Again, she was silent, watching him through narrowed eyes, awaiting with interest his next words. She already knew his intentions. Niall's men were clever and efficient, and they had seen the danger to their new homeland. They were determined that it should not be overrun with Vikings.

Hingamund looked around with some satisfaction. The city was greatly to his liking. "Lady," he said, "we have come to thank you for your past generosity with us. This is a rich land and we have prospered."

"So I have noticed," she observed drily.

He ignored her and continued. "We, my friends and myself, would like to stay here, but," he eyed her with disarming modesty, "we find the lands you have granted us, while very good, do not compare with this city and its wealth."

"I would expect not, since Lord Ethelred and I, with Aethelfrith's help, have taken great pains to enrich this place. I am sorry you feel you cannot stay. We cannot hold you here if you choose to leave." She looked him unwaveringly in the eye, preserving a bland countenance and had the satisfaction of seeing his gaze drop momentarily.

He recovered quickly. "Lady," he explained hastily, "we do not choose to leave!"

"Oh? Then I am sorry you are not happy, for there is nothing more I can do for you." She leaned back and regarded him with polite disinterest. He did not see the steely glint in her eyes.

"But there is!" His bright blue eyes flashed again and this time there was no mistaking the greed in them. "Though our lands be fertile and the harvest good, there is not enough to meet our needs." He looked down at her, almost apologetically. "We have come to ask you, nay, implore you, Lady, to give this city and its lands to us." The sound of breath, suddenly indrawn in astonishment, arose from the levies surrounding Aethelflaed. She thought of Edward. He would have thrown back his head and roared with laughter, then drawn his sword and run this brazen fool through on the spot.

Aethelflaed did not move a hair; from the look of readiness on Hingamund's face, he had expected of her a response such as Edward's might have been. Niall had prepared her well. Hingamund had at last blurted out exactly what she had expected of him from the second he set foot in Mercia. She caught Athelstan's angry murmur of "wanton treachery" and raised her hand without turning her head to silence him. She did not wish to break the tension, or to move her eyes from Hingamund's face, and she was pleased to see him disconcerted by her calm indifference.

"I can understand your needs and your desire, Hingamund, but you cannot ask me to give you the city. I must have payment for it." She heard Athelstan gasp in astonishment. "What do you intend to give me in payment?" she asked imperturbably.

Hingamund's eyes widened with surprise. "I cannot give you anything. I have said, Lady, our lands are not rich enough." She caught the look of annoyance on his face. He had thought to intimidate her with the veiled reference to his "friends."

"I see. Then you cannot expect me to give it to you without ransom. After all," she paused to smile knowingly at him, "I can expect you to understand the matter of ransom. Your kinsmen have practiced it on us to great advantage these many years."

"Lady!" Hingamund's voice was edged with impatience, for he did not understand the game she was playing with him. "Lady!" he exclaimed, "You must hear me. If you do not give us the city, there will be great trouble for you. I wish to do this thing peaceably."

"No!" Her snapped reply hung flatly in the air between them.

Hingamund started, then flushed with anger. "You do not understand." He glared fiercely at her.

She stood up, her face finally growing warm as she released the anger she had been restraining. "Hingamund, you forget that I am your Overlord;

you have sworn loyalty to me. I see you are as careless of oaths as your kinsmen."

Anger contorted his features, and his voice, when he spoke, grated harshly. "We give oaths or you would not give us land. You must give Chester to us, for we will have it one way or another. We are trying to do it in peace because of the favor you have shown us."

"Hingamund." Aethelflaed leaned forward over the table separating them, speaking very softly. A hush fell over the company. "I am tired of your arrogance, your perfidy, your dishonor." He opened his mouth to reply. "Be silent," she commanded him. "I will hear no more of your outrageous demands and threats, nor shall you play the innocent any longer with me. I am aware that you have had secret meetings with your Danish brethren and with Ragnall." She heard Athelstan's twitch of surprise and the angry murmur of the company. Only Niall, herself, and Aethelfrith had known of this. "You come in peace, to spare us, you say. I say it is to spare yourself trouble."

She drew her sword and laid it on the table, unsheathed. Its steel blade, honed and polished by David to a dreadful shine, glinted at him, the jeweled eyes of its hilt glaring up at him with implacable intent. "You shall not have Chester, and if you think to possess it, you will have to cross this," she pointed to her sword between them, "before you do. Tell your Northumbrian kin and Ragnall's horde that your treachery has been uncovered and its stink offends us mightily. It is against your perfidy and theirs that Chester has been fortified."

Hingamund blanched but did not move. His eyes narrowed and his mouth turned down menacingly. Now she did as Edward would have done: she threw back her head and laughed, not with amusement but contempt. "Did you think to win me by flattery and, failing that, to frighten me with threats? Am I to wilt before such foolishness? You said yourself that women are more to be feared than men when angered." The smile left her face abruptly. "Then know that I am angered. And know also that I expected nothing else of you. Did I not tell you when I gave you lands that I did not trust you? Did you think that I would allow you live amongst us unwatched?" She looked at him with immense loathing and was gratified to see the shock on his face. "Now go, and let me not see you again lest I kill you myself, for if you once more set foot in Chester your life is forfeit!"

Hingamund's face blazed with rage and frustration and he was momentarily speechless. Before he could recover, two of the guards had grabbed him roughly by the arms and propelled him toward the door. He went, resistless with shock.

"Bar the gates as soon as he leaves," she said to Aethelfrith. Have all the villagers been gathered in?"

"Aye, they have."

"Then at supper we will have our council. Bring Athelstan with you for his thoughts must be heard also." She saw the quick flare of gratification in Athelstan's eyes. He was sixteen and not inexperienced in battle. It was time his voice was heard. "Now I am tired, Aethelfrith, and wish to rest until then."

"Lady, my wife begs to be allowed to attend you, since you have brought no one with you."

Aethelflaed smiled and accepted; it would be restful. She was dismayed when Leofwyn presented herself, because the girl was obviously with child. Had she known, she would have been unwilling to allow her to come to Chester. She took Leofwyn's hand and drew her to the bench beside her. "Ae'lfrith did not tell me," she exclaimed. "What can he be thinking of? You would be much safer in London."

Leofwyn smiled. "You must not be angry with him. He told me of the danger and entreated me to stay there. I wished to be here."

"My dear," said Aethelflaed heavily. "What lies ahead of us none can tell. It will be very hard and the sights you will see will not be good."

"I know. Ae'lfrith has told me of that also."

"If we do not prevail, it will be much the worse for you, being with child. Are you not afraid?"

Leofwyn's grip on her hand was surprisingly firm and strong. "Of course I am, Lady. Only a fool would be otherwise. But we cannot hold off living for a better day, can we?" She rose from the bench and set about her tasks. She undressed Aethelflaed and washed her with water from a steaming, herb-scented pot brought by a thrall and dressed her in a clean robe and mantle.

"I am glad you have such heart," Aethelflaed said at last. Leofwyn picked up a carved bone comb and began to draw it through Aethelflaed's hair. "There is naught else to do, she said simply. "I cannot worry my husband, since I asked to be here. I would rather share his trials and duties as you have shared your husband's."

Aethelflaed smiled up at the girl, then suddenly looked away. If only this child had been her daughter! She was ashamed at the thought. Leofwyn accepted her life, if not without question—she was too spirited for that—then with grace. Small wonder that Aethelfrith was proud of her.

By dawn, matters were well underway: the fortress was packed with freemen, including Niall's Irish companions, and levies drawn from western Mercia. She had kept these out of sight during Hingamund's visit. One group of levies, their ranks enlarged by the addition of the wiliest and most experienced of the local freemen, were arrayed outside the walls, for it had been agreed that the first battle must be joined on a field some distance outside the fortress and by men of the city. The best of the levies and horsemen remained concealed inside the fortress. She paced the inner ramparts of the wall and saw that all was disposed as she and Ethelred had planned.

They had not long to wait. The Norse approached and the levies waited for their advance until they had almost reached the field where they planned to join the battle, then rode out quickly to meet them. They dismounted, engaged them for a brief skirmish. After a while, the freemen of Chester broke away from the fighting and made as if to flee from the Danes. The north gate was standing wide, ready to receive them, and they rushed back toward the city, the Vikings breathing hotly at their backs.

Aethelflaed and Aethelfrith, watching from the ramparts, checked the inner yards with a quick glance and ducked out of sight. The streets and timbered houses were silent and deserted. All gates other than the widely yawning north gate were secured, and the seemingly empty houses concealed the best and most experienced horsemen among her thanes.

The Norse, thundering toward the north gate behind the men of Chester, were too engrossed in their pursuit to consider the strangeness of the open fortress gate, or the unlikelihood of so carefully prepared a stronghold of being deserted. Their desire to possess Chester overcame all caution. The Lady had made a brave stand and they admired her courage and anticipated taking her as hostage. She could be used to great advantage against her husband and her formidable brother. Hingamund had seen with his own eyes that there were few levies in Chester; otherwise, the freemen of the city would not have been sent out in so disorganized a fashion. Hingamund had smiled with cold zest. She had humiliated him. Brave she might be but very stupid and ill-considered was her threat.

The men of Chester poured through the gate swiftly, the Vikings, behind them, their feet pounding dust into clouds, their battle cries rending the air, their swords and axes brandished with great menace above their heads. In the dust raised by the pursuit, the freemen melted away into the shadows of the buildings. English levies, concealed behind the gates, swung them to with a swiftness that belied their ponderous weight.

The rearmost of the Norse, who saw this, drew up in surprise, but they were too few for the great numbers of the English behind the gates. The other Vikings had lost sight of their quarry in the clamor, and as they turned to check the disturbance at their rear, Aethelfrith, watching, gave the signal.

From the wide entrances of the houses, as if from the maw of Hades, the Mercian horsemen erupted upon them, yelling their war cries. Levies on foot followed by the score and threw themselves into the fray.

Aethelflaed braced herself not to look away, though her stomach churned. Dreadful cries filled the air and clouds of dust, beaten into the air by rampaging feet and stamping hooves, turned the glaring sun red as blood as the horsemen rode down the Vikings. Those that were left standing were cut down by the foot levies. The din was terrible.

Aethelfrith had insisted that she stay back from the fray, but she remained, astride her horse, her sword drawn and ready, at the edge of the clamoring battle. Athelstan charged in at Aethelfrith's side, splendidly fierce and glittering in his burnished helmet and ring-mail. The two together were imposing leaders: Athelstan was nearly six feet tall and was endowed with Edward's large frame. Aethelfrith was as tall and sturdy as Athelstan, though wiry and thinner. Their presence had the same effect on the levies as a strong draught from the mead-jug: the levies followed their leaders into the battle with ferocious and unholy gusto. She was relieved that it was they who led the charge. She doubted that she could have inspired in her thanes such bloodthirsty ardor for battle. She was the planner and Ethelred had told her firmly that she was not to be risked in the brutality of hand-to-hand fighting with the Vikings.

She held her lurching stomach under control until the slaughter was over, and then left to relieve her distress. She found a deserted spot and when the spasms of retching subsided, she rinsed her mouth with clear water. It annoyed her that she seemed to have inherited her father's sensibilities, for this was not the first time she had viewed such carnage, and she was grimly sure it would not be the last. When she returned, Aethelfrith had already set the men to cleaning the gory yard. The hideous cries of the battle still rang in her ears, and there was the stench, the awful stench that always hung over a place of battle. By the next morning, all was quiet, except for the soft "chunk" of shovels, still digging, and the sound of clattering carts, carrying the last of the grisly loads out of the fortress to the fields. For the time, the Norse were gone.

It did not last. When she went to the upper rampart only a few days later and stared out over the clearing, her heart sank. "They are still out there!" she exclaimed to Athelstan, who had followed her to the topmost walk. She pointed to the edge of the clearing where the thicket began. She would not have known they were still there, but for the movement of the brush at the edge. Occasionally a form or two separated themselves from the dense background of the forest to watch the carts rolling out through the gates. "There cannot be many," she said to Athelstan, "or they would have attacked the carts."

He knit his brows and brought his hand up to shade his eyes against the morning sunlight. "They are doing something, but I cannot see what it is."

The sound of axes ringing against tree trunks now reached their ears. They watched for a while, waiting, and saw the Norse emerge from cover to strip the brush away from the edge of the thicket. Soon more came out with shovels and dug pits, into which they poured water, carried from the river. She watched them shovel the dirt back into the soggy holes they had dug. "Mud-pits!" she exclaimed suddenly, beginning to understand. By afternoon she knew she was right and sent for Aethelfrith.

"They are building hurdles," she said. He nodded in response. They intended to force the walls. Several of the fence-like structures had already been put aside to dry. They watched in silence as the Norse wove the hurdles into rectangles big enough to shelter several men and long enough to throw across the ditch. When the weaving was finished, the hurdles were carried to the mud-pits and covered thickly with mud, then left to dry.

"How long?" she asked Aethelfrith.

"Perhaps two or three days, if the sun is good."

"Then," she said, tersely, "we must be about our business."

The Norse, instead of leaving when their companions had been slaughtered, had decided to stay. The hurdles would be used to bridge the ditch and to shelter the men from spears and rocks while they attacked the walls of the fortress.

Athelstan took charge of laying the wood for fires on the upper ramparts and had them set at thirty-foot intervals near slots in the outer wall. Three men; a guard, a spearman, and a fire-tender, would be posted at each woodpile. Rubble stone gathered from the yards below would be piled at the rest of the wall-slots. Harness makers were set to work cutting and sewing slings, for Aethelflaed had found great heaps of fine, sharp pebbles among the heaps of rubblestone, sharp enough to cut and sting the bare arms and legs of the hostile wall-climbers. Like a million bee-stings they would feel. They were shoveled into great earthen pots and hauled up to the walkway. Most of the water supply, and even the ale, was poured into iron kettles hanging in readiness over the unlit fires on the upper ramparts. The fires would be lighted early on the day of the siege, so that they would be boiling by sunup. Bracing herself, she checked the cesspool and found it to be full. That also might be useful.

Leofwyn came to her room in the *haga,* where she and Aethelfrith, along with Aethelflaed and Athelstan, lived, to bathe and dress her. Aethelflaed demurred, but Leofwyn insisted. "It is only fitting," she said, "that a queen have an attendant of rank. A thrall will not do, Lady." Aethelflaed twisted around so quickly that Leofwyn had to drop the plait of hair she was twining.

"Who calls me so?"

"The Irish, of course. They say you have saved them from the Norse by your quick wits and cunning. Truly, Lady," Leofwyn's face softened in the candlelight, loyalty gleaming in her wide eyes, "of all women, you are the most fit."

"I am not so," Aethelflaed insisted stubbornly. "I do this only out of necessity."

"As you think, Lady," Leofwyn agreed amiably, "but it does no harm not to contradict them. They are more in awe of a woman who lifts a sword than they are of a man, for they say it is a man's nature to fight. A woman who takes the sword is thus more greatly to be feared, since in going against the sweetness of mind that God has bestowed on woman she becomes the more fierce and has terrible powers over the minds of men." Leofwyn's eyes sparkled with amusement. Aethelflaed threw back her head and shouted with laughter, though even to her own ears, it sounded a trifle hysterical.

"You see," said Leofwyn reasonably, "such glee from a woman strikes them dumb, for they think it is unnatural for a woman to laugh like that."

Aethelflaed recovered her composure and eyed Leofwyn with friendly suspicion. "And do I terrify you, little mother?"

"Oh, most dreadfully," exclaimed Leofwyn, her eyes brimming with amusement. She gave Aethelflaed's hair a tender pat, arranged her blue embroidered robe carefully, and accompanied her to the Great Hall of *haga*.

In spite of the enemy lying in wait, they feasted, partly to show the host that a siege would not inconvenience them, and above all, to give their people the victory feast they deserved for their skill in the recent battle. Their spirits would be whetted for the coming assault, and Aethelflaed silently prayed, as she raised her drinking horn to salute the gallant Mercians and Irish who loyally followed her, that when it came, they would fare as well as they had in the first battle. She sipped and handed the horn first to Aethelfrith, then to Athelstan, and finally to Niall, whose eyes communicated his thanks for the honor.

"Friend," she said, smiling at him, "I trust you, for your service has been given from a faithful heart." He drank and handed the horn back to her. "Our work is just begun," she added.

He returned her smile, thus assured of her friendship. "I will serve you as long as you have need of me," he promised.

In the next few days, while both sides made ready, Aethelflaed sought to turn aside the coming assault. Through Niall, she got word to the Irish still among the Norse in the fields outside the fortress that the King of the Saxons and his Queen, having authority over her countrymen, were their friends and with them, desired to rid the lands of Chester of the pagans. She bid them go to their Viking masters and ask treasure for those Irish who would betray the city. Then they should bring them to a secluded place for the swearing of oaths, for which it was the Viking custom to disarm.

The Norse, unsuspecting, agreed, so desperate were they to possess the city. For three days, many of the Vikings succumbed to the temptation, and each time, the Irish led them to a hidden place for oath-giving. The Norse laid aside their shields, swords, and spears, and the Mercian levies hidden in the dense cover sprang upon them and killed them.

Early on the fourth day, Aethelflaed could see no lessening of the Viking forces outside the walls, despite the loss of so many of their kindred by the actions of the Irish and Mercian levies. She gave the order to lay torches to the wood under the cauldrons and Aethelfrith sent the levies to their posts on the wall.

The Norse assembled on the far banks of the ditches and laid their hurdles across to the inner edge, forming a temporary bridge. They crossed to the turf, pulled their hurdles after them and stood there, gazing up at the walls, assessing's task ahead of them.

They launched their assault as the cauldrons began to boil. Looking down through one of the slots, Aethelflaed saw the mud-caked hurdles, held over the heads of the Norse as they moved slowly to the foot of the walls, the hardened clay forming a stone-like barrier against weapons from above. When they drew near enough for closer observation, she saw that they had hewn logs and sharpened them, and were now preparing to set the points against the Roman foundations of the rubblestone walls.

"Aethelfrith," she shouted, and he appeared quickly at her side. "They are going to pierce the old wall!" She pointed down at the advancing wall of hurdles. He had no need of explanation. He swore briefly and strode off, stopping at each station to give brusque instructions. The levies, in spite of the grimness of the situation, grinned and nodded vigorously. When the Norse were beneath them, the edges of the hurdles braced against the wall for cover while they set the pointed logs in place, the levies hurled the first volley of rocks down onto the hurdles. Little happened at first, and she could hear only the peppering thud of rocks on the baked clay. They rained down unabated; the mud began to chip and crack. The chunks fell away from the woven frame of the hurdles and she could see the Norse underneath, working feverishly at the loose spots in the lower wall. A breach had been made, for she could see a cascade of shaped Roman stones lying on the turf.

Now posts were set under the hurdles for support, so the Norse could free their hands for the work of driving the points into the wall. The last fragments of the clay covers on the hurdles directly below those on the ramparts broke away from the frame in a shower of crumbling mud and dust. Continued pounding with rocks and heavy beams from above weakened the hurdles, tearing through them, leaving gaping holes.

"The cauldron," Aethelflaed yelled, "swing the cauldron over!" Her throat was scratchy from screaming above the din. Two levies set their forked sticks against the rim of the pot, and straining against the ungainly burden and poor leverage, slowly tilted it. She stole a quick look over the wall, then ducked back: several of the Norse had started to climb. Two more levies wrapped a heavy iron chain around the lower bulge of the pot and pulled it back. As the Norse came almost level with the top of the wall, the levies gave a sharp tug on the chain and the pot tilted its sputtering liquid down the wall, soaking the men who were clinging to the wall with boiling liquid.

In spite of the clamor of the battle, the screams carried above all other sounds, and for an instant, it seemed as if both sides stopped, listened, comprehended, and then resumed the fighting with renewed ferocity. She closed her eyes, gritting her teeth against her usual malaise. Their skins had been stripped raw by the boiling effluent. She turned back to the levies. "Now," she said briskly, "be ready with your slings."

While the shocked and burned men below sorted themselves out, the levies filled their leather slings with sharp pebbles. She ducked again as they raised their arms. The slings described great, whistling arcs overhead, gaining force. A few loose pebbles scattered over the ramparts until the speed was great enough to hold the charge in place. They let them go suddenly, and the air was thick with the hissing and buzzing of thousands of knife-edged pebbles, singing through the air like enraged bees. The wall-climbers reeled backward as if a hive had been let loose upon them, and the pebbles rained stinging fury on the scalded men.

She strode back the way she had come, checking each post and ordering the cauldrons ready as soon as the rest of the hurdles were broken up. The thralls brought fresh loads of rock; the fearsome din of pounding rocks, howls, as more cauldrons were tipped, and the battle yells of both sides went on throughout most of the day. One or two places in the foundation were cracked, and while the pointed logs had not pierced through the wall, they had badly damaged it. Some of the Norse had gotten over before the boiling water and ale washed their screaming kinsmen back down the wall. The swordsmen were ready for them and they were cut down as they swung themselves over onto the ramparts, their battle cries ending in gurgles as they choked on blood and steel.

She went back to her post and saw Athelstan waiting for her. He looked up to shout to her, but she saw his eyes widen, his mouth agape in horror, and even before she saw his expression, her scalp prickled with deadly warning. She wheeled around quickly, her drawn sword raised, gripped firmly in both hands. Steel struck against it and was deflected. Before she could pause to breathe a quick thanksgiving for the fortuitous parry, the Norseman's arm was drawn back and raised for a swinging thrust. But he had overbalanced himself by swinging too high and for an instant, the space of a blink that it took him to regain his poise, she thrust, and making contact, leaned hard against her own sword hilt, throwing her full weight against it until she was chest-to-chest with the Norseman. He roared with pain, swinging his sword arm wildly, trying to pluck her from him. She clung fiercely, for the safest place away from the thrashing arm was next to him; his heavy sword could be wielded effectively only away from the body. Still he thrashed, and she hung on desperately. He lost strength rapidly for her thrust had been deadly accurate. Alfred and Ethelred had taught her well. The sword slipped from his hand, and he turned his failing attention to dislodging her. She clung more firmly, and since he could not shake her off, he gripped her fiercely instead, trying to crush her ribs. Her own sword hilt dug into her stomach painfully and she was drenched with the blood of her adversary.

When she thought she could not bring in another gasp of air, and her ears buzzed loudly, the man's grip suddenly slackened: two Mercian levies had pulled his arms away from her. She was released and fell backward as the Norseman slumped forward against her. One of the levies caught her and pulled her away, steadying her until her vision cleared. She saw the Viking sprawled unconscious and dying at her feet. Athelstan stood over him, sword ready, but there was no need.

Athelstan turned his affrighted gaze on her, for she was covered with blood, and when he had reassured himself it was not hers, he stripped the gory mantle from her shoulders and wrapped her in his own dry cloak, hugging her with relief. She was momentarily weak and dizzy until someone handed her a cup of hot wine, and the fluid burned down her throat, restoring the power of action to her numbed limbs. She smiled finally at Athelstan and he grinned back at her.

They returned to their posts. It was close on sundown and only a few of the attackers were left still skirmishing at the foot of the walls. When one small group gathered for a final charge, Aethelflaed signaled her own levies forward with their special, stinking burden. Unpleasant as their job would be, when she related her intention to them earlier, they roared with laughter and promptly volunteered their aid. They would enjoy such a fitting finish.

The pot was raised, and as the Vikings made one last, angry rush against the wall, the hooting levies tilted it. Its reeking contents drenched the gasping and astonished Norse below. There was dead silence as the stench filled the air, telling all the levies and the host below what she had done; the final insult, her answer to Hingamund's arrogant presumption.

"My God, Lady Mother!" Athelstan was torn between shock and unholy glee. The latter won. He howled with laughter and soon the levies joined him until, at sundown, Chester still firmly in their possession, the ramparts of the great and ancient Camp of the Legions echoed with the laughter of the Mercians who had kept it for their own. Lady Aethelflaed had cleaned the city's cesspools and dumped the contents on her enemies by way of answer.

They came back a few weeks later; after all, Chester was a prize coveted by the Norse, and even though they had been repulsed, they came back again and again, never to succeed. Chester belonged to Aethelflaed and she would not surrender it.

The feasting in the Great Hall went on, day after day, and she was in a haze of disbelief, because it was in her honor. Niall came forward, bowing deeply. "Queen Edelfleda," he said in his peculiar accent, addressing her as all his Irish countrymen did now, "it was the most fortunate day for me that I came and was received kindly by you. You have defended us and saved our lives. We are your people as long as you live and on this do we give our solemn oaths."

She was elated and humbled, and in this triumph, she was saddened that Ethelred was not here to savor it with her. His own reputation among them was great. To them he was the great Saxon king who had kept his kingdom out of the greedy hands of the Norse. At what cost to himself, she thought and was touched with premature grief. She looked up and smiled at Niall. Despite her own sad musing, she could not be ungracious.

Weeks later, she had cause to smile again on him and rewarded him with grants of land for himself and his people. During the summer, he proved his loyalty again and again. When he had finished with the errands she had asked of him and he had settled into his new homeland, the Scots and the Strathclyde Britons, the men of Alba, as they were called, were firmly allied with the great Saxon Queen, Edelfleda. The power of the pestilential Northmen was slowly being limited.

Athelstan was privy to these negotiations, for she wished him to take his part in all things. Leofwyn insisted on serving her, until Aethelflaed, laughing, called Aethelfrith and ordered him take her away and pamper her until the birth of their child.

The four of them, Aethelfrith, Leofwyn, Athelstan, and herself, were bound fast by friendship, having shared a common threat, prevailed together against it, and now shared the victory over their adversaries.

Athelstan and Aethelfrith had become close friends even before Chester bound their fates together, and Aethelflaed had grown inordinately fond of Leofwyn. It was no surprise to her when Leofwyn's husky firstborn thrust himself eagerly into the world that Aethelfrith called him Athelstan. As Leofwyn had told her, and Ethelred, too, no matter what, one cannot stop living. Things have a way of going on, and one could never tell whether it was because of or in spite of one's actions.

Aethelflaed found herself looking backward, but it was only by way of understanding the path by which she had come. One never knows where one is going until one gets there, and when that advantage is gained, the doubts and hardships along the way at last become intelligible.

CHAPTER TWENTY-SIX

(909 – 914)

$\mathcal{E}$thelred was far worse than Aethelflaed had ever seen him, though he insisted that he was better. Their old friend, Bishop Asser, had died quietly in his sleep at Sherborne, and Ethelred received the news with great sadness. David now attended him constantly, since he was too ill to be burdened further with the governing of London, and so again, the rule of London fell on her. She had, of necessity, taken over all of Ethelred's duties in Mercia as well. It was fortunate that the year remained relatively quiet; and that was owing to Edward's quick aggressiveness.

It was well known since Chester that Lord Ethelred of London was sick. Aethelflaed held off rumor as long as she could, but when he grew too weak to manage his duties in London, he took to his room, and his condition could no longer be ignored by the Mercians. At evening, he was always worse. By morning he was somewhat restored, but always he was bright-eyed with fever. Elfwyn redeemed herself in Aethelflaed's eyes by nursing her father devotedly, with no apparent distress that her mother had assumed full overlordship of Mercia. She was content to care for her father, and for that Aethelflaed was grateful.

Sick as he was, Ethelred held council with herself and Edward, and they decided it was now time to put some of the Vikings' own tactics into action. Edward assembled a large force of West Saxon and Mercian levies and marched to Northumbria, where for five weeks he harried the Vikings after their own fashion until they were subdued and offered, for the time, no more trouble.

Edward came home, and Elfled, who had, surprisingly, been without child for almost a year and a half, was soon pregnant again. The rest of the year drifted quietly into winter. In spring, the Danes from Northumbria, still angry from Edward's harrying of them, crossed into Mercia. They waited until Edward was known to be in Kent, where he awaited his fleet from the coasts of Wessex. He left Kent as quickly as Aethelflaed's messengers reached him, rode hard across Wessex to the Bristol Avon in Somerset to intercept the Danes, who had harried all the way to the Bristol Channel.

Edward was too late to catch them there. The word had gone out that Edward, with emergency levies from Wessex and Mercia, was on his way. The Danes turned back and harried up the west bank of the Severn to Bridgnorth. Edward followed relentlessly. They turned eastward, having nowhere else to go: the prospect of being caught between the Welsh and Edward was a dismal one. What lay in store for them was more dismal than they could possibly have imagined. As they harried their way into Staffordshire, Edward caught up with them at Woden's field, near Tettenhall, on the fifth of August. The battle that ensued was brief, bloody, and decisive: the Danes were annihilated and three of their kings were slain.

Aethelflaed rejoiced in Edward's victory, with tears of exultation and relief running down her face as she read the missive from Tettenhall. She hugged Edward's burgeoning wife and they wept together.

After Tettenhall, Aethelflaed rode to Bremesbyrig and quickly fortified it. Elfled went to London and, pregnant though she was, would have helped to nurse her brother-in-law, for the sake of her growing friendship with Aethelflaed, but Aethelflaed's refusal was obdurate. "Your presence here, dearest sister, will be a joy to my daughter, but you must risk neither yourself nor Edward's child. I would not have the venoms touch you; you would not be proof against them." Elfled knew that Ethelred's room had been festooned with herbs and sacred relics to prevent the transfer of the flying venoms, and for herself, was satisfied that these measures were effective; however, she contented herself with staying in London to be near Edward.

The winter of 910 to early 911 was bitter beyond belief: the winds howled unceasingly, and even London had more than its usual snow. The hunting preserve at Oxford lay deep in drifts, and so bitter was it that many of the forest animals starved and froze to death. Spring came, pale and wan, after the long winter. Elfled's daughter, Elgiva, named for the Abbess of Shaftesbury, came peaceably into the world. Shortly after she arrived, her uncle Ethelred fared forth out of the world, his spirit strong, his body wasted and drawn with the disease that after eight terrible years had finally worn him down.

The winter tore at his lungs, he coughed and choked on his own blood, and nothing eased the paroxysms that wracked him; once the coughing began, it seemed impossible to stop. Aethelflaed marveled that he had fought it off so long. At times, she thought it had been for her sake alone that he clung so tenaciously to life. "I cannot go," he whispered often, "without I know that you will be well able to care for yourself and Mercia. Edward cannot carry on his fight unless you will be at his back, protecting him."

She sat with him, night after night, holding his frail hand in hers, reassuring him that all would be well, and telling him how much she loved him and would miss him. They minced no words, for death was no stranger to either of them. She made no attempt to call him back when he slipped into unconsciousness for the last time, her name on his faintly smiling lips. Werferth came to anoint him; Theodred knelt by his couch and prayed. Edward held his other hand, and Ethelred fared forth on his last journey as he had lived; supported by the two people most dear to him in life.

All left his side, save Elfwyn and Aethelflaed, and after a while, Aethelflaed sent Elfwyn away to rest. They had shared so much in life, and she wished to share with him alone those last moments in the empty hush that he left behind him. She spoke to him gently, as if he were still there. He was still smiling faintly, as if in death he heard her. In the morning, Elfled came and led her, exhausted and unresisting, away. It was time for the others to take away what was left of the vital, vigorous man she had married twenty-five years ago, and send him off into his new life.

She smiled unaccountably as she stumbled groggily to her couch and let Elfwyn and Elfled tuck the fur rug around her. She saw them watching her anxiously, but she could not tell them what it was. Ethelred told her the night before he died that when the time was right he would come back for her. It helped for a while to stave off the torrent of grief that she knew would come later.

She slept as one dead, and it was Elfled who attended her. Elfwyn, she told Aethelflaed, was too distraught and had exhausted herself. When Aethelflaed at last arose and forced herself to drink a tumbler of wine, she went back to Ethelred's empty chamber and sat down beside his couch again, looking blankly around her. She had been prepared for this so long. Why then was it so hard to tell herself that he was gone? She tried to convince herself that he would not be back and found every nerve, every fiber in her tired body shrinking from the knowledge.

She had forced herself to sit dry-eyed throughout the long and magnificent requiem for Ethelred; his sorrowing people loved him well and needed to say their farewell. Elfwyn was stony with grief and Aethelflaed had watched her with sympathy. She reached out to touch her arm by way of comfort, but the girl was cold as marble, seeming to prefer the ministrations of her own attendants.

Aethelflaed was too stricken herself to do more for her daughter and drew strength from Edward and Elfled, who sat on either side of her, then rode flanking her protectively on the way back to the garrison. The reason for Elfwyn's chill became apparent shortly. After a short council with Aethelflaed and the principal nobility of London, it was decided that

Edward, for the protection of London, must take possession immediately of the lands bordering on the Thames. The people would still look to Aethelflaed as their overlord: this had been Edward's promise to his father, reaffirmed at Alfred's death. Ethelred had always held these lands in Alfred's name and, by agreement, in his own name until his death. She now agreed to hold these lands in her own name, but Edward would hold them on her death. She could see from Elfwyn's face that this was unacceptable. Her face, already drawn with grief, now tightened perceptibly.

Once back in Ethelred's empty room, as she tested the dreadful reality of his death, she was swamped with agonizing loneliness, straining to reach the husband, friend and lover with whom she had shared so much. She could not reach the world that now claimed his spirit. She bent her will to it; instead of calling him back, she found her spirit retreating to a distant spot, a private, desolate vale, ringed by mountain peaks whose granite heights defied penetration. Ethelred was far away where she could neither speak to him, nor touch him, nor ask his counsel, or draw comfort from his presence.

She wept, at first a trickle, then a torrent, flooding down her face. She subsided finally, feeling worn to the bone, and Elfled found her there in the evening. She spoke quietly to her, stroked her hand, and when she got no response left to fetch a hot tisane to comfort her parched spirit. Aethelflaed sipped it wordlessly, staring at her sister-in-law with blank eyes, and refused to be led to her own room at nightfall. She sat by the empty couch all night, fearful of sleep, clinging to what might remain of Ethelred's spirit and person in his room.

Near dawn, the door opened soundlessly and Edward's frame filled the entrance as he studied her with shadowed eyes. He crossed the room in a few swift strides and stood over her, looking down at her bent head. Gently, he lifted her from the chair and sat down on it himself, holding her on his lap as if she were a child. He held her against his chest and rocked her, crooning words of comfort to her in his deep voice until she could stand his sympathy no longer and wept again; not quiet tears, but hard, grief-wracked sobs, cries that began the process of acknowledging Ethelred's death. When at last her weeping abated, he rose from the chair, still holding her, and carried her back to her own room. He laid her on her own couch, pulled the fur rug over her, and sitting down beside her, held her hand while she slept.

When she awoke, many hours later, he was still there. He smiled wearily as she sat up, but pushed her back as soon as she tried to get up. He was right. She had forgotten about food for the past few days and was weak with hunger and shock. He fed her himself and did not permit her to rise until he had given her every last spoonful of the hot broth that Elfled had prepared with her own hands. His eyes told her how he understood her grief: she had lost her husband, he had lost a wife once, and now he had lost his dearest friend and battle-companion.

She spoke finally. Her grief and rage poured out; rage at the implacable enemy that had worn his life, made him sick to death. Edward listened wordlessly, his eyes on hers, silently telling her that he knew. Had he not drained this same cup himself, choking on the bitter dregs of anger? Did he not also taste her own despair? Ethelred was gone beyond recall; never again would they see his face, share a council-table, a drinking horn, a battle, nor taste a victor's feast together. All that was gone, all that and more. This man had been Alfred's dearest friend; the last of Alfred died with him.

Edward shivered involuntarily. "It is just the two of us now," he whispered, his voice gruff with his own weariness and grief. Edward was thirty-nine, and while he was a strong and imposing man, time and hardship had etched lines into his face. Looking at him, she felt a rush of gratitude for her brother. No one but Edward could have reached her in her grief. As Ethelred had done years ago in Worcester, Edward had stepped in and brought her back.

He left her, and Elfled came to wait upon her and help her to dress. Aethelflaed protested weakly, though she was grateful for her help.

Elfled's smile was touched with sadness. "I am perhaps a bit envious still," she said almost shyly, "for I know that Edward needs your help and companionship more than he needs mine." Aethelflaed opened her mouth to object, but Elfled cut her off. "I know what you are thinking. I am always with child and Edward is happy in his wife."

Aethelflaed reached out to take her hand. "I thank God daily for that, Elfled, but you are wrong. He has always needed you and never more than now."

Elfled bit her lip nervously. "I have wanted to tell you often how wrong I was...."

Aethelflaed interrupted quickly. "Oh, you must not, for you have nothing to regret. You have been right for Edward and have made him happy!"

Elfled smiled ruefully. "I have learned much myself. I did not know Edward as you did—as you do! I must help you now, for Edward needs you. You told me once that I must put my own feelings second to the needs of the kingdom. Now you must do so, too. Your grief cannot overshadow your duty: Edward cannot rule nor hold his lands and inheritance without your help. You know that, do you not?"

She did know it and nodded, searching Elfled's solemn face. "I have battled myself, sister," Elfled continued, "that my jealous nature might not endanger Edward in the carrying out of his kingship. You must battle yourself also, and put aside your grief quickly. It must take second place, even as my envy must, to the needs of us all." She took Aethelflaed's cold hand and held it firmly. "You must even," she said shrewdly, almost casually, "put aside your unspoken sadness for your daughter."

Aethelflaed turned her head and looked into Elfled's face. "I cannot reach her, Elfled. My only child. She is a stranger to me. What have I done to her?"

"You have done what you have been doing all your life. You have carried out the responsibilities laid on you at birth by your father. So have we all; myself, Edward, and most of all, Ethelred. Your daughter has not accepted what was given as her lot."

"I pray to God she will not oppose Athelstan!"

Elfled nodded, understanding. "She is jealous, there is no doubt. I have seen it in my own children." She smiled reassuringly. "She will not oppose Athelstan." What she did not say was her growing certainty that Elfwyn's enmity was being transferred to Edward. "Your responsibilities increase, sister. Elfwyn is a woman grown and must give account of herself. You must attend to more important matters."

Aethelflaed heard, and inwardly acknowledged how right and fitting it was that she should speak thus. One thing above all filled her with gratitude. Elfled had at last called her sister.

She set all things aside then, for as Werferth had warned, the hardest work of her life was ahead of her, in this her forty-first year.

She and Edward immediately set themselves to the labor they had discussed with Ethelred before his death: English Mercia must be fortified, for Norsemen surrounded it on all sides. There could be no more delay, and both Edward and Aethelflaed now knew where their weaknesses lay.

In the summer of 912, Edward went to Maldon in Essex and built an earthwork at Witham, six miles inland from Maldon, thus guarding the old Roman road from Colchester to London. His message was clear to the East Anglian Danes: Lord Ethelred's death had not weakened the rule of King Edward of Wessex, nor had it weakened the Mercian overlordship in any way. At the same time, Aethelflaed built a fortress at Scergeat, and most importantly, another at Bridgnorth. That lonely scarp, brooding high over the Severn river, was too commanding a point to allow it to fall to the Vikings: twice had that happened already and it must not occur again

Brother and sister carefully planned their fortifications, and as Edward secured the boundary of English and Danish Mercia along Watling Street, pushing further into the Danelaw with each new fortress, Aethelflaed secured the western border. The following year, Aethelflaed went to Tamworth and Stafford.

The ancient capitol of Mercia, the village of Tamworth, was on Watling Street, the Roman road from London into the west country, the agreed boundary between Danish and English Mercia. The confluence of the Rivers Tam and Anker, both of which emptied into the Trent in Danish-held Nottingham, guarded the village to the south. The history of the village was great: King Offa had chosen it for his royal residence, and such had been its influence as a market town that the Danes sacked and destroyed it in 874. It had been rebuilt, and, like Bridgnorth, destroyed again. The Saxons, however, were not easily turned from ancient patterns. Their lives centered around Tamworth's church and market, and therefore, in the face of constant disaster, the church rose again, the mud-and-wattle huts by the river reappeared, and life went on.

Aethelflaed's life went on also; though the sting of Ethelred's death was always with her. Her heart searched every face she saw, hoping for a glimpse of a familiar feature. Athelstan saw and understood, for he was very close to her now. He had loved his foster-father dearly, and with a sensitivity inherited from his mother, entered compassionately into her grief. He was deeply religious and growing more so, his fierce piety having been instilled and encouraged by Theodred. More and more did he resemble his grandfather, Alfred.

He saw her attention wander from time to time as she searched each new face, and quietly drew her attention back to matters at hand. They both loved Tamworth and somehow, here, and in neighboring Stafford, her sorrows eased a little. There was a reason. It seemed to her that in this ancient Mercian stronghold of Tamworth, Ethelred's spirit and personality spoke to her, as if his own heritage had begun in this place. He spoke to her in the faces of the Saxon villagers and the thanes, in the green forests in the distance, in the flat green pastures and fields surrounding the village: she heard his voice comforting her in the gently lapping waters of the two rivers.

As the stepped palisade arose under her direction, surrounding this ancient place with protection, she saw in it Ethelred's strength. She loved Tamworth for Ethelred's spirit, as she loved Worcester for the spirit of her dead child, and Chester for the energy she had invested in it. When the fortification at Tamworth was finished, and the village ensured against another disaster, she left almost reluctantly for Stafford, where she and Athelstan built a fortification similar to that which she had built at Tamworth.

She did not know of her reputation, which was greatly enhanced by the dispatch with which she erected the borough at Tamworth. When she and Athelstan arrived in nearby Stafford, the village was turned out and waiting eagerly for her. If Tamworth was a market center, Stafford was the religious center, founded in the eighth century by St. Bertelin. An ancient preaching cross of oak was the earliest relic of the religious importance of the small town, for people came here on pilgrimage to hear St. Bertelin and other, later, itinerant holy men. It was still in use, and as soon as the fortifications were built, Aethelflaed planned a wooden church to be built on the site. It was small and could hardly accommodate all, but the clergy preferred to give their sermons in the open air.

It had been a summer of intense and vitally necessary activity. Necessary, because once the Norse left for Ireland, another Viking menace erupted: Ragnall, grandson of Ivarr the Boneless, and his men left their temporary place of exile in Strathclyde and set sail northward into the Firth of Clyde and marched overland to the Forth, pillaging the Scottish lowlands as they went. When they reached the River Forth, they set sail again southward down the coast past Lindisfarne, haunted by the spirits of their ancestors who sacked it in 793. They landed, finally, at Tynemouth. Ragnall seized the lands of one Ealdred, reeve of Bamborough, who at once set out to ask his friend, King Constantine of the Scots, for help. Constantine was willing, but Ragnall proved himself a grandson of Ivarr by scattering Constantine and his Scots at Corbridge and slaying the English noblemen. Ealdred and his brother were left to grieve their losses, and Ragnall divided the land between two Norse jarls.

Ragnall, emboldened by his success, returned unopposed to the Scottish lowlands, then sailed out to challenge an old Norse rival, *Bardr Ottarsson,* off the Isle of Man. Again, he won and headed to Waterford to savor his victories.

It was no coincidence that Eddisbury was built when Ragnall appeared in Northumbria. Aethelflaed and Edward now saw that it was one man alone who coveted the crowns of Dublin and York, and that man, grandson of Ivarr, had shown himself strong enough to take both.

When Eddisbury and Warwick were finished, Aethelflaed summoned Niall to her *haga* at Chester. "How fare your kinsmen and the people of Strathclyde?" she asked.

"In spite of Ragnall, who stalked among them as the ravening wolf he is, they fare well." He saw the thoughtful look in her eyes. "They are unhappy that their king fled from Corbridge. Not," he added hastily, "that they could condemn him. Being Scots, they would rather be able to fight again, and Ragnall inspires a hatred that renews their will to live."

She waved him to a bench. "There was little chance from the start at Corbridge, but we cannot tolerate these Norse jarls who now rule Corbridge and Bamborough. Know you also that the Norse come in great numbers to Waterford from their homeland in the north?"

"I know that Ragnall rests there, bending his eye upon Dublin."

"And also upon Chester," she reminded him. "It is certain they plan to come back. Ragnall is determined that he will have his grandfather's throne and all of Mercia as well. We will be surrounded from the north if our Strathclyde friends do not resist."

Niall nodded, understanding. "Lady, they wait only for the best time."

"Ragnall sits in Waterford, gloating over his booty and victories. He is too secure. Shall your friends be ready in a month? And will they be counseled by me?"

Niall rose and bowed happily. Life had been much too inactive for him of late. His friends at Strathclyde, experts at scattering and coming together again, were growing restless. It was only their high opinion of the Lady's good judgment that held them in check.

"Constantine's and Ealdred's mistake," she was now saying, "was to face Ragnall openly and challenge him. They would better have waited until his back was turned and his bloodlust sated for a while, as it is now." She raised her eyebrows questioningly as if asking his opinion. He knew better. Her mind was already set. She was ready and nothing would turn her intention aside. Would her friends in Strathclyde follow?

Niall bore the good news to the Scots and Britons of the lowlands and the islands, and they made themselves ready. Like Aethelflaed, they were only waiting; her leadership and guidance was assured. Revenge against the Viking bloodlust ignited the embers burning in fierce Celtic hearts. The Queen might be a Saxon; nevertheless, the Northmen were hated more bitterly than the Saxons. Besides, the Lady had been more generous, more understanding than had her ancestors. As soon as word arrived that Edward had finished his burhs at Buckingham and Bedford, the Scots set out to harry, in true Norse fashion, the Scandinavian strongholds in Strathclyde.

Aethelflaed was right. It was certainly much easier to do with Ragnall in Ireland.

CHAPTER TWENTY-SEVEN

(915 – 917)

*E*lfled was with child again, and Aethelflaed was impatient with her brother. His wife was pale and this twelfth pregnancy was not going well with her. Nine of her children had survived childbirth and infancy, but Elfled was worn with birthing. Her face was drawn and Aethelflaed, who had just returned from the Welsh border, bone-weary herself, forgot her own weariness when she saw her sister-in-law.

Elfled was almost forty-three and her change was upon her. Her hair was not as gray as Aethelflaed's but it showed sprinkles at the temples, and now, five month gone, she walked like an old woman. Her bones were frail from too many children, and it was obvious that she was in constant discomfort, though she rarely complained.

Sudden resentment against Edward's thoughtlessness flared in her and it must have showed in her eyes, for Elfled, looking up at her, smiled wearily and said, "You must not blame Edward only, sister. I am as much at fault as he, for I cannot refuse him."

"Oh, Elfled, you know you have had too much of this. Could you not have sent him away for a little until you were certain you could bear no more children?"

Elfled smiled again, wryly. "I have never loved Edward wisely, and you know that well." She sighed. "Besides, I could not have borne it if he turned to another while he waited for me."

Aethelflaed stroked her hand, without replying. Elfled was right. It was a way of reasserting life and vigor in the face constant threat and sudden death, not just for Edward, but for Elfled, too. She did not just submit; she invited, not knowing when she would see her husband again, or if, when she saw him, he would be alive.

She left her sleeping. From the dark smudges under her eyes, Elfled would need all the rest she could get. So did Aethelflaed. She yawned profoundly and silently blessed David for the crackling fire that kept the January chill somewhat at bay. It was not a month for building fortresses, yet that was what she had done.

Signs of restlessness on the Welsh border had dismayed her. It was enough that they had determined enemies on both the eastern border and across the Irish Sea. Now they must have border skirmishes, as of old, with the Welsh. She had picked Chirbury to build. It was a good spot, within two miles of Offa's ancient dyke, and from there, the earthwork boundary could be well-patrolled. The Welsh might be only a nuisance, but if they chose the wrong time, they could be dangerous nuisance. She returned to London for a brief rest.

She feared for Elfled, but could not stay. Elfwyn assumed the rule of London in her mother's absence. Aethelflaed was dismayed at the extent of authority Edward invested in her and tried to discourage him. He refused. He needed his sister to be strong, for it enhanced his own threat to the Vikings. He treated her as a sovereign leader. "You are," she told him with exasperation, "strengthening Elfwyn's claim every time you defer to my rule." Edward only laughed and told her not to worry. Elfwyn was now certain that her parents' authority would be transferred to herself when the time came.

Even Elfled tried patiently to explain it to her. "I am acknowledged Queen of Wessex," she had said, "but here, I must step back, for the Lady of the Mercians is not a queen or a consort, she is the rightful Overlord of Mercia. You are only her deputy."

"I shall be Overlord of Mercia one day!" Elfwyn was unmoved.

"You cannot and will not be. Her right to govern is given by agreement and is not hers to bequeath. You are as capable as she is, though you have not her military experience. But if you think to inherit, then you and the King are not of one mind." A rueful smile twisted her lips. "I was envious of her when I was younger, but that is past. She is my family now, and even as I understand Edward, I understand her. They are truly of the same womb, and I believe they have shared the same mind and heart since birth. It is not possible to separate them. If you love one, you must love both." She looked her niece in the eye, her own eyes showing a flash of Ethelhelm's doughty spirit. "Edward gave me his body, and his children, and all the love a man gives his wife, but his sister has a part of his mind and heart that will be given to no other. Do not expect it to be given to you when she is gone!"

"Surely she loved my father above all others!"

"Of course she did. But Ethelred understood from the start what I had to learn over the years. He knew they were always as one mind. The old King, your grandfather, saw it, and saw in it a gift from God. Ethelred had an advantage that I had not. He shared their life as warriors, he taught them his skills, shared in their plans. He was part of them in a way that I am not."

"And you accepted this?" Elfwyn's voice was tinged with contempt.

"To interfere would have been to oppose fate. Aethelflaed did not choose for herself, she accepted in spite of herself."

"What do you, mean, in spite of herself? She is the most determined woman I know!"

Elfled looked at her with pity. "Did I say otherwise? But you have not seen that all the while she drives herself, she has never understood her own strength and capacity? She found her fate and gathered just acclaim for her skill, but her determination has not been for herself. Everyone has seen her destiny for years; she sees it as doing what is her duty to do. But it is not for you," she added gently, with concern. "You must learn to let go, for your duties are only temporary."

Elfwyn's cheeks were hot with anger. "The people of Mercia wish to be ruled by a Mercian!"

"And so they shall be..."

"By myself!"

Elfled shook her head. "No, my dearest child; if not by Edward, who has as much Mercian blood in him as you do, then by Athelstan."

The distance between aunt and niece told Aethelflaed all. Even so, she kissed them farewell, knowing Elfwyn could be depended upon and when she returned from Weardburh, she saw how right she had been. Elfled was much better than she would have hoped.

Elfwyn's care was to no avail. The birth at midsummer was long and hard. Aethelflaed and Edward sat with her for hours, each holding her hands in theirs. The child was born, and before the mother left them, she looked from one to the other and all she said was, "I love you," to both of them. They wept together and comforted each other. Aelfweard, Elfled's oldest, and Athelstan, with Edward, escorted her to her grave and watched over it themselves for the first few days.

Neither she nor Edward retreated this time from their sorrow; he did not take refuge in anger and she did not refuse to acknowledge Elfled's permanent absence. There was no need to remind Edward that their hardest work was yet to come. There was much yet to be done. Now they were more than ever painfully aware of their own mortality, for such is the feeling that possesses the heart as family and friends fare forth ahead of one. Each felt an urgency to be on with the task while the other was still alive. It could not be done by either alone.

The Norse that Edward had driven from the Severn in 914 overran Munster. Now they were joined by more of their kinsmen from the far north, who sailed to Waterford to join them. Ireland ran blood again at Viking hands, and Aethelflaed, late in the year, went to Chester, where she and Aethelfrith joined forces to build the burh at Runcorn. By the end of the year, Runcorn on the Mersey was complete, and with Eddisbury, the western defenses were secured.

Her heart, still heavy with Elfled's death was stricken further by the death of Bishop Werferth, who died peacefully in his palace by the Walbrook. This man had been a tower of strength to her, he was as indestructible as a parent: he could not die. Her distress showed on her face, and he comforted her on his deathbed. "I have died many times, child," he whispered, his eyes tranquil and filled with joy. "I fear it not. I cannot have you grieve for me when I am happy."

"For my own loss," she wept. "Now when I need your counsel and your presence above all things."

"Shame on you, daughter," he said sternly, but smiling. "You have no need of aught but the strength you possess in yourself. Must you still doubt? All is well. You shall see."

She left in a daze. She had gone to give comfort and instead, her weakness had betrayed her and she had been comforted by the dying man. Werferth saw beyond his own death and the new life was breaking upon him even as she left him. Faith or no faith, it was so final to her. Ethelred's death still stung at her heart, and she wept often, alone, on her couch at night. Nothing, no one, could replace him.

Edward returned from Bedford in East Anglia, heartened by a successful campaign. He had secured the submission of the Danish jarl Thurketil by patient, forceful negotiation. Thurketil's men submitted with their jarl: more importantly, many men of the more powerful and dangerous army of Northampton submitted along with Thurketil. To reinforce his control, Edward sent English families into Thurketil's territories to settle there. This strengthened his newly established authority greatly, and if events turned against him, they could be counted on to provide a defensive edge. Edward then assured his control by fortifying Bedford.

Athelstan took over the boroughs of Chester, Eddisbury, and Runcorn, for Edward had long had his eye on Aethelfrith, now one of the most powerful ealdormen of Mercia, and a man of great military ability. If he would be willing to settle among the East Anglian Danes with his family, Edward would reward him handsomely, with land grants that would make his family the most powerful family in East Anglia. He was willing, but first he sought Aethelflaed's approval, which she unhesitatingly gave.

The establishment in Edward's territory of so powerful and accomplished a warrior helped to decide Thurketil's wavering judgment. Edward offered him and his men safe conduct overseas, and he quickly took it. The south was, year, by year, coming firmly under Edward's protection.

One incident marred the orderly progress of Aethelflaed's and Edward's carefully laid plans. The Mercian Abbot Egbert was slain by the Welsh in one of their frequent border raids. Aethelflaed was tired and her patience had worn thin. The Welsh behaved as if the world outside their mountains did not exist. They could not understand that without her protection, the Vikings would overrun them. No matter how they hid in their caves and forests, the Vikings would, as they had before, find them and slaughter them.

She sent an army of western Mercians and Londoners into Wales, with David as translator. "Do not waste words with them," she instructed brusquely. "Bring me hostages, important ones. I wish to talk with them." They returned with the wife of the king and thirty-three others. Together, Edward and Aethelflaed, through David, explained to the king's wife the necessity of a peaceful border, though the woman was so terrified that they doubted she comprehended the danger. Before they released her, Aethelflaed gave her a parchment to take to the king, telling him that the thirty-three hostages she would accept in place of a wergild payment for the bishop's death. Any further disturbance and the hostages would be hung. They returned the woman to her husband by way of Hereford, which was fortified and full of Mercian levies. She intended the queen to carry tales of English strength to the king. It worked: the border simmered down. Aethelflaed and Edward turned back to their interrupted plans.

Their system of fortifications was almost complete. Edward planned another at Towcester: the south must be well secured before the Danish midlands could be taken. They dared waste no more time, for the advantage was now with them. It might not always be so, because early in 917 the news reached them that Sigtryggr II, known as *Caech*, the squint-eyed one, had arrived in Dublin to help his kinsman Ragnall. His arrival would sooner or later free Ragnall to pursue his ultimate ambition: the throne of York.

Towcester and Wigingamere were besieged by the Danish shortly after Edward took them, but to no avail. Edward, for the moment, was invincible. With his son and heir at his side, and his beloved Aelfweard also, he moved as inexorably as the hand of fate. Nothing appeared capable of stopping him. He marched to Tempsford, recently fortified by the Danes, and laid siege to it. The advantage usually lay with those inside, but Edward did not understand defeat. Tempsford fell before him.

Aethelflaed left London early in the spring and established herself at Tamworth. The fortification there pleased her immensely, and after crossing the River Tame on the west side of the village, she rode around the outside of the ditch and back to her starting point to check it out herself. A six-foot-deep trench, interrupted by the gates, surrounded the three sides of the village that did not front on the confluence of the Rivers Tam and Anker. From the inner edge of the ditch to the outer palisade was a twenty-foot stretch of turf. She had built a low mound in her *haga*, which she had chosen in the southwest corner behind the confluence of the rivers. A timbered building, surrounded by a low palisade, had been erected for her, and this gave her a vantage point on the river for unobstructed observation of the flat clearing on the far side of the river and the forests to the south.

A wooden church had been built here, as at Stafford, in 913 when the boroughs were constructed, and trade was increasing. The fact that a Danish settlement came almost to the east wall of Tamworth—the closest was only about six miles to the northeast—had earlier discouraged most of the English villagers to the west from prolonging their visits to Tamworth. Now Aethelflaed's patronage of the village encouraged frequent and longer stays.

In the past, the royal demesne of King Offa, near the west gate, had added to the importance of the town. That had been over a hundred years ago. The village was once more important because of the new fortification. Its position was strategic, and she and Edward had seen this years ago. They could not tell which one of them hit upon the idea first. They had both seen the Danes' success with fortification as they had removed larger and larger chunks of Mercia from English control.

They studied the Danish bases, quickly built to support their invading armies, and started on their own carefully planned string of fortifications. Edward built in the south; Aethelflaed built in the north and west. When the system was finished there was an English fortress opposing every Danish fortress along the border of English-Danish Mercia.

Tamworth was not only on that boundary, it was also the center of a rough semicircle on whose circumference were situated the Danish bases of Derby, Nottingham, and Leicester. The campaign centered about Tamworth, the campaign that would bring their patient, years-long struggle to an end, when all of Mercia would once again be brought under English rule.

Edward's rapid and resounding successes at Towcester and Wigingamere caused great anxiety across Watling Street from waiting Tamworth. Aethelflaed kept men watching Derby and Leicester, and it occurred almost simultaneously that news of Edward's successful pressure on the Danish base at Tempsford reached her, followed by the news that a large force of Vikings had left Derby to reinforce their kinsmen at Tempsford. Aethelflaed laughed aloud when she received the news, and perhaps the messengers that brought her the news stared a little uneasily at her. How she wished Ethelred were here! The Vikings had walked into the trap that she and Edward had laid for them, and there was naught left to do but spring it.

And that she did. *Deoraby*, the place of the deer, as the Danish called it, fell. Aethelflaed herself led the attack: there was a swift breaching of the gates by the Mercian levies. Once inside, the battle was fierce, bloody, and costly. The defending force was greatly reduced, as she expected. Those that were left fought to the death. It was quickly done. Four thanes dear to her died in the skirmish, two of them defending their Lord: herself. Aethelflaed rode into the city and claimed it without further resistance. She sent Edward and Athelstan at Tempsford the message that Derby was back in Mercian hands. Edward returned her message with a gleeful one of his own: besieged Tempsford had fallen to him. It was not a mere victorious edge for Edward; it was a resounding defeat for the Danes, whose losses were disastrous. The Danish king and two jarls had been slain, many others had been slaughtered, and the rest were taken prisoner. Edward, Athelstan, and Ealdorman Aethelfrith seized the entire fortress and everything in it. What few Danes escaped did not return to Derby. East Anglia was no longer a haven for the Vikings.

After a brief rest, Edward collected his men and stormed Colchester with unparalleled ferocity. The Danes were stunned. Edward himself could not be dislodged by storming, yet when he took to the field and did the storming, all seemed to crumble before him. Colchester fell: again, it was a disaster. Few escaped from that siege, and Aethelflaed breathed more easily still. Colchester, Witham, Maldon, all formed a direct line to London and all were now in Edward's possession.

The Danes tried to lay siege to Maldon, but were thwarted by Aethelfrith, who attacked them from the rear. Seeing this, Edward's armies streamed out of the fortress at Maldon and attacked the Danes from the other side. The Danes fled.

Athelstan brought the armies of Wessex to Passenham in Northampton and rebuilt the wall at Towcester with stone. The Danes there quickly submitted to Edward and declared him their Lord and Protector. Edward was now in control of most of the south. By the end of the year, the Danes at Cambridge elected Edward as their Lord and Protector, ratifying it with oaths and treaties. The remaining Danes of East Anglia and Essex submitted voluntarily to Edward's terms.

When they met in London for a well-earned rest, Edward, Aethelflaed, and Athelstan embraced each other, all filled with hope and anticipation: the end was in sight. Their plan, Alfred's before them, and Ethelred's and their own, was nearly complete.

CHAPTER TWENTY-EIGHT

Historical Note

In the year 918, the spirit of Lady Aethelflaed fared forth on the twelfth day of June. She was in her eighth year as Overlord of Mercia. At her request, she was buried at Gloucester in St. Peter's Church. She was forty-eight years old.

The twelve days of Christmas of the year 917 was a time of profound thanksgiving and relief. Edward and Aethelflaed spent part of it at London—for Edward made himself very much in evidence there these days—and part in Winchester. If Elfwyn noticed that the King appeared on the streets of London more than he usually did, she made no comment, nor did her behavior show any disfavor toward her uncle. Edward's fame had, at one and the same time, enhanced and eclipsed that of his father, Alfred, whom they had formerly loved as the deliverer of London. Danish Mercia was back in English hands, and Edward and their own Lady were the agents who brought this about.

Elfwyn paid her respects and kept her counsel. Had she not been approached by nobles whose loyalties still lay with her dead father, and whose sentiments now attached to her heroic mother, she might have been less circumspect in her words and actions. To these men, Edward was merely Ethelred's thane, an ally in the struggle against the invader. Something had happened in the years of dual overlordship: Offa's kingdom was reasserting itself, though faintly, and Elfwyn, alive to the undercurrents favoring her own lineage, was aware of it.

Certain of these thanes voiced to Elfwyn their disappointment with the strict limits the Lady had set on her daughter's authority. Elfwyn was gratified. She had worked hard to gain the affection of these men, and her own following had increased most satisfactorily. When the time was ripe, she would move to assert her authority. She was astute enough not to put herself forward at the height of Edward's popularity. Instead, she smiled and deferred.

The Christmas procession to St. Paul's was led by the King of Wessex and the Lady Aethelflaed of Mercia, to the hoarse shouts of *"Hael"* from hundreds of throats. The more thoughtful among the observers noted that the Lady unobtrusively ceded honors to the King, acknowledging the cheers directed toward herself with only a faint smile. They took careful note of her deference; if such was her wish, they would abide by it.

The rest of the twelve days were passed quietly at Winchester, in the company of Edward's children and Aethelflaed's daughter. One great surprise awaited them, and both Edward and Aethelflaed wept to see her: Elgiva, sister and saint in her own lifetime, joined them. How like Werferth's was the light of joy that shone in her eyes! A spirit of clear flame burned in the lean and disciplined frame. She had healed many with a single touch, this once-frail daughter of Alfred. The people of Winchester flocked to see their King and his Lady sister, and the folk from the shires around crowded the city for a glimpse of the holy Abbess of Shaftesbury: they waited for a touch of the hand from the saint and a glimpse of her invincible brother. Both truly carried the spirit within them; the one, the Grace, the other, the Power.

She laid her hands on Aethelflaed and Edward and blessed them, then turned to the children, but not before Aethelflaed had seen the veiled look that suddenly shadowed her eyes.

She restrained Elgiva with a light touch. "What is it, sister? You see things, as did our mother, do you not?" Elgiva smiled reassuringly, but the look did not leave her eyes. "What do you see?" Aethelflaed persisted. "Shall not Edward and I complete our work?"

Elgiva smiled again, and the look left her eyes. "Fear not, sister, it shall be done."

Nevertheless, the look remained in Aethelflaed's memory, though it did not disturb her. Whatever Elgiva saw, Aethelflaed felt only peace within herself. Edward was happy being with his children, and instead of shunning Edytha, named for her half-sister by Elfled just before she died, he bounced her fondly on his knee. Elfled's death had not embittered him as Ecgwin's had, and he loved his children too dearly for themselves to hold them to any account but their own.

It no longer jolted her painfully when thoughts of Ethelred rose unbidden in her mind, so responsive was she to sudden jogs of memory as she chanced upon anything they had shared or loved. She welcomed memories now, for they eased and comforted her when she was tired and lonely, and but for Edward, she was tired and lonely often. Edward maintained her with his strength and drive, though she knew he experienced the same soul-weariness with fighting that she did.

She often wondered if his extraordinary strength came from a desperate will to be done with the struggle to prevail. She looked up to see him standing over her, extending his hand to her. She smiled into his eyes and saw there her own feelings and musings so precisely mirrored that for an instant, quickly passing, she felt as if she had looked into her own mind and past and saw there all her thoughts and memories, as he saw his own in her clear eyes.

They were as if young again that Christmas, Edward as a young Atheling with his warrior sister, laughing, sparkling, but sharing between themselves and Ethelred's unseen shadow, a childhood, a lifetime, nearly half a century of joys and sorrows; of Athelney in the mere, of long-dead, much-loved Asser's gentle schooling, of Alfred's patient wisdom, and Ealhswith's gentle hand upon them. These things they shared unspoken, and Elgiva, their clairvoyant sister, watched them fondly and sadly. They jested and drank together in the Great Hall of their childhood, united in spirit, the blood of Cerdic and Cenwalh, the bond they had been born with, flowing warmly in their veins. Their children rejoiced to see them happy again, not realizing the longing they felt to see the faces of those they saw no more; Ethelred, Ecgwin, Elfled, and battle-companions who had fared forth on the field. Elgiva smiled, full of love for the fleeting moment. She knew it could not last forever.

Early in the next year, Ragnall left Waterford and descended again upon Strathclyde. They were ready for him, and for a long time, repulsed him. But Ragnall, knowing the ferocity of the Britons, brought reserves with him, and at the last, as the battle appeared to be given to the defenders, threw in the reserves and slaughtered the Britons. With his eyes fixed on York, he marched to Northumbria and attacked Corbridge, for much resistance to his rule had grown there in his absence, as it had also at York. The Danish of Corbridge, though they were not fond of him, offered no resistance: that came most strongly from the Northumbrian Angles and the Scots. Ragnall lost two of his jarls; despite this, he eventually drove off the Scots.

It was neither victory nor defeat for either side, and in that, Aethelflaed had played her part. Ragnall's presence had alarmed her greatly: she had never underestimated him, but her and Edward's plans must not be disrupted by Ragnall's presence this close to completion. She sent a large force to Corbridge to aid the Northumbrians, and if at the end there was neither victory nor defeat, it was to her advantage that Corbridge was still, as before, in mixed hands.

Three boroughs yet remained. The Danes held Nottingham, near Derby, and also Stamford, east of Danish Leicester, and further east, Lincoln. Ragnall, after driving off the Scots, retired from Corbridge, leaving Northumbria to settle itself back into uneasy peace. Aethelflaed kept watch on all these events from her *haga* at Tamworth, where she had been since

Epiphany; in fact, since she first learned of Ragnall's return to Strathclyde. Athelstan rode with her this time, and Aethelfrith returned to East Anglia with Edward. By the end of the year, she had said exultantly to Athelstan on their ride north, all but Northumbria would be united under Edward, and York, Ragnall or no, would be their final move.

Athelstan smiled agreeably and thought of Elfwyn, but said nothing. Rumors had come to him—he had always been good at hearing things—and he knew his aunt was ignorant of the rumors.

Edward rode along the south bank of Welland to Stamford: there was no battle. Stamford submitted and Edward built a fortress there. Leicester was now ringed about with English fortresses in the heart of Danish Mercia.

When Aethelflaed clattered out across the little wooden bridge that spanned the Tame, she turned east and rode boldly into Leicester. There was naught to fear here. They knew Edward was close by in Stamford. They smiled, opened the gates, and English levies flooded the city. The Danish army at Leicester, as one man, shrugged and threw their spears, swords and armor in a heap as they prepared to take their oaths of submission. The brief, fierce battle at the gates of Derby was everywhere known, by Dane and Mercian alike. The Lady was as formidable as her brother, and since she kept her face and head covered with the bronze boar helmet, its nosepiece curving down over her face, they could not see the weariness etched upon her countenance. Until she chose to remove the helmet, they saw only the grey-blue eyes, stern and triumphant, staring, unwinking, at them as their armor and weapons clanged noisily into the growing heap. Leicester fell without the drawing of a sword.

Nottingham was all that was left on the road to Lincoln. She rode back to Tamworth, conscious that the struggle was almost at and end, her mission nearly over. She, who had wondered most of her life what her work was to be; she who had envied Elgiva her sense of purpose. She thought of Werferth, dead these three years, constantly reminding her that her work lay ahead of her. Now it was almost behind her.

Her horse stumbled on the rough split logs of the bridge and she steadied him as they crossed into Tamworth. Nottingham would submit soon of its own free will, or wait to offer Edward their allegiance. For the moment, they would do nothing and she welcomed that. She was tired and wanted to rest, for the pace of the past few years had been hard. Once Nottingham submitted, the way into Lincoln would be clear, and Edward would not hesitate to make his next move. York was his target and he would get on with it; even though Ragnall was leaving them alone he would not do so for long, certainly not if Edward marched to York. She agreed with Edward in the matter. York was ready.

It was only a matter of days after Leicester submitted that a group of riders entered Tamworth and begged audience with the Lady. They had come, not from Nottingham, as she had expected, but from York. She surveyed them wearily, almost balefully. They stared back at her, not with contempt and arrogance, as Hingamund had done some eleven years ago, but with great respect. The grey-haired ageing woman before them was Edward's sister, whose will was known to be as implacable as the King's. Her strength was never to be underestimated, and they had come to beg assistance against a man for whom they cared little. She had made alliances with the men of Alba against Ragnall; surely she would listen to them.

The head of the delegation cleared his throat nervously. "We have come to beg your protection, Lady."

She did not reply. She looked at them somewhat absently, waiting for them to continue. The place was suddenly full of Ethelred's presence and she wished to call out to him to stay until these wretched men finished their business and left her alone. The spokesman misunderstood her cold stare and shuffled uneasily. "It is not our wish to submit ourselves to you, but we have seen lately at Corbridge that the men of Strathclyde, under your hand, are able to oppose Ragnall. Indeed, his jarls *Krakabeinn*, the Crowbone, and Ottarr, were slain at Corbridge by your timely intervention. Had this not been so, Ragnall would have come against York."

"He is your kinsman. His grandfather, the Boneless One, was King of York."

The spokesman nodded. "We are sensible of that. But we know also that Ivarr's brother, Halfdan, was driven from York by his own men, for he was drunk with battle and with blood. Ragnall descends from this terrible family, and though he be our kinsman, we bear him no love. We have lived peaceably among the English these many years. We have married their daughters and raised our children in this land."

She thought back briefly. There was a change here, some civilizing hand had tamed them. She was about to ask, though she already knew, when the man continued.

"Our Archbishop, Ethelbald, has preached peaceful ways to us, and helped to feed and comfort us. He is of our blood and yours. He knows our needs."

She smiled at last. "And you desire peace among yourselves and with your neighbors?"

"We do, Lady. If Ragnall were to invade York, there be many to oppose him, including the Archbishop himself, though he might rather submit than shed blood."

"Then he is still the man I knew at London." Over the years she had come to understand Ethelbald better. Wars went on, invaders came and went; the needs of the people, their safety and well-being were always his first concern. "You have not come here only to speak of your dislike of Ragnall."

"No. We will resist Ragnall when he comes—for he will come—if we have your strength to help us. He cannot prevail against his own kin and your strength as well. We are prepared to give you oaths."

Aethelflaed surveyed the group gravely, stifling an urge to laugh. A woman, considered a fit opponent for a grandson of Ivarr! Nonetheless, it was a great honor, and these Danes, old enemies, stood before her, proposing, beseeching her in all sincerity to accept them as allies, to be subject to her overlordship.

"It must be," she said finally, for she could see they were desperate and it had never been her intention to deny them aid. She sent word to Edward that York was ready to be fortified against Ragnall, with their help, as soon as Nottingham and Lincoln submitted.

She spent the next week relaxing, along with Athelstan, occasionally taking her peregrines out with her as they had done when he was a child. Often she took her morning ride alone, as she did this morning. She returned, feeling refreshed and exhilarated, feeling livelier than she had for some time. After York was taken, she might return to London and settle into a peaceful life, such as she had not known for years. Perhaps she would start a school like her father had done. Just thinking about it gave her a lift.

She urged her horse forward, seeing Athelstan in the yard of her *haga*, waiting for her to return for breakfast. She raised her arm to wave to him, but it felt unaccountably heavy. She felt light-headed and was puzzled because her arm was suddenly full of pain.

Athelstan, watching her, saw her arm drop, saw the startled look on her face, and heard her gasp of pain. As she slumped forward in her saddle, the horse stopped; the hand on the reins had fallen away. Athelstan ran swiftly to her side as he saw her face, and caught her as she slid unconscious from the saddle. He carried her to her *haga* and sent David for the Leech. He rubbed her cold hands, though he knew it was to no avail. By the time the Leech arrived, Athelstan looked up and shook his head.

Aethelflaed opened her eyes and tried to move. She had been floating in a dark and confining place, but light at last broke in upon her. Her body felt heavy and cumbersome as she struggled ineffectively against it.

"Do not try to move, *dearling*," said a familiar voice, "it will not help. You cannot move." Tears seemed to well up at the sound of the voice. Over the years she would come to herself with a start on occasion, thinking she had forgotten the sound of it, and she would jog her memory to recall it, and despairing, could not. Yet now, a few, short words and there was no mistaking it.

She blinked away the tears and opened her eyes and saw him standing at the foot of her couch. "Oh, Ethelred," she sighed, "I feared I would never see you again."

He smiled and the warmth that shone from his face made her feel strong again. "It is finished," he explained simply, "and I have come back as I said I would."

"But Ethelred," she struggled against her immobility, "there is Nottingham yet, and Lincoln, and York. The work is not yet over."

"Ah, but yours is. Nottingham is secure; there is no need for you there. Do not fear, Edward will prevail. You have seen faithfully to that. York will be Athelstan's fight." Ethelred's luminous gaze rested on their foster son's head as he knelt in prayer by her couch. Aethelflaed felt a rush of love for the Atheling and reached out to touch him. This time her arm moved and obeyed, but her fingers seemed insubstantial and Athelstan appeared not to notice her caress.

She looked back at Ethelred, whose presence surrounded her with peace and comfort. "I am no longer needed here," she agreed, her plans for the future erased from her mind. She felt no disappointment, only relief. The burden of heaviness and lassitude lifted from her body and she felt as if she were a girl again. Ethelred, young and handsome, as she so vividly remembered him, stretched out his hand to her and she took it eagerly, laughing.

Athelstan raised his head, not needing to look at the still form on the bed. He felt the soft breeze that brushed a farewell against his cheek. His adopted mother, the great-hearted Lady of the Mercians, had fared forth and gone to her new life this twelfth day of June of the year 918.

He rose heavily to his feet and prepared himself to ride to Stamford. The King, his father, must be told at once, for they must deal immediately with certain matters.

EPILOGUE

(918)

Historical Note

In this year, Elfwyn, with the help of some Mercian followers, took over the city of London. She held control for about six months before Edward deposed her. She was taken to Winchester before Christmas, and placed in Nunnaminster.

The clear December air had a snap and sparkle to it that on any other occasion would have filled Athelstan with pleasure. A fire crackled in the Great Hall of London's garrison and he warmed his hands absently at it. The Great Hall, indeed, all of London, was filled with the Lady's presence, though she was irretrievably gone. He had ridden through the city on his return, visiting the places she had taken him as a child, his heart aching with grief as each familiar spot took on a new significance.

He looked at Elfwyn's closed face, and marveled how she, so different in nature, could so strongly resemble her mother. She did not seem to understand, even now, that she ruled London these past six months only at the King's pleasure. She was thirty now, and determined to hang on to her overlordship with the aid of a small but powerful group of Mercian thanes who encouraged her in her folly. Athelstan had come early in hopes of dissuading his cousin from her opposition. He could not bring himself to desert Aethelflaed's daughter, though he had seen her ambition and jealousy years ago and was never deluded into thinking she would behave any other way.

The King had ridden to Tamworth with all speed, and he was hardly in the gate before the village submitted to him. He had intended that, of course, for he could not afford the loss of so crucially situated a fortress, but sorrow drove him harder than necessity. When Athelstan tentatively mentioned Nottingham, Edward only raised his hand for silence, saying, "They will wait," and continued to stare down at his dead sister.

Athelstan had never seen him look so old and forlorn. Edward wept as though he had lost his dearest friend; they both knew he had. For once in their lives, he and his father shared something deeply, this shattering loss. Edward's sister was part of their lives; she was as indestructible as this land they stood upon, this land they had shed their blood to hold. As deeply as Athelstan felt the loss himself, he knew his father had received a blow from which he would never recover. His heart contracted with pity as he watched Edward wring the dead hand, saying over and over, disbelieving, "Only a few more months we needed. She will never see it now." And he wept.

Athelstan consoled him as best he could and was relieved when Edward finally allowed the Church to perform its duty.

"What of Elfwyn?" he asked his father later.

"Let her stay where she is. She will do less harm where she is."

Athelstan thought otherwise, but held his tongue. The King was in no mood to listen. Edward was thinking of other things.

Tamworth's submission was prompt; next to his sister, the King was the most powerful protector they knew. They were, at the moment, in no position to take exception even if they misliked the rule of Wessex. They reminded themselves that this was Offa's ancient kingdom, a kingdom of Mercians, not of West Saxons. But the alternative was Ragnall, so they pledged their allegiance to the King of Wessex, secretly thinking that Edward was not likely to find the rest of Mercia, or Wales, for that matter, so compliant as themselves.

Edward took his sister's body to Gloucester for burial in St. Peter's Church, for she had been especially attached to the community there and had always loved the west country. Not long after, in early autumn, Nottingham submitted and the King fortified it without delay. The rest of Danish Mercia followed Nottingham's example, but York lay further in the future than ever, for when Aethelflaed died, the men of York repudiated their treaty with her. York needed a strong king: it would be Ragnall or Edward, and while many disliked the grandson of Ivarr, if it was to be a choice between him and the King of Wessex.... They shrugged and said no more. It was agreeable to have the aid of Edward's sister. They had not believed that she could remove York from their control. Edward could and would. If they took his help in place of hers, he would freely give it and he would also take York as his price.

For the moment it mattered not. Mercia south of the Humber was now pledged to Edward. Except for one place. And that place, where thirty-two years earlier Alfred had forced the gates, setting in motion unseen forces that would bring his son back to demand it for himself, was ruled by one, who, like the men of York, cared not for the King of Wessex.

By December, the time had come. Edward had given his son a knowing look and said, "It is time we went to London." He laid a hand on his son's shoulder. "Would you care to ride ahead of me? I have work elsewhere." Athelstan smiled wanly, but gratefully. The King possessed a sensitivity he had not known of before.

So he was here ahead of his father. Although London had officially submitted to Edward on Ethelred's death in 911, many were still openly opposed to West Saxon rule. Edward had let it go, honoring his promises to Alfred and Ethelred. His sister should hold it as long as she lived: he had allowed the daughter to do so only in her mother's name. The time was ready, for all of Mercia was under Edward's Lordship and protection, and a few thanes, whether they were peaceful or not, could not hold out once Elfwyn's submission was secured.

"Elfwyn," said Athelstan, a little desperately, "the King will be here shortly. You must reconsider."

She regarded him in tight-lipped silence. Finally, she said, "He is not King here. I am heir."

Athelstan shook his head vigorously. "You never were; my father always was, for he received it from our grandfather through Ethelred's overlordship. Neither Ethelred nor your mother ever held this land except as Overlord, never as king."

"Mercia will never accept Edward!" she exclaimed hotly. "They loved my mother. She had the royal blood of Mercia in her veins, as do I."

Athelstan looked at her pityingly. You are not your mother, he thought, but did not say it. "We are all of the same line," he observed drily. "Mercia, except for London has already taken Edward as King," he explained patiently. "You have no choice."

She must have known it all along, regardless of what she said. Edward rode into the Great Hall, with a rattling of hooves on cobble in the courtyard preceding him, and approached to within yards of where Elfwyn sat stonily watching his entrance. Still astride his horse, he looked down at his niece, and Athelstan was surprised to see not anger, but compassion in his eyes. The King had understood all along that this would happen. Edward would treat her gently.

He did, but he was as inexorably unopposable as ever. "Do you submit?" he asked softly, patiently, even sadly.

"No!" retorted Elfwyn angrily. "I do not."

Edward heaved a great sigh. "Then I am sorry. I loved your mother as dearly as I love my own life, and it grieves me to do this to her child."

"You are ill-advised, uncle," she said coldly. "There are those who will rise against you if I am taken prisoner."

Edward regarded her steadily from under his bushy eyebrows, a faint smile of incredulity crinkling around his eyes. "Do you mean to tell me, Elfwyn...?"

"Lady Elfwyn," she snapped. "I am Queen here!"

"...Elfwyn," he went on as if she had not spoken, "that you will defend London with a handful of men, surrounded by Mercians under my protection? Do you think, as Ethelwold did, to find help in Northumbria?"

She colored hotly, for the thought had occurred to her. She had sent two men on a mission to York, but they had not yet returned.

"Nor will they return," said Edward, reading her thoughts. Athelstan looked up at his father's face, startled. The eyes were cold as ice. "They have been," Edward hesitated, preparing the way for his message, "turned aside from their journey." Athelstan drew in a quick, astonished breath. This was, no doubt, the King's "work" elsewhere.

Elfwyn blanched and the hands that gripped the arms of her chair showed white at the knuckles, but she was silent and unmoving. Only her eyes betrayed that the last thread of hope had snapped.

The silence stretched between them tightly and Athelstan waited for his father to pronounce sentence. Edward had not called her traitor, but she was, and traitor's death she might earn. He misjudged his father. Edward, too, had Alfred's blood. Alfred had loved his brother and battle-companion, King Aethelred, and could not pronounce against Ethelwold, his brother's son. Nor could Edward pronounce against his niece, for the sake of his sister and battle-companion. This much he owed her.

He signaled the guards, who moved to either side of her, too abruptly for Edward's taste. "Do not mishandle her!" he snarled at them suddenly. He looked again at his niece. "I am sending you to Nunnaminster, there to spend your life. You will be amongst your own kinswomen and you will be treated with honor."

"But as a prisoner," she hissed at him, her face twisted with anger.

"If you will, yes," replied Edward wearily. "I cannot have more conspiracy."

They took her away, and she went with them unresisting, her eyes still glistering with fury. Edward turned to Theodred, who had come in with him. "Do you, Theodred, submit your city to me?"

Theodred knelt. "I do indeed, my Lord King. I beg your protection and I thank you for your kindness." To Elfwyn, he meant.

Athelstan mounted his own horse then and rode out into the streets of London with Edward, his father, King of Wessex and now King of all Mercia, he who was descended from the great line of Cerdic and Cenwalh, and of Ecgbert, conqueror of Mercia, and of Alfred, his father: Edward, who would, God willing, hand all of this and more one day to him.

SOURCE MATERIALS

Source materials are listed below by category.

PRINCIPAL HISTORICAL SOURCES

The Anglo-Saxon Chronicle, G. N. Garmonsway, translator, (Dent, 1960).

Two of the Saxon Chronicles Parallel, Charles Plummer. Revised, D. Whitelock Edition (Oxford, 1972).

An Introduction to Anglo-Saxon England, Peter Hunter Blair (Cambridge, 1959).

A History of the Vikings, Gwyn Jones, (Oxford, 1973).

Anglo-Saxon England and the Norman Conquest, H. R. Loyn (Longman, 1962).

Scandinavian York and Dublin, Vol. I, Alfred P. Smyth, (Templekieran, 1975).

Anglo-Saxon England, Sir Frank Stenton, Second Edition (Oxford, 1955).

Tacitus: The Agricola and the Germania, translated by H. Mattingly, translation revised by S. A. Handford (Penguin, 1970).

Scandinavian England, F. T. Wainwright, edited by H. P. R. Finberg (Phillimore, 1975); especially the articles, "Northwest Mercia," "Ingimund's Invasion," and "Aethelflaed, Lady of the Mercians."

BIOGRAPHY

Asser's Life of King Alfred, L. C. Jane's translation from the Latin (1926).

Alfred the Great, Eleanor S. Duckett (University of Chicago Press, 1956).

MISCELLANEOUS: SOCIAL, RELIGIOUS, CULTURAL

Anglo-Saxon Pennies, Michael Dolley, (British Museum Reprint, 1970).

Viking Coins of the Danelaw and of Dublin, C. J. Godfrey, (Cambridge, 1962).

The Making of the English Landscape, W. G. Hoskins (Pelican, 1972).

Life in Anglo-Saxon England, R. I. Page (Batsford/Putnam, 1970).

The Old English Herbals, Eleanor s. Rohde (Dover, 1971).

Preparatory to Anglo-Saxon England, Sir Frank M. Stenton, *Collected*

Papers, edited by Doris Mary Stenton (Oxford, 1970).

The English Woman in History, Doris Mary Stenton, (George Allen & Unwin, 1957).

The Audience of Beowulf, Dorothy Whitelock (Oxford, 1967).

The Beginnings of English Society, Dorothy Whitelock, (Pelican, 1968).

ANGLO-SAXON LITERATURE

The Anglo-Saxon texts that I used for my translations, excerpts of which are used in Chapters Two, Twelve, and Eighteen, are included in this list. These texts were also used for the study of other Anglo-Saxon material: *Ine's Laws, Alfred's Laws, Leechdoms,* Alfred's *Preface to the Cura Pastoralis,* Selections from the *Anglo-Saxon Chronicle,* and selected Poetry.

An Introduction to Old English, G. L. Brook (Manchester University Press, 1955).

Sweet's Anglo-Saxon Reader, Revised by Dorothy Whitelock (Oxford, 1967): *Dream of the Rood.*

An Anglo-Saxon Reader, A. J. Wyatt, editor (Cambridge, 1953): *Grant to Worcester Monastery, Alfred's Will.*

ARCHAEOLOGICAL MATERIALS

Archaeological sources on which descriptions and reconstructions of cities and fortresses are based are given below.

Excavations Near Winchester Cathedral, 1961-1968, Martin Biddle (Winchester, 1969).

"Late Saxon Planned Towns," Martin Biddle, and David Hill, reprinted from *The Antiquaries Journal, (1971).*

"The Ancient History of Shaftesbury and its Abbey," compiled by Phyllis Carter from *Shaftesbury and Its Abbey,* Laura Sydenham, (1969).

"First Report of the Excavations at Tamworth, Staffs.,—The Saxon Defenses," J. Gould FSA, Extract from *Transactions (IX)* of the Lichfield and South Staffordshire Archaeological and Historical Society (1967-1968).

"Third Report of the Excavations at Tamworth, Staffs., 1968—The Western Entrance to the Saxon Borough," J. Gould FSA, Extract from *Transactions (X)* of the South Staffordshire Archaeological and Historical Society (1968-1969).

Londinium, Peter R. V. Marsden (Ginn and Co., 1971).

Deva Victrix, (Chester), Dennis F. Petch (Ginn & Co., 1971).

ORDNANCE SURVEY MAPS

Roman Britain, Third Edition (Her Majesty's Stationer's Office, 1956).

Britain in the Dark Ages (410-870 A.D.), Second Edition (Her Majesty's Stationer's Office, 1971).

MUSEUMS

British Museum, London: The Sutton Hoo Collection.

London and London Guildhall combined Museums, Kensington Palace, London.

Stafford City Museum: Scale model of Aethelflaed's fortress.

Tamworth City Museum: Scale model of Aethelflaed's fortress.

Winchester City Museum.

Worcester City Museum: Plans of the Saxon Burh.

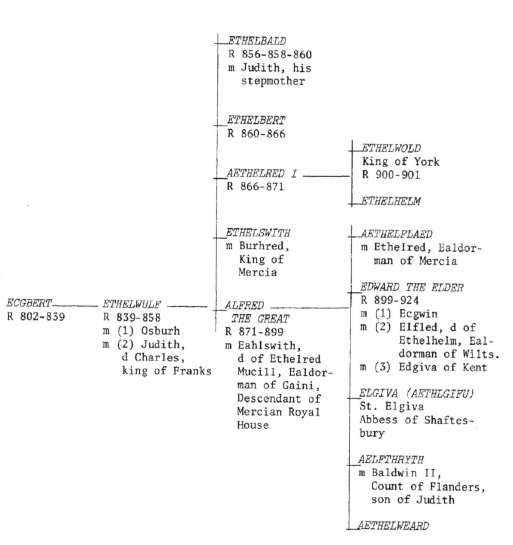

ETHELBALD
R 856-858-860
m Judith, his
   stepmother

ETHELBERT
R 860-866

AETHELRED I ——————— ETHELWOLD
R 866-871   King of York
                       R 900-901

                       ETHELHELM

ETHELSWITH   AETHELFLAED
m Burhred,   m Ethelred, Ealdor-
   King of   man of Mercia
   Mercia
                      EDWARD THE ELDER
ECGBERT———— ETHELWULF ———— ALFRED ————   R 899-924
R 802-839   R 839-858   THE GREAT   m (1) Ecgwin
            m (1) Osburh   R 871-899   m (2) Elfled, d of
            m (2) Judith, m Eahlswith,   Ethelhelm, Eal-
               d Charles,   d of Ethelred   dorman of Wilts.
               king of Franks Mucill, Ealdor- m (3) Edgiva of Kent
                              man of Gaini,
                              Descendant of ELGIVA (AETHLGIFU)
                              Mercian Royal St. Elgiva
                              House   Abbess of Shaftes-
                                             bury

                                             AELFTHRYTH
                                             m Baldwin II,
                                                Count of Flanders,
                                                son of Judith

                                             AETHELWEARD

Brief Genealogy of the House of Wessex

CPSIA information can be obtained at www.ICGtesting.com
Printed in the USA
BVOW06s0835031016

463994BV00008B/58/P